Broken

THE JOURNEY OF TWO SISTERS

Linda M. Prenger

TRILOGY CHRISTIAN PUBLISHERS
Tustin, CA

Trilogy Christian Publishers
A Wholly Owned Subsidiary of Trinity Broadcasting Network
2442 Michelle Drive
Tustin, CA 92780

Broken: The Journey of Two Sisters

Copyright © 2024 Linda M. Prenger

Unless otherwise noted, all Scripture quotations are taken from the King James Version of the Bible. Public domain.

All rights reserved, including the right to reproduce this book or portions thereof in any form whatsoever.

For information, address Trilogy Christian Publishing
Rights Department, 2442 Michelle Drive, Tustin, Ca 92780.

Trilogy Christian Publishing/ TBN and colophon are trademarks of Trinity Broadcasting Network.

For information about special discounts for bulk purchases, please contact Trilogy Christian Publishing.

Trilogy Disclaimer: The views and content expressed in this book are those of the author and may not necessarily reflect the views and doctrine of Trilogy Christian Publishing or the Trinity Broadcasting Network.

10 9 8 7 6 5 4 3 2 1

Library of Congress Cataloging-in-Publication Data is available.

ISBN 979-8-89333-243-8

ISBN 979-8-89333-244-5 (ebook)

Endorsements

When I first heard Linda Prenger speak, it was at a Christian women's conference in 2022. Don't let her tiny statue fool you..... She was a powerhouse. She spoke and shared a small portion of her life and how it shaped her to become a Christian.

I was beyond honored when she asked me to read the book she was writing, her life story. I was hooked from the first page. Her words gutted me. I cried so much while reading the first four chapters, and I would continue to cry until I read the last page of the last chapter of the book.

Her life story needed to be written. When people read this book, they will know about God's never-ending love. His patience and the redemption of a beautiful little girl. Who had no idea who God was. That is now this powerhouse of a godly woman who will never depart from His ways.

To know Linda, you could never imagine all she endured. She has the sweetest smile, the sweetest demeanor. She gives the best hugs and is one of the strongest people I know. I am honored to call Linda M. Prenger my friend, my role mode, and most importantly, my sister in Christ.

—Rita Blanco

This book has forever touched my life. Knowing someone else's story puts your own life in perspective. This book has kept me in suspense of what would happen next and how God would turn what was meant for evil into good.

Laura and Linda captured my heart. While some of the others, I hoped, would eventually see the truth. This is a story of the unbelievable love of the Father and how His forgiveness for us can be given to others only if we are willing to see His truth.

This is a testimony of lies and heartbreaking and painful events in the lives of two young girls, tangled in a web of bitterness and unforgiveness, but it ends with the Father's love. This story is one of spiritual blindness, abuse, murder, and so much more dysfunction, but it is also a story of God and how He doesn't leave you, how He goes before you, and most certainly how He forgives us and how we can forgive others. The two main characters, Linda and Laura, I wanted so badly to free them from the parents and the grandparents.

This is a must-read book.

—Stephanie Harvey
President and Founder of Women's Encounter North

Contents

Introduction vii

Chapter 1. A Visit to the Park 1

Chapter 2. A Little Lost Girl 20

Chapter 3. Daddy, Please Let It Go By 39

Chapter 4. A Little Girl No More 60

Chapter 5. Once Upon a Time, There Were Two Sisters 94

Chapter 6. Different Directions 108

Chapter 7. The Promise 135

Chapter 8. Choices 162

Chapter 9. The Bitter Years 176

Chapter 10. The Final Battle 192

Chapter 11. A Sister's Unfailing Love 217

Chapter 12. Love, Truth, and Loss 231

Chapter 13. The Unexpected 263

Chapter 14. Shattered 277

Chapter 15. Exposed 312

Chapter 16. Judgment and Justice 327

Chapter 17. Time to Dig 348

Chapter 18. Will You Go? 369

Chapter 19. The Letter 393

Chapter 20. The Shocking Truth 408

Chapter 21. Secret of My Heart 430

Chapter 22. Reflections 450

Chapter 23. The Journey's End 467

Chapter 24. Forgiveness: Just Let It Go By! 482

Introduction

This book is based on a true story; some of the names have been changed.

My name is Linda Marie Prenger; I was known as the girl in the white patent leather shoes.

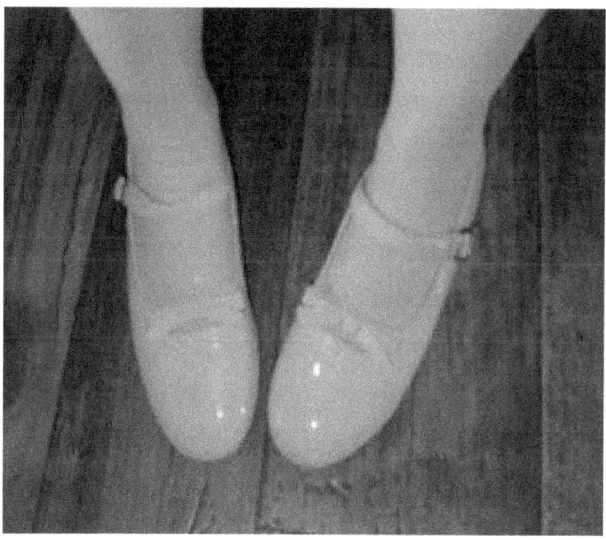

As a result of the emotional damage in the early years of my life, I closed all doors to my soul. I was never going to let anyone get close to me, period. However, there was one person who was always by my side. She wiped my tears away when they escaped and put her arms around me when I was afraid. We shared our secrets and our fears. We laughed and cried together. There was very little happiness in our lives and never a shortage of sadness. I was close to this girl who loved me, and I trusted her. She brought joy to my life when there was no joy to be found in the dark hall of our lives. She was the only one who was constant in my life. Laura and I were truly broken; still, we both had a life shared together. We had a past, a present, and a future.

I realized that in order for anyone to understand, the whole story must be told. I pray that you, the reader, will truly come to know and love the real people in this story. I hope that you will not only come to understand the battles we faced and fought alone but also come to a place where you become a part of this amazing story of compassion, mercy, and forgiveness as you extend it to others. I pray that you will understand the ashes we rose up out of and how our lives were changed by God's amazing love.

I realize that this is out of the ordinary and will not be considered normal for a book, but I have never been one who is predictable or typical. As strange as it may seem, I am inviting you into our lives to get to know us, the good and the bad, the tears, the laughter, the losses we suffered, the victories we shared, the emotional pain we endured, and the hope that filled our hearts. I ask that you open the door of your heart and walk into our lives and the experiences that molded and shaped Laura's future and mine.

It is my prayer that when you put this book down, you will feel you have been a part of something special. I pray your heart will be touched, that life will become more precious to you, and that those around you will suddenly know how much you love them. Most of all, I pray your life will be changed by this story and that in the midst of who you are, all you have done, and all that has been done to you, forgiveness will begin to flow within your soul.

I invite you into my life and into the painful journey of brokenness, bitterness, and anger, which lead to healing and forgiveness.

Linda M. Prenger

CHAPTER 1

A Visit to the Park

This is a personal note to those who read my story. It was with much prayer and tears that I came to the place where I am willing to share this story. It is here that I feel I need to start. To share a little piece of what my home life was like as a child. I feel this is the place where it would not only be most understood but also help you see my life through the eyes of the one who lived through it. Me!

Our house was truly the house that Satan shook. Inside the walls of that house, it was more than the fact that my dad drank. More than the fact that my mom had affair after affair... more than the fights, the yelling, the screaming, and cussing. More than the fact that my sister and I were products of the anger, rage, and greed that infested our parents. More important than all of this was the fact that we were being taught there was no way out. Our lives belonged to them.

In our home, there were rules—rules to get up by and rules to go to bed by. Rules for each task given to us. Rules even for whom we could listen to. Rules on how to deal with people we were not to listen to, rules for bathing, dressing, and taking care of our clothes. We had seven dresses for each day of the week, with one nice dress for special days and the bonfire at the end of the harvest. We had seven pairs of white panties and seven pairs of white socks. Two pairs of shoes, one for spe-

cial days and one for everyday wear. There were rules for everything. They were enforced! Each task was carried out with perfect precision. There was no room for error.

As we grew up, there was no television in our home until 1965. The television was moved into my parent's bedroom. We were not allowed to watch it. I had never seen a television in my home as a child until that year. Nor do I recall hearing it, or ever seeing it on, after it was moved into our home. It was for my parents. We were warned, and we knew the consequences if we were caught messing with it. Not that we would know how to turn it on or operate it.

It was a rule my parents had: as children, we were not allowed to watch television. It was not a religious preference; it had nothing to do with God. It had nothing to do with what they believed or did not believe. We were just simply told it was a rule. However, I believe the real reason was to keep us from hearing anything that had to do with the Lord. I think this because it truly was, at that time, the only place we could have heard anything concerning God, Jesus, the cross, or the Word. Whatever the reason was, I grew up without a television.

Now I have given you a small idea of how it was in my home and that I did not watch television in my childhood. We worked; we were not like the other children in our neighborhood. Most of the children in our neighborhood made fun of us. It was because we were so different. We were taught from an early age to work. The most important thing was our family. To protect our family from outsiders who would corrupt our family's seed and spirit. That was it.

I shared all this with you here before the beginning of my story because I wanted you to be able to understand, as a child, how I lived. I wanted you to fully share and possibly connect to the shattered life of the little girl who grew up to write this book.

My mind is so crystal clear when it comes to my childhood, my past, and my conversations. I remember many things about my childhood. Some of those things are not word for word. But there are certain things that I do remember word for word, exactly what was said. How it all happened. How it all unfolded. I do not have any remembrance of movies or advertisements. If I read something in a book, for example, it stayed with me.

If I was told something, it stayed with me. I have an incredible memory of my childhood. Whatever the reason for my ability to retain information and knowledge of past events and so many experiences remains a mystery to me. Once, I was told that I had a photogenic memory. I didn't understand what that was. Then I was told and, in many ways, believe it had to do with the fact that I did not watch television. I am just saying what happened in my life and how it affected me. I was told there was nothing in my mind to crowd out my thoughts, to occupy my mind, or to numb me from the events that happened in my life. I had to live my story.

So here is where my story begins.

My dad came from a large family. He had eighteen brothers and sisters. Out of them, he was the first to leave Kentucky. He settled in Virginia and later moved to Texas. Later, three of his sisters and their husbands made the trip to Texas as well. All that happened long before I was born. I had heard the story often. My dad and his siblings grew up in Kentucky.

My dad left the farm and married my mom in 1949. Moved to Virginia and lived there until I was born in December of 1953. In the spring of 1954, my dad moved us to Texas. He purchased the house that I grew up in, and I called it home. It had been decided that four families would leave the farm and go to different places and find jobs to help support the farm. All four families ended up in Texas because that's where jobs and opportunities flourished. At least, that is what my dad said.

Every year, all four families made the drive to Kentucky for the planting season in the spring. My grandpa and grandma had a big farm. Each one of my grandpa's children was allotted a portion of the land to farm. In the planting season, my grandpa's children, all eighteen of them, would bring their children, "the grandchildren," to plant the seeds and care for the crops. At harvest time, our parents returned, and we all left a week after the harvest bonfire.

I am not sure how all that worked. I just know we went in the spring and planted seeds. In the fall, we harvested all that we had planted and had a big bonfire. It was a big celebration. I had done it all my life. I did not understand all of it. It's just the way it was.

All the children went. Our parents stayed for a few days, getting us ready for the work ahead. Our moms would help us get settled in our sleeping areas. There were two large rooms with little beds along the walls. There was a small chest by each bed. One room was for the boys and one for the girls. In the fall, our parents returned for the harvest. After the harvest, everyone returned home, taking a portion of the crop and a portion of meat back with them.

It was springtime. The year was 1963. I was nine years old. I had just turned nine in December of 1962, and I was in the third grade. The family was getting ready to go to Kentucky for the planting season. It was a time of celebration. Before the trip, the four families in Texas would gather for a big picnic.

The next day, we would leave early in the morning for the long drive to Kentucky.

We always went to a park for this big picnic. We stayed the entire day. It was the only time I can remember when the children, including myself, were allowed the freedom to play, not under the fearful watchful eyes of our parents. We would run and play. We would get on the swings, the slide, and the merry-go-round. This was the one day we were children.

My favorite was the swings. I loved swinging back and forth, higher and higher. It made me feel like nothing could hurt me. I loved feeling the breeze, as the strands of my hair would tickle my face. I would spend most of the day at the swings away from the other children, in a little world all of my own. One I had been creating since I was four years old.

The other children always talked; it went on and on every year. It was always the same thing. They talked about which boys would get to help with the pigs and cows, which boys would get to hunt, who would be chosen to plow the fields, which girls would pluck the chickens, which girls would remain in the fields, and who would be chosen to go into the house to cook, can, and bake. The girls who went into the house enjoyed sewing as well. However, the main topic was always about the harvest and which child would be chosen to sit by Grandpa.

The most important topic was whose father would be chosen to light the bonfire at the end of the harvest. It was a great honor for that family. The bonfire at the end of the harvest was the biggest event of the year. My grandpa would get his guitar out, and we would all stand around the bonfire singing and shouting. There was laughter and special hugs from grandpa.

I really did not care for the things they talked about. I would always go to my favorite place, the swings.

After lunch, I was on my way back to the swings. I noticed one of the picnic tables where a little girl who lived in our neighborhood sat. I had seen her many times outside playing with her mother. I had never seen any children at her house other than the girls from our neighborhood.

As I look back, I realize now that she was an only child. She was with her father and mother, talking and laughing. They were just getting ready to eat. They looked at me and then back to where my family was. I glanced over to see my dad and mom watching me. I smiled at my dad and went running to the swings.

I wasn't there long before I heard a voice. "This moment is for you; remember it always." Then I saw her standing there. She smiled. A smile like none I had ever seen. It was an expression of complete peace and joy. Crystal clear eyes full of innocence, the sweetest voice, gentle and soft. She spoke with purpose and words of truth, with a conviction I had never witnessed before. "You are Linda." It was more of a statement than a question. Before I could answer, her words stopped me. "You are the younger one." This time, she waited. So, I said. "Yes, I am Linda, and I am younger than my sister, Laura."

She walked over to the swing as if to get in it, stopped, looked at me, and said, "I'm going to be with God in heaven when I die." I told her, "There is no God, and there is no heaven." She sat down in the swing and looked up. "Yes, Linda, there is a heaven, and there is a God, and He has a Son." I just could not comprehend that. It was at this point that I told her what my parents had said to me so many times. I said, "There are all kinds of people who lie, and even little girls like you will try to tell me lies. I shouldn't listen to you. I'm supposed to run away from you."

She didn't try to debate it. She just said. "I pray for you every night." I did not have a clue as to what she was talking about. Something in my heart grabbed those words, and I thought, *She thinks about me every night.* That was huge to me. Someone thought about me. I remember thinking I wished my mommy would let me play with her. But I knew she wouldn't.

Then the little girl said, "We don't have much time. Can you remember something?"

I said, "Yes."

She said, "This is our secret: when you see me do this, it means I'm praying for you. Okay?" She folded her hands together, smiled, and bowed her head. Then looked up at me and smiled again. She did it three, maybe four more times. "Can you remember that?" she asked.

I said, "Yes, I will remember that." It was at that point I heard my dad holler at me. I just acted like I did not hear him.

She reached over, put her hand in mine, and said the words I had never heard before. It is the reason or, at least, part of the reason I never forgot this event. "I love you. I would not lie to you. There is a God." My dad hollered again, and I knew it was going to be bad. I wanted to stay there with her just a moment longer. I was nine years old, and I had never heard anyone say, "I love you." Nine! I stood up to leave the swings as she said, "We are friends. Remember what I said."

For some reason, I did not care that I was in trouble. I had a feeling that I could not explain, not then. I had never felt that way before. I was so overpowered with emotion that I wanted to cry. It was not because I was hurt or because of feelings of emptiness I had so many times. Instead, it was a reaction to love and an expression of tenderness, which, as a child, I had never experienced. I didn't even care if my dad saw me. I walked over to her and said. "I will always remember. I promise." Then I turned and started running towards my dad as he hollered a third time.

I knew that I was going to be punished severely for this action. I just did not realize the extent of that punishment. All four families were there, and they all saw it. It would be hours of being questioned by my parents. The other children would ignore me during the planting. I would be staying in Kentucky for the whole summer. It meant my punishment would not end until after the harvest.

My dad met me halfway, and when we got back to the picnic table, I looked into the eyes of my family, and I saw hatred in their eyes. I didn't understand how talking to one little girl made them so angry. My dad sat down and called me over to where he was. No one said a word. My dad was the first to speak. "Linda, you tell me the truth; you hear me, girl? What did she say to you?" I looked up at my dad. With my head held high, I said, "She told me there was a God and a heaven!" They all started laughing at me. "There is no God, and there is no heaven." They all said it so loud. Everyone in the park was looking at us.

Then it got silent. It was like a hush fell over the whole park. I could hear the wind blowing. I thought this must be what it is like when you die. I was afraid. Then my dad stood up, looked down at me, and said, "What did you tell her?" It seemed like I stood there frozen for hours. Yet, I am sure it was a minute or less. Suddenly, I was not afraid. I could see right past my dad to where the swings were. There she was; she folded her hands, smiled, and bowed her head. I truly did not know what all that meant. I just knew she had shown me a kindness I had never experienced. The only thing I truly understood was when she folded her hands and bowed her head, she was thinking of me in a special way. As for God, well, I just didn't think she was right about that. I thought she might be confused because someone had lied to her, to her father, and to her mother. In my little girl's heart and through my little girl's eyes, I was not able to understand. I could only see the world I lived in. I loved my dad and mom, and I wanted them to love me. I believed them. They would not lie to me. They would tell me if there was a God.

My dad looked back over his shoulder to see what I had been staring at. The little girl had just left the swings and was running back to her parents. My dad asked me one more time, "Linda! What did you say to her?"

He was angry; I could hear it in his voice. His face had no expression at all. I looked at my dad and told him the truth. "I told her there was no heaven and there was no God."

My dad said, "That's right." I do not remember word for word everything he said after that. He was angry with me, and it did not go well for me. We left the park early that year. When we got home, I had to go to my room and was not allowed to finish the celebration with the rest of the family.

Early the next morning, we were on our way to Kentucky. It was a long drive, and I had lots of time to think. I thought a lot about the day before. About the little girl, the way she had talked so kindly to me. Her words came back to me: "I pray for you every night." It was nice to think that someone liked me and thought about me every night in a special way. I smiled and said to myself, "I will always remember. I promise."

When we left Texas, we were taken out of school. When we got to Kentucky, our parents stayed for a week. They had to enroll us back into the Kentucky schools. Then, they got our releases for the planting season. Kentucky, along with several other states, had laws for farmers that had large crops who depended on the children from those farms to work. The children could be removed for both the planting and harvest season and still be passed on to the next grade. There were no repercussions for those children. (Those laws have been changed.)

I know the bittersweet of the planting and harvesting seasons. I just want to say that today, that knowledge is very important to me, but for very different reasons. I see it with new eyes and in a very different light. The planting season and harvest time were very important to our family. It provided food year-round. It brought us together, and we all learned how to live and work together. Some plowed, preparing the fields for the seed. Some planted the seeds, while others covered the seeds with the soil. However, everyone took care of the crop. The children would walk through the fields day after day. We were all trained. We knew what to look for and what to do when we found anything that might destroy our crop. I learned a lot about planting and harvesting from those long seasons spent in Kentucky.

During the planting season, the field must be prepared and ready to receive the seed. If the field is not ready for the seed, no matter what you do, it will not produce. The timing must be right, too soon or too late, and the seeds will not root. Seeds must be planted at a certain depth. Too deep or not deep enough, and they will not grow, nor will they produce. You must inspect the seeds you are planting; some seeds are bad. When all conditions are right and everything is ready, plant the seeds. The rain will come, and the seeds grow.

It is very important to take care of the crops during the tender stages. We must keep the weeds out and the bugs off while they grow. We must keep a close eye on each and every plant for a problem. Worms can be very damaging to a crop. They are small and hard to spot at first. If unattended, they will destroy a whole crop. It is everyone's job to take care of the crop.

When the harvest comes, you separate the good from the bad. The good crop that grew and was not damaged was put in a special place to get it ready to be used. But the rest was put in a different pile. It is good for nothing but to be used in the bonfire. It is burned because it is useless. It cannot be used for anything. It didn't produce; it didn't take root. It was choked out, and it did not grow.

There are many reasons why certain seeds do not take root and produce. It is the same with our life. We plant seeds in the souls of others. We wait for the rain and growth. Some grow, and some do not. We must care enough to take a careful look so we can discover why someone is not growing and producing. Was the soil ready? Was it the plowing or the timing? How about the depth? Was it covered? Maybe it's the seed. Did we examine what we planted? The crop must be cared for and tended to. Our position should always be to protect the crop.

In many ways, we spend our whole lives planting and harvesting one thing after another. In our own lives, we plant good seeds and bad seeds. When it comes time to harvest what we have planted, we would rather forget about dealing with the harvest because we do not want to deal with the bad seeds we planted and the crop that those bad seeds have produced. However, there were good seeds in that crop as well. Why do we choose to destroy the good with the bad because the bad is too painful to face? So, the ground of our heart becomes hard and must be plowed. It needs to be broken up and cultivated so it is good, soft ground, ready to receive seeds and rain again.

We must honestly look at our lives. It does not matter that there are things hidden in our past. No matter how well we hide them, they are still there, and they are not going anywhere until we honestly look at the seeds we planted and the harvest in our lives from those seeds we planted. We cannot do that alone. We need to connect with someone. Take a risk. We can plant alone, but we cannot take care of a crop and harvest it all by ourselves. We need help to walk through that field and pull those weeds. Find the worms that infested our crop and stole all our joy. We need to see the worms as they are. They torment, they undermine, and they corrupt from within.

At my grandpa's farm that year, I learned some valuable lessons. I had to work in the fields that year. No one would talk to me. I had a long time to think about my final punishment because it would come at the end of the harvest. I didn't think about it a lot at first, but the closer it got to the harvest, the more I thought about it. I knew I had messed things up that day at the park. I had been disobedient. I knew I should be punished. After all, we were at the park to celebrate the life spirit in our seeds and in our family seed. I was not sure what all that really meant. I kind of knew and understood some of it. I just didn't understand all of it. That would happen when I turned thirteen. I would receive a book and have a year to read it, and then I would receive my passage.

The end of the harvest finally arrived. The harvest ceremony would be just as it always had been, except I knew that I was going to be punished for breaking the rules in the park that day for talking to an outsider about God. That night, the bonfire was started, and the family stood around the fire in one large circle. I was not in the circle. I was on the outside of the circle. I had to wait for my dad to call for me. The circle could not be broken at this point. I had stood in this circle since I was one year old. I had always held Laura's hand; we were always so excited singing our songs.

As always, my grandpa said, "Let the life spirit choose us again." Then they sang the song as they had done ever since I could remember: "There's no God. / There's no Satan. / There's no heaven. / There's no hell. / There's no wrong. / There's no sin. / We are the family in this circle. / We are the family the life spirit chose. / We are the family that continues to grow." Then, my grandpa stepped into the middle of the circle. He was a big man. He took his guitar and played the song one more time. Then he held out the guitar in front of him and walked through the fire. I do not know how he did it; I just know he did. I know it seems impossible, but then again, there are many things that happen in life that are impossible. I have really battled as to whether or not to include this portion of the story in this book or any book. I choose to speak loud and clear. It happened!

The circle could now be broken. Everyone clapped and started shouting. (They were chanting. Back then, I did not know what it was called.) Then, my grandpa would call for his big chair. When he sat down, all the children ran and touched the guitar and sat on his lap. The children could touch him and the guitar only on this night. In the backwoods of Kentucky, my grandpa was the head of this clan, and he was a man to be feared.

I watched as all the children took their turns and received a breath from him for protection and strength until the next harvest. Each child stood in a line and received the breath. One by one, we would stand in front of Grandpa and open our mouths as he would lean over us and blow into our mouths. That is how we received a breath from him. It was so we would have strength and protection for the whole year.

I am not in the circle. I don't know what I am going to do. If I am not in the circle, I can't touch Grandpa or his guitar. I will not have any life spirit in me. Now, I am not going to receive my breath from Grandpa for protection and strength. I am going to die. I can't live without that breath. Those were my thoughts as I sat on the ground during the ceremony.

The time had come. My dad spoke next. He talked about my act of disobedience as I stood behind him. I was still on the outside of the circle. I do not remember what he said word for word, only in general. He spoke about how my one act could have destroyed the planting season celebration. My actions could have destroyed our crop and caused the life spirit to leave us. When he was finished, everyone said with one loud voice, "Punishment!" I then stood in front of my dad with my back to him. One by one, all the men and boys walked up to me and spit on me. Last of all, my grandpa. I turned around and faced my dad, and he also spit on me.

I then went to where my mom was and stood behind her. It was her turn to talk. I never heard a word she said. When she was finished, everyone said with one loud voice, "Punishment!" I then stood in front of my mom with my back to her. I stood there once again as all the women and girls did the same. One by one, they walked up, spit on me, and walked away.

When Laura came up, she had such sadness in her eyes. I smiled at her. Just to let her know it was okay. I knew she did not want to do this. She had no choice. At last, I turned around and faced my mom. My heart was screaming, "No, Mom! No, Mom!" She never even looked into my eyes. Three deep breaths and three times she spit on me. Something inside of me broke.

I had to go sit down on the ground outside the circle again. I had to wait for the festivities to end. I cried; I just cried. I had spit all over me. It was in my hair, on my face, on my clothes. I had no spirit life, no protection, no strength, and I knew I would die before the next harvest without those things. When the night was over, all the children, aunts, and uncles walked by me as if I did not exist.

I just sat there on the ground with my head down. The shame was too great. I did not think about the little girl in the park anymore; I just wanted my family back. My dad was the last one to walk by. He stopped and said, "Come with me, Linda." I didn't get to take a bath or go to a nice, warm bed. I had to sleep in my clothes with a blanket on the back porch.

The next day, I learned what the three breaths meant. It would be three days before I would be allowed to take a bath. No one could talk to me for three days. I had to eat by myself outside for three days. I could only have bread and water for three days. It seemed like the three days would never end. When they did, everyone still seemed different to me. I felt something was wrong with me. I thought that I was dying because I had not received my breath from Grandpa.

The women were shelling and bagging the last of the peas. I had to go to the outhouse. They still had outhouses in Kentucky. (A lot of places in Kentucky had outhouses, even in the late sixties.) Well, I had to go, and the door to get out of the house was blocked.

All the women and girls were working in the house, getting the last of everything finished before the long drive back to Texas. Grandma had a door that went outside in her bedroom, and she told me to go out that way. I was surprised because everyone was forbidden to go into Grandma's room. I went to her bedroom and headed for the door that would take me outside. I reached for the door, getting ready to walk out. I stopped where I was standing. My eyes fixed on my grandpa's guitar. I just froze.

It is my heart's desire to portray this moment as it happened and as closely as I can to the thoughts and pain I felt. It is not my intention to shade over or to color this moment into anything other than it was. I cannot honestly put all my thoughts in order as they were back then. I can only share this moment as close as I can to the memory of the mixed thoughts and emotions I had as a nine-year-old little girl whose world just fell apart.

As for the previous nine years of my life, they were spent focusing on rules, my dad's drinking, my mom's affairs, and my dad's raging anger. I lived in fear, waiting for his next explosion, never knowing what was going to set him off. Fearing what he would do when he was set off.

There was no love, not one "I love you," and in the midst of all of that was the false beliefs we were all being taught and living by. These are the times, moments, and memories forever forged in my heart. The fear, the disbelief, and the pain of this moment remain inscribed in the halls of my mind. The moment everything I had been taught lay in ruins. I was too young to deal with this type of deception.

If I touched it, I would die. I was going to die anyway. If I touched it, I would get all of its power. Then it was clear: it didn't matter either way because I was dying. I wasn't in the circle; I didn't get my breath. And everything was different now. I was going to die, and everyone knew it. I was cursed and rebellious, just like they said. Now, I was going to die because of it. Even after the three days were over, everyone still treated me differently.

Part of me said, "Don't touch it!" But there was something in me that day that was stronger than all the fear I felt, and with my hand shaking, I reached out and slid my hand across the guitar. Nothing happened; I didn't feel anything. I touched it again, but still nothing. I looked around for another guitar—no, this is it. This one belongs to Grandpa. I picked it up and turned it over—nothing. I put it back as it was. I walked out the door, shutting it very quietly.

Walking down the path, I knew my grandpa lied to me. From that moment on, I saw him as a bad man. He had lied to me, and he was lying to everyone. There was nothing, no breath. I didn't need any breath from Grandpa to live. I didn't need any life spirit to give me strength and to protect me.

Grandpa is a bad man, and he made my dad a bad man. I hate him! I went behind the outhouse and just cried. There, broken and all alone, I knew that there was just this time, nothing beyond that. A life to live, and then we die. What then? What was going to happen to all of us, this family who believed my grandpa? There was no healing or power in his breath. There was no special power in his guitar. There was no seed life or spirit life. There was no place called heaven, and there was no God.

I lay there and cried until I fell asleep. I must have slept for a long time because it was getting dark when I woke up. I stood up and dusted myself off. I was walking back to the house. There was a gentle breeze blowing, and I just stopped so I could feel it. It was the most wonderful feeling. It was all around me. My hair was blowing in all directions; the way it felt on my face made me think of the park and the swings, and then I thought of the little girl in the park. I thought about our talk, and I looked up at the sky and said in a loud voice, "I will always remember. I promise."

The next day, we left early in the morning for the long drive home. The harvest was over, but spring would come again. We would go to the park again to celebrate the life spirit in our seeds and in our family seed. Then, make the long drive to Kentucky again.

I did not know it at the time, but I would only make that trip three more years. For all three years, I was chosen to work in the house. I would add to my knowledge of cooking, baking, and a host of other things, from sewing to setting tables to preparing for company. Those were lessons and information that I use today as I serve guests in my home.

Also, I was the one chosen to sit in the place of honor all three years. That place was right by my grandpa at the evening meal on the eve of the bonfire. I stood in the circle and sang the songs. Clapped and shouted. Touched the guitar, hugged my grandpa, and took a breath from him. I was known as one of the most obedient children of the family.

I had learned to pretend. I pushed all the hurt, the pain, the deception, the confusion, and the shame of that year deep down inside. I made myself become what they wanted me to be in order to survive. They had not let me take part in the harvest celebration that year. They withheld the hug from my grandpa. They would not let me touch the guitar, and my grandpa would not give me the breath of life and protection for the next year.

But in doing so, I lived, I survived, I didn't die, and I knew something was very wrong with what I had been taught. Oh, yes, there were moments that I questioned it because I thought I had to touch the guitar while Grandpa was holding it because he's the one that gave the power to it, but a little bit of truth took hold, and that truth could not be denied especially for a hungry child who craved and desired truth.

I never forgot that visit to the park in 1963, and I always remembered the little girl, as I promised, and the things she spoke into my life. Some questions rose up in my heart because one little girl told me there was a God, and He loved me. The conversation we had that day at the park was no more than three minutes. Those three minutes and the words spoken within those three minutes had within them the power to change my life. "Remember!" she said, and I did.

CHAPTER 2

A Little Lost Girl

In the fall, when my family returned home, Mom enrolled us back into a Texas school sometime in February. We did not go to school in November, December, or January. Once a week, Mom would go to school. She would pick up our work and turn in what we had done. Then, in February, we would return to school. It is just the way it was. I would see the little girl from the park at school and in front of her house. Sometimes, I would see her walking with her mother around the block. Each time I saw her, it was the same: she would fold her hands, smile, and bow her head. We were always careful to make sure no one was watching. I would always smile back at her. I was always so happy when I saw her do that. It let me know she had not forgotten me, that she did love me, and she was thinking about me in a special way.

I really did not understand what she was doing or why. I just knew that, somehow, it made me feel better. The children at school always made fun of me in one way or another. I had learned to live with it and ignore it. I struggled in every area at school. I knew it was because we missed school so much. But Dad said the only important thing was that we could read, write, and do a little arithmetic. I was a good reader even though I had missed so much school. Writing and arithmetic were the two areas I struggled in. The two together were a deadly combination and the greatest source of embarrassment. I was always so humiliated in class.

I was glad I didn't have to go to school all year like the other children did. With every passing year, I noticed more and more differences. Those differences were based on never feeling good enough. It was a feeling of knowing I was never going to measure up at school. One of the things that seemed different to me was the fact that all the other children went to class earlier than my sister and me. School started at eight o'clock, but Laura and I did not get to go to class until eight twenty. When the bell rang for school to start, Laura and I went to the office. We would wait in a little room. One of the women from the office would come and get us. Then we would go to class.

When we were younger, we didn't notice it. As we got older, the other children gave us a hard time about it. I understand it all now. However, as a child, I was torn between two worlds, and I did not understand either of them. We were not allowed to go early because of prayer. I know that now. I understand now why I was always put in the back of the classroom and why the teachers always seemed very friendly with the other children. Yet they would never smile at me or even make eye contact. The teachers all knew that my parents didn't believe in God. They knew we were being taught the same. I know and understand now that my parents made it known to the principal, office staff, and teachers. They did not want their children exposed to any kind of teaching from the Bible or on the existence of God.

There were many times I was removed from the classroom. I would be taken to a small room with my paper, pencil, and a book. I would be left there all by myself; sometimes, Laura and I would be in there together. We never knew why; we thought they did it to all the children, not just to us. The teachers would check on us occasionally, but what comfort was that in the face of what we were going through.

We needed more than just being checked on; we needed someone to talk to us. The sad truth is that no one at school was willing to take the risk! I am sure the teachers had many problems in dealing with the situation. I can understand, and I imagine that the teachers did not know how to reach out to us. They didn't know how to communicate with children who were being raised in such conditions.

However, as a child, I did not know or understand these things. Growing up, I felt rejected, pushed to the side, not good enough, not pretty enough, not smart enough, unloved, unlovable, and unwanted. I didn't bother the other children. Laura and I always sat together at lunch. No one would ever sit with us. I played alone on the playground. I walked down the hall alone.

I always looked down to avoid the little gestures that hurt me. I didn't understand most of the gestures. It was the knowing that, in some way, it was to mock me. For reasons I could not understand, the children enjoyed making fun of me. They would laugh at me and make fun of how I was dressed, my shoes, how I wore my hair, and the fact that I was not smart. I couldn't spell and write, and while I could read, I couldn't read as well as they could.

The list of the names I was called was long. I was looking forward to turning thirteen. I would be taken out of school, get the book of truth, and receive my passage. I did not know what it was, and I didn't care what it was. All that mattered to me was that I would never have to step a foot back into a school. But for now, these were my school days. School, well, it was just as unbalanced as my home life. The memory of my school days was very hard for me to look at and examine as a part of my life.

There were so many days full of tears, emotional pain, and rejection. There was, however, one day that stood out above them all. It's truly amazing how one day can change your life. How can one event tear you down or build you up? How can one moment, bad or good, change your destiny, even if you cannot see it at the time? That was true of this day, this event, and this moment.

On that day, for the first time in a long time, I woke up and felt pretty. That same night, I went to bed, knowing that I was ugly and hated. My heart was shutting down. I was beginning to refuse to cry. I was pushing the pain deeper and deeper down into my soul. I had finally come to the place where believing anyone was vanishing. It was February and the first day to return to school after being out of school for three months.

On December 19, 1963, I had turned ten, and I thought three more years and no more school. Now, the year was 1964, and I was ten years old, that winter day in February of 1964 when my life would take a turn, and not trusting anyone became my rule.

My dad surprised me with a new winter coat. He gave it to me the night before we were to return to school. We did not acknowledge Christmas, nor did we know anything about it, so it was not a Christmas gift. My dad said I had been doing all my work and following all the rules. I had not been disobedient since the park. He said Mom told him that the coat I had was two years old and I needed a new coat.

My new coat was beautiful. It had fur around the neck and deep pockets for my hands and gloves that matched. It was the most beautiful coat I ever had as a child. I would have slept in it that night, but I didn't want it to get all wrinkled and messed up.

The next morning, it was cold outside, and I was very happy. I was going to get to wear my new coat. I put it on and looked in the mirror and thought for a moment, *I'm pretty too*. For whatever reason, I stood there for a moment and looked quickly at the door, making sure it was shut. I looked back in the mirror, folded my hands, smiled at myself, and bowed my head. I giggled just a little. I wanted to see how I would look doing it. I gave myself a serious look and said, "I will always remember, I promise!" As I headed for the door, Laura yelled, "It's time to go!"

I was so proud of my new coat. Laura said the strangest thing to me. She said, "Linda, you are pretty, and the coat has nothing to do with it." We were on our way to the bus stop. Laura was the one person who was constant in my life. Faithful and unweaving, we were laughing, and she reached over and rubbed the fur on my coat.

The bus stop was about four blocks from our house. I always loved this time with Laura. It was really the only time we were able to talk and laugh with each other. The bus was pulling up as we arrived at the stop. We were both getting on when Laura slipped and fell. From what I could see, she was crying, and I thought she might be hurt.

I didn't get to talk to her after she fell. So, I was not sure why the bus driver sent her home. I tried to go with her, but he would not let me go. It was a rule we were not to separate from the time we left home until we got to class. It was a rule; we were always to stay together on the bus.

The children on the bus were not going to pass up an opportunity when the weird sister was alone. They pulled my hair, called me names, and said my coat was ugly. They laughed and said my sister and I were so ugly that even the bogeyman was afraid of us.

Then four of the prettiest and most popular girls in the school told all the other children to stop it. Two of them sat by me, and the other two sat in front of me. They all were talking to me. One fixed my hair, and they were all being so nice. When we were getting off the bus, they asked if I would sit with them at lunch. I was so happy; at lunch, I sat with them. I didn't say anything; I just listened to them. They seemed very different to me. They talked loudly and laughed at stupid things. I didn't really understand anything they were talking about. I just felt different sitting there with them.

It's hard to admit, but the truth is I was proud sitting there with them. All the children were looking at me, smiling, and saying, "Hi." It was great. I didn't like the way they acted, and I knew it. But yet, I wanted to be like them and liked by them. I hated going to school. I liked learning. I just hated the way the children called me names and teased me. Now, for some reason, they liked me, and I liked the way it made me feel. However, the truth is, even as a child, pride had a hold of my heart.

Lunch was ending when one of the girls asked me if I would like to be in their secret club. I asked them if Laura would have to know. They said no. I told them I wanted to be in it and asked them what they did in the secret club. They told me to meet them in the restroom after school, and they would tell me then. I asked them about the school bus. I was worried I might miss it. They told me the bus always waited fifteen minutes after it arrived.

As I was walking out of the cafeteria, I saw her—the little girl from the park. I was overflooded with emotions that were all new, different, and mixed up. It was as if I was happy to see her but embarrassed at the same time. I watched her closely as she folded her hands, smiled, and bowed her head. I turned and walked away. I looked back quickly to catch a glimpse of her wiping her tears away. I wanted to run back and tell her I was sorry, but it was too late.

The bell rang, and the four girls were just saying forget about it. "She is not cool; she will not fit in our secret club. You want to be our friend or hers?"

I said, "Yours," and quickly ran to class.

The afternoon was long. I jumped at every sound. Finally, the bell rang, and school was out. I rushed to the restroom as fast as I could. It wasn't long before the restroom was filling up with girls. Then, the four girls walked through the crowd. They said, "Welcome to our secret club." Then they just started hitting me, pulling my hair, kicking me, and calling me nasty names. The worst of it was they spit on me, not just a little.

When I was laying on the floor crying, they just kept kicking me and spitting on me. I am sure it didn't last long, maybe five minutes or less. However, I thought it was never going to end.

One of the girls yelled, "Bus!" They all took off running. I was just lying there on the floor. I was afraid to get up at first. I was hurting all over. I saw blood but did not know where it was coming from. I slowly started moving around. I was all alone, there in the restroom; not even one girl had stayed behind to see if I was hurt. Out of at least twenty girls, not one cared enough to check to see if I was okay. Within minutes, I remembered the bus.

I got up and grabbed my book satchel. As I was leaving the restroom to go get on the bus, I saw myself in the mirror. My nose was bleeding, and there was blood on my pretty new coat. My hair was a mess; my eyes were puffy and red. I wanted to cry. Instead, at that moment, I made a vow to myself that no one was ever going to see me cry again. I swore that not one person would ever see me shed a tear. *Not even one tear*, I swore. I really did not understand what had just happened to me or why. *Why did they do that to me? I have never done anything to them. Why did they do this? Why do they hate me so much?*

I realized I was going to miss the bus, so I took off running. I did not care what I looked like; I had to make a run for the bus. I would try to fix my hair when I got on the bus. As I was coming out the door, the bus was pulling off. I threw my book satchel down and ran as fast as I could. All I could see was the back of the bus. In the window, the four girls were making faces and laughing at me.

I just stood there. I didn't know what to do. It seemed like the only thing going through my mind was, *Why?* I don't know how long I stood there. I started to cry. I was trying to hold the tears back. I did not want anyone to see me cry.

Without any thought, I walked over, picked up my book satchel, and started walking. I didn't even know where I was going. I walked a long time; my nose stopped bleeding at some point. My new coat was ruined. My eyes hurt, my legs hurt, and it was getting dark. I didn't know where I was. Nothing looked familiar. I was afraid and all alone. Tears began to fall, blinding and freezing. I just kept walking. The pain in my heart outweighed my physical pain. My mind flashed scenes of the girls in the restroom. I could see them calling me names, hitting me, laughing, pulling my hair, and, worst of all, spitting on me. I was so hurt and confused. It was getting colder and colder. My mind would go back to the cafeteria, then to the restroom. Tears would fill my eyes, and I would tell myself, "No! No more tears." It was so very cold, but not as cold as my heart was turning.

At some point, I looked up, and there it was—a big "plus" sign. What was a "plus" sign doing on top of a building like that? It was shining bright. I started staring at it and just began walking towards it. It was getting darker and darker outside. But the plus sign was getting brighter and brighter. I was very tried, and it was colder. I was looking at the "plus" sign and thought that it was the most beautiful one I had ever seen. I remember wondering why there was a light shining on it. I kept walking towards it.

There were many thoughts in my head. *Why did I act like that in the lunchroom? They didn't really like me; they were just pretending so they could hurt me. That much I have figured out. But why did I act like that? Why did I do that to my friend? The little girl from the park, I could have sat with her. Maybe I would have found out what her name was. I hurt her for no reason. Why did I do that? She has never done anything to me. She has always been nice to me. She would not have done that to me. She thinks of me in a special way. Now, what am I going to do? I have lost the only friend I had. She probably hates me now, after what I did.*

Then, with one huge stab to my heart, I realized, *No! No! No! I am just as bad as the other children. I am worse than those four girls are. They didn't know me, but she knew me, and I knew her, and I hurt her.* It broke my heart as I realized that they also hated her, and then I remembered how I had seen them making fun of her as well. *Why? Why would I do such a thing? I don't deserve her as a friend.* About the time I was thinking, I hated myself for the way I had acted. I found myself standing right in front of the building with the big "plus" sign on top of it. I looked at the building for a few moments, trying to decide what kind of place this was.

A man came out of nowhere and said. "Everyone will be here soon; it's too cold out here. Let's go inside. Your parents dropped you off a little early." He unlocked and held the door open for me to walk in. He vanished. I didn't know where he went. I went in and went through some more doors and immediatcly felt the warmth.

I noticed these long skinny couches, but they were not couches; they just looked like them, in a way. They were all in rows, like a classroom. I noticed an area like a stage, but not like the one at school. It reminded me of the auditorium at school, only not as big. Maybe it was a different kind of school.

All I knew was I had not seen a place like this before. I thought, *This is a strange place...*

I saw the man again; about that time, he was getting up from off the floor. He had been on his knees.

"Are you okay?" I asked him.

He told me he was.

Then, I asked him, "Who is everyone?"

"Well, everyone who attends here," he responded.

I didn't understand, and he was busy doing something. I wasn't getting anywhere with this man. It was plain to see. So, I just asked him the only thing I could think of, "What is this place?"

He stopped what he was doing and turned around. I guess that's when he really saw me for the first time. He wanted to know what had happened to me. I told him I was lost and asked him if he could call my mom to come and get me. I gave him the phone number of our house. My mom had written it in my book satchel on the name tag inside.

He called, and my sister answered the phone. I talked to Laura for a few minutes. My dad and mom were out looking for me. Laura talked to the good man. When he got off the phone, he said, "She has the number of where you are, and she will give it to your dad and mom as soon as they get back."

While we were waiting for my dad to call, he asked me how I ended up getting lost. I told him about what the girls at school had done in the restroom and how I missed the bus. I told him about how I had been walking for a long time until I saw the "plus" sign on the building. Then I asked him again, "What kind of place is this?" He got a funny look on his face. He told me that was a cross, not a "plus" sign on top of the building.

Then he told me we were in a church. I asked him more questions. Things like what a church was and what a cross was.

Last of all, I asked, "What do they do in this place called church?"

The look on his face was one of shock, confusion, and sadness. I have always remembered what he said: "Well, little one, this is God's house. It's where people come to learn about God and His Son. We pray here and sing—"

I didn't let him finish, asking, "What does 'pray' mean?" I told him about the little girl from the park, everything we said to each other, and how she showed me our secret sign.

He said, "Praying was when you talk to God about somebody or something." He added, "You have a good friend."

I was very sad then. I remembered what I did to her, and I told him all about it. I also told him I knew I had hurt her and I had made her cry. "She hates me now..."

He said she would forgive me.

"What does to forgive really mean?" I asked.

"Forgiveness means you let it go by," the man responded. I was confused, and it was easy to tell. He said, "When you do things wrong or sin—"

"There is no such thing as wrong or sin," once again, I did not let him finish.

Then, the man said, "If there was no wrong or sin, why do you feel bad?" Then he asked me all kinds of questions. I liked it. No one ever asked me anything. I just felt like I could talk to him all night.

We talked and talked; I liked him. He was different. He didn't talk to me the way everyone else did. I thought to myself,

This man is a good man. He just might be the only one I would ever meet. At some point, my dad called and said he was on his way.

People had started coming in, and they kept saying, "Good evening, Pastor." He pulled one couple to the side and talked to them for a few minutes. Then he came over to where I was. He wanted to tell me a story while we waited for my parents. He said he wanted to talk to my dad and mom. I told him I didn't think that was a very good idea. We waited in this little room. He said it was his office. I asked him, "What is a 'pastor'?"

"They teach, train, and take care of the flock," the man answered.

I laughed and said, "So, you take care of the sheep?"

He was serious now for some reason. He had this look on his face. It seemed for a moment that he himself would cry. "I am going to ask you to remember something. Can you do that?"

I said, "I remembered the little girl in the park, didn't I? Yes, I can remember." I smiled and added, "I promise." I waited for him to speak.

This good man who took care of sheep said, "Linda, what you called a 'plus' sign is called a cross. No matter what ever happens in your life, just look for the cross. If you're hurt, alone, frightened, or just need help, look for the cross, Linda, and go there." Then he said, "You must remember this: if you are ever in danger, fear something bad is going to happen to you. Scream out, 'God, save me!' and He will." He asked me to repeat it three or four times. He told me that he would be praying for me.

He started talking about God. I listened for a few moments. I told him there was no God. As I said those words, he looked past me. I turned around, and there was my dad and mom. I ran to them.

My dad looked at me and asked, "Who did this?" I didn't tell my dad and mom everything, just about the restroom and missing the bus. Then the man wanted to talk to them. They didn't talk very long. Dad and Mom came out smiling, but as we all walked away, I could see the anger.

When we were in the car, I asked, "Am I in trouble because I didn't do anything?"

My dad asked me, "Linda, tell me the truth. Do you believe what he said to you about a God?"

I told my dad with a smile on my face, "Dad, the girls at school hurt me, and I missed the bus. It's not like the park. I was lost and cold. I did not know what kind of place that was. Dad, you know that there is no God. I know it too." That's what I told him. My dad didn't say a word after that.

When we got home, he sat me down and talked to me. I did not want to stay on the outside of the circle at the end of the harvest again. I just listened, smiled, and agreed. I knew there was no such thing as a life spirit, but I thought it would be stupid for me to be spit on again over something I knew was a lie. But if I believed in something, well, that made it different. I could stand and be spit on, but I was not going to be spit on for something I did not believe in. In my little girl's world, I was learning to reason things out in my mind. Inside my mind, I knew they could not touch me there. They could not know my thoughts. I had figured it out.

Laura helped me get all cleaned up. She cried when she saw all the bruises on me. I didn't even know I had any until she said, "Look at what they have done to you!" Laura hugged me, and we cried together.

I asked her, "Laura, why do they hate us so much?"

She just said, "I don't know, Linda." Then she whispered in my ear. "Dad and Mom are going to the school tomorrow."

It was a very long night; my head was full of thoughts. I went over and over what happened in the restroom and the long walk in the freezing mist. My beautiful new coat was ruined. I thought about the good man who tended sheep. I thought he didn't look or smell like the boys in Kentucky who tend to the sheep. He must have really clean sheep. I kept thinking about all the things we talked about. They just kept flowing into my mind. Over and over, like rivers of water that would keep these memories washed clean and clear for some future use. In many ways, these memories kept me alive. They kept me going and kept me looking for that cross. Every time I saw a cross, the memory of that night flooded my soul again. I would smile and look at the cross carefully, but then, when I realized it didn't look like the cross I had seen that night when I was lost, sadness filled my heart. Would I ever find that cross again?

I thought a lot that night about what he said, how he talked about praying, and what it means to forgive. I didn't believe in God, and I didn't believe in praying. However, I had reasoned that the little girl in the park did. I had a plan: I would make the secret sign to her, and then she would know I understand now. If she does it back, she is still my friend.

That night was also a night of bad dreams about the girls in a circle spitting on me, calling me names, hitting me, and pulling my hair. I had dreams about a little girl in a park, folding her hands, smiling, and bowing her head. I would wake up and go back to sleep, only to dream again. I dreamed about bonfires and people spitting on me and trying to find water to wash myself off. I would wake up again and fall back into a world of dreams and nightmares where sleep is not really sleep.

Laura was right. The next morning, Dad and Mom took us to school. On the way, Dad talked to Laura and me. He reminded us that we would be taken out of school when we turned thirteen. Mom would find us something to do to bring money in to help. He would find us husbands who would accept our ways. He told me not to worry about the girls at school. They would never bother me again. He told me those girls were going to pay for what they did. Their parents were going to get me a new coat.

They were going to a meeting at the school about what happened to me. I could hear my dad hollering from where I was sitting. It was not the first time. I had heard him many times. He would holler so loud, but I never understood why. Now, he was in the principal's office with the parents of the four girls, and even the ladies in the office sat at the desk, giving each other looks. The four girls were sitting across from me outside the principal's office. They seemed different today. They did not look at me. If they did and I looked at them, they turned away quickly. The parents finally came out.

Their parents told me they were sorry for what their daughters had done and that they would be punished. They looked at my black eyes, swollen nose, swollen face, and bruised legs and kept saying to their daughters, "I cannot believe you would do a thing like this."

That day at lunch, none of the children would look at Laura and me. The cafeteria was full of whispers. Laura and I sat at a table alone, as we had always done. I looked around for the little girl in the park. I spotted her standing by the door, ready to walk out. I looked at Laura and said, "Please, please don't tell on me; I have to do this." Laura nodded, and I knew it was okay.

I got up and started walking towards the little girl from the park. I yelled, "Hey!" She immediately looked over to where I was standing. Every eye in the cafeteria was on me, and not a word was said. I bravely folded my hands, smiled, and bowed my head. I then looked at her and said in a loud voice, "I know what it means now." She folded her hands, smiled, and bowed her head. The bell rang at that time, and we both smiled at each other. We both knew we couldn't talk. Laura and I headed for our classes.

Laura asked me, "Do you believe in God, Linda?"

I told her, "No, I don't, but my friend does. When she does that, she thinks she is talking to God about me. I just wanted her to know that I know what it means when she folds her hands and bows her head. That's all."

Laura said, "Good, because there is no God. You will just get in all kinds of trouble for nothing. I will not tell Dad or Mom about this, but you need to leave her alone. Okay?"

I said, "I will, Laura." Then I ran to my classroom.

After I had gotten lost that night and ended up in a church, Dad told Mom to take Laura and me to a pay phone and teach us how to use one. He never wanted that to happen again; he wanted us to be able to call home if we were lost or needed help. For that purpose, from that day forward, a dime was put in our shoe and a piece of paper with our phone number on it wrapped in foil. I was so excited; I knew how to use a phone.

However, as a direct result of that cruel act of hatred, the memory of that day has been hard for me to think about. The emotional damage it caused in my life took years to overcome. At ten, my little world had changed. I learned that just because someone smiles at you, it doesn't mean you can trust them. *A smile can be as dangerous as an angry look.*

It was March 1964; soon, we would be checked out of school again. We would go to the park for the celebration of the life spirit and then head for Kentucky, the harvest, the bonfire, the circle, and Grandpa. Then, we would go home again. Was life just one big circle with no rhyme or reason?

Had three little words taken flight in my heart and rocked the foundation of all that my family believed? Everything they had taught me meant nothing. I had always believed that there was no God. Now, there was nothing for me to believe in: no God, no spirit life. I was still a little lost girl, looking for understanding and a road that would lead me to the truth. Three words had been planted in my mind and heart. They were three words small and gentle that would breeze through my mind, three words big enough to change the course of my life. Those three words were "cross," "pray," and "forgive," and let it go by.

I was different. The world that used to seem so small was getting bigger. I was noticing things I never noticed before. I knew that not all families were like mine; each family was different in one way or another. They believed in different things and did different things. Families were people in cars. For some reason, in 1964, I started looking at people in cars. I knew that in every car was a family, and even if they were alone, they belonged to a family somewhere. In some cars, the families didn't seem to be happy. In other cars, I could tell they were yelling at each other. In a few cars, the people would be talking and just seemed happy. Some cars only had one person. He or she would be patting the steering wheel in a certain pattern. I decided that was the kind of car I wanted to be in, one all by myself.

I would go to a place where no one would treat me badly, a place where everybody was happy and people did not lie and hurt each other, a place where I could find the truth, a place where people are not mean to you just because you are different, and a place where you are not hated by people who don't even know you. I decided to go to a place where I was not hated by people who have never even taken the time to talk to me—a place where there are swings and everybody says, "I love you."

The wounds and scars from my first day back to school in February of 1964 would be sealed in my memory. Every time I saw a cross, I remembered when the girls at school used me as the object of a cruel joke. My beautiful coat was ruined. But I also remembered a good man, the only one I had ever met, and he tended sheep. Days went by, weeks, then years, and I never got a new coat. I never forgot my beautiful coat, how warm and wonderful it felt. I can still see it in my mind. It was the only thing my father ever gave me.

CHAPTER 3

Daddy, Please Let It Go By

Planting season was approaching; it was still a time of celebration for my family. However, the event meant nothing to me. I did not see it the same way as I did when I was nine years old. Things at school had not changed at all, if anything. They had gotten worse. Then there was the planting and harvesting; nothing was different there either. It was still one big circle of events in my life. It seemed that life was like the circle at the end of the harvest: It began with planting and ended with the harvest. So, it was with life. It begins with birth, and it ends with death, just one big circle. Nothing had changed, and yet everything was changing in me.

My thoughts were taking me further and further from my family and their beliefs. On the outside, I appeared to be the perfect picture of all that my family lived by and believed. On the inside, however, there was pain and confusion and so many unanswered questions. At home, I obeyed the rules and endured all the fighting between Dad and Mom. There were fistfights and devastating destruction of things inside the home.

My dad's raging anger and drinking had carved a course that ran wild and rampant. However, it could never be compared to the course that was being carved out for two young sisters. Carved out by the very things we were being taught and had learned to endure.

It was a beautiful day, sometime in early March. The year was 1965, and I was eleven years old. Four months earlier, on December 19, 1964, I had turned eleven. I had my countdown going: two more years, no more school. I would get the book of truth and then take my passage, and I would finally know the truth. But for now, it was rules, planting, harvesting, celebration in the park, celebration at the end of the harvest, more rules, obedience, and disobedience. It just seemed I couldn't get it all straight in my head.

Mom was having some friends over for tea on the patio overlooking her garden in the back yard. It was one of her favorite places to have tea in the spring. The garden was full of pansies. Mom loved pansies, and she made this salad that included pansies in it. Today, it is still one of my favorite salads to make and eat. Mom always made her tea parties a big event. She would have us get out her crystal glasses, fine china cups, and saucers. We had to wash and dry them. Everything had to be perfect. The table was set with a sterling silver teapot, a sterling silver creamer, and a matching sugar bowl. There were sterling silver spoons to match that had to be polished. Everything was checked and rechecked; all the silver had to be polished. Mom had four different tablecloths for her outside table. The one she had chosen was emerald green with a beautiful lace border that was just a shade lighter than the cloth. It was beautiful.

I had never served one of Mom's tea parties; this one would be my first. Laura had gone over everything with me. Mom double-checked to make sure I understood all the rules: Do not speak, always smile, and say, "Yes, ma'am" and "No, ma'am" when spoken to. Do not embarrass her. Do not spill, drop, or break anything. I received instructions on how to pour so that no drop would drip on the tablecloth. I had been prepared for more than a year just to learn how to serve a tea party properly. I was ready.

Laura would stay in the kitchen doing all the baking this time. It was normally me in the kitchen, and she would help me as time allowed away from serving. This time, it was going to be the other way around, and I was excited for the first time in over a year. This was going to be a very special day for me. I thought about it almost all night. I am sure that I fell asleep long after everyone in the house. I woke up the next morning and put on my nice dress for special days.

My mom came into my room; my long-awaited moment had come. In her hands was a beautiful apron for me. It was white with lace and emerald green ribbon to match the tablecloth. Mom had made the apron for me to wear on this special occasion. I put the apron on after she handed it to me with special rules and instructions. My mom tied it for me and told me it was her special time with her lady friends and for me not to mess it up. I looked up at her, smiled, and said, "Mom, thank you for making me this apron; it is so beautiful."

She opened the door to walk out, looked at me, and said, "The apron will be put up after today, and it is not yours; it is mine. You are only wearing it to serve my friends." She closed the door behind her. I just stood there. I was so hurt. I thought about all the hours of practicing pouring water and tea without spilling a drop and the hours I had spent learning how to serve from the right to the left, setting the table, and pulling out the chairs for the ladies to sit. All of a sudden, it meant nothing to me. I didn't want to even serve her or her friends. I didn't care anymore. I just wanted her to love me and notice how hard I was trying to make her proud of me as her daughter.

It was time to go sit in the living room with Laura and wait for Mom's friends to arrive. This was one of the rare occasions we were allowed in the living room. One by one, they arrived, and Mom would always introduce Laura and me to her friends. We knew them all, but Mom would always say, "As you know, this is Laura, my oldest," and pointing to me, "This is Linda, the youngest." They were always polite to Laura and me, always told us we were pretty, and every now and then made a comment on how big we were getting.

They all went out to the patio and were talking and laughing somewhat loud. I went out and pulled the chairs out as I had been taught. They all sat down. I poured the water and the tea. It was perfect. I served the dessert and picked up the plates after they were finished. I was getting ready to place the ashtray on the table when my mom said, "Tell Laura to get my new diamond ring your father got me last week."

Well, I knew that was a lie; my dad did not give her a ring. It was from one of the men that came to see her. The ashtray slipped from my hand and crashed into the table. It bounced, hit her glass, and knocked it onto the saucer, which caused the cup to fly up in the air and land in my mom's lap. As all of the contents in the glass poured out into her lap, amazingly not breaking one item on the table, the ashtray landed in the center of the table, bottom side up.

I saw my mom's face, and I just started laughing. Everyone was laughing, and then my mom started laughing. After a few moments, my mom got up from the table to go inside and asked me to go with her.

When we got inside, she was very angry and told me I would never serve her and her friends again. Mom told me that after her friends left, I was going to do all the cleaning and that Laura and she were going out for a while. Mom changed and went back out with Laura. Mom had Laura sit down at the table with her guest. It wasn't very long, maybe ten minutes, and everyone came in, and soon the house was empty.

I went to the front door to see if all the cars were gone. Laura and Mom were standing on the front porch. Mom was showing off the ring and just smiling like nothing in the world was wrong, but I knew better. She was angry, and I knew before this day ended, I was going to get punished. I went to the patio and started to clean things up. I thought it would help. I took everything inside, including the tablecloth. I ran the dishwater and prepared the tablecloth to be handwashed. I went back outside, washed the table off, and put everything back the way it should be on the patio. I went inside to the front door to see what was going on. They were all still on the front porch. I was getting ready to go back to the kitchen when I heard my mom say, "Yes, Laura is very special."

I went to the kitchen and washed all the dishes, then dried them. I was putting them away when I started talking to myself. I was standing in front of the china cabinet saying things.

I said, "When I grow up, I'm going to have lots of money, lots of pretty things, and lots and lots of jewelry. I'm going to have a lot of friends, and I'm going places. My mom will want to spend time with me, but I will tell her, 'I have more important things to do. I just do not have time for you.'" I continued talking, "I am going to be too busy with my things, my money, my jewelry, and my friends." I was going to have good friends like the little girl from the park, not half dressed, loud friends that say many bad words. "How does Mom even know these ladies? They are not from around here; they are not schoolteachers, and I don't believe they are nurses. I'm glad Mom doesn't want me to serve them anymore because I don't want to."

As I was speaking out loud to myself, I heard my mom say, "Linda!" I jumped. I didn't have time to say anything. She walked over to where I was and said, "Young lady, you will take all the dishes from the china cabinet. Then you are going to wash, dry, and put them away, starting right now."

I believe it was at this point in my life that something started shifting. I looked at her and said, "No! I will not! I will break every dish in this cabinet before I wash all these dishes." Then, outrolled the words, "Mom, do you love me? Do you love me even just a little? Is there anything that you see in me as special?" The way she looked at me was unforgettable. Even now, I cannot describe the look on her face.

Mom asked me to give her the cup and saucer I was holding. I told her, "No! Not until you answer me. Have you ever felt anything for me? I have never even seen you shed a tear, even when you know that I have been hurt. Please answer me. Do you love anything at all about me?"

Once again, she did not answer but asked me to give her the cup and saucer I was holding. That's when it happened. I raised my arms as I heard her scream, *"No!"* I threw the cup and saucer to the floor, and it broke into pieces.

I watched my mom; she went to her knees, crying over her cup and saucer lying on the floor, now broken and shattered into tiny pieces. Calmly and silently, I walked away, knowing in my heart my mom loved her things more than she loved me because things were more important than me. She could cry over the broken cup and saucer but could not shed one tear for me, her broken daughter. I turned and watched as she cried over the broken cup and saucer. I remember having a hard time processing what was in my heart. I wanted to hate her, remembering that a year ago, I had bruises, black eyes, a busted nose, and not one tear for me. She just walked by me as if I didn't exist. Now, here she is, crying over a stupid cup and saucer. This is how I, as a little girl, processed and handled the hurt that day.

Suddenly, I felt as though my heart would break for her. I saw her as that broken cup, and I was the broken saucer. All her brokenness was being poured out into me. However, I liked the saucer, which was not big enough to handle the contents of what was in the cup.

At that moment, I wished to see my little friend from the park fold her hands, smile, and bow her head. I wished I could run down some street and find that cross and talk to the good man who tended sheep. But there was no one. With tears in my eyes, I walked over to where my mom was and knelt beside her, and I began to pick up the broken pieces. I thought for a moment, *These are the broken pieces of our lives.*

I told her I was sorry. There was this hurt look in her eyes that I cannot explain, not even to this day. That day in March of 1965, I believe that I saw a brokenness in her that no one had ever seen. A brokenness that she did not want anyone to know existed. It was not just the broken cup and saucer that I saw in her eyes.

I cleaned it all up and helped her get to her feet. I was really very sorry that I had broken her beautiful china cup and saucer. I told her once again, "Mom, I am so sorry about the cup and saucer. I love you, and if you need me, I will be in my bedroom." I had forgotten what had led up to this moment, but now it had flooded my heart. I added, "Mom, I am also sorry about dropping the ashtray at your little tea party. It was an accident. It really was."

I was almost in my bedroom when I heard the dreaded words. "Linda Marie! I'm telling your father when he gets home." I turned around and walked back to where she was. I looked at her and said, "No! You are not going to tell him. I will tell him. I can go to my father and tell him. I am going to sit on the front porch and wait until he comes home. I am going to tell him myself that I refused to wash everything in the cabinet because I did not drop that ashtray on purpose, and I laughed because I couldn't help it; it was funny. I will also tell him that I broke your precious cup and precious saucer and that I did it on purpose."

Mom, true to her word, left that afternoon with Laura. Everything had been cleaned and put away. Mom left me on the front porch, waiting for my dad to come home. Even though she knew she would return long before he came home, Mom left me on the porch and locked me out of the house. I had lots of time to think, and there was a wide range of thoughts that afternoon. I have laid them out here as I remember to the best of my ability. They are not in order; I am sure of that. However, they are the things that I thought about that afternoon. I do recall that I did spend the first part of that afternoon thinking about the things that would be taking place over the next few months.

I thought about the trip to Kentucky, Laura, and all the things that surrounded her thirteenth birthday and when I would turn thirteen. She would be receiving the book of truth, read it, and the following year, she would receive her passage. School had changed some; Laura and I no longer went into a little room in the mornings. We went directly to class in the mornings. That was a little confusing for us. A few days later, after going to class instead of that little room, I heard a girl say in the lunch line, "My mom says we cannot pray in the mornings anymore; it's the law. Isn't that silly?" The other girl said, "My dad said our school had done it for years when they should not have, and they got in trouble. That's crazy." At that point, I thought I understood what it meant; I just wasn't sure. There was no one to talk to who could help me to understand.

In about a week, we would be heading for the park for the planting season celebration. Then, the next day, we would leave for Kentucky. My thoughts turned to Grandpa, his guitar, and the truth concerning the life spirit. There was a chance I thought I could be wrong, that I was cursed, like they said. It seemed like a long time ago when I had believed in the life spirit. Still, sometimes, I would think about it and think that maybe it was real. After all, Grandpa really did walk through the fire. I did know that; I watched it very closely during the last two years. I don't know how he did it. I just know that he did. It's like how he stands up on the guitar and dances on it. I don't know how he did it; I just know he did.

Sometimes, I would think I was wrong about everything, and the life spirit left me that day at the park, and I was left to wonder all the days of my life. I cannot say I had not thought of it ever again after that day in Kentucky when I touched Grandpa's guitar because I did. I often thought I could have been wrong the day that I touched Grandpa's guitar. Maybe it was Grandpa who had the power and gave it to the guitar only when he was touching it. Sometimes, I would wake up in the middle of the night, and fear would fill my soul. During those times, I thought the life spirit was real, and I had disobeyed so much for so long it would not reveal itself to me.

Laura would be turning fourteen on April 29, 1966, and she would receive her passage. However, from thirteen to fourteen was the preparation for receiving the passage. Then she was going to tell me all about it. Laura had promised me a long time ago that she would tell me how wonderful it all was.

We both had looked forward to it for as long as we could remember. I believed that when I received my passage, all my questions would be answered, and I may even find that the life spirit was real. I believed that the life spirit would come to me when I received my passage and that I would be forgiven for all my disobedience. I am not sure how I came up with that conclusion. I guess I just thought that's how it was going to work.

In many ways, I was waiting to turn thirteen, too, so I could read the book of truth. It would answer all my questions, and I would be set free. I wanted to read the book of truth so I could learn the truth, then I would take my passage, and I would finally know the truth and be free. Then I could start living my life; that's kind of how the plan had been laid out to us ever since we could remember, so to Laura and me, there was no life until after our passage. It was on days like this, and when I thought about it, it all made sense. However, there were times that I thought the whole concept was crazy.

Laura had already received the book of truth. She would be turning thirteen on April 29, 1965. For some reason, Dad gave her the book early; she had not shared anything with me from it.

That was the main reason for us going to school, so we could learn to read. All the children in the family who turned thirteen would receive the book. After reading it, the book would be given back to our dad. Then we could go once every three months to a feast for the reading and instructions. We both knew that at fourteen, we would receive our passage. But neither of us knew what it was.

I thought about the little girl in the park who believed in a God and in a place called heaven. I thought about a building that was called church. This place called church had a cross on top of it and a man inside. He was a good man and the only one I had ever met, and maybe the only one I would ever meet. I did so want to talk to him that day.

I always went over and over that night in my mind. All the things we talked about. The parts of the conversation that were most important to me. The one thing he wanted me to remember was the one thing I reminded myself of often: No matter what ever happens in my life, look for the cross. If I am hurt, alone, frightened, or just need help, look for the cross and go there. Then came the words I tried so hard to understand, "If you are afraid and fear something bad is going to happen to you, scream out, 'God, save me,' and He will." I remembered him well. He was a good man who tended sheep. I would think about all kinds of things. I was always looking and asking myself questions. But even after all the looking, all the seeking, and all the asking, I still had no answers. I was still just a little girl locked out of her house, sitting on the front porch waiting for her father to come home.

Last of all, I had thoughts of my mother, her life, my secret, and the shattering truth. It was here, on this day, on the front porch, that thoughts of my mother and the reality of her life were going to shape and change my little girl's view of her. I would no longer see her through the eyes of a little girl after this day. In my eyes, there was nothing or no one more beautiful than my mother. She was truly a beautiful woman. She had long blonde hair, deep green eyes, and a beautiful complexion. She was around five and a half foot and had a figure that most women envy. She was a woman who was admired by men… lots of men. She knew how to attract them and get their attention.

My mother was a woman who knew how to get what she wanted. No matter what my dad did, it was never enough. Mother wanted more, so she used her body and her looks to get what she wanted. She received money, jewelry, clothes, and many beautiful things in our home from the men she saw. Mother had many possessions.

I believe she had become no more than a possession herself to those men who had given her those beautiful things. Deep down inside, she knew she had been bought and paid for and that she had become their possession. Maybe that is what I saw in her eyes that day; she was grieving what she had given up for that little broken possession.

That day in March of 1965, I came to realize my mother seeing men for money was at least part of the reason my dad drank and was so angry at her. As a child, I feared for my mother's life.

Many nights, my dad was out of town, and a man would come in the late-night hours to be with her. I was a very light sleeper and would always wake up to the tapping, loud noises, or the lights flashing in the house. I would get up, go down the hall, and hear the whispering and laughing. I was so afraid my dad would come home and catch her with a man.

I would get my pillow and blanket and lay by her door so I could warn her if Dad came home in the middle of the night. When I heard a lot of movement and laughing again, I knew it was time and the man would be leaving soon. I would quietly get my things and go back to my bedroom. I had done this for a long time.

There are times when your mind will wander and take you places that you don't want to go. Things in the past that, even as a child, sometimes you are painfully aware of. This was true of that day in March. I did not want to think about my secret that day, but it slipped into my mind like a gentle breeze. Once it was there, it was too late. I had fallen back into time that afternoon.

I had gotten off the porch and was walking around in the yard, and there it was—that little shovel. I looked at it for a minute. *No, that cannot be it.* That was a long time ago. I went back to the porch, but it was too late; my mind went back, back,

back… Back to a time and place where the truth was too painful, and the shattered life of a little girl lay in ruins.

It was a beautiful fall day. I have no knowledge of time, day, month, or year. I just know it started out a beautiful day. Laura was at school; I had not started school yet. I would start the following year.

Mom had told me to go take my nap, but I wanted to slide down the hallway with my white socks on. That's what I was doing, sliding down the hallway when the doorbell rang. I took off running to open the door. There he was, J.D., my dad's best friend, and he just patted me on the head, called me special, and gave me a dollar. He smiled at me and gave me a wink.

The next thing I knew, I was skipping to the store at the end of our street with my dollar in hand. I don't recall it being a big store. It carried a few items: sugar, milk, eggs, flour, and things like that, and in the back of the store, it had a little countertop and stools to sit on and have ice cream. The stools didn't have backs on them. When you sat on them, you could twirl, going round and round. There I sat with my little feet just dangling, going round and round. I had an ice cream cone—strawberry—my favorite. They had chocolate, vanilla, and strawberry. That was it back then, but strawberry was my favorite.

I was having a great time, and then I looked up, and there was a big jar full of all kinds of candy. The jar was huge and had a big silver top. I looked on the counter at how much money I had left. I was able to get a bag full of candy. I thought of my mom and got her a beautiful sucker that looked like the rainbow. I skipped all the way back home. I still had two pennies left, a bag full of candy, and a sucker for my mom. I was a child; I thought like a child, and I acted like a five-year-old child.

I opened the door and went inside; it was very quiet, and all the lights were out. I thought Mom must be taking a nap. I wanted to surprise her with the sucker. I was just going to open her bedroom door very quietly and put the sucker on the little table by her bed. I could not move. I just stood there. I did not know what to do. My mind was spinning. There they were, J.D., my dad's best friend, in my father's bed with my mother. At first, I could not move, out of shock, then out of fear. I felt a pain like none other I had ever felt. It didn't make sense; I could not move because of the pain, but I was not hit, kicked, or slapped, but I felt worse than all of them put together.

Neither one of them heard me or saw me. Even as a child, I knew it was wrong; it hurt me so deeply as if someone had just spanked me for something I did not do. I don't know how long I stood there watching them and not fully understanding, but somehow, it was hurting me, and deep inside, I knew this would hurt my dad.

I somehow managed to get out of the bedroom and shut the door. I was standing in the hallway where, not long ago, I was a child running, sliding, and laughing, and I was happy. Something happened to me in that moment. At five years old, my life had been shattered. What does a five-year-old do with that? How can a five-year-old process something like that? I saw my hand and felt it getting tighter and tighter around the bag of candy. I did not know or understand the feelings I was experiencing. I felt rage, hate, and anger but was unable to identify or process any of it.

I started walking down the hallway. I went through the kitchen. My hand was hurting from holding the bag so tight. I went through the large family room to the back door, and out the door, tears streamed down my face. There it was, a little shovel. I bent down, grabbed it, walked over to a tree, sat down, and began digging.

I don't know how long I dug, but when I stopped, I slammed the candy down in that hole and buried it right along with myself. I was shattered, and there was no way to put me back together. I buried it, and I refused to think about it.

I had not thought about it in seven years, and I didn't want to think about it now. I was still unable to look at that moment when I walked into that room. There was still so much pain in the memories of that day and emotions that I still could not understand. They just seemed to be pieces and fragments of a day that I chose long ago to bury. I once again pushed it back into the secret place in my heart.

Now, I sat on the front porch waiting for a man whom I called Dad. I was painfully aware of his presence in my life. He was a man I did not know, a man who seemed to disappear from time to time and for no apparent reason. A man who returned home drunk and angry more times than not. A man I had never really seen smile. A man I feared because of the words, "I am going to tell your father when he gets home." This man spit on me and then turned around and was angry when someone else did the same. A man who bought me the most beautiful coat I had ever seen. That man was my father; on this day, I came to a truth, and that truth was my mother crushed my father's heart.

I knew my mom had hurt my dad by always wanting more than he could give her. My mom hurt him by doing all those things with men. However, no matter what she did, he stayed with her for reasons only he knew and understood. It was getting dark when Mom and Laura returned.

I went in, used the bathroom, and got a drink of water. Mom told me I needed to get back on the porch and wait for my father. I went back to the porch and realized I had no plan. What was I going to tell him? At that moment, my father had become the most important person in my life.

My father was still the same, but I had changed. If my father had not been drinking, I knew I would get a good hand spanking, and it would not last long. However, if my father had been drinking, I knew it meant a belt and would last until his anger diminished.

I thought to myself that it was a good thing I had spent the whole afternoon thinking about so many different things. I just didn't sit around all that time worrying about what was going to happen to me. I knew just sitting around worrying about it was not going to help or change the outcome. But right now, it was time for me to be thinking about what I was going to do and what I was going to say. It was getting later and later, and I knew the later it got, the worse it was going to be.

I thought I could run away, but where could I go? I had an idea. I thought about what the good man who tended sheep had said about forgiveness and what it meant. He said, "It means to let it go by." For a long time, I sat and thought about what it really means to let it go by. I did not fully understand it. But it was a good idea.

I was going to tell Dad about what had happened, how I accidentally dropped the ashtray and then got mad at Mom, and then I broke her cup and saucer on purpose. Then I would ask him, "Daddy, please let it go by." I made a promise to myself that no matter what happened that night, I was going to try to talk to my father.

I went in to get another drink of water and use the bathroom. I looked at the clock—it was nine. I knew what that meant—he was drinking. I knew that this night would not end well for me. I went back out on the porch and kept saying the words repeatedly, "Daddy, please let it go by. Daddy, please let it go by. Daddy, please let it go by." It was getting late, and I was having a hard time holding my eyes open. I was tired; it had been a long day.

This day had started out with such excitement. Now, it was ending with unpleasant thoughts of what might happen to me. I saw the headlights coming down the road; I knew it was him long before he pulled up into the driveway. My heart was beating fast and hard, so hard that I thought it was going to beat right out of my chest. I realized I had never spoken to my dad for myself. I mean, I would answer his questions when he asked, but I had never just gone to him about anything. My mind started racing, and I just forgot everything.

Dad was getting out of the truck, and I could tell he was drunk. I recognized that old, familiar walk. Dad had a surprised look on his face when he saw me; he wasn't accustomed to finding his children waiting for him on the front porch. I am sure that this was the first and last time this had ever happened, at least to my knowledge. He asked, "You can't sleep and just decided to come out here and wait for your old dad?" I looked at him for what seemed to be hours. I noticed the lines on his face and his dark, tired eyes.

He looked very different to me that night. My thoughts were not very organized at this time, and I couldn't seem to get the words to come out. He asked me if I was planning to answer him, and I said, "Yes, I need to talk to you about something."

Dad said, "Well, then, speak up. What do you get to tell me, girl?"

I took a deep breath and told him everything, from the time I dropped the ashtray to breaking her cup and saucer on purpose. After I told him that, I said, "I hurt Mom today, Daddy, when I broke her cup and saucer. I know it was an act of disobedience, and I am not sure I would ever do something like this again, but just this once; can you—"

I did not get to finish; he grabbed my arm and jerked me up to my feet. He was pulling me into the house. Once we were in the house, he shoved me into the hallway, and I slipped and fell. He told me to get up and get in the bathroom. I was heading towards the bathroom when I knew I had to say the words. I said, "Daddy, you didn't let me finish." I waited to see what he was going to do.

He said, "I told you to get in the bathroom."

I walked on into the bathroom. I turned around to face him as he walked through the bathroom door. I said, "Daddy, I know you are going to punish me no matter what, so can you just give me a few seconds to say something? I have waited all afternoon to say this to you." He didn't answer my question. I looked up at him, tears running down my face as the words came out, "Daddy, please let it go by, just this one time. Please let it go by."

He was taking off his belt as he said, "No!"

I went to my knees and said, "Daddy, please let it go by; Daddy, please let it go by..." My hands were holding onto his ankles. Dad told me to let go and move away from him. I backed up into the corner of the bathroom, looked at him one more time, and said, "Daddy, please let it go by; Daddy, please let it go by!"

I was watching him as he pulled his arm up into the air with the belt in his hand. He was ready to make his first swing as the words came out, "Daddy, please let it go by; please, Daddy, please, let it go by." He was now in full swing motion as I covered my eyes and said, "Let it go by, Daddy, please..."

I waited for the full blow of the lash to strike somewhere on my body. From the position he was standing in, I knew that the first lash was going to strike across my shoulder area or possibly across my face, so I covered my eyes and was in the process of turning away from him.

When the first lash hit somewhere, I heard it hit, but I felt nothing. I waited, but nothing. I slowly started moving out of the position of a rolled-up ball. I saw my dad's feet and moved my head upward very slowly.

When my dad's face was in full view, I looked into his blue eyes, which were now filled with tears. There was this look on his face; what was this look? I had never seen this look before. I wanted to reach up and wipe away his tears, but I dared not. At that very moment, this one moment in my life was being inscribed in the depths of my soul. I felt a rush of peace and joy I had never experienced in my father's presence.

He said no words; there was no need, for the daughter had captured the heart of the father, and the father had granted forgiveness. It was truly a feeling like no other I had ever experienced. Tears had worked their way to my eyes and were now rolling down my cheeks. The silence was broken. I said, "Daddy, thank you for letting it go by. I know, even now, that all my life, I am going to mess up and even be disobedient at times. But I will never forget what took place here. I will always remember that you let it go by this one time. I love you, Daddy." With my final words, my dad turned and walked out of the bathroom. It was never spoken of again, but it was, indeed, always remembered.

I stayed in the bathroom, as was the custom of our family, to think about my disobedience. I got a towel out of the cabinet to cover up. I curled up on the floor and covered up with the towel. There was never a bending of the rules; I would have to wait the two hours required after a punishment. It was very late that night, and I knew no one was going to stay up just to let me know when my time was up. I also knew that if I left the bathroom before morning, I would have more trouble. Mom would think I left before the two hours was up. No, I knew it was best for me just to sleep here.

I tried to go to sleep, but the day's events filled my thoughts. I went over everything: what happened, my thoughts, what I did, what I said, my mom, my dad, what they did, and what they said. Over and over, I thought about this day, like I did with the events that happened with the little girl from the park and the results. I thought about the day I was lost and all that had happened to me that day. So, it was with this event. I went over and over it for weeks, months, and years. They were the events that marked the seasons of change in my life.

As the days and the years went by in the shadows of my heart, that day, I was a little girl standing in the presence of her father. What transpired in those few moments between us can never be erased from my memory or from my heart. Forgiveness has a powerful effect on those who truly experience it. I may not have known it by name, but I have never forgotten that my father let it go by...

CHAPTER 4

A Little Girl No More

Turning the pages of my life once again to an event that stripped away all that was left of a little girl. It is strange to look back on these four events; they truly were the defining seasons of my life. The spring, summer, and fall of my life had come and gone. Now winter was coming. It would be a long, cold winter, and from the snowbanks of pain and suffering, I would emerge a little girl no more.

I always thought about the little girl at the park. Three years had passed, but not a day went by that I didn't think about her. I would think about everything she said that day at the park. How I had promised I would always remember. It was as if I needed to see her put her hands together, smile, and bow her head. It seemed to do something in my heart that just made me feel better. I had come to know that the word "pray" meant talking to God. I understood what she did was a sign that she was talking to God about me, for some reason, about something. But what the reason and "something" was, I did not know or understand. I did not understand what it truly meant to pray for someone.

I did not comprehend that she was praying to God for me and on my behalf. To me, she was giving me a sign that she still cared about me and was thinking about me. It had been two years since I had been a little lost girl. It was as clear in my mind as the night it happened. I relived that day over and over, just like I did the little girl in the park. Everywhere I went, I was looking for that cross. I had not forgotten the good man who tended sheep. The man who lived in a building with a cross on top. All the time, I wished I could find him and talk to him. I still remember what he said, "Linda, what you called a 'plus' sign is a cross. No matter what ever happens in your life, just look for the cross. If you are hurt or alone, frightened, or just need help, look for the cross, Linda, and go there." I wanted to go there, and I wanted to find that cross, but it was nowhere to be found.

What can be said of a little girl standing in the presence of her father in the power of forgiveness? I never forgot that moment; it only happened a year ago, but it was as fresh in my mind as the little girl in the park and the good man who tended sheep, but another event was going to be added in the coming year.

I had learned that when I looked inside other cars, to look at the mirror. Some mirrors had dice or hula girls hanging on them. There were other mirrors that had hands folded together, and others had crosses on them. I had not put it all together, but I thought when I got older, I would follow one of the cars that had a cross. They would lead me to the building with the cross on top. I would go inside and surprise the good man who tended sheep.

I knew if I could just find him, he could answer my most important questions: If there is a God, then where is He? If there is a spirit life, then why doesn't everybody know about it? Why are the most important things in life so hard to find and understand? Is either one real? What's going to happen to me when I die? What is the truth?

I thought a lot about the night my daddy let it go by. How I had such excitement fill my heart that morning, and then my mother hurt me. I thought about all that led up to the broken cup and saucer and how I broke it. Every time I looked into the china cabinet, there they were—the rest of the set. My constant reminders.

Then, like fresh water washing away all the bad memories, I would see my father and his hand swiftly letting the belt pass over me, and though he never said the words, I can hear them now: "I am letting it go by, my child." Then I would go back to the very beginning again: to the park, to when I was lost, and to my daddy letting it go by. I was always thinking about one of those events in my life. They were the spring, summer, and fall of my life, and now it was winter. The snow began to fall.

It was September of 1966. My family had returned from Kentucky early this year. For some reason, we did not stay, not even for the bonfire. Everything was different right from the beginning. I was now in the seventh grade and considered a junior high school student. I had no idea how I got there. The grades and schools were different back then.

All I knew was that elementary went from the first grade to the sixth grade. The junior high school went from the seventh grade to the ninth grade. The high school was the last one, and it went from the tenth grade to the twelfth grade. But my dad and mom told me I was not to think about that ever. I would never make it there. I don't recall ever hearing anything about kindergarten.

For now, I was in a junior high school. To Laura and me, school was like "check-in," "check-out." It was hard to tell where and when. We did not question it, not us. We checked into school in February and checked out sometime in March. Checked into a school in Kentucky in March and got our releases for planting season. So, in reality, we only went about three or four months out of the year, sometimes more, sometimes less. The rest of the time, we learned at home. We were given books; Mom would go over some things with us. For the rest of it, we were pretty much on our own.

Even now, it is hard for me to understand because, for some years, we didn't check in until February of the following year in Texas. That was because our mom checked us into school in Kentucky in March and August. Got our work releases and didn't think to check us out before we left Kentucky. We didn't always leave the same month from Kentucky every year, but always before the end of November. Mom always checked us back into school in February in Texas. So, we didn't even go sometimes in the fall or the beginning of winter. It was very mixed up. One time, I thought I was in the fifth grade, but I was in the fourth grade. Very complicated to understand. We were torn between two states, two schools, and family rules. It was evident that no one from the schools knew how to deal with our parents. Talking to my parents was difficult, to say the least.

This was the year that I was enrolled in a different school, a junior high school. It was a big school, and I remember the first day as I stood in front of that building. At this point in my life, it was the biggest building I had ever walked into. Three stories high, which, of course, meant more children to pick on me and tease me. I had come from a very small elementary school, and this was like six of them put together. I was lost, frightened, confused, and very alone. Laura received her passage that year, in 1966, on a beautiful mid-summer night in Kentucky, and she had never returned to school; her last schooling was sometime in March of 1965.

I had to walk to the bus stop and ride the bus all alone. I looked for my little friend from the park, but I could not find her among all those children. I was late to every single class. I no longer stayed in one room all day. I had to go to six different rooms every day, and I could not find my way around that building, and no one would help me.

Two weeks later, I was still having a hard time making it from class to class. I still had not seen the little girl from the park. I walked by her house daily on my way home from the bus stop. The car was in the driveway, and the curtains were still open. I could not understand why she wasn't at school. She never rode the school bus; her mom took her to and from school. I just knew I had to see her. I thought that I would just walk right up to her house and knock on the door. The fear of the trouble I would get into if I were caught stopped me in my tracks.

I decided I would talk to Laura. I thought she might have an idea to help me find my friend in that big school. I asked her, and she called me stupid; it really hurt me. I was walking away crying when she asked me to come back. She told me, "Your friend is two or three years younger than you. Linda, she is still in elementary school. I believe she is in the fourth grade this year." I was happy with that and said thanks. Laura told me not to go around the little girl's house and that it would be best just to forget about her. I did not understand. I thought to myself, *I cannot forget about her. She's my friend.*

Laura had changed a lot since that day of the tea party. I couldn't figure out what was different, but I knew she was different. In my heart, I felt she had been hurt deeply somehow, but Laura had stopped talking to me since the tea party. I thought for a long time that it was because she was mad at me for messing things up and breaking Mom's favorite china cup and saucer. However, that was a long time ago, and Laura never stayed mad about anything very long. But on that day, the way she smiled at me, I knew she loved me. I decided that I was wrong about everything; I decided that Laura was just grown up now, and she didn't have time for my silly little things.

After two weeks of looking for the little girl from the park, I finally had an answer. I would take my time walking home. I was hoping to give her enough time to finish her homework. I was really wishing she would be outside.

I spent one Saturday working out in the yard, pulling weeds and the dead flowers out of the flowerbeds. I volunteered for the job because sometimes, on Saturdays, I saw them walking. I thought the chances of seeing them were good this Saturday morning. I worked very hard that day but always kept my eyes on the sidewalk. Just when I had given up, I saw their car coming towards my house.

I sat down and looked around at the front of our house. I wanted to make sure Mom or Laura was not looking out the window or had stepped out on the front porch. As their car went by, I lifted my hand high and waved. I was so excited, waving my hand back and forth and looking back over my shoulder, that I didn't get to see into the car as it went by. I didn't get to see her; I cried the rest of the afternoon. I knew I should have just sat down and waited. Her mother would have stopped the car long enough for us to exchange our secret sign. But I had messed it all up.

The next Saturday morning was the first day of October 1966; I was dusting in the living room when the doorbell rang. On the fourth ring, I knew Mom was still putting on her make-up, so I answered the door. It was the little girl's mother from the park. She smiled at me; it was hard for me to understand her smile. It was beautiful, not fake or forced, but sad.

She asked if my mother was at home. About the time I was saying yes to go and get my mom, she rounded the corner. Mom was not very nice to her at all. She said, "Linda, go to your room. Now." I went in that direction, and by that time, Laura was coming out of our room. I looked at her and shook my head.

Laura knew there was trouble; she would go hide in the closet. I went back down the hall to hear them talk. The woman was talking very kindly to my mother and crying softly. She said, "Please, let me talk to Linda; I have asked you repeatedly. I will not mention God to her, I promise. I just want to tell her that my daughter Deborah died while she was gone this year. I know Linda looks for her, and well, frankly, I think she needs to know."

My mom told her to leave, to get out of our house. I was standing in the hall. Her name, my friend from the park, was

Deborah. I could not stop myself; I ran to her and said, "Please, lady, tell her I am not mad at her. Tell her I love her, I miss her, and to come outside in the yard."

The woman was crying and so sad. I could hear the words she spoke through her tears, "Deborah is dead, Linda. My daughter is gone..."

My mom was yelling and kept saying, "Get out. I told you I did not want you to tell her. Stay away from my daughter. She is my daughter, not yours. Stay away from her; now get out of my house!"

I didn't hear anything after that. There was so much going on, and it was all so fast. Suddenly, I understood, and I screamed so loud, "No! No! No!" I was trying to get away from both of them. I turned around and ran. I saw Laura as I went through the kitchen; she was just standing there like a stone statue. She really didn't know what to do or what to say.

I kept running and went out the back door. There I was in the backyard. I looked past the fence toward a field. It had grass that was taller than I was. The field went as far as the eye could see. Beyond the field and far away was a highway. A friend of my mother's had told me at one of her tea parties, and I still remembered her words, and those words had frightened me. She said, "Linda, it's a big, big world out there, and all kinds of things happen, bad things."

I knew I was disobeying. I opened the gate and went out of the yard. I went into the field and ran through the tall grass, leaving a trail behind me. I finally collapsed somewhere in the field. I was just too weak to go on. I would never make it to the highway. I just lay there crying and exhausted. I finally knew her name, but what good was that? I said her name over and over, "Deborah! Deborah! My friend, Deborah, is gone."

I looked up at the sky. I had never really taken a lot of time to look at the sky before, and I didn't know if it always looked that way, but today, it was beautiful. Suddenly, I just wanted to know, and maybe I needed to know. I asked the questions aloud: "Is there a heaven out there beyond those clouds? Deborah, did you make it to heaven? Why don't I understand?" I said those words repeatedly.

What will I do now? She was the only one who ever smiled at me, and she was the only one who really thought about me. The wind blew, and I could hear the rustling of the grass. The pain went deep into the core of my being. I felt as if I couldn't breathe. I had never experienced this kind of pain. There was nothing to ease my pain; I did the only thing I knew to do. I stood up and said it out loud, "Deborah, I will always remember. I promise!"

That's when I heard Laura say, "No! Linda, no! They will hear you." Laura came up and pulled me down and held me while I cried. It seemed as if we were there for days. Laura told me some things that she had known since we had come back home from Kentucky.

A few days after we got back, Deborah's parents came to our house while I was at school. They came to get permission to speak to me. They told Mom that a drunk driver had killed Deborah while we were away. They wanted to talk to me and share some things about their daughter with me. Deborah really loved me, and they wanted me to know things like her favorite color, her love for flowers, and the happiest day of her life.

Laura looked at me with such hurt and sadness in her eyes and said, "Deborah's last words were about you, Linda."

I asked her why Dad and Mom wouldn't let them tell me.

Laura said, "I don't know, Linda, I really don't know." Laura told me Mom had made her go to her room, and she didn't get to hear everything.

Laura shared with me why Dad and Mom had allowed her to come and get me. She had begged them to let her. She told me I wasn't in trouble and that I needed to go back and just act like nothing had happened. She said it was the best thing to do.

We sat in the field for a long time and just talked. It had been a long time since we had hugged each other. Even longer since we had talked and laughed together. Laura told me before we left that things were different than she thought they would be. She told me she was sorry about the book and that she did not tell me about her passage.

Laura told me that if I could, I should run fast and hard and never look back. I did not take her seriously. I thought she must really be mad at Dad and Mom. Laura told me to keep all the money the men visiting Mom gave me. If we were around when the men came to see Mom, they would give us money. It started out small, but as we got older, it seemed like they gave us more. It went from a dollar to three, to five, then tens. I kept all mine in an old shoebox in my closet. I didn't want it, really, and I never knew what to do with it. Mom never took me anywhere, and the last place she would take me was to a store. I used the money when I was younger to go get ice cream and candy at the little store at the end of our street. I had decided there was only so much candy and ice cream one could eat.

Laura shared with me many things that day. She wanted to ask me some questions and made me promise not to tell. She asked, "Do you think Deborah was right and there is a God?"

I decided to tell her what I thought. I said, "No, I don't think so. I know if you want to find out about God, you must look for the cross on the top of a building. Go there, and a good man will tell you all kinds of things. The good man tends to sheep. The cross is a 'plus' sign, but he will tell you it is a cross." I added, "Laura, I don't believe there is a spirit life. Please don't be mad at me, but there is no spirit life, and I had known it since that summer when I had to sit outside the circle. I think Grandpa is a bad man."

Laura said, "You're right about Grandpa. How do you know about the building and the... Is it a 'plus' sign or a cross?"

We talked a lot about the night I got lost and all about what had happened to me that day at school. I just broke down and began crying when I had to tell her how I had acted towards my little friend from the park. Somehow, it eased the pain in my heart, knowing Deborah was her name.

I told Laura all about the day at the park when I met Deborah. Then I asked Laura, "Do you believe in God?"

Laura took a long time to answer; she finally said, "If there is, I am sure you will find Him."

We both laughed. Then we got up and walked back to the house. We talked all the way to the house, and with our last words to each other, we went inside. Things were just different. Laura and I talked and laughed again, but back home, she didn't have much to say to me. I was still hurting over the loss of my friend, Deborah.

I would hide in the bathroom or in the closet and cry. School was horrible. I was falling further behind in every class. The teachers and children didn't see me. I was invisible, I was out of place, and I didn't belong. There was no place for me to hide there. One day, I just walked out of the school. I crawled behind the bushes on the side of the building and cried all afternoon. Right before school was out, I went to the restroom and washed up. No one even missed me, at least not one I know of. I got on the bus and went home.

It was the beginning of November 1966; my mom had taken me out of school, and it was time for the pumpkins. The children had already done the Halloween thing. We did not celebrate Halloween, Thanksgiving, Christmas, or Easter. The only holiday I knew anything about was Halloween, and only what I had heard at school, not at home.

My mom had brought my schoolwork home early, about eleven o'clock, and left shortly after. She told me she would be back late in the afternoon and told me I could take a walk to the store later if I wanted to. I thought it to be funny. She rarely ever told me she was leaving and never told me when she would return. She didn't tell me where she was going. She just said she was leaving and would be back. About an hour after she left, I finished the housework. I thought it would be nice to go to the little store at the end of our street. The couple that ran it was always very good to me when I went in. I just thought today would be a good day to get in my shoebox where I hid all my money, take a little out, and just step out and do something on my own. I had never done that. I just thought I would go down and have some ice cream, take my schoolwork, sit there, and do some of it.

I decided I was going to have a hamburger because the little store had added hamburgers and French fries to their menu, as well as drinks with ice in a cup. It was great, and I was just going to be a big girl today. I got my money out; I recall getting ten dollars from my shoebox. My purchase wasn't even close to that, but I had it just in case. I took my book satchel with me and all my homework. I had a good time. I had a hamburger, some French fries, and a coke. It was the first one I ever had. I remember at first thinking I didn't like it, but before I left, I had two more and some ice cream. I finished all my homework and then thought I should head home.

One of my favorite times of the year was fall. I loved cleaning out pumpkins and making pumpkin pies, but my favorite thing of all was roasting the pumpkin seeds. They are great, and it is fun and easy to do. As I headed home, I remembered Mom promised she would get a pumpkin for me and had forgotten about it five or six days in a row. It hurt me, so I was really in a hurry to get home to see if she remembered to get my pumpkin. Normally, I liked taking my time and thinking about things. On this day, things were about to change for me.

This day in November of 1966 would bring the cold winds of change. In many ways, it would mark the end of childhood. The days of my childhood would soon disappear, and all our lives would be altered forever. One moment in time was about to change everything.

I was deep in thought when I heard someone call my name. I stopped and looked around, but I saw no one. I started walking again. I heard someone calling my name out again, "Linda, I'm over here." I looked around and realized I was standing in front of Deborah's house. I looked to the side of the house, and Deborah's mother stood there. She was calling and motioning for me to come to her. I looked towards my house, but my mom's car was gone. From what I could tell, no one was at home. Deborah's mother motioned for me to come to her again. I walked up to her; she took my hand and led me to the side of her house. I could tell she had been crying, and she seemed to be nervous and upset as well.

She took my book satchel and said as she opened it, "I am giving you a book; it's the real book of truth. I know you do not understand now, but hide it, Linda, and only get it out when you know you will not get caught with it." She said it four or five times, and then she reached into a box that I did not see until that moment, and she pulled out a black book with golden pages. She told me it was Deborah's book, and she and Deborah read it together every night. With those words, she shoved it into my book satchel.

She told me Deborah wanted me to have it. Then she said, "Please try to remember all this: Deborah's favorite color was lavender, her favorite flowers were lilies, and her best friend was you. She prayed for you every night." She told me that Deborah asked her to make sure I got her book.

Deborah made her promise to give me a message and to make sure I promised to remember it. She repeated everything again and then said, "This is the message: when you are in danger, call out to God; He will save you. God loves you, Linda." Deborah's mother repeated everything from the beginning again.

Then she reached into the box and pulled out a beautiful picture in a frame. The picture was of me from the side, bent down, wiping off Deborah's knees. Lying on the ground next to us was a tricycle turned over. She asked me, "Linda, do you remember this?" I did remember it. I was about eight. I was walking home from the little store on the corner. Mom had sent me to buy a little bag of sugar. I saw a little girl fall off her tricycle. Some children were laughing at her. I ran to where she was and helped her up. I bent down, looked at her knees, and wiped them off. Deborah's mother told me it was Deborah's first tricycle.

She decided to take a picture and went in the house to get the camera. When she came back outside, the two of us were there. She said it was like a picture from heaven. Deborah saw the picture and asked if she could have it. She and Deborah picked out a frame together. She kept it by her bed. From that time on, Deborah would hold that picture and pray for me every night. She was four years old when it happened. Deborah's mother also told me that Deborah had asked them permission to talk to me that day in the park. They had looked around and thought no one was paying attention to me. None of them ever meant to get me into trouble. She went over everything one more time and then put the picture into my book satchel by the book.

I knew by the way Deborah's mother was acting that time was up. I had been there at least fifteen minutes, maybe more. Before getting up off her knees, she bent over, hugged me, gave me a kiss on the cheek, and said, "I love you." It was a big hug, and her words were sweet and gentle. I believed them, and I liked the way it made me feel.

She asked me if I could remember all of this, and I told her I could. We walked out from the side of the house into the driveway. She stopped in the driveway, and I went onto the sidewalk. I noticed my shoe was untied and made a comment about it. She walked over and bent down to tie my shoe. I looked up and saw my mother coming. I could see the anger in her eyes. She was yelling, "I told you to stay away from my daughter." Mom grabbed my arm and told me to get home right now. Mom stayed and continued to talk to Deborah's mother.

When I got to the house, I noticed Mom's car door was still open. I knew then that Mom must have seen us standing in the driveway or, worse, coming from the side of the house. I went over to Mom's car and stood by the door. I looked down towards Deborah's house and was content when I realized the only thing Mom could have seen was me standing in the driveway talking to Deborah's mother.

I could see Deborah's mother and my mom standing on the sidewalk, talking. I knew I was in trouble, but I didn't care. I missed my friend and cried every night because she was gone. I would never again get to see her fold her hands together, smile, and bow her head. I felt bad that I never knew all the wonderful things about her that I was only beginning to discover.

I had no friends—not one. No one ever talked to me except to call me names and make fun of me. None of the children at school or in our neighborhood ever talked to me. Deborah and I had only talked that one time in the park. However, I was sure of one thing: Deborah had been my one and only true friend.

Now, I felt alone. I felt in my heart I had been deserted. I thought, *If only I could find that cross.* I remembered it; I knew exactly what it looked like. I had looked and looked for it, but I could not find it. I had seen some crosses, or "plus" signs, whatever they were, but none of them looked like the one I was looking for.

I shut Mom's car door and went in the house. I looked out the window and saw Mom still talking to Deborah's mother. I watched for a few minutes, and then I remembered I had the book of truth and a picture. I decided that I needed to hide them both. I went in my bedroom and carefully took the book out of my satchel. I put it between my mattress and box springs. I needed to think about what to do with the picture, so I left it in my satchel.

However, for right now, I decided the best thing for me to do was get busy doing my work. I checked to see what had been put on the counter for supper. That's when I saw it—the biggest pumpkin I had ever seen. Mom remembered my pumpkin, and she brought me the biggest pumpkin ever. I was so excited I started jumping up and down when Mom walked in. I asked her when I would get to do the pumpkin. She told me I would not be doing anything with her pumpkin. I told her that it was my pumpkin, which she had promised me for over a week. She went over to the counter, picked up the pumpkin, and said it was hers and that she was going to throw it in the trash. I asked her if I could have it. Mom looked at me, and I thought for a moment she hated me. I asked her to please let me have the pumpkin. She said, "No, you are not good enough for this pumpkin."

She started walking out the back door with the pumpkin. She was heading toward the trash cans. I ran after her. I was begging and crying, "Please, Mom, don't throw the pumpkin away. Please, Mom, let's take it back in and put it on the counter." I was in the middle of saying I was sorry when she raised it high above her head and threw it to the ground. It busted into several pieces.

She just looked at me and said, "Now, just look at what you made me do. Linda Marie, clean this mess up right now." She laughed and said, "Remember the teacup and saucer? How does it feel?" With those words, she turned and walked back to the house, saying, "You are my child, not hers."

Tears were streaming down my face. I knelt down, picked up the broken pieces, and put them in the trash. My heart was so broken, more broken than the pumpkin I was now picking up off the ground.

My dad was drunk when he came home. I did not even make it to the bathroom before I felt the belt hit across my back, and then I was shoved into the bathroom. When it was finally over, Dad turned on Mom. They spent the rest of the night fighting. By the time I got to sleep, it was time to get up.

My morning started with cleaning up the mess from last night's fight. I found a picture of Laura and me that had been in a frame that was now broken. I asked Mom if I could have it, and she said she didn't care. I went to my room and got the picture of Deborah and me out. I placed it in front of the picture of Deborah and me. They both were the same size.

I thought it was a good way to hide my picture. I had my sister and my only friend in the same frame. I put the frame back in my satchel. At this point, I did not know how to explain where the frame came from. I could leave the pictures in my book satchel, and they would be safe there. Mom never looked in my satchel, and I knew I could get my pictures out and look at them from time to time.

I didn't see Laura much anymore. Mom said she was a working girl now. All I knew was Laura was not there. Laura was not there when I went to bed, and she was home when I woke up. Laura was home on most Sundays, but she was different. She would sleep almost all day, and then she would yell at me.

One Sunday morning, Laura caught me with my picture. I showed her the picture and told her everything. Laura surprised me when she gave me a big hug and said, "I love you, Little Sis." I couldn't help but wonder where that came from. When I had my picture put back in the frame the way I had it, Laura grabbed the frame and took off with it. I went running after her. She said, "Hey, Mom, look at this nice picture frame I got for Linda. I wanted her to have a nice frame for the picture you gave her of us." Mom didn't even look; she just shook her head and said, "Laura, I will let her keep it, but don't buy her anything else." Laura walked over to me. She smiled at me and handed me the picture frame. She told me I did not have to hide it anymore and to go put it on my nightstand. Laura did have her moments, and at that moment, I wanted to hug her and tell her I loved her, but she had already walked away.

I was very shocked at what she had done. That was all disobedience. We were taught that there was no right or wrong. There was no good or bad. There was only obedience or disobedience. There was nothing in between. Any variance from a rule to be obeyed was disobedience, and punishment would always follow. I had never seen Laura just outright disobey like that. Laura was always afraid. She would hide in the closet when Dad and Mom fought. Laura always did as she was told, never broke the rules, and seemed to say just the right thing. I had only known her to be in serious trouble one time.

A week later, on a beautiful Sunday, I remembered the book was under my mattress. I thought a lot about it that day. I had to change my sheets on Sundays and clean my bedroom. Sundays were the only time I got to stay in my room most of the day. It was considered my free time.

I wanted to read the book of truth. I was trying to figure out how Deborah and her mother had the book of truth. I was a little confused. I thought you had to be thirteen to read the book of truth. Deborah had read it, and she was not even close to thirteen. I spent the entire day going to my bed to get it out, then to my window, just looking outside at all the different colors. I went back and forth, from the window to the bed, from the bed to the window.

I had been asking myself questions for almost two months. I finally decided that if I had the book, it would be stupid if I didn't read it. I had turned thirteen on December 19, 1966; I should have been given the book of truth. I was sure of it. I should have received the book on my thirteenth birthday, but I did not receive it. As always, I never asked questions. No, not me. I was not going to ask any questions. The last thing I wanted was to get in trouble. I kept my mouth shut and did not understand why they didn't give it to me.

My thought was, *How could I ever prepare myself for my passage if I did not read the book?* That's when I decided that they wanted me to fail. They did not want me to succeed. They wanted me to look stupid and already knew I would fail the passage. I would be like Laura because deep in my heart, I thought she failed. That's why she wouldn't talk to me. That's why she changed.

I was not going to fail; I was going to be the one that made it through the passage. Maybe because I received my passage, my dad would be picked. My dad would be the next master, then he and Mom would love me, and maybe at last, I would understand. Maybe the spirit life would come back to me. I didn't know, but I thought it left me that day in the park because I wanted to believe there was a God. Now I knew there wasn't, but just maybe the spirit life was real.

I made up my mind that night when everyone was sleeping. I was going to use a flashlight, go into the closet, and begin to read it. That way, I could start reading and studying early and be far ahead. Dad and Mom would be so proud of me. That night, when I took the trash out, I went in the shed and got one of my dad's flashlights. I took it to my room and put it under my pillow.

When everyone was in bed, I got the flashlight out. I turned it on so I could see to get the book of truth and get to the closet without bumping into something and waking someone up. When I got in the closet, I turned on the closet light. It was one of the things I really liked about my room. I had a big walk-in closet. I got settled down and comfortable. I opened the book of truth. It took me a few minutes to find the beginning, and it seemed like there was a lot to read. I thought that was why Laura was so different; she was not an exceptionally good reader. I took one look at the book and knew that it had to be it. Laura could have never read that book in a year. Silly girl, she should have let me read it to her. Then she would have been able to answer all the questions and pass the test, and she would have gotten her passage, which she never told me about, and now I know why. Cause she did not make it. Well, I was not going to be like her; I was going to make it.

I remembered the night of her passage. She was beautiful. The white gown, all the lights going down the path, everyone singing that song, and her entering the white tent. I did not remember her coming out. I was told to go to bed. I felt something was wrong, very wrong. I just did not know what it was. Now I knew. She did not make it. Laura had failed her passage. Well, that was not going to happen to me. I had the book of truth in my hands. And I was going to read it, and I was going to know the truth. I remembered her telling me to never read the book of truth. She wants me to fail too. I decided to read it, but she was wrong.

Something was very different about this book, different from any other book I had held in my hands. Even the paper on which the words were written was different. The pages were thin and so fragile. It seemed as if they would be easy to damage and tear. I felt as if I were holding something unbelievable, valuable, and delicate in my hands. I had heard about this book of truth since I was old enough to understand words. Now, at last, I was holding it in my hands, getting ready to read it. I did not feel the way I thought I would feel at this moment. I rubbed the pages as I flipped through them. I knew that this was the book that Deborah had read; it was a real treasure.

I finally turned to the front of the book. I knew that was where I was supposed to start. I saw Genesis at the top of the page, and down a little lower were the words "chapter 1." As I began to read, something amazing happened. Every word was like music to my soul. There was such power in those words.

> In the beginning God created the heaven and the earth.
> And the earth was without form, and void; and darkness was upon the face of the deep. And the Spirit of God moved upon the face of the waters.

> And God said, Let there be light: and there was light.
> And God saw the light, that it was good: and God divided the light from the darkness.
> And God called the light Day, and the darkness he called Night. And the evening and the morning were the first day.
>
> Genesis 1:1–5

I never got past those words that night. Those words alone were making an impact on my life as they flooded into my soul. There are no words to express the heart of that little girl. All attempts have failed. Even the best attempts have been feeble. I read those words and reread them that night repeatedly. My heart was alive in a way I had not known before. I felt different holding and reading this book. My heart could not answer the questions now forming in my mind. How can one little girl read these words and not be affected by them?

So many things I did not understand. There is a God, and He created the heavens and the earth. Why didn't Dad and Mom just tell me that? It was so simple, God said, and it was.

Why would anyone keep this book away from children until they were thirteen? There was a host of questions now flooding my soul. The words I had read were now forming a wall around my heart, one that would keep alive in my soul the memory of the spring, summer, fall, and winter of my childhood memories. To keep alive the memories of the winter that was all around me now and that was soon going to close in on me. These words would remain alive in my soul for all the seasons to come in my life. These words alone would be preserved to keep alive the heart of a child who had read from a book with golden pages. "And God said, Let there be light: and there was light. And God saw the light, that it was good: and God divided the light from the darkness" (Genesis 1:3–4).

I was exhausted, and I had to get in bed; I had school the next day. I turned on the flashlight and turned off the closet light. I made my way back to my bed. I put the book under my mattress and the flashlight under the bed. I would put it back in the shed in the morning when I left for school. I would get it again when I took out the trash the next night. It was a simple plan.

All that week, I developed a routine at night. I would do the supper dishes and put them away. Then, I would take the trash out and stop by the shed to get the flashlight. After everyone was in bed and asleep, I would get up. I would get the book of truth and the flashlight. I would turn it on and go to the closet. There in my closet, I read repeatedly, again and again, the words I had read that first night. I just could not get past those words; they were being engrafted into my soul.

The next week, I finally turned the page. I read how God created everything. How God created the sun, the moon, and the stars. My heart was overwhelmed as I read how God made man from the dust of the ground. The next day, I could not wait for school to be out. I had a lot of questions, but I knew if I just kept reading that somehow, they would all be answered.

As I read chapter 3 that night, my heart broke as I read how Adam and Eve disobeyed. I understood because I, too, had disobeyed. I read about the punishment and how they had to leave the garden. That night, after I was in bed, I could not sleep. I kept thinking about all that happened and how God made a beautiful world. He made a man and a woman to live in it.

The serpent kept coming to my mind. *Who was the serpent? Where did he come from?* I sat straight up in bed. I knew who he was; somehow, I knew the serpent was Satan. I fell asleep sometime in the early morning hours. Now, there was a God and a Satan.

Why have Dad and Mom kept this from me? From Laura. We both should have been told. Was it because I was from the family that had to get bruised? Was that the reason all the children at school hated me? I decided that I would start reading more every night so I could find out which one I belonged to and see if there was a way to find God. I thought there just had to be a way. I wondered if God knew about me.

Laura woke me up the next morning. I had overslept, and she told me she would make my bed for me. She told me to just get dressed and run to the bus stop. All day, I worried about the flashlight and the book of truth. *What if Laura finds them? What will she do?* I thought. It was the longest day and the longest bus ride. I thought the bus would never get to my bus stop. I ran all the way home from the bus stop. Laura was gone to work when I got home.

Mom was just getting home, and she was all dressed up. I knew what that meant; she had spent a few hours of the day out with one of her male friends. She was in an exceptionally good mood. She told me to go to my room for a while and not to worry about supper. She told me she had something special just for me. She added with a smile that I could have the white apron with the emerald ribbon if I was a good girl. She even told me I could go outside later. I went to my room and looked under the bed.

There was the flashlight, but it was too late to take it out now. It would be okay. I put my hand between the mattresses and felt for the book of truth. My heart was beating so hard; the book was there. I smiled and took a big breath. I could not get it out; Mom might just walk in my room. She never knocked. I would just wait until nighttime.

Later, Mom came to my room and told me I was her special girl. She told me I could go out and play on the old tire swing. Mom knew that I loved playing outside, climbing in the tree, and swinging on the tire. It wasn't the same as the park, but it sure was fun. Once outside, I had a feeling of freedom that I had not had in such a long time. I played, climbed the tree, played on the tire swing, and just laughed. I looked toward the sky and knew that beyond that was a heaven somewhere and that my friend, Deborah, was there. My heart was a little sad when I thought of her. I still missed her. I looked up and said in a whisper, "I will always remember, I promise."

Before I knew it, Dad was home, and Mom came to the door and called me to come in for supper. We were all sitting at the supper table, our plates filled with my favorite things: chicken and dumplings. I could not believe Mom had made my favorite meal in all the world. She made my favorite dessert too: carrot cake. Mom told us about the meal she had prepared for us. It was the way we always began our meals. The cook or those who prepared the meal would share everything we would be eating, and then we would eat.

As I was getting ready to take my first bite, my mom stopped me and said the words I would never forget: "Edward, today Linda woke up late and did not have time to make her bed or clean her room. Laura was going to do it, but I told her I would. I know why Linda has been so tired lately. She has been staying up late at night. Look what I found in her room."

My heart was beating so hard that I just knew I was going to die. Then, Mom pulled out the flashlight and laid it on the table. Dad was mad. "You steal from your dad, girl," he said.

I said, "Dad, I only borrowed it; I was going to put it back." He had been drinking, and I knew that this night was not going to end well.

Then he asked me, "What did you need my flashlight for, girl?"

I looked down, not knowing how to answer. Mom answered for me. She reached in the chair beside her and pulled out the book of truth. She laid it on the table and said, "It seems that someone has given Linda this book, and she has been staying up all night reading it." I never saw it coming.

Without warning, my dad hit me so hard that the chair tumbled over with me in it. The physical pain was beyond anything I had ever felt. I had never hurt this bad before. No beating could match that one hit. I was squirming on the floor because of the pain.

My dad had got up from the table and was trying to grab me. He thought I was squirming to get away from him. He kicked me hard, and I couldn't move. My dad grabbed me by the throat and dragged me outside. I was struggling so hard to get away. I was hurting and so scared.

I thought he was going to kill me. He was cussing and screaming; I had never seen him this angry before. All I could hear was, "You are never going to read again, you hear me, girl? You will never read again!" He grabbed the water hose.

I started screaming, "No, Daddy, please!" He just kept hitting me. I could see blood, and I knew I was bleeding from somewhere. From what I could tell, I knew it was bad, but he wouldn't stop.

He was screaming, "Why did you have that book? Why couldn't you wait?" Then he was saying, "You will never read again, you hear me? No more reading. Do you understand me? You touch a book again, and I will kill you." With that, he threw the water hose at me and walked up the stairs and inside the house.

My mom was standing there with the book in her hand. She had such a hateful look on her face, and her eyes were so full of hate. I could not understand this hate over a book and why she wanted this to be done to me. No matter how much I begged, it was not going to change the events of that night.

Dad came out of the house and went to the shed. He came back with the gas can for the lawn mower. I knew it had gas in it, and I knew what they were going to do. Mom put the book on the grill, and Dad poured the gas on it. I was crying and saying, "No, please don't burn it, please give it back to Deborah's mother. Please don't burn it." With that, my mother lit a match and set it on fire. I lay there and watched it burn.

Everything in me died that night. All the little sparks that had been left in my soul, little sparks of hope, faded away. The last of my hopes was burned out that night. All words of hope had left. There were no more questions because I knew I would never find the answers. I felt so powerless against the hatred that was in my father and my mother. They were never going to change, and I was forever their prisoner.

My dad addressed the neighbors that had been accumulating around our backyard. He said it only once: "You need to be minding your own business. My daughter here had a book that is unacceptable." I watched the neighbors as they watched my dad. Then I saw Deborah's mother standing there with tears streaming down her face. I didn't know if she had been weeping for Deborah or for me. She suddenly fell to her knees and screamed, "Why, God? Why?"

I am sure that the man who was with her was her husband. He picked her up and walked away. She could not control her pain. I heard the mournful cries she was releasing as her husband carried her away. There was nothing left to do. I watched as, one by one, the neighbors shook their heads and went back to their homes.

Everyone was gone now; even my mom and dad had gone into the house. By this time, I'm sure they were getting ready for bed. Since Laura was not there and working, I knew that I had to go in and clean up whatever mess was in the house.

I stumbled to my feet. I could barely move because of the intense pain. I managed to get in the house. With tears streaming down my face and every move I made hurt, with thoughts of how much pain this night had caused Deborah's mother. I tried to ignore my own pain until the mess was cleaned up.

I finally made it to the bathroom. I got in the shower and turned the water on. I sat down and cried until the water ran cold. Even after the water was running cold, I remained in the shower for five minutes or so. I knew it would help the pain and the swelling. I went through this several times a year, but never this bad. I knew what to do. I had the routine down. I got out of the shower. I was so cold I had to wait until I stopped shaking to take a good look at myself. I needed to see the damage that had been done.

I could tell from what I saw that I would not be going to school for a few days, maybe a week. I had a lot of red, deep marks that were swelling. There were marks that were already turning into bruises. There was a gash on my left knee. It looked bad, and I tried to clean it up. I also had a small cut on my right hand. The worst cut was on the right side of my head. I had bruises and red marks all around my neck. I knew I would live.

I looked in the mirror, but I didn't see myself anymore. Something had changed in me that night. When I looked in the mirror, there was no shine in my eyes. It was gone, like Laura's eyes had changed over a year ago.

The police came to our house later that night. I stood in the hall and listened as Mom told them that it was all a lie. She explained that Deborah was killed by a drunk driver, and her mother had been trying to get me to sneak up to her house. Mom said that she was giving me things that belonged to her daughter.

Then my mom told the police that Deborah's mom was trying to turn me into her own daughter, and my mother said she just wanted it to stop. Dad told the police that he and Mom had tried to stop her from telling me to sneak up to her house. Now, she was making up lies. Dad even asked the police officer if he would like to see me. He said no.

I went to the doctor the next day. I had stitches in my head, hand, and my knee. When the doctor asked what happened to me, Mom told him that my father had caught me with the wrong kind of book. When my father tried to talk to me about it, I ran and fell out the door and down the stairs. The doctor gave me a look of disapproval and said this is what happens to bad little girls.

It took about six weeks to heal completely. I did not return to school until mid-March of 1967. On my first day back at school, a teacher asked me to read in front of the class. I could not read at all. I tried, but it was as if I had never read in my life. I could not see the words; they were all scrambled up together.

Mom took me to the doctor about it. Mom told me something had happened to my head that night when Dad was upset about the book. It was now affecting my vision and made me see the words differently. Mom told me the doctor said it probably happened when I hit my head. He said they could take some X-rays and run some more tests. I never went back to the doctor about it. It didn't really matter to me because the doctor told my mom there was a chance it could not be fixed. The damage had already been done and may not have been discovered in time. All I knew was before that night, I could read, but after that night, I could not. I could not put words or letters together. They were backwards and all mixed up.

I went by Deborah's house in March of 1967 on my way home from the bus stop. They were moving. Deborah's mother was not the same; she was no longer weeping. She was smiling again. The way I had seen her smile long ago when she would take long walks with Deborah.

Deborah's mother was no longer the woman I had seen that night, the night my dad beat me and mom burned the book of truth, with pain and grief written all over her face as she asked the God she believed in why. I looked at the moving truck that was now being loaded. I glanced at the sign in her yard. I knew what that meant. I saw her, and I wanted to run to her one minute, and the next, I wanted to hate her. I did not know how to feel or to act. So, I kept walking.

With more love and courage than I have ever witnessed from that day until now, Deborah's mother folded her hands, smiled, and bowed her head. I watched every move, carving the image in my heart, for I knew it would be the last time I would ever see her. I have watched that scene unfold a million times in my mind. I never responded. I just turned around and kept walking.

After I got home, I wanted to go back and tell her I was sorry. It was too late; Mom would never allow it. I knew by tomorrow afternoon, the moving truck would be loaded, and Deborah's mother would be gone. Now, for the first time since I had met the little girl in the park, I knew I was going to be alone. I would be alone in a world that somehow, and for some reason, I just did not fit in. I was in a trap with no way out. *Who will think of me now? Deborah is dead, and now her mother is leaving me too. Is there anyone to fold their hands and bow their head for Linda? Would anyone ever, again, think about me in a special way?*

A few days later, I walked by Deborah's house, and it seemed so empty. I thought about how it once was a home where a family lived. How there was a little girl and a mother who lived together, played together, and loved each other. They watched the flowers bloom together, they took long walks together, and they read together. I remembered: The little girl's name was Deborah. Her favorite color was lavender. Her favorite flowers were lilies; she believed in God, and her best friend was me.

I looked up at the front porch, and in the corner by the door was a flower. I looked towards my house, but my mom's car was gone. I ran up to the porch, but it wasn't a real flower. It was just one single lily. It was silk and had been beautifully made. It looked so very real. I reached down and picked it up. I knew she left it for me; I just knew it. I thought it was her way of letting me know she understood. She still loved me, and she knew I loved her and Deborah. Somehow, that day, even though I did not understand all the things that had happened or even why, I knew she, too, would always remember.

We were supposed to go to Kentucky. We were supposed to go to the park for the celebration. But that was not true this year. This year, in March of 1967, would be my last days of school. The school doors closed behind me that day in March when my mom picked me up and checked me out of school. Now we would go to the park for the celebration; our clothes were already packed and in our suitcases. I thought we were on our way to the park, but instead, there would be no celebration. There would be no planting season, and the school doors were closing for good. Without me even realizing it, my school days had ended. I never return to school. Nor would I ever return to Kentucky. Instead, a mighty wind would blow hard enough to change the direction and course of my life.

The only reminders I have that I was ever a little girl is the gentle mixing of the ingredients in the heart of that little girl into these four events. It is indeed hard to look back at these four events because with them came severe emotional pain, physical pain, and the pain of rejection, but with them also came a strength, a determination, a fight to survive, and the courage to continue looking for the truth. At the end of the seasons of my childhood, winter was over, and I was a little girl no more.

CHAPTER 5

Once Upon a Time, There Were Two Sisters

The spring, summer, fall, and winter had passed for me, and of truth, I was a little girl no more. My life had forever been altered. However, before the seasons of my life, there was a time of innocence for two sisters. A time short and bittersweet. A time before the day of awakening. A day when all innocence faded away, and there remained two little girls forever bonded together.

A day that was remembered more than any other day in our life. A moment in time that could never be taken away. The memory forever burned in our hearts; it was the beginning of all the things I always remembered and cherished, going over and over them in the corners of my mind, the day in the park talking to Deborah, the day I was lost and met a good man who tended sheep. The only one I had ever met, and he told me to look for the cross. The memory of my father letting it go by and me in the shadow of forgiveness. What can be said of a little girl who has been touched by the pain of death, not fully understanding it, watching as my mother took the only thing Deborah wanted me to have and burned it? These are the events that lived in my heart and kept me alive, kept me looking, and kept me hoping that one day would come understanding.

We were sisters forever, Laura and Linda, the two L's. She was the Big L, and I was the Little L. The Big L's job was to watch over and take care of the Little L. That's what Laura would always tell me, and she did a great job. As little girls, we shared our hearts; we were all we had.

Together, we felt safe, and in our own way, we believed we were protecting each other. We cried with each other. We hid together when the fighting between Dad and Mom got out of control.

Laura and I were just two little girls who, like in most families, loved and trusted our father and mother. That love and trust were shattered, and what we needed most was denied time and time again.

The love and comfort we needed were never granted to us. We were trapped with no way out, and all shreds of hope were stripped away from us. From the outside, everything about our family seemed to be normal. But inside that house, there was a darkness that overshadowed our lives, making it anything but normal.

The only love we knew was the love we had for each other. Words like "I love you" were never heard in our home. Even school was a place of rejection, which only added to our already emotionally damaged and broken lives. As far as we were concerned, life had very little to offer us. But no matter how hard our home life was, with the harsh boundaries and control that our parents had over us, it was still "safe" for us. The world was so big and terrifying to two little girls who had been taught not to trust anyone outside the family circle.

I believe our lives are marked by events, and it is those events that are remembered. For most, those events are cherished. When all else has faded, they become the memories that comfort us and bring us joy and laughter. That was not true of Laura's life or mine.

Our childhood was not marked with dolls, pretty dresses, playing with other children, birthday parties, or celebrating holidays. Our childhood was marked by very different events, like poker parties, with drunks who filled the air with foul language while smoking and fighting as Laura and I emptied dirty ashtrays, served them beer, made and served them mixed drinks.

After the parties were over, we cleaned the house. We did not question things; that's simply how things were. It was normal for Laura and me to clean up the vomit and spilled drinks. It was normal to help men and women who had too much to drink to a room where they could sleep it off.

There are also other well-remembered events of beatings and fights between our parents. There were times when I thought for sure Dad was going to kill our mother. Laura and I were trapped in this war zone between Dad and Mom. For two little girls, it was impossible to understand. My dad loved my mom, without a doubt, but Mom wanted more than what Dad could give her. My mother was beautiful and used her beauty to get what she wanted from men. This was just the beginning.

There were other things that played a part in the midst of all that was wrong with the home that I now call "the house that Satan shook."

It was not just the fights between our parents or even the beatings. When Dad was away or at work, Laura and I saw lots of men come and go. When we were younger, quarters and dollars that were placed into our hands with smiles and confirming words made us feel good: "What special little girls you two are." These men would say things to us that made us feel special. In time, Laura and I did not feel special at all. The amount of money given to us increased as the years went by. Eventually, we were getting fives, tens, and twenties.

As we got older, not only did the amounts of money change, but so did the words. The men would say things like, "Well, you two are just blossoming into beautiful young ladies" and "What beautiful daughters you have." Or they would point to Laura and say, "Now this one, she's a real looker." The looks they gave Laura when they placed the money in her hands were different than the way they looked at me.

Although we didn't quite understand why, it just seemed wrong to us. It amazes me that as children, even though we were told there was no right, no wrong, no God, and no Satan, our young hearts told us that something was very wrong with our mother's behavior. We were confused about why it felt that way to us, but we dared not ask.

Laura and I talked about it sometimes. We knew that no matter what Mom said, all of this was terribly wrong. We knew that not only what she did was wrong but also the fact that she was teaching us to do the same. At first, it was in small ways. She would dress us up in our special dresses and have us twirl around in circles in front of men or sit on their laps and accept money from them. It all seemed terribly wrong to us, so

Laura and I stayed together as much as we could. We knew if we stayed together, we would be safe.

As I said before, there were so many things that were very wrong and deceptive about the home we were growing up in. The walls of evil were high, the bars strong and enforced with hate. We were pinned in on every side with no way out. All of this was going on in our lives; we were powerless to change it. Laura and I had to live it. In addition to all we were going through, we believed there was no God, no Satan, no absolutes, and everything was by chance.

We were products of our parents, and we belonged to them. They would tell us when to leave, when to get married, when we would be finished with schooling, and where we would work. It was all up to them. They were in control. My dad and mom had very different views about family, life, and our destiny. God did not play a part in any aspect of our lives. God simply did not exist. We were told if someone talked to us about God, we were to walk away because they would hurt us and take us away, never to be seen again. That is exactly what we did; well, not exactly—we would run. There was no God, and Laura and I were forbidden to talk about it at all. We were forbidden to ask questions or even discuss such things. To do so would mean that we had disobeyed, and punishment would be the result.

In reality, Laura and I had been stripped of all hope, and we believed that this was all there was to life. This was our life, what we knew, what we believed. We believed what they taught us. Why wouldn't we? They fed us and clothed us. They were our parents. We had no reason to doubt what they told us. We believed the only one who had power was my father's father. It had been that way for generations.

My grandpa had complete power and authority over all his children, and all the grandchildren obeyed as well. To refute his power or authority meant severe punishment, maybe separation from the family. To be separated from them forever. The entire family would never speak again to anyone who objected or said anything against the master. He was the one who had all authority over this family. That man was my grandfather. We learned to do our work and keep our mouths shut for fear of such punishment. This was our everyday life. It all seemed very simple to two little girls who knew nothing else.

We were taught only two words mattered in life, and one of those words was "obedience." That is, *complete obedience*. Grandpa was the master of the family. Grandpa and Grandma had eighteen children, and they all answered to Grandpa. If there was a problem with one of the children in a family unit, the father of that unit would talk to Grandpa, and whatever Grandpa told him to do was carried out in full measure. It was our duty to obey the *master*. For our family to survive, we had to conform, submit, and respect our *master*. We were well-trained, loyal, and devoted to our family. We were taught to protect our private laws, rights, and beliefs. As a result of complete obedience, we would receive benefits. We would obtain special privileges, gifts, and special treatment from the *master* at the end of the harvest.

"Disobedience" was the second word that mattered because all disobedience was dealt with harshly. Punishment was calculated as to when, what, and how long by Grandpa. Unless it was a small matter, then the father of that unit took care of it. *All disobedience was punished*, sometimes with very severe punishment. Complete obedience was expected at all times. Age did not matter. When asked to do something, our response was to do it without questions.

There were rules for everything, and they were not taken lightly. These rules were strictly enforced. To disobey and break any rule or command ended in punishment. There were no exceptions, no mercy, no forgiveness, and no compassion. Rules were rules, and they were enforced. Laura and I were taught and believed that we were merely the product of our parents. They owned us, and they controlled us.

We did not celebrate any holidays and knew very little about them. Birthdays were not celebrated. The only days that were looked at in our life as special were the spring celebration, preparing the soil for the seeds, planting the seeds, harvesting the crops, the harvest celebration, and the day we celebrated turning fourteen. The day we came of age was all we knew, and it was a great celebration for the girls in the family when we took our passage.

Laura and I were not allowed to play as other children. By the time we were twelve years old, we could cook a big breakfast and prepare a nice lunch, and for supper, we could prepare a full five-course meal, set the table, and do the dishes afterwards.

We were good at serving parties, making mixed drinks, and taking care of guests, both sober and drunk. We could clean a house from top to bottom. We could do laundry, yard work, iron clothes, mend clothes, make dresses and quilts, bake, and do any housework that was put before us; we could work in the fields planting, tending the fields, and harvesting without help or supervision.

The events that marked the seasons for us were the trips our family took in the spring to Kentucky and in the fall to Texas. Dad and Mom took us there in the spring to work on Grandpa's farm. Up until the age of five, we would only stay for two weeks and return home with our parents. Then, in the fall, we would return to Kentucky for the harvest. After the age of five, we were left on the farm to work all summer. After the harvest celebration, we would return to Texas with our parents.

Grandpa's farm had 590 acres that had been passed down for many generations. There were cows, pigs, chickens, and sheep on the farm. The land was marked off in sections. Every child worked, from the youngest to the oldest. If we were on the farm, we were working. The provisions from those many days of working provided for our families year-round.

I do not remember playing games or sitting at the supper table talking and laughing. When I look back at my childhood, the events I remember are marked by fights, beatings, and trips to and from Kentucky. This was our life, and in the middle of all of this, there were two little girls who were very hurt and very confused. The reality of our life each day was the fear that Dad would beat Mom or one of us to death when he came home drunk. There were times that Dad was gone from home for long periods, but for the most part, he was home.

Laura and I loved each other. We knew that we would never want to hurt one another. It was for that reason we could not understand why Dad and Mom did such terrible things to each other and to us. We wanted to be loved by them, even though we did not fully understand that it was love we wanted or was even what we were looking for. We just knew that there was something missing in our lives, something that we both wanted and desperately needed from our parents.

Everyone needs moments of kindness, compassion, and even laughter. For Laura and me, those moments did exist, but they were as brief as they were rare. I believe the reason those rare moments were so cherished and remembered, no matter how small or insignificant they were, was because those short moments became living water to our souls.

Laura loved telling me the story of an event that happened when I was very young. I remembered very little about it, but I loved hearing the story. It was the story of a day when our innocence was lost. It was the day of awakening, and it was truly Laura's story. I believe she loved that moment in her life because she was the hero, my hero. Laura told me the story many, many times, and I never got tired of hearing it.

This is the way I heard it from Laura and from my mother. Together, it will make the story complete.

The things I remember, which are very few, I have put in italics:

It was the summer of 1957. From all accounts, an argument had started between Dad and Mom late the night before. Early the next morning, they were up and at it again, and it had escalated as the day continued. Laura remembered this to be the first real fight between Dad and Mom. Before that day, Laura said she never remembered them fighting; there were only a few disagreements here and there. This argument was different; Laura and I were afraid.

Laura and I went upstairs, and I headed for the closet. However, she said, "No! We are not going to stay here." She took me out of her bedroom, and we hid under twin beds in one of the other rooms upstairs. *Laura was under one bed, and I was under the other one. We were laughing at each other and making faces. Then it started getting hot, very hot, and the room was filling with smoke.* Laura said she saw the smoke coming into the room from under the door, filling the room fast. She got out from under the bed and told me we had to get out of there. I got out from under the bed and ran to the door. Laura said she screamed at me to stop. She told me, "No, Linda, not that way!"

Laura said I tried to go into the closet, but she took me to the window. There, she talked me into climbing out of the window onto the ledge and hanging on until she came out. *Laura and I were hanging onto the ledge outside as the fire spread. I could see the fire and remember it well.* I do not remember how or when we got down. Laura and Mom said a sixteen-year-old boy and his father, who lived next door, got a ladder and rescued us. They told my parents that everyone was so busy trying to put the fire out on the sides and at the front of the house that no one had seen us in the back.

Laura always continued the story by telling me, "I saw our pictures on the bed, Sissy Linda. The room was all filled up with smoke. I could see fire coming through the door. I could not let our pictures burn up. I ran back to the bed, and I grabbed our pictures. I could not hold them and get out of the window. So, you know what I did? I put them under my dress.

"When that boy and his dad got us down, you were so afraid. You were crying and saying the fire was trying to get you. I took you by the hand and said, 'Let's go sit under the big tree, Sissy Linda.' Then, you know what I did? I took you by the hand and led you to the tree. Then we sat down on the cool grass, and I showed you the two pictures." She said I fell asleep looking at them.

She told me it was important that I always remember it, and I should never forget it because, that day, we became the two L's bonded together for life, and it could not be broken. I believed her, and she would always end the story with, "I get to be your hero now, but when we grow up, you will be my hero." Then Laura would laugh and say, "Go to sleep now; I need to get back to my room."

Our house burned to the ground that day, along with everything in it. Nothing was left. We never really knew how it started. Dad and Mom were the only ones who knew the truth. They both said it was an accident. But later, when they would fight, the fire was always brought up.

Mom would say Dad set the house on fire to destroy her beautiful home and all her beautiful things. Dad would scream at her, saying he wanted us all to die in the fire and that he did not care about her things. Every fight they had ended up with Mom telling Dad she hated him for destroying her beautiful things. However, when she told the story to her friends, she would say it was an accident and that Dad saved her.

Whatever really caused the fire, at this point, did not matter to Laura or me. What mattered was how that fire changed both of them. Laura always said that after that day, the fighting between them changed into an ugliness that she did not understand and that Dad's drinking from that point on also changed; he was drunk more times than not. Whatever happened that day remains with both of them. However, the results of that day were carried in the hearts of two little sisters. They lost their innocence and freedom that day and became prisoners of fear, never knowing when, how, or why the next fight would start. Before that day, Dad would only drink at our house parties; they didn't fight, but after that day, everything changed. I never remembered it being any different; all I knew was they were fighting.

Laura and I were found curled up together, asleep under the pecan tree in our backyard. Laura was holding two pictures, the only things that survived the fire. The pictures were taken about a month earlier. One was a picture of Laura, and the other was a picture of me. Laura told Mom she had put them under her dress and held them close to her tummy. This is what Laura told me. This was her story more than mine, and she told it so well. I also heard my mother tell the story to her friends many times over the years. I guess it was part of her history as well. To be honest, I believe all of us looked back on this event because it had truly left its mark on our souls. I believe we all saw it from different perspectives.

The picture of Laura was damaged, but she didn't care. She asked Mom if she could keep them. Mom told her she could have them but to keep them in her room and out of sight. Laura kept both and took those two pictures everywhere with her over the years.

Our life was spared that day. From all the stories that I have heard, no one even knew we were hanging on the ledge outside the window. We never heard our parents even acknowledge that they had put us in harm's way that day. Neither one of us knew if they were thankful that we did not die in the fire that day.

What I know to be true today is that God knew we were there in the midst of that fire. The God, who loved us, sent a young boy to the back of the house. He may have thought he went to find a water hose, but what he discovered were two little girls hanging from a window ledge.

God sent him to rescue us, for the ending of the story is the cold, harsh fact that just minutes after the young boy discovered us and we were rescued, the house went up in flames. There was nothing anyone could do but stand back and watch it fall to the ground in a flaming heap.

Two of God's children slept in His arms, curled up together under a pecan tree that day. We were not even aware of the danger we had been subjected to. We may not have known that there was a God, but He knew us, loved us, and delivered us that day. God has always known where Laura and I were, and He carved a path for us to find Him, and I find that to be most amazing.

It seems so strange to look back on all this, but I really feel it is important to lay this foundation for all who read this book. I believe it is important to see two little girls who never really got to be children. We lived in a world of physical, emotional, and verbal abuse and a home filled with violence. We were neglected, exploited, and told there was no God. We had no hope and no one to help us. All we had was each other.

As I look back to that time, I believe God wove it into the fabric of our lives so we would always have something to look back on, such as our time of love and innocence, with the evidence of two photos. Two photos of two little girls with smiles and innocence shining in their eyes. We were not broken then; fire and hatred had not touched our lives; we were young, and we were innocent. But that day was the day of awakening; that day, we understood the hate and destruction that existed between the two of them, and we would never again hide under the bed and laugh or make faces at each other during their fights because fighting was something to fear. We could become the subjects of that hate at any moment during any fight. We always had to be on guard because a fight could start at any moment, and we both knew and understood that. We had to make sure we were always together and stayed hidden and quiet when the fights broke out.

Before the fire, we were just two little girls. After the fire, the beauty in those two photos was the only proof we were very young and innocent. Those two photos Laura would drag around with her. The photos were damaged by the fire and water, but it did not matter to Laura. They were torn and faded, and the edges were damaged and discolored, but she kept them and carried them everywhere for many years. However, that was not Laura or me in the years that followed; we were very much like those two photos: torn, fading, and very damaged.

CHAPTER 6

Different Directions

The years passed as Laura and I stepped out of our childhood and into our teenage years. The end of our life together as little girls had come to an end. Our lives were being shaped, and roads were forming before us. Our moments together were brief, and a deep sense of abandonment overshadowed both of our lives. We were indeed pulling away from each other.

The day I found out that Deborah had died, that afternoon out in the field was the last time that Laura and I shared our hearts as little sisters. A moment that was marked by our love for each other and one of my cherished memories of us together. We had never been granted any time at all like that before, but that day, God opened a door for us to spend one amazing afternoon together. That was the day I asked her if she believed in God, and Laura said, "No, Linda, but if there is a God, I am sure you will find Him."

Laura told me that day that if I ever had the chance to run away from home, I should run. She said, "Run, Linda. Run fast and never, never look back, and never come back." Laura told me where she had hidden some money and the name and number of someone who would help me.

Laura said to just call them and tell whoever answered that Laura was my sister and that they would help me and be good to me. She smiled and said, "Linda, don't be afraid. It will be fine." I asked her if she was sure about running away, and she told me yes, it was something that I must do. I asked her to come too; she said no, it was too late for her. She said, "I'm broken, and all value is gone; the spirit life left me." I told her that was not true, and I tried to tell her that I thought there was no spirit life, but she would not listen.

We hugged each other. Laura said, "I want you to know that I love you no matter what ever happens." I never forgot my reply to her; it just rolled out. I said, "Laura, someday I will come for you. I will; I promise I will. Please know I will always love you too, no matter what."

We hugged each other one more time and walked into the house with a memory that was sealed in our hearts for all the days of our lives. I now see that we said goodbye to each other that day before, and we went our different ways. It was also the day she showed me the two photos from the fire. We looked at them and cried for all that was lost; it was the last time she would ever show me those photos.

I believe that God arranged that moment for us because He knew we would need something to look back on. We both needed a special time and place to remember as a precious moment between us. Maybe somewhere deep in our souls, we knew the time was coming that we would be leaving home and going in different directions.

I have always remembered the year 1966 as the last year that Laura and I went to Kentucky. The next year brought our little world crashing down around us. We would never see our lives the same after 1966. It would take us years to face and deal with the emotional damage these events would leave in their wake. It was the year that changed the course of our lives.

The year 1967 brought so many changes into our life. I knew something was wrong; Laura did not talk to me at all anymore. She would not look me in the eye when I tried to talk to her. When I would ask her about her job, she seemed to be upset with me and would tell me to leave her alone or go to my own room. Laura's words only confirmed what my mother had told me about her: she did not want to be around me anymore; she was saving her money so she could leave, and she would be leaving me behind.

It was around this time that my mother started telling me that Laura said she did not care about me and was going to leave me behind and never come back, not even to see me. Those words my mom spoke tore into my soul. What I did not know was that my mother was telling Laura I was mad at her and hated her because she was Mom's special girl.

Mother was telling Laura I was jealous of her because she was prettier than me and had a job. Our mother was telling us both terrible things about each other and telling us both that each was her special girl. For reasons unknown to us, Mom wanted Laura and me to be divided. She wanted us to hate each other. Neither one of us realized it until it was too late.

At home, things continued as they always had, except for a reason unknown to me: we did not go to Kentucky in the spring of 1967, nor did we ever go back there again. Laura and I got ready as we always had. It was the planting season and time for the picnic at the park, then the long drive to Kentucky.

Planting season came and went, but we did not go to the park for the family picnic, nor did we go to Kentucky. Not that year or ever again.

Laura was not talking to me. I did not know why, and I did not dare ask. It was like the whole family just split up, and everyone went in different directions. Laura was so distant, and I wondered what had happened, but I knew better than to say anything. I wasn't brave enough to ask any questions about why we did not go to Kentucky that year. We had always gone for the planting and the harvest; they were the two biggest celebrations we had as a family. Now, without any explanation, it was over.

Nothing was ever explained to the children. I do not know about Laura, but I was very lost and confused at this point in my life, and in the midst of this, we were being pulled apart from each other. *What do I believe now? Do I believe in anything?* Everything I was taught and everything I believed in was suddenly gone.

The year 1967 was not only the first year we did not go to Kentucky but also the year that would close the door between Laura and me. I never returned to school. My school days were over at thirteen. After March of 1967, there would be no more school for me. I was still a young girl; I had no dreams of a future. No, I just tried to live through each day. I did not know if Laura had dreams. I just knew she was very unhappy, and she could not hide it from me. I did not know what was wrong or how to help her, as my life was just as unbalanced as hers, and I myself was unhappy.

In April of 1967, Mom came into my room with bags and a few boxes. She said, "It's time I teach you how to dress up, how to walk, talk, and act with men. You are not a baby anymore. I need you to work now. You can bring home enough to pay your own way so you can live here. If you do not listen to me, you will have no place to live, nothing to eat or wear. Do you understand me?"

I said, "Yes, Mother."

Then she started saying things and showing me things. She was messing with my face and hair. Then she grabbed my face hard and said, "Listen to me, Linda; you are different." She then grabbed me by the arm and dragged me into the den. She said, "Look at the china cabinet. You see those beautiful china cups?"

I said, "Yes."

Then she went around the counter into the kitchen and got a coffee cup out of the cabinet. She said, "Pay attention to me, Linda, this is important. You are a china cup—precious, expensive, beautiful, and very valuable. Laura is a coffee cup—inexpensive, cheap, and has chips. She is unable to make enough money to pay her way. Some girls are made for the streets, and other girls are made for mansions. On the streets is how Laura makes money, but you belong to the rich man. Laura's a waste of my time. She got her looks from your dad, but you got yours from me. It just occurred to me as I was watching you yesterday dusting just how beautiful you are. You need to understand, young lady, that this is to our advantage."

Day after day, she talked, and I listened. I felt important, even though I really did not understand a thing she was talking about, except that Mom was upset with Laura for some reason, and I was her very special girl now. Yet the truth was she was drilling me, teaching me, leading me down a path of lies and deception. It hurt me that she said Laura was a cheap coffee cup; that was not true. Laura was beautiful. *Why did Mom say those things about her?*

The day came when I understood what my mother was talking about. It was early in the afternoon; I had finished my housework and was getting things laid out for dinner when Mom came in all excited.

Mom put my hair in a ponytail, took clothes out of a bag, and told me to put them on. I did as I was told, but something did not feel right. The clothes she gave me made me look like a kid instead of a thirteen-year-old. I mean, I was small for my age and looked younger, but now I looked like a nine-year-old. I did not say a word, not me; I did not want to get in any trouble.

We got in the car. She said, "We are going shopping." Instead, she took me to a house and told me to wait on the porch. As I was walking to the porch, she said she would come back in a little while, and we would go shopping. It was not long until I heard someone talking. I looked up and saw that it was my mom and a man. I saw her grab something from his hands. I realized it was his wallet and that she took money from it and handed it back to him. She was laughing and saying something to him, but I could not hear her.

I knew I was in trouble, and now the man was walking towards me. I knew this man. He had been to our house to see Mom. I did not know what to do. He told me not to be afraid, but I was. After we were in the house, he took me downstairs into a basement.

I remember thinking, *It's really nice down here.* There was a dollhouse and dolls. He said, "You are a very special little girl.

That is why you get to come here to this very special place. Only special little girls get to come here. You need to listen to me and do exactly what I tell you, and you will get a special present. Now, be a good little girl and take off your clothes." He said he wasn't going to hurt me; he was going to take some pictures, and we would play a game after.

I was afraid, and one thing was for sure: I did not feel special. I told myself, "It's okay; nothing is going to happen." As painful as it is to admit, I took my clothes off. He took pictures of me with dolls. Then he said it was playtime. He gave me an ice cream, which he had gotten out of a refrigerator, which I had not noticed before. He then wanted me to eat the ice cream a certain way while I sat on his lap, and he watched me. After that, he said, "I'm going to give you some money, and you tell your mom I want her to buy you a princess dress with lace and wear it the next time you come and put your hair in pick tails." Then he said, "Don't you worry, we are going to have fun, and I want you to get to know me so we can be real friends."

After it was all over and he was gone, my mom came in and told me it was time I grew up, that I needed to know what life was all about, and it was time I stopped acting like a baby. She told me to put my clothes on and to hurry up about it. That is when my eyes were opened. There was a picture on the dresser right in front of me. It was a picture of the man with his wife, two sons, and a daughter that I thought to be around my age. Suddenly, I was extremely sick, and I told Mom I wanted to go home. She just kept talking, and I said, "Now."

Mom started cursing at me, then slapped me and said, "Grow up; you are not a baby anymore. This is the real world, and you will learn to like it. At least no man is going to do anything to you till I say so and get a fair price. This man will not touch you unless he pays full price. Do you understand? For now, he just wants to play and pay. He likes to take his time; you should be happy about that. We're going to make lots of money from him."

We did not go shopping that day or any day after. It had never really been her intention to take me shopping that day. Deep down in the core of my being, I knew that it had all been planned, and it would not be the only time.

On the way home, I asked my mom, "Did you do this to Laura too?"

She said, "Laura is not your concern; she is doing what she needs to do, working. Laura is paying her share; all the things in our house cost money, and now it's your turn to start helping, maybe once a week. Stop acting like you did not like getting your picture taken. You're not a child anymore, and you are worth a lot to me. I want you to stay untouched, so for now, I will make sure that the men who see you will only take pictures and play around. They will not go all the way with you for now. Understand? You are pure, and men desire that, Laura. She has been used, a cheap coffee cup, remember?" With that, it was the end of the conversation; what I felt, or even thought, did not matter.

Late that night, I got out of bed and went to my closet, where an old shoebox was hidden behind a few things. It was full of money that had been given to me over the years by the men who visited Mom. I took it out and stuffed it into a pillowcase, along with some of my clothes and a few other things. I went to the place Laura told me about, where she had hidden some things for me. I found money and a number for me to call. In June of 1967, at the age of thirteen, I ran away from home. I could not handle the pain of what my mother had done to me. I felt ashamed, confused, and broken. I did not know much about the world, but I was sure of one thing: I never wanted anyone to do such a thing to me again, and I did not like what happened that day, regardless of what my mother said or thought.

The number Laura had left for me led me to a place where six beautiful young women lived; they had not seen or heard from Laura in months. That's what they told me: They told me I could stay there until they found Laura. They were all talking among themselves about whether I could stay or not. One of them said, "Yes, she is." Then one of them said, "Well, I am not going to cook and clean up after her."

I spoke up and said, "I know how to cook. I can fix any meal, and cleaning is really all I know." I fixed breakfast that morning for them, and they ate every bite; nothing was left. While they slept that day, I cleaned the whole place and had everything laid out for dinner to fix a big meal for everyone. From that day on, I was like a housekeeper to them. I did everything for them: laundry, cooking, cleaning, sewing, and everything that had to do with a clean house.

They tried to find Laura, and one of them told me she was not on the streets anymore and no one knew what happened to her. I asked what they meant "on the streets." They told me not to worry about it and that they would explain it later. The six girls were quite different; they were not bad girls, just different. They were like my mom in some ways, getting all dressed up and going out. They talked of college, families, and their hopes and dreams. One of them was loud, they cussed, they all smoked, and most of the time drank, but they were good to me. They said I was their little sister, and they all watched out for me. They gave me money and brought me things. Yes, they were good to me. It was October. I remember because of the pumpkins. The girls talked about Halloween, but I didn't care about it.

There was this one man that came every day, and they all told me to stay away from him. They did not have to tell me that because I knew already that I did not like this man. One day, he came early and told me they were all in jail, and my free ride was over. He grabbed me and said, laughing, "They are not here to protect you. I have a plan. I am going to take you with me this evening, and you are going to do what I tell you to do."

Later that day, he took me to a room, took clothes out of a closet, and threw them at me. He said, "Get dressed." The man stood there and watched. When I was ready, he took me down to the kitchen table and told me what I was going to do. I told him I cannot do that. He said I would, or he would kill me himself. Before I knew it, the sun had gone down. I was in a car doing something I did not want to do; how could I do this thing that he wanted me to do?

We pulled up in front of a gas station. I did as I was told; I got out of the car, pulled the hat down low, pulled the mask up, opened the door, walked over to the counter, pulled the gun, and said to give me all the money. I saw no fear in the young girl's eyes. She smiled at me, opened the register, and said, "I will pray for you." Then she said, "Father, keep me safe and give me the right words."

I looked around, thinking, *Where is her father?* I told her I did not want to do this and that a man was making me do it. Then I said, "I will not hurt you or your father." She had this look on her face as she handed me the money; there was no fear on her face or in her eyes. *How can that be when I am holding a gun on her?* I was puzzled by this.

Then she said, "I forgive you."

As I turned to walk out the door, I said, "Yes, just let this go by…"

I went out the door and jumped into the car; we drove off. He said that was a good practice run and that tomorrow would be better. When we got back to the house, we sat at the table, and he counted the money. He handed me a ten-dollar bill and said that was for me. I told him I was going to the bathroom. I left that ten-dollar bill on the table, went to the bathroom, opened the window, climbed out, and started to run. I kept running for a long time. I was so lost, so hungry, and frightened. I had no money, no food, and no place to lay my head. I had left everything behind. I had nothing but what I was wearing.

All night, I looked for the cross with a light shining on it, but I could not find it. *The man long ago who told me to look for the cross when I was frightened or lost must have taken that cross and left, or he just got old and forgot to turn on the light,* I thought. I did not understand, but I kept looking.

I thought about the seasons of my life and how it all happened. Everything was so different; I was different, and this time, I was really lost. I slept under a tree that night. The next morning, I was hungry. I had never been that hungry; I looked in trash cans and, after hours of looking, found something I felt I could eat. I just roamed for what seemed to be years. People would holler at me and call me names. Sometimes, people, for no reason, would give me money. No one ever asked me any questions. They just stared at me, mostly in disgust. I was lonely and scared. I didn't know where home was, and I didn't want that man to find me.

One night, I was looking at the stars, and I remembered reading the book of truth. I remembered how I read that God made the stars and the moon. I was looking at them, and the sky was so beautiful that night, full of stars, and my heart just cried out. *I need to find the cross so I can talk to that man again. I need to know the truth.* I did not find that cross; instead, I was picked up by the police.

I confessed to robbing a gas station and that I had run away from home. I was a minor, so my name was never disclosed to the papers. I was told that I would get a record, but because I was a minor, it would be expunged. This would not affect my future, but there would be consequences for my actions. During the trial, the young girl I had pulled the gun on not only testified on my behalf but also came up to me and talked to me. She told me she had been praying for me. I told her how sorry I was that I did that. I told her that I really didn't have a choice. He said he would kill me. She said it was all right, that she knew. She told me she had asked God to get me away from that man and that he wouldn't hurt me. She said she asked God to give her the opportunity to meet me again. I asked her how she knew God. But before she could answer me, they took me away. As I was walking away, or should I say as they were taking me away, I heard her say, "Linda, I will pray and ask God to send someone to you to show you the way." With that, she was gone.

I was handcuffed and taken back to jail to wait to be transferred to a rehabilitation center for runaway teens at a state hospital. It was a facility of some type. I missed juvenile hall by one year. The law for juveniles was passed in 1968, starting first in Iowa. It was not long before juvenile detention centers were in every state and almost every county. I looked it up while I was working on this book. I wanted to understand why I was sent to a state hospital because I was just a runaway.

It was not long until I was transferred to the state hospital. The lady handling my transfer looked at me and smiled. She said, "Honey, do you know that today is Thanksgiving? It's November 23, 1967, sweetheart." I made no reply. I just looked down. I was so full of guilt and shame that I could not even look that lady in the eyes. And what was I supposed to say about Thanksgiving? I had no idea as to what it really was. Even when she said, "Linda, you still have things to be thankful for. You are alive, and as long as you are alive, there is hope." But I can tell you, that was not my thoughts at all. I was thinking about home, and I had been gone for six months, so I wanted to go home. But that was not going to happen.

At the state hospital, I was to be placed on a ward for troubled teenagers until I was released and returned home. But that was not what happened. My papers were lost or misplaced. I was placed on a wing for the mentally ill. Two days later, a girl jumped on me and was pulling my hair. I just pushed her away from me when I was grabbed from behind. They were putting me in this thing; it was white and very tight.

When they were done with me, I could not move. Then they threw me into this square room that was not big at all. It had mattresses all the way around the room. There was a horrible smell in this room. I wanted to vomit; the smell was so sickening. There was this funny-looking thing for me to drink water from. Food was placed under the door; the only way to eat was to eat like a dog. Occasionally, they would turn the water on; it would gush out and wash everything down the drain. I thought that it was possible I could die in there, and no one would ever know it.

Time was lost to me, no days or nights. I was alive but dead, lost in a place so lonely, void of life, and so dark. I saw no one. I talked to no one. There was no human contact whatsoever. I was empty. I do not know how and why, but deep down in the very depths of my soul, I heard: "There is a God, and He loves you. No matter what, look for the cross. Let it all go by. Linda, just let it all go by..." I saw Deborah's mother folding her hands, smiling, and bowing her head. Even here in the darkest place, so empty where there's nothing but silence, God was speaking to me and reminding me. Giving me a reason to hold on and to fight. However, I had nothing left to fight for. I did not want to fight. I did not want to live. How was I ever going to survive this? I thought I was losing even my mind. If anyone opened the door, they would have thought I was a mad, insane girl.

Something happened again. I heard, "Remember, Linda... Remember, Linda, you promised you would always remember. You must live, you must survive..." It was at this point that I started with the fire, remembering Laura and the two photos. Then Deborah at the swings telling me there is a God in heaven. Then, the good man, the only one I had ever met, who tended sheep and lived in a building with a cross on top. My father, letting it go by and remembering how it felt. Suddenly, I wanted to live. I wanted out of there. I had no idea what I was saying or who I was talking to, but I just kept saying, "Please get me out of here." Then, I let those thoughts wash over me again. I let all those memories come alive again.

Then, one day, this lady was tapping on the window. It took her time, but little by little, she was able to open the door without me acting like a wild animal backing into a corner. Little by little, she was able to get close enough to me to release me from the bondage that I had been in. Then I understood that she was not there to hurt me, but she was there to help me.

I began to cry, and she reached out and hugged me. I had never been hugged like that by anyone, but my sister and I just could not let go. I needed that hug; she let me hug her, and she did not let go. She let me cry until there were no more tears. Then she said, "I have been looking for you for five months. Well, here you are. I knew you were a special girl. You are going to be all right, Linda." I took a shower, and they had to shave my head. I was so skinny my arms and legs looked awful, like string beans, but I got clean clothes and moved to the ward for troubled teenagers.

When I looked in the mirror, I just stood there so shocked at my image. I looked nothing like I should have looked. Nothing like I thought I would when I looked in the mirror. I was so different. There were dark circles under my eyes as if I had not slept in a year. There were blotches all over my skin, and it seemed so white and wrinkly in some places. My head shaved. I felt so ashamed. I really deserved this for pulling that gun on that girl. What had happened to me, I deserved it for what I had done. It was so disobedient to take that money. Pulling a gun on a helpless girl while her father stood by. He was so afraid he could not even come out of hiding. This was my punishment. My punishment was to lock me away. For a while, and then if I lived, they had to shave my head so all would know the terrible things that I had done. It was a just punishment, I thought. I was so skinny. I did not look like I should be alive. But here I was—alive. My question was, why was I alive?

It was all explained to me that they lost all my paperwork and that it was the persistence of my therapist, Sandy Cheatham, who was given charge over me, who had my paperwork. She believed I was in the hospital somewhere and would not give up until they knew what happened to me. They thought I had escaped. Sandy Cheatham told me all the paperwork showed I arrived and was checked in, but then I just disappeared, but she knew I was there. They had been looking for me for five months. At the time, I truly did not understand any of this. I thought it was part of my punishment, ordered by the court. I accepted it as my punishment, something I deserved.

Two months later, I got to go home. I had been gone for a year. I was worn out, crushed, emotionally defeated, and disappointed by my vision of the world. I had risked everything only to find out that the world was bigger than any imagining I could have ever done. I was lost and drowning in a world that I could not understand. There was a longing in my heart as I looked for something that would bring meaning into my empty shell of existence.

Once I was at home, my mother did not waste any time. She told me she had something different in mind for me and that

I would like it much better. She said it was easy, and I would make so much more money. She would take the money I made each day and save it for me. She would take out so much every week, of course, for my expenses and extra for a car. I did not agree or disagree.

For days and days, she coached me. It was like I was never gone. She never asked me any questions about what I did, where I was, where I stayed, or where I slept. She never asked what happened to me, why my hair was all gone. She never asked me anything about what happened to me while I was gone, nothing. She just went straight to prepping me, training me, working with me, teaching me how to talk, telling me what kind of things to say to different kinds of men, and telling me what I needed to do and how I needed to do it. She told me she was going to teach me to play games with men and how to get money from them. She spoke to me day after day, filling me with information of how I could tell a rich man from a poor man, a lonely man, a married man, a man who would only want to use me and abuse me. She taught me how and what to look for in a man. That I could use for money and just how to do it. I wanted out, but how? Where would I go? I did not know where the cross was nor the man who tended sheep. I did not know what happened to the girls I had lived with or how to find them. I did not know what to do, so I just stayed and did everything my mom told me to do. I was too frightened of the world now.

After all the test runs we did in different clubs, her pointing out men, all the things that she was teaching me and training me had come to an end. Now, it was time for me to go wherever she was going to take me. She said, "You are finally ready; it is time for you to go to work." She dressed me up and took me to a club. Mom did all the talking. A man had me stand up and turn around. He told my mom I would do fine, so I went to work there. I served drinks in a gentlemen's club, and I gave all the money I made to my mom. She continued to coach me, constantly telling me what men liked and what they didn't, how to walk, how to talk, how to use them, how to lie, and how to extort money from them. But never, never let a man touch me. She was training me how to pick out certain men. They were men who wanted what they could not have, and they would give just about anything to get it. That's what she said. I certainly didn't understand the change in that area. It was as if she was training me, guiding me, and leading me on this path of self-destruction, and I didn't know how to stop it.

I wanted to believe that she was sorry for what she had done. She told me she only did it because Laura took all her money and had left. She needed to pay a bill, or the police would have come and arrested her. She cried as she told me they would have put her in jail, and she would never let anyone hurt her special girl. I felt that if I just stayed home, followed the rules, and did what Mom asked me to do, it would all be okay.

I had reasoned that at least at home, I had food and clothes. I had a warm bed to sleep in and a room with everything I needed. It was a safe place for me, and even with all the things that were messed up, I knew at least here I could survive. I knew the rules at home, but out in the world, I did not know the rules, and I was lost. I learned that the world was big and full of all kinds of things that I could not understand. The world outside was just as confusing as the home I had grown up in. There was really no difference. I was safe at home and believed my mom would not let anyone hurt me again.

When I was home, I would stay in my room so I could rest and think. I would soon be sixteen, and since my return home, not one time had a belt, hand, or fist been placed upon me. Still, I knew I was trapped, and there was no way out, at least not for me. Laura was gone. Was she happy? Where was she? Did she have money and a place to live? I missed her, and I longed to see her. What was happening to her? I wanted to know what happened to her and why she would not come home, even if it was just to visit Mom. Did Laura hate Mom so much that she did not even want to see her?

I was quickly learning the ways of the world. It was a world that I grew to hate increasingly more. All I could see was this ugly force that seemed to control men and women who used their looks and their bodies to achieve their own selfish goals and desires. I saw greed, perversion, lust, adultery, envy, pride, and corruption. Filth gushed out like a nasty cistern, and I saw drunkenness in its ugliest form. It was truly as if all the sewers in the world were poured into the place that was called the gentlemen's club. It was an evil place with a title it did not deserve. It was Satan's territory, and looking back, I believe it to be the very gates to hell itself. That is where my mother chose to take her fourteen-year-old daughter.

I lived in a world of darkness. There was no light and nothing to show me any different. I was lost, and I was dying a little more each day. I believed in my heart that this was all the world had for me. I was shattered, and I did not know how to put myself together again. How could I ever mend all the brokenness in my life?

I had been working at the club for one and a half years. It was December 19, 1969, my birthday. I finally had the courage to ask about Laura. I asked Mom where Laura was and what she was doing. Mom said, "Your sister got married and has her own life now. She wants nothing to do with you. Did you forget what I told you?" I was very hurt, and I felt betrayed. I still missed Laura, and I wanted to see her. So, about a month later, I asked Mom about Laura again. Mom and I were sitting outside the club, waiting for it to open. This was also the time Mom would do extra coaching and instructions to make me better at my job.

I felt like Mom was in an exceptionally good mood, so I asked her to take me to see Laura. She slapped me and told me that Laura did not want to see me and I needed to forget about her. She said Laura did not care about our family. With tears in her eyes, Mom looked at me and said, "Linda, you are all I have got. You must work and give me all your money now, or we will lose our home. Laura does not care about us." I told Mom she could have all the money she had been saving for me. She smiled and spoke. "Now you get on in there, and you make lots of money for your mommy today." I got out of the car, and as I walked into the club that day, I was truly broken and had finally acccpted that this was my life.

It was now February of 1971; I had been working at the club for almost four years. I had grown up a lot, but still, in many ways, I was like a lost child. In February, at the club, I met a man who was in the US Navy. His name was Thomas, and he told me he was only there because his friends had dragged him in. He then asked me what I was doing there. I did not say anything. The man kept talking to me. He told me he was leaving for Vietnam in May. He came back to see me every day and would talk to me for hours. One day, I told him about my mother and why I was working there. I do not know why I told him. However, this man made me feel special. I believed he really cared about me. He was not like any of the men who filled the club day after day. I knew I could trust him and wanted to share things with him. I mean, like, tell him about my life and all the things that had happened to me.

Then, one day, Thomas came into the club and asked me to marry him. He told me he wanted to get me out of that club and away from my mother. I certainly did not want to be in that club. I hated everything about it. Everything my mother told me to do, I did, thinking I was going to be happy. I thought that somehow, I was going to find what it was that I felt was missing in my life. I did not understand, but I knew there was something wrong in my life. There was this emptiness and longing for a moment like the afternoon Laura and I had in the field. That was the day I thought the entire world had stopped turning for us. It was truly the only time I had experienced total joy and peace.

I will admit that when Thomas asked me to marry him, I saw it as an opportunity to get out of that place and away from my parents. I did not really know him, but I felt it was all going to be okay. He said as soon as he got to Vietnam, he would get all the paperwork done and send enough money for me to get a place to live. He said I would get a check every month to pay the bills and buy food. He assured me everything would be all right.

I am not sure as to why my mother signed for me to get married, but she did; maybe Thomas gave her money, maybe because she knew once he was gone, she could still control me and take the money he would be sending and put me back in the club. Maybe she had some underhanded plan of her own. I will never know, but what I do know is that I was finally out of that club after four years.

We got married, and we spent seven days together before Thomas left for Vietnam. They were good days. He talked to me and asked me how I felt about things. He said when he came back, if I still wanted to, we would build a life together. If not, he said he would understand and still help me get a place to live. He would help me with the things I needed and even get me a job. I promised him I would wait for him to come home. I would be waiting for him, and there was so much I wanted to share with him. He was a truly kind man. He did not hurt me in any way. In a time of darkness, Thomas brought light into my life. As he was getting ready to board his plane, he said, "Pray for me." I told him I could not and didn't know how or to whom to pray. He told me, "To God." I told him, "There is no God, and if there is a God, where is He?"

My heart and the hardness that had been developing melted away in one moment as the man I had married looked at me with such love and compassion and said, "There is a God, Linda. He knows you, and He loves you; remember that."

"How can that be?" I asked.

He looked at me and said, "It's too much to explain now, but it's true, and you can call on Him anytime, and He will hear you and save you. I'll write you and tell you more. For now, just know God is everywhere."

With that, he hugged me and stepped onto the plane. Just like that, he was gone. However, his words lingered for days, weeks, months, and years.

Laura's life and mine seemed to parallel. It had been almost five years since we had seen each other. I thought about her every day. I wanted to see Laura, to find out if she was okay and if she had found the love and happiness we both had longed for as little girls. I wanted to find out if she felt something was missing in her life the way I did. I wanted to know why she left and why she did not want to see me, and I needed her to know that no matter what, I still loved her.

Laura and I were still the same, but we were different somehow. We were both married, and yet neither of us was mature enough to understand what marriage really was, and for sure, neither of us had an example of what it meant to be a wife. Certainly, neither one of us had married for the right reasons. We knew how to take care of a home and cook and prepare good meals, but it takes more than that to be a wife, as I am sure so many unsuspecting young girls have discovered.

I did not get to talk to Laura, nor did I get to move out of my parents' house. I waited and waited, but nothing: no letters, no money, and no way out. My husband had been gone six months. I felt abandoned and deeply hurt. I did not feel that way because I genuinely loved him; I really did not even know him. I felt that way because I had believed him, and I thought he saw value in me. Now I was just gaining weight and getting bigger and bigger. I had gone to the doctor, and he told me that I was going to have a baby. Not exactly what I had planned. There had to be a reason that he had not written to me. Why would he pick me out just to hurt me like this? I would think about the children at school. They had no reason to hate me and treat me the way they did. They called it "fun," never realizing the pain and damage they caused in my life as a result of their so-called "fun." What reason would Thomas have to do this?

I could not understand. I just thought, for some reason unknown to me, Thomas had deserted me. But death was not among my thoughts. I was not prepared for it. I was informed of my husband's death in October of 1971. He was shot down five days after he had arrived in Vietnam, right outside of Da Nang. He was gone. I just did not know how to feel or how to respond. There were no tears because I really didn't know him. However, there was this sadness in me, a feeling that someone incredibly special had just slipped out of my life. It was over as quickly as it had begun, and at seventeen, I had no idea what I was supposed to do with all this. I did not know how to act or how to feel. I met his family very briefly. I could tell right away they did not care for me. Time and distance never allowed for a relationship to develop, and it was best to leave it that way. They never saw his child and did not believe the child to be his. Nor did they ever acknowledge me as his wife.

I was going to have a baby. Now, I could say I knew what that meant, but I had no idea about having a baby or taking care of a baby. And the cold fact was, I was of no more value to my mother. I feared it would be a matter of time before she would throw me out on the street. I knew I was alone.

It all seemed to be so hopeless until the Navy contacted me again. It seemed I had money coming to me. The Navy officer talked to me without my mother. She received twenty thousand dollars from me for the sole purpose of leaving me alone to live my own life. The Navy officer Oliver and his wife, Nancy, then helped me map out a plan to get me out of my parents' house. This plan also included a private PO box of my very own. My own apartment and furniture. I had enough money to take care of myself and my baby. I did not have to worry about it anymore. I would receive a check every month, and I had my very own checking account at a bank where I could put the check in. I also received a generous sum of money from an insurance company and one from the Navy as well. The man I had married kept his promise to me. Thomas had indeed taken care of me.

In January of 1972, I moved into my very own apartment. Oliver and Nancy put an ad in the newspaper for a roommate. I needed someone willing to help me take care of my baby in exchange for rent. They would help with childcare. I was looking for someone to show me how to take care of my baby. The ad was quickly answered by a young girl; she was a year older than me. She had graduated from high school and was taking time for herself before going to college. She told me she was not sure she wanted to go to college. It was perfect. Her name was Rhonda.

It would give Rhonda time to teach me how to take care of my baby. She said she would teach me more about banking and shopping, which I was already learning from Oliver and Nancy. I was so comfortable with her, and everything had gone so well. She was with me the night my baby was born. My baby girl was born February 5, 1972, and suddenly I was a mother.

I named her Jasmine Marie, and she was beautiful. From the first moment that I saw her, I knew I would never do anything to hurt my beautiful baby. Everything in me wanted to protect her, but from what, I was not exactly sure. I knew I did not want her to see the things I had seen or to be hurt in any way. I never wanted her to be treated the way I had been treated by my mother.

My heart was filling quickly with hopes and dreams for Jasmine. One of those dreams was that I would find my sister because I wanted my daughter to know Laura the way I did. I wanted Jasmine to know and to love her aunt, Laura. I wondered if that would ever be possible.

I asked Mom one last time for information about Laura in April of 1972. "For a price," Mom told me where Laura lived, her phone number, and that Laura also had a baby boy in February of 1972. I could not believe it. We both had our babies in the same month and in the same year. I had to see her. Still, Mom told me it would be best not to see Laura or call her. I asked Mom how often she saw Laura, and she told me once a week. I asked Mom if she had told Laura about me and that I wanted to see her. Mom told me again that Laura did not want to see me. I was so hurt by what Mom said that even though I had Laura's phone number, I did not call her.

Dad and Mom were going through changes as well. Mom's beauty was slowly beginning to fade, and she did not have her two daughters to depend on anymore. When I went to their home, things were different. There were still men, but they did not wear suits or drive fancy cars.

I tried to go there only when my dad was home. If I was there when a man came, I would leave without saying anything to them. I kept going to see Mom because I loved both my parents and hoped that someday they, too, would express a love for me. I also hoped that Laura would come to their house while I was there. I needed to see her, and I had to find out what I had done that made her hate me so much.

The years went by so fast, and two little girls emerged into a world for which they were not prepared. We were still just young girls who, with the help of our mother, had been separated and thrown into the world and a life that neither of us chose. Life had taken us in different directions, some by choice and others forced upon us. The older we got, the more we started taking control of our own lives. But control without knowledge can be dangerous. We made choices that were based on the idea that, somehow, we would be taken away from the place that had created the brokenness and pain that filled our souls. We were damaged and had no idea how to fix what was wrong. The very foundation of our lives had been utterly shattered at such an early age. We were in a world full of darkness, without hope, and surviving in the only way we knew.

Laura and I did not get to choose anything; we had been thrown into the world. We were trying to figure everything out for ourselves. Life was changing for us, teaching us and taking us away from each other instead of towards each other. It seemed as if neither of us had a choice. We were the products of our parents. They owned us. They controlled us, but we were slowly breaking away, and in truth, we were going in different directions!

CHAPTER 7

The Promise

The year 1972 was the year I stepped into motherhood. It started out as the best year of my life. Motherhood seemed to come to me naturally. With the help of my roommate, Rhonda, the Navy officer, Oliver, and his wife, Nancy, I learned about banking and investments. I taught Rhonda how to pick out the best fruits and vegetables and how to tell when they were bad, and she taught me all about coupons.

Rhonda and I had become close. She was enjoying her break between high school and college. She talked to me about how it would help me to go back to school, but I dismissed that idea right away. She taught me how to drive, and I got a driver's license. She went with me and helped me pick out my first car. She taught me how to laugh. Without realizing it, Rhonda had become my friend, and I was learning how to trust someone outside my family.

Rhonda loved the fall season as much as I did. I was going to teach her how to bake pumpkin seeds. I told her of my love for pumpkins, and she said, "Let's go get a pumpkin, and we can make the seeds tonight." We did not waste any time. We went and bought a pumpkin that night.

While we were at the store, she said, "Let's have a party, and I will invite some of my friends over." I did not want to have a party, but she kept saying it would be fun and that she had never gotten to have one before. I thought about all the parties my parents had, serving drinks, cleaning up after all those drunks, and how they smelled and talked. I told her no, I did not think it was a good idea with Jasmine. She told me to get my mother to babysit. I do not know why I agreed to have the party. I took Jasmine to my mother to keep for the night. I told Mom I would be there to pick Jasmine up the next morning at nine o'clock sharp.

It was October 31, 1972. Rhonda chose to have the party on Halloween night. The whole time, I was telling myself not to do this, even asking myself why I agreed. I just wanted to make Rhonda happy. When I said yes, she jumped up and down, shouting, "This is going to be so cool!"

As I got dressed that night, something inside me just kept saying this was all wrong. I opened my little jewelry box and took Laura's phone number out. I looked at the number. I wanted to call but asked myself, "Why? She hates me, and she will just hang up on me. Rhonda's my sister now." I hated the thoughts I was having, and I knew Rhonda was not my sister, nor could she ever be. She was a friend, and that was all.

I thought about what my mom said, "Laura does not want to talk to you." I thought about the price I had paid in order to get her number. With that thought, I wadded up the paper and threw it back in the jewelry box. I told myself I was having a party tonight with my friend, and I was going to have fun. As I was closing the bedroom door, I glanced back at the jewelry box. Right then, I knew deep down that I should go get that number, call Laura, go get my baby, and go see my sister. I knew that was what I should do. It was a deep-down sense of knowing I should not stay for the party. I was taking my first step toward the jewelry box when the doorbell rang, and Rhonda yelled, "Let's party!" I turned and shut the door behind me.

The party was not all Rhonda had hoped it would be, and I was relieved when only four people showed up. The party was over before eleven o'clock. I told her I was sorry about her party not turning out the way she had planned. She said, "Linda, when I was growing up, all I ever got to do was go to church. I never got to have any fun. I never got to drink or go to parties, and if God was not in it, I didn't get to do it."

My face must have lost all expression and all color. She looked at me and said, "What's the matter with you? Are you sick?"

I said, "You believe in God, and you are just now telling me? Did you know that I do not believe in God?" I must have talked for thirty minutes or more and never let her say a word. I told her about my childhood, the parties, the beatings, and left nothing out. I was angry! When I was finished, she said she was sorry. She told me there was a God, and she could answer all my questions about God. I asked her if she knew where the church with the cross on top that the light shined on was. I told her there was a good man inside who tended sheep. She looked at me, kind of funny, and changed the subject. She said, "No matter where you are or what is happening, you can call out to Him. He will hear you and save you."

I thought, *Why do people keep telling me that? What does it mean, "He will save me"? Save me from what?*

The phone rang, and she went to answer it. She came back about ten minutes later and told me it was her mother just checking up on her. Rhonda said her mother sounded worried, but she had assured her we were at home and getting ready to go to bed. Rhonda looked at me with her big, sad brown eyes and said, "I'm really tired." She promised me she would spend the next day with me, and we were going to talk about God. She said, "I've got a book, and you need to see it. I'll read you some things from it, and we will go get you one." She told me if I had questions she could not answer, we could go to her church, or we could always talk to her dad.

I told her to go to bed and that I would clean up. I smiled at her and said it was not that big of a mess, and we both laughed. I started cleaning up, and she went to her room. There were two small bags of trash in the kitchen. I thought I would go ahead and run them out so I would not have to mess with them in the morning. I put the trash bags by the door and finished what needed to be done in the kitchen. I wiped off the coffee table and looked at the clock. It was eleven thirty.

I grabbed the two bags and walked out the door. I tossed the trash bags, and at that very moment, the strangest thought crossed my mind: something my husband had said to me before he boarded his plane: "There is a God. He is everywhere; you can call on Him anytime, and He will save you. He loves you." I lingered there a few moments, caught up in my thoughts. I was just looking at the stars and thought that Rhonda basically said the same thing: God would save me. What did that mean, "He would save me"? I shook my head. "But there is no God, and there is no Satan. I am so confused by all this and have been for years. One day, it is the spirit life, and the next day, there is a God. Then I think there is nothing, no spirit life, no God, but then what? I am going to go crazy before I figure this all out." I turned and walked back to the stairs. On the way up the stairs, I realized I had left the door open.

I walked in and shut the door before I noticed a man sitting in the chair by the door. I looked down the hall, and Rhonda's light was on. I really did not know her friends, and I had never met this man before. I went back to the kitchen, got a drink of water, and put the glass in the sink. I looked at the clock. It was eleven forty-five. I walked out of the kitchen into the living room and turned the corner that led down the hall when I noticed Rhonda's bedroom light was off.

I turned back around and faced the man still sitting in the chair by the door. I knew deep down that this was all wrong. I realized Rhonda did not know he was in the house, and I felt fear as the full weight of the realization that she did not know him at all sank into my heart. I can still hear the words slowly coming out as I asked him what he wanted.

That is the last thing I remember. I was on the other side of the room, and I should remember him getting up and moving towards me, but I did not. My mind just does not remember. Maybe deep down inside, I don't want to remember. When I say I remember nothing, I am referring to that moment in time when I should remember him getting up out of the chair and coming towards me, but I simply do not remember. There was a small time frame when I felt like I was waking up from a bad dream, and I realized what was happening to me. It seemed like he was waiting for me to be conscious. I looked down and saw blood and noticed part of my clothes were missing. This was the only part of the ordeal that I remember in detail. I do not know what had happened or even how I got there, but I was on the couch. He was sitting beside me. He bent down and lowered his left hand to the floor and, with power in a horrible-sounding voice, said, "Satan, give me the power to do what you sent me to do." When he spoke those words, the room started spinning, and my mind was racing. It was as if, in that moment, time had no meaning; the world just stopped. "There is a Satan, there... is... Satan... Satan is real!" Something inside me snapped; I remembered the good man who tended sheep, and I knew there was a God. At that moment, with all my strength and with everything that I am, without thought, without reasoning, and without hesitation, I screamed, *"God, save me!"* That is all I remembered.

On November 3, 1972, three days later, my body was found in a field nine miles from where I lived, almost dead. I do not know what happened to Rhonda. I never saw her again after that fatal night. Her body was never found.

I was in the hospital for over two weeks before I really understood where I was and what had taken place. I had been through two major surgeries. I was waiting for a decision from the doctors about what would happen to my right eye because there had been severe damage done to it. The results of that night were difficult to even begin to process. The bruises were fading, and I was beginning to heal on the outside, but inside was a different story. It would take years to overcome all the damage done to my body, mind, and soul that one dark night in my life.

Nine surgeries and five months later, covered with scars and bruises and mentally unstable, came the final blow: I would never have children. I saw it as a punishment, what I deserved. Broken… so broken, that was me. My life was… There are no words for the empty, lost girl I had become or maybe had always been. What would become of me now? I could not explain it, but I felt as if something evil was around me now, just waiting for me to close my eyes, shut the door, or open it. I do not know; I just felt the evil around me. It was as if that night, I fought the evil and escaped, and now the evil was angry and wanted to torture me and make me live in fear.

I looked up one day, and there was Laura. She said she had just found out I was there. Neither Dad nor Mom had been to see me and had no plans to come. She told me she was at our parents' when the police came to talk to them. She knew that Dad and Mom had kept all of this from her. So, she just asked the police officer where I was. She knew it made our parents mad, but she said she did not care. She wanted to know where I was and what had happened to me. Laura looked at me and said, "I still love you, Little Sis, and I just wanted you to know. No, Linda, I need you to know that. You are still the Little L, and I am the Big L, and I am so sorry I wasn't there for you."

We talked, we laughed, and we cried. I discovered so many things that day. Laura never said she did not want to see me. She was told that I did not want to see her. Mom had lied to both of us. We could not understand why Mom would do that to us, even though we both knew in our hearts that money and control were the main two reasons. But neither one of us voiced our thoughts about the matter.

Big L came to see Little L every day at the hospital. We spent our time together talking and sharing the things we had been through. She told me the night I was raped, she knew something bad was going to happen, and she thought I was going to die that night. She was in a car, going over a bridge around midnight, when suddenly she felt fear, and she knew I was in danger. Laura looked as if she were going to say something else and then just stopped.

We shared many things, and one of those things was extremely hard for Laura to tell me. I saw her pain, and I knew it well, but I remained silent. Laura had fallen into the lifestyle Mother had carved out for her. Mom had complete control of her. What I had not known was that after the tea party in the spring of 1965, Mom had taken Laura to a house where a man waited for her inside. She said there was so much more to her story, but she just couldn't talk about it now. Maybe later, when things were better, when things might be different. But I knew in my heart that man was the first in a long line of men who paid for a moment of pleasure with my beautiful sister. I know that destroyed her. It crushed her. After two years, Mom told Laura that she did not have what it took to be a high-class lady of pleasure, and Mom had no more good offers for her. Mom told Laura the street was her next stop, and Laura continued living that way. Laura told me that she felt so dirty and so ashamed. Laura lived this lifestyle for a year, hidden away in the dark, alone, with no one to talk to. Laura believed I wanted nothing to do with her because she was Mom's favorite. Laura told me that in April of 1968, Mom told her I was coming home. At Mom's request, she got her first apartment and left home the week before I was due to arrive. She admitted she stayed working on the streets for almost a year, and then she took a job at a restaurant.

Laura met an older man while she was working there. She told me his name was Kevin, and they got married in March of 1970 and had a son in February of 1972. She said her husband was good to her and that he had never hit her. She was not happy, but her life was still better than it had ever been. She looked up at me and smiled. "Oh, Linda, my baby boy is so beautiful, and I love him so much; Kevin named him Kenneth. I would bring him up here, but my husband does not want him here at the hospital around all these sick people."

During one of our visits, I finally decided to tell Laura I believed there was a God and that I didn't know how to find Him, but I knew He was real. I also told her there was a Satan and that I did not fully understand, but he was real, and he was very evil. I told her about the night I was raped. The whole experience: the party, wanting to call her, taking the trash out, that man sitting in the chair, how I was on the couch, and what he said. I told her that was when I knew that God was real and He existed, and I called out to God to save me, and He did. I did not know how, and I did not know why, but somehow God saved me. I knew she thought I was weird, but I told her that I did not imagine it; God saved my life. I tried to tell her something happened when I called out to God, but I was not sure what it was. Laura was asking questions I could not possibly answer, and I felt like she was testing me, so I finally said, "Laura, nothing you say to me is going to change my mind. I believe in God; I do not know how I know, I just know, and I am going to find Him, and when I do, I will be able to answer all your questions."

Later, I told her that before my husband, Thomas, got on the plane to Vietnam, he told me that God was everywhere. Laura just looked at me in shock and asked, "How can that be?" I told her I did not know. I asked her if she ever heard anyone talk about God. Had anyone ever told her there was a God? She told me that no one had ever talked to her about God. Laura said she just did not know if there was a God because if there was, why didn't anyone ever talk about Him, or why wouldn't someone tell us about God?

Laura said the most amazing thing: "If God is so big and powerful, then everyone would be talking about Him all the time. So where are all the people that know Him? Linda, in all our lives, only two people have ever talked to you about God. I have only heard one family in the restaurant talk about this great God that you believe in now. Why would our parents tell us there is no God if there is a God?"

I looked at her. I loved her more than my own life, and I just wanted her to believe me. I said, "Laura, I do not know why no one talks about Him, and I do not know why our parents don't believe in Him, but I believe that God exists; I know He is real. He is out there somewhere. I am going to find Him, and that is what I do know." I looked at her, and for the first time, I realized how truly broken she was. My beautiful sister was hurting, too, and she was just as confused as I was. We both had been damaged by our mother. I did not have an answer for her. With all the wisdom I could have at eighteen, I spoke the words I knew Laura would hold on to. "Laura, I do not know why Dad and Mom would tell us there is no God. Maybe it's because no one ever told them either. This is a big world with millions of people, and someone knows where God is. Someone out there knows the truth, but I think it may be a secret. Maybe it's like a club, with special rules and stuff. I do not know, but what I do know is there is a God, and there is a Satan."

I was released from the hospital the first week of March 1973. My parents still had Jasmine, and I could not wait to get my baby away from them. She was over a year old now. When I arrived at their house, I was informed that they had custody of her and that if I did not sign the papers, the state was going to take her away, and I would never see her again. I did not know what to believe, and I wasn't willing to take any chances. My mom told me that after a few days, the state would be out of it, and I could come back and get my Jasmine. I did what I was told; I went with her, and I signed all the papers she put in front of me.

As with most things in my life, it all happened very quickly. Jasmine now belonged to my parents. I was not allowed to see her. I tried, but Mom kept telling me no, and the last time I tried, she called the police. That day, I learned I had signed all my rights away as her mother. The last time I saw Jasmine was the day I dropped her off at my parent's house, October 31, 1972. I felt I had failed as a mother and walked away defeated. I knew not to trust my mother, and yet I let her lie to me and deceive me again. Now, what would become of my little girl? I hated what I had done, and now my little girl would pay the price.

My next step was to go back to the apartment and try to start my life over again. The apartment manager was kind and understanding. I had sent Laura there to have the lock on the door changed. Laura's husband took care of a few things until I got out of the hospital. He went to my apartment and took care of everything after the police finished. He allowed Rhonda's parents in to take her belongings. He said they left almost everything there and took only a small box. I thought to myself, *So little for someone's life, a small box of memories.*

Laura's husband, Kevin, handled everything. He threw all the things away for me on a list I had given him and sold the rest. I told him to keep the money. He also went to the post office and bank and took care of some business matters for me. I gave him checks for the apartment, which I continued to pay because of the lease I had signed, and of course, I needed a place to go when I got out of the hospital. *I will fix it all back up with everything new, clean, and with a fresh new beginning,* I thought.

When I got to the apartment, I stood at the foot of the stairs for what seemed like hours. Fear had a hold on me. I finally pushed past it and walked up the stairs. I was telling myself that I would be okay once I got up the stairs and in the apartment. But once I was up the stairs and standing in front of the door with my key in hand, I could not open the door. I just stood there outside that door, shaking. I could not go in, and no force on this earth was going to make me.

I went to a little café and called Laura. I told her where I was and what had happened. She came and got me. We left my car at the café and took her car so she could do all the driving. She took me to the post office and to the bank. After we were finished with my business matters, she took me back to the café where my car was and followed me to a nearby hotel. I rented a hotel room, and we talked for a few moments before she had to leave. Laura said she would talk to her husband to see if I could live with them for a while until I got better and found a different place to live.

The next day, Laura came to see me, and I told her I did not want to move in with her. She wanted to know why. I tried to explain it, but she could not understand. I did not even realize it at first, but slowly, day by day, it took control of my life—*fear!* That is the only word that expresses the condition of my life. I could not sleep, eat, or even take a bath. I was afraid of being inside, and at the same time, I was afraid of being outside. *Fear had taken control of my life in such a short period of time!*

I told Laura I was going to move to a small town about an hour away. At the time, neither one of us foresaw the events that would once again keep us apart. It was March 1973; she was so beautiful that day. She said, "Linda, I am trying to understand why you are going. So please tell me one more time, why are you going away?"

As honestly as I could, I answered her question. I tried not to let fear control my answer. I told her, "I have to go, Laura. I must find God. I know now that He is out there, but I know Satan is out there too. It is Satan that wants to take me over. I do not know how or why, but it is not my body he wants. I fear it is something else, and it has nothing to do with what we can see or touch.

"I cannot tell you what I do not fully understand, and I know you don't understand, but it's time for me to go; I need to go. I will find God, and when I find Him, I will come back and tell you all about Him. Then I will take you to where He is so you can meet Him too. I will come back, Laura. I promise you I will come back for you."

We both cried, but I knew I had to go. I told her to visit our parents often and keep an eye on my little girl. She promised she would. With a hug to seal the promises we made to each other, I got in my car and drove off.

It would be twelve and a half years before we would see each other again, and our lives would be vastly different. Laura and I were once again separated, but this time, we both knew we loved each other, and neither time nor distance could change that. Mother knew she could not put a wedge between us again. Laura and I may have been broken, and we may have been lost, but God knows how to find that which is lost and how to restore broken lives.

I was nineteen; I did not feel young or old. In many ways, I was still a young girl standing in the hallway of the home where I grew up, asking myself why my mother did not love me. In other ways, I felt that I had lived a long, long time and had been through more than my years should have allowed. Now I was on my way to find God, the God I was told did not exist. The God I knew almost nothing about. One thing that I knew for sure was that God was out there somewhere, and I had to find Him. When I did, I was going to tell Him, "I would have come sooner, but no one ever told me about You, and I didn't know where You were. Well, there was the good man who tended sheep, and he told me to look for the cross, but we just did not get to talk much, and there was so much I didn't understand."

I called Laura once a month to let her know how I was doing. She always asked, "Did you find God?" I did not have a phone, so I called her from pay phones. She asked me many times to get a phone put in where I lived in case something happened. I told her that I moved so much that I felt it would be difficult to keep up with, but I felt I could not manage it. If the phone were to ring, it might frighten me, and I was afraid of how I might react to the sudden noise.

I knew myself, and the fear I lived in had pushed me past all reason when it came to certain things, and sound was one of them. I had no television, no radio, nothing that made any kind of noise, not even an alarm clock. I could not deal with noise, especially sudden noises. I had to have it silent, and I liked it silent.

I tried to call her in September of 1974. Kevin told me she was no longer there, but he would see her in court and let her know I had called. I did not understand what he was talking about, but I knew it could not be good. I called a couple of times over the next few months. No answer; later, the number was disconnected. Again, Laura and I had lost touch with each other. I did not know where she was, and she had no idea where I was. I hung onto the fact that as soon as I found God, I would return home. It was all I needed to give me hope. Hope that I would find the truth and take that truth back to my sister.

The years passed; I had moved more times than I could count, but thanks to the Texas Department of Public Safety, who kept up with it for me, I discovered I had moved and requested a new driver's license thirty-four times. I had lived in various places in Texas: Hillsboro, Waco, Athens, Mount Pleasant, Gladewater, Malakoff, Seven Points, Gun Barrel, Mabank, Terrell, Brownsville, Winnsboro, Whitehouse, Canton, Longview, and Tyler. There was the panhandle and the coast. West Texas and East Texas, I had moved a lot, never in one place long.

The list was long, and there were so many little towns. I would get a change of address, but before I got my new driver's license, I was already on the move. Fear kept me on the move. However, the Texas Department of Public Safety thought I had done something illegal with all the licenses issued to me over a five-year period.

I had no choice but to tell my story; of course, I left out the part about me looking for God. I was not going to make the mistake of telling them that. What if they did not believe, like my parents, and I might never get another driver's license? After hearing my story, I was told I would be issued a license, but it would be the last one for a two-year period, and by order of the court, I had to seek professional help as well, whatever that meant. I asked them, and they were kind enough to give me directions.

I was living in Tyler, Texas, when all of this occurred. I moved there in January of 1978. I was living in constant fear, and I was still looking for God. I sat down one night and put a list together in my head of everything I knew about God. I went all the way back to Deborah, the little girl I met in a park. She had told me there was a God. So, I knew some children believed in Him. The day I was lost. I wandered around until night came, and I could not find my way home. It was very cold, and I found a building with a cross on top of it that I called a "plus" sign. The good man inside told me it was a church, and people came there to learn about God.

I remembered the words Thomas, my husband, spoke to me before he got on the plane that took him to Vietnam. He told me, "God is everywhere." But I just did not know where.

Rhonda told me that God would save me, the same words the man who tended sheep and my husband had said to me.

She also told me that night if she could not answer my questions, we could go to church. That was the sum of what I knew. Four things I had been told, and none of them made any sense to me. I could not get the word "church" out of my mind, and now, Tyler would be just one more place I would check off my list. God was not in Tyler, Texas. Check!

I had a deep fear that Satan was waiting for me in some strange way. A fear that he wanted more than for me to die overshadowed every day and every minute of my life. I knew he wanted something else. I feared Satan was going to take something away from me, and I would not be able to stop it from happening. These thoughts were pushing me over the edge.

I bought a map of the world. As I looked at the map, I started weeping, and the words just rolled out. It was not like I knew I was praying because I really did not know how to pray or even what praying was. I honestly believe, however, that this was my first prayer. "It is all so big, God. I have tried to find You, and I have failed. Who are You, God, and where are You? I am so lost and frightened; I am trying to understand."

I had finally realized and accepted that the world was too big and there were too many places for God to be. What if He had just left that place right before I got there, or worse, what if I left, and God was on His way there? After all, God was everywhere. It was something I was never going to figure out. I knew October was right around the corner; it was always the hardest time of the year for me, and the nightmares were getting worse.

Every night was a night of fear and hopelessness. Looking for a cross on top of a building all seemed so useless now. However, on this night in March of 1978, I was completely taken over with fear, along with the fact that I was suffering from a severe lack of sleep. The truth was I wanted to end my life. The idea of ending my life had taken over most of my thoughts. I had reasoned that if I could not find God, I would rather die than have Satan come and take from me whatever it was he wanted. I decided to end my life, but how? I had two prescriptions for sleeping pills and thought that would be painless and easy. Still, my heart said to wait a little longer, wait until May.

The next morning, I was on my way to my little garage apartment after a long night of looking for the cross on top of a building. I had finally given up, and that's when I saw three crosses. I had this habit of always looking at crosses and comparing them to the one in my memory. If it did not match, I would keep driving. These three crosses somehow captivated me. There were cars, lots of cars, in the parking lot. I had already passed the church; I knew it was a church. I don't know how I knew; I just did, so I turned around and went back.

My heart was beating so fast, but not with fear. This was a new feeling; it was hope. That is the only way I can explain it. In a moment, something happened to me. *Hope!* Even though I did not know it by name, it changed everything in a moment. I had driven around many times before and looked at buildings where there were crosses, but no one was ever there. No cars, no people, and I had long given up on finding the good man I had talked to so long ago on a cold winter night. In my heart, I believed that all the buildings were empty because all the people had gone away with God somewhere. But now, here was this building, and cars filled the parking lot. I parked my car across the street and got out. *What do I do now?* I thought. *I will just go, knock on the door, introduce myself, and ask to talk to God.*

Then I heard it: "Amazing grace (how sweet the sound) / that saved a wrench like me! / I once was lost, but now am found, / was blind, but now I see." I sat on the curb and cried; it seemed like hours had passed. I looked at that building, making mental notes. I wanted to remember everything about it. I could hear singing and music; I heard the words but could not make out what was being said.

After a while, people started coming out. They were all smiling and talking to one another. I could not believe my eyes. Children were running around and laughing! My eyes were drawn to a woman. She was beautiful, but not in the way my mother was beautiful. This lady was radiant. She had her hair up and was wearing a long green dress with heels to match. She had a black book in her hand. She had opened it up and was pointing to something in it to another woman. I could not believe the scene unfolding before my eyes. Slowly, the parking lot emptied, and I just sat there on the curb with tears streaming down my face. My heart was filled with something I could not explain. There was joy and sadness all mixed up together in my soul.

What I experienced amazed me, and I was overwhelmed with hope. I went back there the next day at about the same time. Nothing. My heart was broken. I kept going back every day. Nothing! Every day for six days, I was ready to give up, but I could not. I would try one more time.

The next day, the parking lot was full, just like before. I parked across the street and listened. I heard the singing and the music again. After a while, they all came out. I watched again in amazement, and I saw people hugging each other, talking, and laughing. I saw the lady I had admired the first time again. It was her voice that sounded out across the parking lot that day as she said, "I will not be here Wednesday, but I will see you next Sunday."

I went home and looked at the calendar. It was Sunday. I believe I was the happiest person in the world that day. I knew if I just kept going back, maybe somehow, I could figure it all out. As it turned out, I sat across the street on the curb for five months. No one noticed me; I sat there and cried, all that time hoping someone would notice me and, well, I don't know, maybe invite me in.

There was a big void in my life, and I had no idea how to fill it. I had no idea how I was going to find God if I continued sitting on the curb! After all, God was not going to come out of the building and introduce Himself to me. I had to figure out how all of this worked. I had no idea how I was going to get from the curb, where I sat in fear and darkness, to inside the building to find God. I certainly did not have the courage just to walk up there and knock on the door and ask, "May I come in, and by the way, is God here?" I just did not see that working for me. They might think I had lost...well, my mind. The church I had found was like a special treasure I had discovered. I would always just head in that direction; it had a special place in my heart. Then, one Sunday morning, I heard a lady yell across the parking lot to someone, "I'll meet you at Sambo's."

I knew where Sambo's was. I had a plan. I would go there and get a job. With what little courage I had, I dressed up the best I could and went to that restaurant to get a job. Sambo's was a family restaurant popular in the sixties and seventies. I talked to the manager, and I got a job there as a waitress. I told the owner I would like to work on Sundays. The man who hired me laughed. "No one likes to work on Sundays. I will give you the job based on that alone."

I went through a small training session on Saturday afternoon. I returned to Sambo's on Sunday evening. A group of people came in, and my two tables were put together; because I was in training, I only had two tables. Then I noticed the lady who wore the green dress from the church. I was so excited she was at my table. I did the best I could. I know I made mistakes. But I smiled the whole time. I kept the coffee coming and delivered the food while it was hot. I did the best I could. I listened to some of their conversations and heard the word "Jesus" more than once, and they kept saying "God's word." "What's that all about?" I said to myself.

The dining room had long closed before they started leaving. The oldest couple left first; then, they kept leaving from the oldest to the youngest. Finally, the last couple left. I walked over to the table, and I was shocked. I reached down, grabbed that penny off the table, and walked out to where the couple was checking out. I stretched out my hand with the penny and said, "I do not want it." I told them how I had sat on the curb across the street from their church for the last five months and that I knew they were coming here to this restaurant. I got a job just so I could get close to them and find God. But if this was how it was, I wanted no part of it. I knew that I was useless, unwanted, unloved, and there was no value in me, but they did not have to hurt me. I took my hand and turned it upside down, and the penny made its presence known as it hit the floor with a clinking sound. I was done, and it was over for me.

I turned around and walked into the dining area. Closing the door behind me, I walked over to the table. Knowing that I was going to lose the job, I slowly looked around the table. I saw it: money, money all the way around. I just collapsed in the chair behind me and started to cry.

God is really going to be mad. I had done something against His people. I was in serious trouble. I was not only going to lose my job but the only connection I had with people from that church. This was it; I was looking at a glass of water. It was the most beautiful glass of water I believe I had ever seen. It was so cool, with drops of water sliding down all around the glass. I had never felt so thirsty in my life, and I just thought if I could reach out and satisfy this thirst, this longing to know the truth. If all it took was just water, I would drink that water, all of it, every drop. I thought, *Well, nothing is that easy...* Nope, it was over for me.

I had been hateful to God's people, and then I heard her voice, "Linda, no one meant to hurt you."

I knew that voice. It was the oldest lady at the table. I said, "I am so sorry. I didn't see the money that was all around the table. All I saw was that penny, and it hurt me so badly. Please, let this go by."

The lady said, "Mary found a penny on the floor and just picked it up and laid it on the table."

I did not know what to say, and the only thing I wanted to know was, "Am I in trouble? Is God mad at me and going to punish me?"

The lady came and knelt beside me and said, "No, God loves you very much. I see how God allowed these things to happen so we can share His love and His word with you."

Over the next few weeks, I got to know Pat and Naomi very well. They brought me a Bible in a box, which I had never opened after they said it was a book. I immediately gave it back to them with the words, "I cannot read."

They did not leave it there; however, they came to see me again and brought me this little box-looking thing and a big box of what they called eight-track cassettes. There were so many; at first, I thought there were a million or more in that box, but it was the entire Bible on those cassettes. They said, "It's God's Word, and now you can hear it."

They showed me how to use the device, which I called a "box." In truth, it was a small stereo with a cassette player on it. I took it home with me and plugged it in. Turned it on, put a tape in, and waited. There it was, truth for the first time plunging into my soul: "In the beginning was the Word, and the Word was with God, and the Word was God. The same was in the beginning with God. All things were made by him; and without him was not any thing made that was made" (John 1:1–3). For a long time, I listened and heard the truth as never before.

I told Naomi the story about what had happened to me as a little girl the night my dad burned the book of truth and how I was never able to read after that. They asked me questions. How good of a reader I was before the incident. I told them I was a very good reader. After that, they took me to this big store. Naomi told me it was a Christian bookstore. As I was looking around, they took me to the back, and on this wall were all these black books. Those books, those black books with golden pages. My heart was so full at that moment. I was overwhelmed. And I began to weep. I said, "This is the book of truth." I thought about Deborah and her book. That had been given to me. I picked one up off the shelf and flipped the pages. I remembered: "In the beginning God created the heaven and the earth" (Genesis 1:1).

I remembered, and I said it out loud right then, "I remember. I will always remember, I promise." It was then that things began to make sense. I began to understand things that I never thought I would. God loved me. He sent Deborah to me that day at the swings. God loved me. The girls that had abused me that day led me to a man. A good man who shared with me the truth. He told me to look for the cross, to go there, and they would help me. At the time, I just didn't understand it. God loved me. I finally understood. "Forgive" was truly letting it go by. It all came rushing into my soul; I had finally found the cross.

I came to know Jesus Christ as my personal Savior. I had a long journey ahead of me. I was on the right road at last. I had a lot to learn, but in time, I would face and deal with the pain of my childhood and the damage it had caused. But for this time in my life, it was Jesus, the Word, and me.

The day Pat and Naomi took me to the Christian bookstore, they purchased me the Bible of my choice. They taught me how to line up what I was listening to on the tape with the pages in the Bible. They said it would help me learn to read again. I was not too sure about that. Naomi worked with me and helped me with reading, but it was difficult.

I listened to the tapes over and over, and it kept sinking deeper and deeper into my soul, and then, it was as if it was meant to be; in a second, I understood Psalm 27:1: "The Lord is my light and my salvation; whom shall I fear? the Lord is the strength of my life; of whom shall I be afraid?" It was the truth, and it plummeted into my soul, and every false thing and every lie that I've ever been told, whether it came from my parents or the enemy, was crushed, and the false foundation on which my life stood was shattered; in a moment, a new foundation was laid. That was on November 19, 1978, I was twenty-four.

I did not work at Sambo's long after I got the job. While I was there, I had the opportunity to serve some of the people I had seen outside the church where I had sat on the curb. I was at peace in a way that I had never experienced. It was hard for me to even believe I had sat on the curb across the street and watched them so many times. I had watched them go into the building, smiling and greeting each other. I had watched them come out; I had seen their children play on the front lawn while the adults stood around and talked. I had listened to them sing, and now here I was serving them. I was pouring their coffee and bringing them their food. I listened to their conversations. I did not understand much of anything I heard, but oh, how I loved being around God's people! I knew there was something incredibly special about Christians.

I told myself so many times, "I was going to go back home and tell my parents about God, and I'm going to find Laura." The years went by, and I just kept telling myself, "Someday..." I told myself I needed to learn more so I would be ready to answer all their questions. Oh, I gave myself so many reasons not to go back, but the truth was I feared my father. I did not know what I would say to him or even how to tell him that he was wrong and that there is a God. I knew it was time to go home and find Laura. Somehow, I knew she needed me. I just kept putting it off.

It had been a long time since I had allowed myself to even think about my parents, Laura, and Jasmine, my baby girl. God put a longing in my heart for home. The place that held so much pain was the place where my baby girl was growing up. *What is she like?* I wondered for the first time in years. Then came the sharp pain, and it dug deep into my heart... My baby girl was not a baby anymore; Jasmine was a teenager now.

It was time to go home and do as I had promised. When I left, I promised Laura that I would return with God. I was ready to go home. I had to find Laura and tell her, "I found God, and we never had to look very far because He has always been right here." It would be hard for her to understand, as it had been with me.

I was on the road that led me to everlasting life, and it was time for me to go and share that with my family. I had to find my way back home now. I had to find the strength and the courage to tell my parents they were wrong. There is a God, and He loves us. He wants to save us and deliver us from the power of darkness.

I wanted to go home to tell Laura I had been redeemed and that God's desire had always been to save us. Deep in my heart, I knew I was not ready. I had never really settled in any church. I still did not communicate with people very well; truthfully, only when I had to. I went from church to church, so I never really got to know anyone. Things were changing in my life, but there were so many things I was just not ready to face. Yet I knew I had to go home, not move back, not live there, but just visit and begin to open doors so they could hear the truth, God's truth.

I kept remembering those words I had spoken to Laura the last time I had seen her. Suddenly, I was aware it had been twelve long years, and it was time to keep the promise.

If only I had not wasted so much time, I was still a baby in Christ. I ignored the things I knew that God was trying to deal with in my life. If only I had done more with what I had learned. I may have been ready for this journey as I returned home to keep the promise.

CHAPTER 8

Choices

I pulled up in front of the house I grew up in. It was a beautiful December day in 1985. It had been almost thirteen years since I had been there, but it seemed as if it had been a million years ago, and I was such a different person now.

I noticed right away things were different. I arrived at my parents' house on their thirty-sixth anniversary. It was a good day. My parents introduced me to my daughter as her sister, Linda. She seemed so grown up, and of course, she had no idea who I was. She was unaware that she even had a sister named Linda. Jasmine was almost fourteen, and she was beautiful.

I visited them often over the next few months. Tyler was my home, and I had not planned on moving in the beginning. I will always remember it as the place where I found God and where my life began to change. One afternoon, before I left to drive back to Tyler, I shared with my parents that I was planning on moving from Tyler. They asked me if I would like my old room back.

It still amazes me that, even after all those years, I still wanted them to love me. I still wanted to do the one thing that got their attention. Deep down, I knew it was a mistake, but I agreed to move in with them and help them out.

My mother looked older; the hard life she had lived was now showing. Sometimes, I could see this emptiness in her and wondered if she would ever find what was missing in her life. I prayed often for my parents. I still could not talk about God in their home; they would not stand for it. "Some things will never change around here," my dad would say.

I had been home for almost a year and had not heard one word spoken about Laura. I kept waiting for her to visit. I knew from the past that if something was not spoken about in the home, my parents would not be willing to give out information.

I decided it was time I asked. I took Mom out to eat, then took her shopping. She still loved pretty things and was not going to pass up the opportunity to get a few things for herself or her home. We had a wonderful time together. I felt like her daughter and not her puppet. After we finished shopping, I took her to a little café for a cup of coffee. It was there that I chose to ask about Laura.

Mom just stared at me and said, "She's gone; I thought you knew."

I yelled, "What do you mean 'gone'?"

Mom said, "She's messed up in drugs, and she is in jail."

She did not know when Laura would get out. I asked if she had been to see Laura, and she said no. I told her that I was going to see Laura, but she told me she forbade it.

I had made up my mind to go see Laura, but I got there too late. They told me she had been released a month ago after time served for a drug-related charge. She was not on probation or parole, and they would not give me any other information. I did not know where to go or how to find her. I went back home and tried to find out what I could from Mom, but she was not talking.

About two weeks later, early in the morning, I went to the kitchen to get a cup of coffee; when I looked up, Laura was sitting at the table. She did not see me; she was looking at some papers. I said, "Laura!" When she looked up and saw me, her whole face just lit up.

She jumped up and came running to me and hugged me. She would not let go. She kept saying, "Where have you been, Linda?" When she finally let me go, I told her we had so much to talk about. She followed me to my bedroom, and I asked, "Laura, do you want to get a blanket and go out to the field and talk? Or do you want to go somewhere else? You name it, Laura, and we will do it." She looked at me and told me I was very pretty. I was not used to hearing things like that, but I thanked her and repeated my question. She said no, she had to find a job. She did not have any money, and her rent was due. I told her not to worry. We went to the bank, and I gave her the amount she needed to pay her rent. When we got back to the house, I went to my room to get a blanket, and when I came back, she was gone. It was about four months before I saw her again.

Laura would walk into my life, smile, lie, cry, get what she wanted, and disappear. I would talk to her, but she did not want to hear it. She was cold and very hateful at times, but I kept hoping and praying. There were times I would see her walking down the road aimlessly. I always stopped and asked her if she would like me to take her somewhere. Sometimes, she would get into my car, and other times, she just kept walking. I knew Laura was hurting, but I just did not know how to help her.

In July of 1988, after a long series of events, I adopted a beautiful baby girl. I would so love to share this amazing story, but I believe it is enough to simply say, "God truly blessed me, and it was a miracle that I was able to adopt a baby whom I called Abigail." My own ability to bear children had been taken away from me as a result of the rape in 1972. Laura was so excited for me, but it was not until five months later that she saw Abigail. I had hoped that this day would be different, but once again, she took me for a few hundred dollars, and she was gone. I had no answers, and I had no idea what had happened to Laura or why she acted the way she did toward me. I knew drugs were bad, but I had never been around them or anyone who did them, so I was at a complete loss as to how to help her. I did not understand the power of drugs or the effect that they had on people. I could not see how something so small controlled her. It was beyond my knowledge as to why she would do and say such things, all for the sake of what she called her next "fix" or "hit."

Laura had been in and out of jail several times, all drug-related charges, but in February of 1991, she went to prison again. She was there until December of 1993. It was during this time that I was able to really talk to her. For so long, Laura seemed to have this huge wall around her and never talked or shared her feelings with me. I went to the prison to see her every week on Saturday. It was extremely hard going every weekend, but I made myself go, even when I did not want to go. Sometimes, I just did not feel up to it, and sometimes, it was hard for me to see her that way.

Laura was struggling with the past, her shame, but we were talking, sharing our lives and hearts with each other. We became friends and sisters again. What I learned was that in the fall of 1974, her husband, Kevin, had kicked her out. Laura had no education and knew of just one place to go and one way to make money—back to the streets and back to our parents' house.

Kevin divorced her. Laura was deeply hurt by what had happened. Her lack of education and her inability to prove she could care for her own son, Kenneth, resulted in her greatest loss. Her husband took their son away from her, and I believe that Laura never fully recovered.

Laura rarely saw her Kenneth. She told me on his nineteenth birthday, he came to see her, and she was so messed up and strung out on drugs that she had said some horrible things to him. I told her that when she got out, we would go see him together. I reassured her that I believed he would forgive her.

Laura said that in 1975, she got a job at a nice restaurant. She loved it: clean, honest, hard work. She loved being a waitress, serving all kinds of people. She was doing well and making enough money to take care of herself, and she gave Mom about five hundred dollars a month for rent and food. However, that was not good enough for Mom. Mom pressured Laura to leave her job and return to doing what she wanted her to do. Laura finally stood up to Mom and told her she was never going to do those things again. Mom told her to get out.

During the time Laura worked at the restaurant, she had met someone. Jerry came in often, and they went out a few times. When Laura shared with him how Mom had told her to leave, he came to her rescue and told her she could stay with him. Laura told me she just wanted a normal life but was not sure what normal was.

They lived together for about three years and then decided to get married. Laura said that, at first, they were happy and did everything together. Then, her past began to haunt her, and she had nightmares about when we were little girls. She was struggling with so many memories, and there were times she thought she was going crazy.

Laura started taking pills to help her sleep, and then she took pills to stay awake. Early in 1981, she and her husband, Jerry, both tried meth. They both liked it and continued to use it. Laura said that meth helped her to forget the past. Using meth at first made everything better, easier, and she did not have nightmares. It made her feel good; the bad feelings went away for a while, but by 1985, Laura was heavy into drugs. She no longer used it because it was fun or because it helped her to forget. Laura had become a drug addict, and her addiction was taking her down roads she thought she would never travel.

Laura shared with me that by 1989, there was no turning back. They were both hooked and would do anything for the next hit. They were homeless, off and on, for several years. Laura could not keep up with her drug habit, and she was no longer making enough money from the streets to survive. Mom would not let her come home or help her in any way. She was of no value to Mom now. Laura had become a castaway.

Every weekend, I faithfully took the long drive to see Laura. I listened to her story, cried with her, talked to her, and we even had a few laughs. One day, she laughed and said, "Oh, you are going to like this. Do you remember all those women who used to come to Mom's tea parties? They were dancers from strip clubs."

Laura looked at me with this beautiful smile on her face and said, "I will never forget the time you got in trouble when you told Mom that you did not know where her friends came from, but you knew they were not nurses or schoolteachers?"

We both laughed, and I said, "Yes, I remember, and I also remember how much trouble I was in that day. After the tea party, you went shopping with Mom. I was so mad at you."

Laura said, "That is funny; I was mad at you too. I blamed you for what happened to me that day." Laura took a deep breath and said, "But not anymore; I know you were not responsible for what Mom did. She lied to us and used us both for her own selfish desires."

Laura seemed as if she could not share all her heart with me, things that had happened to her, and how she had been so hurt. She just said, "Things that happened to me I will never talk about; I was so used and messed up that after a while, I was all used up." She told me that life was so empty, and she kept waiting for me to come back, but I never came.

One day, Laura asked me what I had done all those years while I was gone and where I had been all that time. Now, it was time for me to tell her what had happened in my life since March of 1973. For me, it was simple: I looked at her and said, "I found God!" I took it slow, and we just talked about God's Word. Every visit after that was filled with praying and talking about God. I was sharing things with Laura now, all the things that I had been through and what I had learned. I sent her a

Bible in October 1993, and she cried as she held God's Word in her hands for the first time.

I visited every week and made plans for when she got out. I told her we were going to talk to our parents together and share the Word of God with them. Laura said, "Together, we can make a difference in their life." Laura was getting stronger; we laughed and talked about doing things together as sisters. We were never going to let anything come between us again. Now we could do all the things we had talked about when we were young. Laura would soon be getting out, and more than anything, we wanted our parents to know Jesus the way we had come to know Him.

My visits with Laura during this time had brought us close again. We both listened as we shared the choices we had made and the changes those choices had brought into our lives. We talked about what Mom had done to us. Somehow, we always ended up talking about the day in the field. It was our memory, our time, and we never forgot it.

Our parents had changed a lot. Dad did not drink at all; Mother had aged, and the only man in her life now appeared to be my dad. Still, Mother's age could not hide the traces of beauty that once graced her face. Her once haunting eyes were now full of sadness, and there seemed to be such an emptiness in her. Dad and Mom were close now, spending most of their time together. I told Laura it was hard to believe they were the same two people who raised us. Laura said, "Amen to that," and we both laughed.

In December of 1993, Laura was released. I wanted to make it special for her. I got a nice room at a hotel. We stayed up all night, talking and making plans. I decided I wanted to help Laura get an apartment because Dad and Mom would not let her return to their house, perhaps to visit, but not to live. I had been thinking about getting a house out in the country, but that idea just seemed to slip away.

The first Sunday after she had been released from prison, we went to church together. It was Laura's first time to walk inside a church, and she was in awe of everything, from the singing to the preaching. It was great; my sister sat by me on the back pew. She wanted to sit in the front, but I said, "No, I don't think we can do that." Laura wanted to know why. I told her you must go to church for at least seven years to sit in the front. To sit in the front row, you also have to know when to say "amen" and "glory!"

She reluctantly sat down with me in the back row and said, "Are you sure about that?"

I nodded my head and said, "Yep, I'm pretty sure."

Why did I lie, and why did I say that? I knew the truth. I did not want to sit in the front row, and I certainly didn't want to talk to anyone; the thought of it petrified me.

Laura and I went to a restaurant and had a wonderful lunch after church. Then she wanted to go to a park near our parent's house. It was a park well remembered by both of us. We would go there every year in the spring when we were growing up for the celebration before we drove to Kentucky for the planting season. We were sitting on the swings, just kind of swaying back and forth.

Laura jumped out of her swing and stood in front of the swing I was on. Her face was a picture of firm determination as she said, "We are going to make it, Linda, you and me. We are going to go to heaven one day. Can you believe that?" Laura paused; she looked down at the ground for a long time. I asked her what was on her mind. She said, "Linda, I may mess up, but do not give up on me, please. Just keep praying for me." I told her I was not worried and that we were both going to be okay.

The next day, we found a nice apartment. I still had all my furniture in storage from when I moved from Tyler. I told her she could have it. She needed food, so we did some grocery shopping. It was a remarkably busy week. We moved all the furniture and decorated her apartment. We cooked the first meal together in her apartment. It had been a long time since we had shared a kitchen. When we were young, we just did things out of fear or because we had no choice. Now, we were doing it because we both had a genuine love for the kitchen.

The following week, Laura got a job at a little café down the street from where she lived. A few weeks later, I helped her get a car and told her that now it was time for us to do what we said we were going to do. It was time we talked to our parents. It was time they knew the truth. We needed to make a plan. Then, we had to put it into action. It was time for me to get serious.

I let Laura know that I did not know as much as she thought I did about the whole church thing. I felt it was time for her to know the truth. I told her that I went to church all the time and that I did not have anything to do with the people. I would just go, listen, and leave. I told her I had moved from church to church, and Laura didn't like that. She said, "Linda, that is all wrong. We need to get in one church and stay there." That was not what I wanted to hear, but I knew she was right.

I had been saved for sixteen years, but I had not grown in the Lord. I was still just a baby in Christ. Yes, I spent a lot of time in prayer. I listened and read along with the Bible on cassettes, but I was not applying it to my life in any area. I went to church, but I had no fellowship with other believers. I was invisible and undetected in the body of Christ. I had done this myself. I would not allow myself to grow up. It is hard to believe that after sixteen years, I was still an infant in Christ. Now, at forty, I still dressed the same as I did at nine years of age, and I was still wearing white patent leather shoes; I was stuck, and I simply did not know how to move forward. It meant talking to ladies in the church and getting to know them and them getting to know me. No. That would be a disaster; it cannot happen. They would never like me. They would never accept me. I was worse than Rahab, the harlot, and the woman at the well mixed together. They would never have anything to do with me. It just wouldn't work. I tried to explain it to Laura the best I could. She just looked at me and said, "Take off those white patent leather shoes, Linda Marie, and stop being a child. You are not a child anymore. Get over it. Go to church and get to know some of the ladies there and have fellowship, for goodness' sake. You read about it all the time: Loving one another, forgiving one another, and fellowship. It means you too, Linda. Or do you not believe the book of truth? I know you do. Don't let shame drown you." And with that, she turned around and walked off.

A few days later, I was leaving Laura's apartment in the afternoon when she said, "Linda, do you remember what you said about coming back for me?"

I told her, "Yes, I do."

She told me it gave her hope all those years. She said, "No matter how bad it got, I would just remember what you said. I would tell myself, 'My sister is coming for me one day. She is coming for me, and she is going to take me away, and no one will hurt me again.'" I told Laura I loved her and I was sorry I did not come sooner. She was silent for a moment, then said, "Now you are my hero," and hugged me. We both laughed, and then I walked down the stairs and got into my car. I looked back up, and there she was, blowing me kisses. She had this big, beautiful smile on her face, and I thought, *No, Laura, you will always be my hero*. She yelled out, "We are still the two L's."

I talked to Laura about a week later, and she told me she had to work some extra hours for a week or so. One of the girls had gotten sick and ended up in the hospital. She also shared with me that she had run into her husband, and they were going to try to work things out.

I reminded her about talking to our parents about the Lord. I did not want to put it off too long. She said she did not know when she would be able to. I was disappointed, but I did not let her know it. I did not see Laura for a month. When I called, she usually did not answer, and when she did answer, she was on her way to work or just getting home from work and needed to get some rest. I was very frustrated because everything we had planned was not happening. Everything I expected and hoped for was vanishing. It was all out of my hands and out of my control. The more I tried to control it, the worse it got.

It was not long until I knew what was really going on in Laura's life. She was back on meth, and it crushed me. She had sold the furniture, piece by piece. She was sleeping on the floor. The apartment was filthy, and I had my fill of all her excuses. Her husband, Jerry, was done with her and was long gone. No matter what I tried, she kept doing the same thing over and over.

The day came when I could not take it anymore. I was finished. I finally said to her, "If this is what you want to do, fine. Did you forget that we were going to witness to our parents? Share the Word of God with them?" I looked at her and said, "I am your sister; you choose right now: me or the drugs?"

Laura looked at me and turned away. I saw the tears fall as she walked away and said, "The drugs."

I fell to my knees and screamed, "No! Laura. *No!*" I begged her to come with me. I told her there was help.

After about thirty minutes, it was over; she had made her choice. She was in her bedroom with the door shut. I stood up and took one long look around. All our hopes and dreams were gone. Our choices were made, and the line was drawn. I turned and walked out, slamming the door behind me.

I did not want anything else to do with Laura. When she would come to visit Mom, I would just get up and walk out of the room. I would not make any kind of effort toward making things right. I kept telling myself I was finished with her. I was living for God; it was Jesus and me.

I would think about how she had said, "When I get out of here, we are going to do so many things together. We will be the two L's again." Then, I would remember how she looked at me that day. I gave her the choice, and she said, "The drugs." I felt the anger rush in, and I refused to think about how we might resolve the problem. I would not admit to having a problem. She had the problem, and I did not want to be a part of her problem anymore. I was done.

The problem was that I had been offended, and I did not want to deal with it. I wanted to sweep it under the rug, so to speak. I did not want to admit that the problem was my creation. I gave her an ultimatum and passed judgment upon her because my demands were rejected. I was angry because she chose drugs over me. I told myself that I was hurt, and I had every reason to be. Oh no, I was not angry. I was hurt.

I failed to realize that bitterness had taken up residence in my heart. Now, I would need a good solid plow to break up the hard soil. I had truly become bitter and angry. Laura had been set free only to, once again, choose to destroy her life with drugs and once again become their prisoner. I, however, allowed myself to become a prisoner to bitterness and haunting memories of the past, and I was holding Laura responsible for all of it. We were caught in the crossfire of the choices we had made; in my heart, bitterness had begun its reign!

CHAPTER 9

The Bitter Years

It was not long after I had given Laura the choice that my heart turned into stone. I was bitter, and I was angry. I was free, but I was more of a prisoner than Laura had ever been. My heart turned hard, and I was full of animosity toward Laura. She came to see me in September of 1994; I told her to get out of my room. I looked her in the eyes with my prideful, better-than-you attitude and said, "What do you want? Come to see if your stupid little sister will fall for more of your lies and give you some money to feed your drug habit?"

With those words, I bent down and wiped a spot off my white patent leather shoes and said, "You are like that spot I just wiped off my shoe, worthless! It does not bother me the least little bit what will happen to that little piece of dirt, and I do not care what happens to you. So, if you don't mind, get out of my room. Go get your drugs. Remember, you chose them over me."

The look on Laura's face was one of the deepest kinds of hurt and pain as tears flowed down her face. I pushed my feelings of love, compassion, and mercy back down in my soul and allowed the anger to boil. I refused to forgive her or reach out to her in the midst of her pain during the greatest battle of her life.

Laura, with such brokenness and shame, said, "Linda, I didn't come in here to ask you for money. I came to ask you to pray with me and for me. I was wrong that day. I need help!"

I never let her finish. I lashed out with my final blow as if to punish her. "Help? Help! You do not want help. As for praying, Laura, what do you want me to pray for? What, Laura? Just what do you want me to pray for? What? For a good street corner for you to stand on so you can sell your soul for drugs? Is that what you would like me to pray for? No, Laura, I will not be praying for you today or any day, as far as that goes."

My words hit the target: her heart. Laura went to her knees, begging me, "Linda, forgive me, please; I need help, can't you see?"

Laura reached out for me, but I lashed out, "Don't you touch me! Do not ever put your nasty, filthy hands on me again!"

I walked out of my room and left her on the floor, crying, just like she had done to me the day she chose drugs over me. I did not bother to look back at her. Instead, I allowed my bitterness to take over, and the root of it sank deep into my soul at that very moment.

I stormed out of the house and got in my car. Guilt flooded my soul as I looked down at the Bible in the front seat. Abigail walked out of the house, got in the car, and said, "Are we still going to church this morning, Mom?"

Once again, guilt came rushing in and flooded my soul. But by this time, I had learned how to balance my guilt with blame. I looked at Abigail and said, "Of course we are. We go every Sunday. Why would you think we wouldn't go to church?"

Her words pierced my heart: "God wants us to love each other and says not to go to church or even to pray when we are mad."

I made an excuse, "Oh, sweetie, I am not mad. I was very hurt by your aunt, Laura, because she made a bad choice." I justified my actions, and I would live to regret this day: my actions, my lack of compassion, and most of all, my bitter, hateful words.

That day, I pushed away God's grace and mercy that should have been extended to my sister. With love and compassion, I should have gathered her into my arms. Instead, I fed her to the wolves. I stripped her of all hope and condemned her as I passed judgment upon her, believing that God could not change her. I dismissed her as I would have an old pair of worn-out shoes.

I continued to balance the guilt and blame as unforgiveness filled my heart with darkness. I was building a barrier to keep out feelings of love toward my sister. It was my defense mechanism, and I did not want to face the possibility of being wrong. I rejected her and acted as if I was superior and she would always be beneath me.

In November of 1994, Laura was arrested again, and she received a ten-year sentence in the Texas State Penitentiary. In my opinion, she got what she deserved. There was no room in my own heart for compassion or mercy. There were moments of guilt, but those moments were short-lived. I just kept pushing my love down deeper and deeper until I felt nothing.

I blamed Laura for choosing drugs over me. I never once thought about where she was or about the help she really needed at the time of that choice. I placed myself above her, and I judged her with my own human wisdom. And I was wrong. I would not allow myself to see her through God's eyes. God was tugging at my heart in so many ways, wanting me to reconcile with Laura. I just did not want to receive it.

Bitterness had taken root in my heart; it was anchored deep into the core of my being. Bitterness was draining all the nutrients of God's Word from my soul. The result was anger and pride tearing my soul apart while harsh and bitter words poured out of my mouth against Laura in every direction. It was affecting every area of my life, and I would not acknowledge it. I went on with my life as though nothing was wrong.

I received letters from Laura, one every week, without fail. I would see them on the table. I would tell Mom to send them back to Laura. I instructed her to write on each envelope: "Return to sender; person unknown." Mom would do it, of course, but I could tell Mom was reluctant about doing as I asked. Every letter was returned to Laura, unopened and untouched by me. However, Laura did not give up, and she continued to write to me.

Finally, my mother could not bear it any longer. It was so unlike her, but she asked me one day, "Why are you not accepting your sister's letters? You know, Linda, she is the only sister you have, and whatever the problem is, you need to work it out."

Needless to say, my mother's words pierced my heart, but once again, I allowed my bitterness to push them away and responded with, "I thought you would be happy that your two daughters are enemies. Isn't that what you always wanted?

Well, now you finally got what you wanted. I do not want to see her or ever be around her. I cannot stand the sight of her. That should make you exceedingly happy!" The look on my mother's face was one of hurt, and that was something I was not used to seeing in her.

I had been living with my parents for over ten years, and I had not witnessed to them. Oh, they knew I believed in God. I was allowed to have my Bible as long as I did not bring it in the house. It was a trade-off. I paid their bills, and Abigail and I had a nice room, but my life was empty. Oh, I knew I was saved. I read my Bible, and I prayed. I was going to church, but I changed churches as soon as someone noticed me in the back row. "In and out"—that was my motto. I was doing nothing with all the gifts and talents God had given me. The reality was that I did not know what my gifts and talents were.

At this time, I had wasted eighteen years. I did not fellowship with other believers. I did not commit myself to any church. I did not tithe to any one church. I had only witnessed to one person, and that was my sister. Then, in her greatest moment of need, I had turned my back on her. I was a failure, and I knew it. I was holding on with what little strength I had. I knew I had to make a change, or I was never going to do anything. God began pushing me very slowly at first. I would see a house up for sale and think how nice it would be for Abigail and me to have our own place. Little by little, I began to like the idea.

I was forty-three, and I was still reading my Bible in my car in front of my parent's house. In my heart, I knew as long as I stayed there, I would remain "the girl who paid the bills for them." I had to face the sad truth that it would always be that way. I would never be anything more to them.

When I moved in with my parents, it was with the understanding that it was only going to be for a brief time. However, that was not the case; the control and demands placed on my life by my parents became the excuse and the reason I stayed in their home. No matter what the reasons or excuses I may use, I knew the truth. I never prayed about any of it, not about moving into my parents' house or staying in Tyler or even moving from Tyler. I moved into my parents' house, and from there, I did whatever I thought was right. I didn't pray about life or the changing choices I made. It was a recipe for mistakes that came with a variety of repercussions.

I knew, from all accounts, that I had failed in every aspect of what I thought to be the Christian life. I failed with Laura, and I failed with my parents. I believed if I continued in this cycle, it would only diminish what little strength I had left. I knew staying with my parents would certainly continue to pull me down until nothing was left of me. It was as if I suddenly woke up from a long nap and realized that I had been living with my parents for ten years. The truth was, my parents controlled me, used me, and asked me to do things for their own personal gain, with no thought of what it might do to me. What about my little girl, Abigail? It was time to go.

I began to remember the days when I lived in Tyler, right after I was saved. The peace and joy I had experienced then was now missing from my life. I felt lost, alone, and empty. For the first time in a long time, I prayed. I asked for Jesus to forgive me and to help me. Within days of that prayer, I knew what I had to do, and for me, it was a bold step.

In May of 1996, I took Abigail out for a drive in the country to a piece of land that was for sale. We both got out, and I asked, "Abigail, would you like to live here?" I told Abigail I wanted to move out of my parents' house. She was excited about the idea that we would have our own home. I explained to her that I had been badly hurt a long time ago. I wanted her to understand that the main reason we lived at my parents' house was that I felt safe there.

I assured Abigail that I loved her and that her feelings and opinions were important and mattered very much to me. I told her I wanted it to be a decision we both made together. We would both pray and ask God to help us. It was not long before I had the answer. I purchased the property in June of 1996, and we moved into our new home in November. My parents were upset, but I had to do this for Abigail and, more importantly, for myself. I could not remain in their house any longer. I wanted to be loved and accepted by them. I wanted to share the Gospel with them. They knew I believed in God all that time, but they never asked me any questions regarding my beliefs. I just kept thinking if I stayed just one more year, they would get saved, tell me they were sorry, and go to church with me. I wanted them to tell me they loved me.

I was forty-three, and I had never heard my parents tell me they loved me. I wanted so much to hear those words. I just wanted them to say, "Linda, we love you." I thought it would somehow change things or at least give the past and all I had endured some kind of meaning.

I had lost so much by living with them. In 1985, when I left Tyler, I was by no means where I should have been in my

Christian walk, but I had a wonderful prayer life. I loved reading and studying His Word, and I was growing little by little. Now, eleven years later, it felt like I was starting all over. It was hard at first because, for most of my life, I had someone telling me what to do. In so many ways, I was still a child. I was forty-three, and I had only lived twelve years out on my own.

This was a whole new experience for me, one that I was really beginning to enjoy. I was so thankful I did not allow my parents to talk me out of it. Things were much better for Abigail and me. It was wonderful to wake up and put on Christian music. I had the freedom to pray out loud anytime I wanted. I play my Bible on CDs anytime: morning, noon, or night. And I could read my Bible along with it if I wanted to. I could play them all day, and that is what I did most of the time.

It was a daily battle as I began to struggle with who I really was and about my life. I needed to come to terms with the way I was raised and where I belonged as a Christian woman. I certainly felt that I would never measure up to any of the Christian women I had seen, especially after hearing a few of them speak. I just hung my head in shame. I would never be accepted in a godly women's circle. The best thing for me was to keep finding churches where I was not noticed so I could slip in and slip out.

Jasmine also had her battles. It seemed that I never knew where she fit into my life or how I fit into hers. I just tried to be there when she needed me. I never thought I would ever be close enough to Jasmine that she would allow me to stand by her at the birth of one of my grandchildren. Then she called me on the day Daniel was born, and I witnessed his birth.

Daniel was a blessing right from the beginning. He was born December 8, 1994; after Daniel was born, Jasmine had some health issues as well as a drug-related problem. I took care of him. I love all my grandsons; however, Daniel had a special place in my heart. I spent time with him. Daniel had spent most of his life with me, and he loved being with Abigail and me.

Jasmine came to live with Abigail and me in December of 1997. She had some drug-related problems and thought that if she was out in the country, away from everything, it would help her. I agreed and felt it would be the start of building a strong, healthy relationship with her. She did not stay long; however, she found a place nearby and moved out in April of 1998.

Shortly after she moved out, tragedy struck my life. On May 20, 1998, I left home on a Wednesday afternoon, leaving Abigail, age ten, and Daniel, age three and half, in the care of a woman. I trusted her. She had two children of her own. Dakota, I felt, was responsible, and I had only planned on being gone for less than one hour. Daniel drowned; that is the only way to say it. In one moment, my life changed. One choice, one afternoon, turned my world upside down. Daniel was left unattended in the backyard at the swimming pool. I received the call less than twenty minutes after I had left.

It was one of those moments in life that you never forget. The pain was unbearable. It was as if a sword had cut through the very fiber of my life. I kept thinking, *It's only a dream... I must wake up.* But it was real. I was not going to wake up; it was not a dream, and I was... Well, there are just simply no words for it. I was just broken and very crushed and bruised.

On the morning of the funeral, I stood in my closet, unable to move, as the memories of his birth and his life poured into the core of my being. I could no longer stand, and there was nothing left for me to do but fall to my knees. I did not think it would be possible for me to make it through the day of Daniel's funeral. There are no words to describe his life or the pain of such a loss. Daniel was a precious little boy, and his death was a great loss. His death, no matter how I look at it, seems to have been an untimely tragedy.

Just sitting here and writing about this is hard. It seems like yesterday. That I was looking into my little Daniel's eyes. Memories of that day still flash through my mind. What words can ever be said of such a tragic loss? I shall never understand how someone so precious could slip away from my life so quickly. The depth of my pain and the depth of my love are the same, and they cannot be measured. There is within me a great sorrow and a heaviness that crushes my heart and brings me to my knees.

In a moment, a split second, three words had enough power to rip through my entire being, leaving my life in a whirlwind of pain. *Daniel is dead.* As I looked at his little body, screaming, "No! No!" There could be no other words. What other words could be said?

I do not remember the things I said or the things I did in the days that followed. Everything in my life just stopped. It was like a never-ending dream; everything was in slow motion, and I just wanted to wake up. But I was awake, and this was not a dream. For days, weeks, and even months, I just moved through life, not living, just existing.

The pain of his death still overshadows my life. But somehow, I have come to a place where I can smile and even laugh when memories of him flow through my mind of little things he did or said. Sometimes, in the coolness of the day like today, I can still see him playing in the yard, and in the wind, I hear his voice say, "I love Jesus, and I love you too, Grandma." Oh, God. I do miss him. It is in saying this that I am brought to a place where I know that it is okay to grieve. It is okay to cry. It is okay to feel lost, alone, hurt, and even angry. These emotions I have is okay. These are the things that help me to accept his untimely death and face another day to continue the healing process.

He was so pure and innocent, and the only comfort I find is in knowing that my face was kissed by one of God's very own, now safe in the arms of Jesus, where no one can ever hurt him. Where the world cannot corrupt him. Where Satan cannot deceive him or lie to him or take his innocence away. No, Daniel is in heaven, where someday I will join him. This is the very foundation of my faith. Jesus gave His life that we might have eternal life.

It was not by chance or a thing called fate that brought Daniel into my life. No, it was an almighty and loving God. I was truly blessed by God to have had the opportunity to hold Daniel not just in my arms but also in my heart. The winds of adversity blew hard enough to take him from my arms. But rest assured, they will never take Daniel from my heart. We will dance and laugh again before our Lord and Savior someday in heaven.

At the funeral, I saw Laura for the first time since she had gotten out of prison. I had not talked to her since the day I had walked out of my bedroom, leaving her on the floor, crying. I heard she was out on parole for good behavior; she had gotten out sometime in March of 1998, but I refused to go see her. She was living at our parents' house. Dad and Mom had been out to see me and said that Laura was working and doing very well. Mom told me Laura was saving her money and was going to buy her own home. That she gave God the credit for the job she had. I could not believe Mom even said that. She told me everyone said Laura would not get that job and she was wasting her time. Mom laughed and said, "But she got it!"

I watched Laura closely for signs of drugs. She showed no signs of drug use. She tried to talk to me, and I just let her have it. "What are you doing here? You never even knew him. You were in prison when he was born, and you just got out! So, what are you doing here? You never even met him. This is just too much for me right now. I have to deal with Daniel's death. My sweet little boy was gone. It was all so quick and all so very final. One minute, he was there, and I turned for just a second, and he was gone." I just turned and walked away and left her there.

Daniel was gone, and I told myself, "I have to accept that." There were other people in my life who were deeply hurt by the loss of Daniel, but I could not see their pain, nor could I help them. I couldn't even help myself.

Even now, as I write this, I am moved to tears as I remember the shock and pain of a loss that seemed so premature. My heart was being plowed like an untouched field of hardened earth, and the soil was breaking up. My heart was turning back into a heart of flesh. My heart was broken. No, it was shattered. Still, nothing could have prepared me for what lay ahead.

Time, however, was not on my side, as the saying goes. I was not granted the privilege or the opportunity to grieve for Daniel. My father and mother had been diagnosed with cancer about a year before Daniel's death. My mom was not doing well. I would visit her as much as I could. I would see Laura there from time to time. She had a job and was, for the most part, taking care of Mom when she was not at work. Laura looked healthy, and I could tell she was not on drugs. Joy and peace just seemed to surround her.

Mom asked me about God one day. She asked me to get my Bible and read something to her. I went to the car and got my Bible. As I went in the back door, my dad was standing there. He said, "The rules still apply in this house. I do not want that book in this house." He then grabbed me by the throat and pushed me up against the wall. I was about to pass out when he finally let go and said, "Take that book out of my house."

I don't know what happened to me. Just a boldness that only comes from the Lord. I do believe it was the first time I felt that power that He has and gives to us to do or say something on His behalf. I looked at my dad and boldly stated, "I will not leave this house, and I will not take this book outside. It is called God's Word, Dad. I am going to read it to my mother, who has asked to hear it, and I will not deny her the opportunity to hear the truth. You're more than welcome to come and sit as I read to her. But I'm going in, whether you like it or not. I'm going to read God's Word to her. Dad, I would love to read it to you as well."

He had a few choice words. He then turned, walked away from the door, and went on outside. It took me a few moments to gather myself. Needless to say, I was a little shocked and finally thought, *Wow*... I went to my mom, who was lying on the couch, and began to read to her. I sat there and read to her for about an hour. When I finished reading to her, she asked me if I believed Daniel was in heaven. I told her yes.

Finally, after all the years I wasted, I shared the Gospel with my mother. I had convinced myself that Laura and I had to do it together. I wanted to blame Laura, but the truth was, from the moment I first visited my parents, I could have shared the Gospel with them. I could continue to use Laura as an excuse, but I was a coward, afraid of what my dad would do to me if I shared what I really believed with him.

Laura was in the kitchen. I knew she was listening as I told Mom that this was the reason I had come back home so many years ago. I wanted to share this good news with her and Dad. I told her that, somehow, I managed to mess it all up. I had gotten sidetracked, hurt, and mixed up about a lot of things. I started trying to please her and Dad instead of the Lord. I allowed Dad and her to control me, and in the end, that was why I had to move out. I told her how much I had grown since I had moved out two years earlier.

Oh, I gave her a lot of excuses. But I never gave her the truth. Truth was, I was afraid of my dad. Afraid of what he might do to me. How much time had I wasted because of that? Then, in just one moment of standing up to him, he stepped aside and let me bring God's Word into a house where the Word of God had never been allowed. At that very moment, I remembered. God's Word says, "God hath not given us the spirit of fear; but of power, and of love, and of a sound mind" (2 Timothy 1:7).

I had it all along. The love, the power, and the sound mind. I foolishly let it all slip away.

Laura tried to say something, and I told her I was doing fine without her and that if I needed help, she would not be the one I would ask. Mom spoke up, "You two are sisters. You two are going to need each other. Both of you girls know I've done my share of wrong, God forgive me. The two of you were always so close. I did things to put distance between the two of you. I am telling you both right now I have lived to regret it. You two need to work this out so I can die in peace, at least about what I have done to the two of you."

I told my mother she was right and we would work it out. The truth was, I just did not know how to respond to my mother's statement.

I finished sharing some scripture, and then I prayed with my mother. She asked Jesus to forgive her of her sins and to save her. My mother, with tears in her eyes, got up, went into her bedroom, and shut the door. No one could get her to come out. About three weeks later, she was taken to the hospital. The next night, my mother died less than a year after Daniel's death.

My mother's words about Laura being my sister and the only one I would ever have were weighing heavily on my mind at my mother's funeral. I noticed Laura sitting all alone and saw the pain that was lining her face. But I rejected her again. I reasoned it away and justified it. I allowed pride to stand in the way of compassion.

God was dealing with me, but I kept justifying my actions. I was still trying to hold on to the bitterness. I loved Laura, but so many years had passed, and I didn't know how to let go of all the hurt I had held onto for so long. That heavy chain had wrapped its ugly self around me and was choking all the goodness and love of God out of my life, and all that was left was the bitterness.

It would not be long before Laura and I would be faced with yet another death. Less than a year after my mother's death, our father died. At my father's funeral, Laura walked up to me and said, "Linda, you are allowing bitterness to blind you to all the good things that God has for you. It has been six years since you gave me a choice. I made the wrong one, and I suffered for it. I made it right, and I asked God to forgive me, and He forgave me. He was faithful to His Word. I go to church, and I fellowship with other believers. But you are still hanging onto your pain, and you have built a twenty-foot wall around yourself just to ensure that you will never get hurt again. Wake up! You lost your grandson. We have lost our mother and now our father. You're hurting, and you're alone. Linda, you're still sitting on the floor in that apartment, begging me to choose you, and you can't even see it."

I didn't say a word to her; I did not know how to deal with the damaging effects that bitterness had on my life. There was this emptiness in my soul now, and I did not know how to reach out to Laura. I didn't know what to say, so I just walked away.

After the funeral, Laura and I got in our cars and went our separate ways. We were both alone now.

The bitter years had truly left their mark upon both of our souls. I longed to be that little girl in the photo from so long ago again. Could we go back to that time of love and innocence, untouched and undamaged, asleep under a pecan tree? Would we ever be that free again?

CHAPTER 10

The Final Battle

I was sitting at the kitchen table, looking out the sliding glass door. It was crystal clear that morning. I looked across the deck to the swimming pool. My mind filled with thoughts of Daniel, and the tears came. My heart was so full of sorrow. Thinking of Daniel always leads to the other thoughts of my mother and then thoughts of my father. It seemed I was always thinking of one of them. Thoughts of them just flowed through my mind. It was just one big circle. Day after long day, night after sleepless night, I wandered aimlessly; it felt like all life had been stripped away from me.

The night my mom died was so crystal clear in my mind: Dad had walked out. Laura went after him. I was with my mom when I noticed that her bedding needed changing and that her clothes were so dirty. I asked a nurse to come and change the sheets, and I changed her gown. I didn't know why I was so concerned about that and getting it done, but I wanted everything clean and fresh.

After it was all done, I realized why. I knew it was her time, and I knew it was close. I didn't want her to die in a dirty gown, in a bed with spoiled sheets. I wanted everything around her to be clean. She was always that way. Her house was always clean and in order. Even if it was that way because of her two daughters. She was always so clean and fresh. Every hair had to be in place. Every outfit was in style and perfect. Everything had to be perfect. For some reason, that stuck with me. And on this night, I wanted her sheets to be clean. I wanted her gown to be fresh and clean, especially on that night.

She said, "Linda..."

It was the way she said it. That I knew she wanted to talk about the past. I said, "Mom, I do not want to hash out the past right now. I love you, and all is forgiven."

She took a deep breath and looked at me; it was a look I had never seen from her. It was born of sweetness with peace and joy that I had never seen in her eyes before. I thought she was going to tell me that she loved me. She let that breath out, and she was gone. However, it was in that split second that I saw this bright light, but it was just a second.

I looked at my mom, and she was just glowing. My mother was a beautiful woman, but I had never seen her more beautiful. She weighed less than forty-five pounds. Her skin was bruised and just hanging from her body. She didn't have a hair on her head, but she was beautiful. More beautiful to me than she had ever been. I was looking at her face, and there it was, a tear, one tear, sliding down her cheek, just one tear. I wiped that tear and said in a very soft voice, "That's my tear. That's Linda's tear." There was this peace that flooded my soul. I may have never heard the words "I love you" from my mother, but that night, that moment, that second, I knew she loved me.

I could never think of my mother's death without thinking of the death that followed. My father died not long after my mother died. Both my parents were diagnosed with cancer, two months apart from each other. My dad seemed to do much better than my mother. He seemed to be holding up well. He was also given more time than my mother. So, I thought, of course, he was going to be around for a while.

Once again, I put off talking to my dad about salvation and sharing the Word of God with him. It wasn't so much that I was afraid of him or what he might do to me anymore. I had gotten over that. It was more the rejection. The way I saw him treat my mother the night she died. The way he refused to listen to her or hear anything. I remembered him saying that he would never forgive her. It really weighed heavily on my mind.

Then he got sick, and I knew time was running out. I was with my dad on the night that he died. I will never forget it. But oh, how I have tried. It was horrible. It was my three nights to stay with my dad. Laura and I were rotating. He would not allow hospice to do anything in the house. He refused the bed. He allowed them to come in, check him, and leave meds and instructions along with the oxygen machine. But that was it: he refused everything else. Simply put, he refused to go to the hospital. He told me he was going to lay right there in that bed and die. He was not going to go to any hospital. "No," he said, "I will not give her that satisfaction."

It was early in the evening when my dad looked over at me and told me, "I'm going to die in this bed tonight. Right here, in the bed that she betrayed me in. I don't know how many men were here laying with her and had pleasure. Pleasure that belonged to me. It was mine, my place, my bed, my home."

He got this look on his face as he continued, "The first time I remember so well, it cut me deep. You know what I mean? It hurt me, Linda, when I caught her with that man in my bed. Where I should have been. We fought all night long, and when the morning came, the fighting continued. I was going to beat her to death. That's the day I set the house on fire. That's the day I was going to kill us all. But she begged me…begged me, so I untied her. I dragged her out of the house as she was screaming about her things. Not once did she ask about her daughters. I grabbed a water hose and began to put the fire out, but it was too late. A neighbor called the fire department. They arrived twenty minutes too late. The house had already burned to the ground. I thought Laura and you were dead. They told me you two were sleeping under a tree in the backyard. We should have all died that day."

I tried to stop him from talking, but he continued. "I knew your mother wasn't going to change. But I couldn't leave her, couldn't let her go. No matter what she did, I loved her. She was the only thing in my life that mattered. It was her. Always her… But the pain she brought into my life destroyed me. What she was doing was never going to stop. All those years, she never stopped. Then she got old, and she knew no man wanted her anymore. I knew it too. She was old and used up, her beauty gone, yet there were traces of what used to be. I finally got her all to myself; she tried to love me, but it was all too late. I didn't want to touch her. I couldn't even look at her sometimes. I just refused to give her the satisfaction of leaving."

My father got quiet for a moment. Then he looked over at me and said, "Jesus is standing over here right by my bed."

I said, "Daddy, how do you know it's Jesus? I thought you didn't believe in Him."

He said, "It's Jesus."

I said, "How do you know, Daddy?"

"Because I see the holes in His feet," he responded.

I said, "Daddy, He loves you. He's here so that you will believe and accept Him. So, you can go to heaven. That's where Mother is; that's where I'm going…"

That's when he said it: "I don't want to go to heaven if there is such a place. I don't want to be in any place where your mother is. I hate her. I hate what she did to all of us."

It was quiet again for a moment. Then he said, "Linda, do you remember? Do you remember that night? Do you remember the night you asked me to let it go by?"

I said, "Oh, yes, Daddy, I do. I still think about it a lot. I never forgot. Why do you ask?"

He told me he wanted to know something. Then he asked me, "How did it feel? Because you know what it really was now, don't you?" He took a deep breath and said, "It was forgiveness. You know that, right?"

I answered, "Daddy, at the time, I didn't. But I do now, yes. Do you want to know how it felt? Daddy, it was amazing. It was so wonderful. Not because I didn't get the spanking but because it did something inside of me. It made me feel alive, like I wanted to dance forever in your presence. I felt like I was your little princess. I was unashamed, just that one moment. There was this amazing and wonderful feeling inside of me. It was like I could live forever, right there in that moment, with you, letting it go by. It was like I was in the presence of something so powerful. There was no way to explain it then. Now I know it was forgiveness. It's what it feels like when Jesus comes into your life and all your sins have been forgiven and washed away. It's like—"

He interrupted me. "I don't want to hear anymore. There He is. There's Jesus just standing there. But where was He that night when all the lies came gushing out? The night of Laura's passage when I learned the truth. Your mother lied to me. She never believed in the spirit life. She believed in nothing; it was always about what she wanted. She ruled and controlled everything, especially me. When it was finally over in the fall of 1966, she told me she never believed any of it. Why did she lie and deceive me all those years? Because you girls went to Kentucky every year for seven months. She had the freedom to do whatever she wanted. And that she did. Man after man..."

He took a deep breath again, then said, "The night she let you play outside right before you came into the house. The night I beat you, and she burned that book. This will make you hate her. That night, when you came into the house. She had already told me she had something to show me at dinner, and after I saw it, she wanted to burn it. She even made me go out to the shed and check the gas can to make sure there was gas in it. For the right moment, she said. She had already planned what she was going to do, and she was going to burn that book right in front of you. I even sat the grill out and got it ready for her. Your mother knew what was going to happen when I saw that Bible. That is the reason she did not tell me or show me what it was beforehand. She wanted the full effect of my anger unleashed on you. Your mother knew it was going to make me angry, and it did. I never wanted one of those books in my house."

He paused for a moment. "When you ran away, she told me you weren't my daughter. You are not my daughter, Linda. She slept with some man in Virginia. She tried to get rid of you. She tried to end the pregnancy. She never wanted you. That day, she also told me she had gotten rid of three of my brats, but you just wouldn't die and come out. That is why she hated you. If there is any justice, that was it; she had to give birth to you and name you and take care of you. Linda, you were such a little thing. I didn't think you were going to make it. You almost died when you were born. Did she ever tell you that and that it was all her doing?"

My dad paused for a moment, a weary look on his face. Maybe it was just time for him to share all the brokenness of his life. I'm not sure why he decided to tell me all of this. Maybe it's because I was there, or he really wanted me to understand. Maybe of a truth, it was just so I would hate my mother. But here he was, sharing his heart and his broken life with me.

He spoke again, "Later, she told me she wanted a divorce. She was taking my house and everything in the bank. Everything I had, she was going to take. As you noticed, she stayed. Do you want to know why? Because I told her, after everything she did to me, after everything she did to our two daughters, after everything, she was not going to get the satisfaction of leaving me. She was going to stay until the day she died. I was going to make sure of it. I told her if she left me, I would hunt her down. I would kill her, and I would make her suffer. I would torture her over a long period and watch her slowly die. She knew I was telling the truth, and she knew I would do it.

"I told your mother that you were my daughter, Linda. No matter what she said or did, you are my daughter. I raised you. I paid the hospital bill. I provided food and clothes for you. No matter what she said, you are my daughter. I told her I knew she did something to you to make you run away. It didn't matter, though, because it was too late, it was too late for all of us. The damage had already been done. We had all been living in lies for so long because of my father and your mother!"

He was screaming loud. Then he started beating on his chest. He was saying, "There were so many changes. Everything just kept changing. But no matter what, there were always these questions with no answers. My father's lies, your mother's lies, and all their deception. I could never understand any of it. I could never make sense of it. I've never been able to distinguish between the real and the unreal of all they had done. How one book survived everything and still lays over there on top of my dresser. The other book was so easily burned, yet it still haunts me. I've never believed in heaven or hell. I've never believed in God. I've never believed in Satan. Oh, I've heard the stories. But I believed the spirit life and yet turned my back on the spirit life and my family because...."

He never finished the sentence.

Then he asked me, "Why does a book that burned so easily haunt me? And the one that's still here, I can't even touch it, not since our return from Kentucky in 1966. Did you know I was going to be the next master? I was supposed to be. I was chosen by my grandfather, the first one to be chosen by the grandfather in many generations. It was a great honor, but my father, the master, was not going to honor the former master's word. He was not going to honor my grandfather, the master. A real master. All the members of the family knew it. They were all there that day, the day he gave me the book of truth, the only one that was complete. Not handwritten like all the ones they passed around and added to. This one was very old. The only one left of its kind, written by our ancestors. For 2,500 years, we have worshipped the spirit life and the deity that's in our seeds that spring forth life and the breath that's passed from one generation to another. There is no more breath and no more seeds. There will be no more of us soon. Because there is no more spirit life left for us, there was disobedience. They all disobeyed. They have destroyed our family. My father and your mother did all of this and more."

He didn't say a word for a moment, and then he spoke so softly that I could barely hear him. He told me my mother said the book given to me was full of lies. That is why the book burned easily. Because it was full of lies. The only book of truth was the one my great-grandfather had given to him in 1949. That's when my great-grandfather told my dad he would be the next master.

My dad took a deep breath again and then continued without stopping: "She was greedy and consumed with lust. She was a cheater and a liar. I had to deal with all her lies, so many lies. My father lied to me; he was worse because I was his flesh and blood. My own father lied to me. I tried all these years; I tried to sort through all the lies and deception, years and years of nothing but lies. For thirty-four years of my life, he lied to me, and your mother did the same. They were both liars, and I was the victim of those lies." My father just hung his head and said, "How could she say she was forgiven? I never forgave her, and I never will. She doesn't deserve to have that feeling. That feeling you say comes with forgiveness, she doesn't deserve it. I won't forgive her, ever."

He didn't say anything for a moment. I was hoping he was finished. He turned his face back to me and said, "Look at me. You should hate her; you want the truth. I want you to hate her. It was your mother. All the ladies that came to the house, to her tea parties, when you were young came from a gentlemen's club, the only kind of friends your mother ever had, and your mom worked in some of the clubs. She would work two or three times a week. She got to know the rich men. I want you to know these things now, Linda. I want you to hate her too for what she did to Laura and you."

I told my father, "I don't hate my mother, and I don't hate you. I've never hated either one of you. I have always loved you. I've always loved both of you. I've never hated anyone. There could not be hate in my heart for either one of you. Because, Daddy, there's never been room in my heart for hate."

He said, "I'm going to bare my soul to you. I can't carry this to my grave. I feel like I have a huge stain somewhere inside of me. So, I have to tell you, and when I'm finished, you will hate her as much as I do. I hate her, and I hate my father for the lies and the deception. I remember my daughter. Laura was beautiful that night. More beautiful than I'd ever seen her in that white gown with flowers in her hair and a smile that seemed to light up even the sky. She was walking down that path so beautiful, lovely, and so pure in my eyes. She looked at me with those trusting eyes as she walked into that white tent. I watched as your grandfather went into that tent. He came out about an hour later, longer than any time I had known for the passage to take place. Not as he had done with all the daughters of the family and the wives-to-be."

My dad stopped talking for a moment as if to gather his thoughts. I was thinking, *No, I don't want to hear this. I do not want to hear anymore. Why is he telling me this now?*

My dad continued; I couldn't stop him. "Your grandfather came out of the tent. But this time, it was different; he had been in there a long time. When he finally came out, your grandfather went to my brother Sam and said something to him. Sam went into the tent, which I had never seen done in all my years at the farm, attending the passage of many girls of the family and the future wives of my brothers. I noticed a line forming in front of the tent. I knew what it meant, but I was to go in first. I was Laura's father. Your grandfather was talking with each man in the family. Normally, the master would come out and say, 'The spirit life has chosen her to bear many children; she has received the seed, and her passage is complete. She is now a woman.'

"I was to be the proud father and wait for her to come out of the tent. Walk her through the crowd of my brothers, brothers-in-law, and nephews as they honored her with flowers and small tokens. Walk her to the path leading back to the house where the women waited with gifts for her. But not this time. After a long time, your uncle Sam still had not come out. Your grandfather finally told me what was going on."

My dad stopped for a moment. His face was etched with pain as he continued. "Your grandfather told me that my brother Sam was going to be the next master. So, he had the honor and the privilege of going in first, as our laws commanded.

"Then, your grandfather told me the awful lies mixed with truth: 'You know our laws, Son, you must go in next and lay with her. You have to give her your seed, the same seed she was made from. Your seed is the most important. Laura was unclean, not pure; she has been with a man. There was no proof, no stain. She's unclean. She will not produce until we all lay with her. We must protect our family. It's our law. She will be restored and bear children and carry much seed. You know our laws, Son. This has to be; this is the result of her disobedience.'"

My father continued, "I had always known what the passage was. But for some reason, until that moment, I had never really accepted it or let its meaning into my heart or my mind, nor had I truly understood it. However, that night, I knew my father had not only laid with my wife many years before, but on this night, he had also laid with my daughter. Yes, he laid with your mother and your sister."

My dad screamed, "Linda, I deserve hell. If there's a hell, then I deserve to be there. They laid with my daughter...my beautiful daughter Laura. When your uncle Sam came out, I hated that look on his face. I wanted to hurt him. Then your grandfather told me, 'You got to do this; you go on in there and do what needs to be done.'

"When I walked in, I saw Laura. She was like a frightened child. I never saw such pain in any young girl. I was angry, and I wanted to kill them all. I picked up that blanket and wrapped it around her. I carried her down to the stream. I laid her in it and walked away. That's the night that I wished we had all died in that fire. I wish I'd never believed your mother's lies. We should have all died in that fire. I went back up to the tent. All the men, my brothers and their sons, were laughing and talking. I screamed out loud to them, calling out some of their names. I told them all: 'Do any of you understand that the spirit life has left us this night? It's over for all of us. I have the whole book of truth that our grandfather gave to me. The book I have has no pages torn out. You all know the reason my grandfather gave me the true and only real copy of the book. All of you know he told me I would be the next master after our father died. And all of you know this to be the truth. But our father is not honoring our grandfather's word.'

"'Our father has disobeyed the master before him and, instead, has chosen our brother Sam, the drunk and gambler, to take his place as master. Do you really want Sam to rule over you and your family? Sam will gamble and drink this place into the ground. The spirit life has left us all; our seeds are now cursed. Our family has been cursed now. We will die, all of us, and there will be no seed to follow after. I'm to be the next master, and it has been altered, and we all know the "penalty." Well, I will be no part of it anymore. I'm taking my things and my family, and I'm going home; I will never return. All of you best be leaving here as well or suffer the worst of the curse. We will all die in the very near future. Our sons will no longer produce; the spirit life has left us and has taken all seed life with him to find a family more worthy.'

"'I choose not to be a part of this anymore. I do not want to be the next master. I believe the spirit life has left us this night, as the book foretold. I have been disobedient this very night. I refuse to lay with Laura!' When they all heard that and about Uncle Sam, they were all mad, and there was a rebellion that night. Linda, because they all knew Sam was nothing and didn't care about anything except his gambling, his drinking, and wild women, I told them all that night your uncle Sam did not believe as we did; he was a fake. All of us left the farm that night. Never to return."

He stopped, took a deep breath, and groaned. I thought he was finished. I prayed he was finished, but he wasn't.

He finally continued, "Do you know, Linda, that most of our family killed themselves? I thought for a long time that Laura would end her life. When I went back to the stream to get her, I wished she would have drowned and floated away. But there she was, sitting in the water, shaking; so cold and so afraid."

For a moment, I thought he was going to cry; it was silent. *It was Laura's tear I saw rolling down his cheek.* It was not mine to capture, and the moment passed me by. He took a deep breath. "I swear to you, if I had a gun that night, I would have killed her and then myself. I'm glad I left the family that night. I'm glad I spoke up. Because that night tore our family apart, we all went different ways and never saw each other and never spoke again. But I'm still glad I did it. It was too late for Laura and your mother. It was too late for all of us.

"Your mother thought she could tell me how wrong she was and ask for forgiveness when she was dying. She was wrong. I told her I would never forgive her. I told her it was my life and my death, and I was not going to spend any more time with her in either one. The night she died, that's what I said to her. I left you in there with her, and she died before I came back in. I was glad I didn't see her die. How is it possible that I can hate her so much and love her so much at the same time?"

I couldn't speak. I couldn't breathe. I thought I was going to pass out. My father had literally lost his mind. Where was all this stuff coming from? Why was he saying these things? It must be the morphine that's made him go crazy like this. I couldn't think anymore, and I didn't want to hear anymore. But I knew he wasn't finished.

Then my father screamed out, "It was me, Linda; it was all my fault. I knew your grandfather was going in that tent in 1948 to lay with your mother, and I did nothing. She was never the same again. I don't know what he did to her, but she had changed. Your mother was so young and innocent. I wanted to be the first. But I let him take that from me. It was our laws; it was the law. I wanted her to bear many children for me and be my wife. But I let her down. I did not stop my father, and I should have protected her. I don't know what he did, but it changed everything, and I blamed her. Why didn't I stop it?" He screamed again, "Laura, why did I let them do that to you? I knew it, and I did nothing. I could never forget that look of innocence on her face when she looked at me that night before going into the tent. Your mother was so beautiful the night she went in, but when she came out, there was this look of fear that I was never able to wipe from my mind. It has haunted me all these years. That's why I did what I did that night: I was angry and hated my father. I didn't want to live by those laws anymore if they could be so easily broken and changed. I was to be the next master. Me, your father, and he took that from me too."

He called out my name, "Linda!" Then he said, "It's Jesus. He's still here. He hasn't left yet." He looked over at me and said, "What do you say about Jesus, just standing there? What does He want from me?"

I didn't know what to say. I was so confused by all the things my dad was saying. My heart was breaking for this man. He was so tormented and torn between guilt, shame, and blaming others for all the things that he, as a man, knew he should have done. Blaming himself for all the things he didn't do. He was truly a broken man.

I finally said, "Daddy, Jesus loves you, and He wants to let it go by. He has a place for you in His kingdom where there is truth, love, and forgiveness. Please, Daddy, please, just talk to Jesus. I can't make your stain go away, but He can. I can't carry what you have carried in your heart, the things that you cannot bear, the things you don't want to carry to the grave. I cannot help you with all this, but Jesus can. Daddy, He can take that stain. Ask Him to forgive you and to come into your heart and cleanse you and make you whole."

It was like the hammer went down, and the line was drawn. My father said, "I will not yield. For I don't want to be in any place where your mother exists, to be forever reminded of how it was my fault that she changed from the innocent young girl I met so long ago."

I don't know how to explain it. It was like a veil just dropped, and my daddy said, "Jesus is turning around and walking away."

I said, "Daddy, please, please! This is your last chance, Daddy."

He said, "I don't care. I deserve to go to hell. If there is a hell, I deserve to go there."

He looked back at where he said Jesus was standing. And then he looked back at me. His face was so pale, and his eyes empty as he said, "Jesus is gone now."

I said, "Oh, Daddy, what have you done? Please call out to Him."

He said, "No, I cannot, and I will not call out to Him. Where was He all those years? I want Him to go. I am tired now. I want to rest. I want you to go too. I do not need you here to remind me of your mother. You look like her; you know that, don't you? I want you to get out of here. I will not yield to you or Jesus. Get out of here. I do not want to look at you a moment longer. Get out!"

He talked for a long time and then finally fell asleep. After talking and talking, saying the most hateful and cruel things, I could not believe that this man was my father. He was so full of hate. I just wanted to remember him letting it go by and me standing in his presence on that night so very long ago. That's the way I wanted to remember him.

He had been asleep for about three hours when the alarm went off; it was time to give him the morphine. I gave it to him, and I went back to settle down in the chair. But I could not sleep. I could still hear all the words that he had spoken. The harshness, the coldness, and the reality of it all. I knew something now that I didn't want to know. I wanted it to go away. I didn't want to think about it. All this time, he would not listen. Giving into his hatred. His love for her and his hate for her were equal to each other. One could not win. Not the hate. Not the love. The battle was over, and I knew it. These were the final moments of my father's life.

A few hours later, he was really struggling and in so much pain. I tried to give him some more morphine. But I couldn't. I just couldn't. I walked out of the room and went to make some coffee. I heard him scream and went running back into his room. I saw him. He was different somehow. He was shaking, and his face was distorted. I couldn't understand the words at first. Then I knew what he was saying.

He was saying it over and over: "They are coming for me. They are coming for me. They're coming; I feel them. They're here. They're here. Get them out of here, Linda. No, no!"

My father was screaming. It was just for a second. For a split second, there was such a darkness and such an evil in that room, and after it was over, it was cold. It was only for a split second, then it was gone, and so was my father. The final battle was over.

Still, I stood there trying to take it all in, the whole night, the whole experience. I had never had such a long, in-depth conversation with anyone. My dad never said much to me my whole life unless I was in trouble. Why did he choose now? I wanted all the things he said to go away. I wanted to forget them. There was nothing left to do.

It was all laid out before me. *Oh, Daddy. Your spirit is gone now, and you did not choose life. I must carry that with me because I watched you pass from life to death—to hell. I couldn't do anything because it was your choice. You were a tortured soul. Caught in a web of lies and deceit. Torn between love and hate. Lost, you were so lost and so deceived by the people who were supposed to love you. They deceived with so many lies; so much deception was around you. After a while, you never knew who to trust, what to trust, and what to believe. I don't even think you knew how to respond to love. The only thing you knew to do was rely on what you felt, your anger and your hate, for what your father and your wife had done to you.*

It seemed as if he was all twisted up and like there was this darkness around him. Not dark, but like a shadow that seemed to linger. I really didn't know how to feel or what to think. I knew he wasn't breathing. I could not stay in that room a minute longer. I covered him up with a white sheet and walked out of the room, closing the door behind me. My tears flowed freely as I got my phone and called hospice.

It wasn't long. Within hours, my dad's body was removed. From his house. From his bed, where he said he wanted to die. I was left alone in the silence, yet there seemed to be echoes of his words pouring into my heart for me to deal with. My father told me not so I would understand anything; it was so that I would hate my mother, or was it? Maybe he was trying to clear his conscience in the only way he knew how. I have gone over and over that night and the things he said. I believe that in his final hours, he was sifting through all the things he had allowed to happen. Riddled with guilt, torn apart with shame, and blaming Mom for everything. Yet, in the end, I believe that he understood it was his responsibility to protect her. He did not protect her from his father, and it haunted him as to what his father did on that fatal night in 1948 to his innocent sixteen-year-old future wife. Still, in the end, he could not accept the fact he had believed in the lies of the spirit life. Built his life and his family's life on something that could be destroyed in less than three hours. "How easily it crumbled," he said.

Laura was on the road working; she had a car to deliver, so she would not arrive until the next morning. So, I stayed at my parents' house. I was alone for the first time in their house in a long time. Alone in the house that Satan shook. As I looked around, the memories began to flood my soul. I thought, *What is it going to be like to remove all their things from this house, to deal with all of that, selling the house? What will that be like?*

I walked into their room. My father and mother's room. Where my father insisted he must die. For what reason, I don't know. But there it was, that book, that cursed book. It was a curse. A curse to me, a curse to my sister, a curse to my family. There was no truth in it. I grabbed that book, and I went storming into the backyard. I opened the grill; I laid the book on the grill. I searched for the gas can. I went into the shed, found it, and grabbed it up. I went back to the grill. I was in tears. My wound was fresh as I poured gas on that book. The book that destroyed my family.

There it was, a lighter. I picked it up and pushed the button. I watched the flame come up. I looked at the flame for a second, then I reached out and touched the flame to that book and watched it erupt into flames. I, too, erupted into tears as I screamed, "Daddy, look at it burn. It burns, just like paper. That's what you didn't understand. It wasn't the paper that had power. It wasn't the book that had power. It was the words in the book that had power, Daddy, the words. The words in these books had the power to change our lives. One with truth and one with lies."

I continued, "You chose lies, Daddy. And you forced your children to live in those lies. You forced your wife to live in those lies. We chose so many paths that were before us because of those lies. Daddy, it was lies in that book; you chose the wrong one. I am so sorry, Daddy. I tried to tell you the truth. I'm sorry that I was afraid of you; I couldn't risk your anger. I didn't want it unleashed on me. God, forgive me for that. I should have not been afraid. I should have spoken to you openly and freely long ago. But I, too, lied to you and stripped you of a choice that you could have had long ago. When I first came home in 1985. I'm so sorry, Daddy, I was too late, and you ran out of time."

I don't know how long I stood there. Or how long some of these ramblings went on. I just know I stood there until there was nothing left but ashes on the grill, and my broken heart was empty. I just stood there and cried. For all that was lost. For all the lies believed. As it burned, I knew it had no power, no truth, no life-giving seed, and no breath in it. It was lies, all lies, forged in the hearts of men who knew no truth, who lived in its falsehoods and, far worse, taught it to generations.

Grandpa made it known that Uncle Sam would be the next in line, and everything would be passed on to him, including his power. All the families would look to Uncle Sam as the next *master*. It appears that my father and the other seventeen children did not agree with Grandpa's decision. For the first time in their lives, they stood against Grandpa.

Grandpa told them all to get off his land and never return. They did just that, leaving behind a lifetime of teaching and beliefs. My dad was never the same, and to my knowledge, the family never recovered. We didn't see our uncles or aunts after the harvest in 1966. I do know that when Uncle Sam died, only five acres of my grandpa's farm were left. As it turned out, Uncle Sam did indeed like to drink and gamble, and he sold the farm off piece by piece. Uncle Sam died in 1991, and what was left of the farm went to the state of Kentucky for back taxes.

What I still find so amazing, and at the same time hard to understand, is that for generations, my dad's family lived and believed in this cult. They had lived in all its false teachings for many generations. It was well organized, and our practices and beliefs were very involved and controlled. Yet it was destroyed, brought down, and put to an end so quickly. It happened overnight, and not one family ever went back. To my knowledge, all family members never contacted each other again. They all went their separate ways. My dad said it was because of the law. They were all cursed and went to wait for the punishment. Which was all seed was taken, and death would reign until they were all dead. Then, the spirit life would choose another family.

That book, which belonged to my dad, was not the only book that burned on that grill. No, many years ago, in February 1967, thirty-four years earlier, another book burned on that grill. But it was the real *book of truth*—the Word of God. The flames could not burn the words away placed in my heart many years ago; those words stayed with me. And on this night, as I looked to the heavens, those words came alive in my spirit. I knew them to be true.

Nothing can ever burn the words of truth away.

> In the beginning God created the heaven and the earth. And the earth was without form, and void; and darkness was upon the face of the deep. And the Spirit of God moved upon the face of the waters. And God said, Let there be light: and there was light. And God saw the light, that it was good: and God divided the light from the darkness.
>
> Genesis 1:1–4

Now, I also know what the truth is! Because on this night, I burned my father's false book of the spirit life. God opened the eyes of my understanding and poured into my soul the truth. The night that I read those words for the very first time, hiding in the closet in the middle of the night. In 1966, I was such a young girl, but that night, God spoke light into my life. That night, as I read the words on the pages of God's Word, the words were light to my soul. Light was spoken into my life by God. He said, "Let there be light in Linda's spirit." And there was. This is what I believe to be true.

The night my father died, I also saw something else. I saw my father didn't have forgiveness, and he didn't know how to receive it. He had allowed his heart to be full of bitterness and anger. There was so much hurt, and there was so much deception that he could not sort out the lies from the truth, so he died in them, and I felt I was responsible.

I am not the smartest person. Probably don't have a right to say a lot of things. But I do know this: You never want to live with the fact that you could have witnessed to someone. You could have shared God's love with them, and their life could have been different. You could have spoken truth into their life. But you let that chance pass you by, time and time again. Then you realize they are dead; their destination is not heaven but hell. To know that you are going to be eternally separated from the person that you love so much. When you realize that you will be walking in a kingdom full of light and love, and they will burn for all eternity in darkness. Somehow, that changes the way you look at life because you will never want to pass up the opportunity to witness to someone, to show them love, to show them the Way, the Truth, and the Life. At any moment to be ready to show an act of kindness. To be ready to be a witness and share the gospel at any time, any moment. To make a difference in someone's life. Between heaven and hell to change their destiny. Their final destination can change, and it is the responsibility of every Christian to share the gospel, even unto the end of time.

I knew, for the first time in my life, that there was no returning home, and I was out in the world, completely alone. Their deaths seemed to have dropped a dark, heavy cloud over my life, and with it came the realization that I had truly never been loved. It is hard to even speak of this time in my life. As thoughts of their death surrounded me, I couldn't escape them, no matter how hard I tried.

I thought of my mother and how she accepted Jesus Christ as her Savior, how she had repented and had a change of heart. I thought about my father also. I was forty-five years old, and my father had never really spoken to me.

But on the night of his death, he chose to pour out his soul to me so openly and left me with words that now cut into my soul. Words that were more than I could bear. More than I wanted to know. They were too much for me to carry and figure out; at this point in my life, in time, understanding would come. But for now, what I experienced that night, the way he died, crushed my heart, and the reality of my dad's final destination weighed heavily on my mind.

Two residents of the "house that Satan shook" had faced death as they held firm to the final choices they had made. The shadows fell, and the lines were drawn on the nights my parents died. The house I grew up in was now empty and silent. There were no signs of the people who had once lived there.

The dark halls of false teachings, fights, beatings, and the cries of two little girls hiding in fear were forever silenced. Emptiness overshadowed the house like a blanket of forbidden memories. Those who lived them were told, "It is best to forget." My father's last words were instructions and comfort for his two daughters. How was I ever going to forget?

My mother chose life, and my father chose death in their final battle. Laura and I were the surviving residents of the house that Satan shook. We had made our choices as well. Somehow, we would have to find our way back to each other. We would have to find a way to overcome the past and learn to forgive each other for our inability to be perfect in an imperfect world.

CHAPTER 11

A Sister's Unfailing Love

Laura and I were putting our parents' house up for sale, and both of us had to sign some papers in order to sell their home. Laura handled the details, and all I had to do was show up and sign. We met at the real estate agent's office in December of 2000. We did not speak. We both signed the paperwork and went our separate ways. I sat in my car in the parking lot and watched her get into her car and drive off. I wondered if we would ever find a place of peace again. Would we ever laugh together or pray together? Would we ever talk again? Had the bitterness of my own heart destroyed the one relationship I so desperately needed now?

Laura was out of sight when I realized how wrong I had been. I knew she was hurting just as much as I was...even more. I saw the pain in her eyes. Then it hit me: Laura did not even try to talk to me. She didn't even look in my direction. Had my bitterness and anger finally pushed her away from me?

I thought to myself, *What am I doing? I am doing the same thing my dad did. I am acting like a five-year-old child. I have let this bitterness destroy a beautiful relationship between me and my sister. We have both suffered enough. I don't know how to fix this. Laura is my only sister. I should have spoken to her. I should have told her I, too, have a job. I am working, and I am doing well. I should have told her I have met someone on my job. I should have told her I am getting married and he is a good man.*

But nope! I didn't even speak to her. I let her go. Just let her drive off. And I knew she was alone and had no one. The truth, I was afraid she would not understand the mess I was creating. Laura might let something slip to my future husband. Because I had lied to him about so many things, even about her, and he knew nothing about my past. And I just did not know how to approach her. I could not seem to find the words.

Laura had suffered so much more than me. All that she had to go through. She was always protecting me, making sure I was out of harm's way. I could not even begin to imagine the things my sister had suffered. I didn't want to think about the things my father had said the night he died. How she must have suffered the night of her passage. I hate to even think about it. The enormous amount of guilt and shame she must have carried for years and may still be carrying it. I had been so foolish.

Time has a way of continually passing by, whether you do anything or not. Time does not stop just because you do; it keeps on ticking. Nor does time heal all wounds, no matter what we are told. If they are not dealt with, time causes them to fester, and our souls will get infected.

Just like a physical cut that has not been cleaned and properly taken care of, an unattended cut will cause a severe infection in the body and can lead to the loss of limbs or even death. So it is with our spirit: our wounds must be looked at and treated. So, we can spiritually grow and move on with a healthy spiritual attitude and walk victoriously in life.

When we get wounded in our souls, it also must be looked at and attended to. The Word of God says, "[...] but a wounded spirit who can bear?" (Proverbs 18:14b) That is what happened to me. I was wounded the day I gave my sister a choice, and instead of turning to God and asking God to heal my broken heart, I became bitter and unforgiving. That bitterness turned to pride and anger. I was infected! The final result of my wounded spirit, needless to say, I was seeking revenge.

I had ignored all the warning signs, and I pushed the gentle tugging of God away and indulged in my pride and arrogance. I basked in my bitterness and anger, refusing to show any kindness toward Laura. I became the judge and the jury and punished her. What she needed from me the most, I denied her, and now my heart was heavy because I was reaping what I had sown.

Laura and I had lost a lot of time that we could have spent together. We could have helped each other through the death of Daniel and our parents. We could have prayed for each other and encouraged each other as we overcame the pain and rejection of our past. Both our lives had been hard.

Certainly, we had endured and survived many raging storms in our lives. We didn't let those storms fill us with the anger or the hate that was displayed before our eyes as we grew up. We didn't hate or blame our parents for anything that had happened in our lives. All we ever wanted was for our parents to love us. We both longed to hear the words "I love you" from our parents. However, we never heard those words, not even once.

I thought of Laura more often as time passed. It was not long until thoughts of her filled my mind all day, every day. Some thoughts were painful, and other memories filled my heart with happiness and a touch of sadness. Laura's life had certainly taken her down different roads than my life had taken me. We were two simple girls who were thrown into a world we just didn't understand.

Our parents did not train us or prepare us in any way for this thing called "life." Because of the lack of training in money matters, we had no knowledge about how to control or manage finances. We had no skills for jobs, no teaching regarding right and wrong, and we had zero social skills. We were not smart in the ways of the world, nor were we educated. We learned to live and survive by trial and error. That is a very hard way to learn, but the lessons we learned as a direct result of those experiences have become our foundation for making future decisions.

Neither Laura nor I blamed our parents for the outcome of our lives. We had realized our choices had played as much a part in our lives as the things that our parents did or did not teach us. Yes, there were those things that were forced upon us, things in which we had no choice. But in the end, we both knew blaming our parents would only cause us to discard the responsibility for our own actions.

Laura was outgoing, and she was not afraid to strike up a conversation with anyone. I, on the other hand, was not at all skilled in the communication department. I froze just placing an order at a drive-thru window. I told Laura once that I could never be used by God in the speaking arena. I was not one to speak out in front of anyone. That was the reason I wanted Laura and me to speak to our parents together. I didn't believe they would listen to just me. I would have just stuttered and then froze up. And the words would have never come out. Laura was bold and would speak her mind, and I was just the opposite.

I set out to get a job because I couldn't take it anymore. I just couldn't sit around the house and think about the loss of Daniel and my parents any longer. I knew Abigail was also hurting, and she needed to know I was okay. God used Abigail and my love for her to get my attention. I had to move out from my state of isolation, mourning, and sorrow.

I had to step out of the life I was creating and take a mighty big step out into the world. Getting a job, I thought, would be hard for me, without an education or training of any kind, but I got a job my first day out. I didn't want to work in a club, and I didn't want to be a waitress serving food. I got a job on a production line, which was perfect. I had to stay focused and keep my mind on the job. The work I did was repetitive. I had to stay focused. I didn't have to associate with anyone. It was the perfect job for me.

I had worked for about two months when I met Scott Prenger. It was a whirlwind relationship; we rushed into marriage. He wanted to marry me less than a month after we met. He said he was sure, and as for me, I didn't think. I was numb; I just moved, living day to day, empty, just a shell that was faking some kind of imagined life. So, we got married. It wasn't as if I went looking for a husband. It was the last thing I thought I would ever do. A husband was certainly not what I was looking for or something I had on a to-do list, like get a job, check, get a home, check, get a husband, check.

However, Scott brought something into my life that I had never had. He brought love and friendship. I had a friend, and that was very rare in my life. God had sent someone that I trusted for some unknown reason, someone that I could talk to and a strong shoulder I could cry on. I was able to share the pain in my heart concerning Daniel's death. I said very little about the death of my parents; I carried that burden alone in my heart.

He knew that the loss of my parents and Daniel had happened in the last year and nine months. My father's death was the most recent, three months before I met him. The rest of my life remained a secret. He knew nothing about the way I was raised and absolutely nothing about my past. He knew I had a sister, and that was about it. The truth was, I lied to him about my past, and I covered it up as if it had never happened.

I was the good girl raised in a good Christian home. I finished school, graduated top of my class, and went to church every Sunday. Loved the Lord and loved the Word. Worked hard and had my own home. Adopted a daughter who was unwanted by her biological mother. Scott also knew about Daniel, a little boy I was raising and getting ready to adopt before he accidentally drowned. I was the perfect Christian woman. Never drank and never had even stepped into a club of any kind.

I had always identified with the bad women in the Bible. I was a Rehab, the woman at the well, the woman taken in adultery, but now I had the chance to be a Mary, an Elizabeth, or a Hannah. I had a chance to know how it felt to be the good woman in the Bible. I had the chance to be loved and accepted by a whole new family, and I took the chance. I tossed out whatever feelings I had about whether it was right or wrong. For a moment, I believed that to be loved by Scott that way was worth the risk I was taking.

It was a beautiful day in March; I was still trying to comprehend the fact I was actually married. Certainly not something I had planned, but I was married, and Scott was a really good man. I had spent the day resting and reading from the Psalms. I remember the peace I felt that day. There was a calmness that had been absent in my life, filling my soul that day. I thought maybe, just maybe, there was a chance for the words I had just read to be a part of my life after all. I was in the den, sitting on the couch, and I looked up and saw Abigail outside in the pool. I thought about how God had truly blessed my life by allowing me to adopt her.

The phone rang, interrupting my thoughts. Who would be calling? My phone never rang unless it was Abigail, who was in the pool, or Scott, who was mowing the pasture. I looked at the number and did not recognize it. I started to not answer it when I remembered it might be an interested buyer for my parents' house. It could be the real estate agent, I thought, and hit the talk button. "Hello?" It was silent. Again, I said, "Hello?"

I heard her voice, "Linda, please don't hang up. I have been driving around all day, looking for your house. I got your number and address from Mother before she died. I was going to call before I came, but I didn't want to give you a chance to turn me down. Please let me come to see you. Just hear me out, then if you want me to leave, I will, and I will never bother you again."

"Where are you?" I asked.

She told me she was at Brookshire's in the parking lot. I told her I was on my way. She sounded relieved. "Thanks, Linda, see you in a minute. You're not going to leave me just sitting here, are you?"

I assured her I was coming. I pulled into Brookshire's parking lot and looked for her car. I had spotted her and pulled up beside her. I knew this wasn't the place for words of any kind, so I told her to just follow me, and we could talk at my house. I could tell she was nervous. All the way to my house, my mind was racing. *What does she want? Why did she drive all the way out here to see me after all this time? Is she in trouble?*

I knew I only had minutes to decide what I was going to do and how I was going to handle this visit. The Lord spoke to my heart, "Just love and forgive her." I knew it was the Lord, and I knew He was right. So, I began to pray. I asked the Lord to help me to see her through His eyes, and no matter what she told me, even if it involved drugs, to help me show her love and understanding.

I pulled up in the driveway, and she pulled in behind me. She got out of her car first. We were walking toward each other in quick, steady steps. We both stopped at the same time. She spoke first, "Linda, please." Whatever she was going to say didn't matter at that moment. She was there, and that was all that mattered to me. The space between us closed in as we embraced. There were lots of tears and words of forgiveness. My heart was so overjoyed. I had missed her so much more than I realized.

The bond between us that day proved to be strong and undamaged. We shared a lifetime together that day as we talked about our lives, the painful truth of our childhood, the wrongs done to us, our struggles to overcome them, and where we were now. It seemed we both had survived and found peace. We both understood we had made mistakes, and some of those mistakes came with a high price. We spent the whole afternoon and long into the evening by the pool just talking.

Laura surprised me with her memories of our childhood. She wanted to share her heart and her memories with me that day. As I listened to her talk, I realized how much I had truly missed her. She talked about the fire and shared things with me that she had never mentioned before, about how she saved my life the day of the fire in 1957.

Laura told me that when we were trapped in the upstairs bedroom, she heard a voice, and it told her the only way out was through the window and to make sure I went out first because I would not follow her out onto the window ledge. She said she believed it was the spirit life but was afraid to say anything. She never spoke about it because she didn't understand, and sometimes, she felt that maybe it had never happened.

Laura told me that the only reason she got the pictures of her and me was because the voice told her to get the pictures and that we needed them. She asked me if I thought she was crazy. I told her I didn't think she was crazy, and then I asked her, "Whatever happened to those pictures?"

She got this look on her face. She said, "I'm sorry, Linda. I just don't want to talk about them right now. I'm sorry, I just can't talk about them."

I assured her that it was all right and that I understood. The years had been long, and she had dragged them around for a long time. With all the places she had lived and all she had been through, they were bound to get lost, destroyed, or left behind somewhere. "They are gone, and it's all right," I told her. "Because now we have each other."

She had this look on her face. Then she smiled and said, "You're right. We have each other, and we are going to be like those two little girls in those two pictures. Only the grown-up version." And then she laughed. That amazing laughter she had just filled my heart, and I began to laugh as well. Her laughter was so contagious.

Laura said when she was young, she thought about it all the time, but as she got older, she just forgot about it until the night I was raped. Laura said, "I know that I told you I felt something was wrong that night, but there was more to it. I have never shared it with anyone. I heard the same voice that night that I heard on the day of the fire. I felt you were in danger, and I didn't know what to do. I stopped the car right where I was on the bridge, got out of my car, went to the rail, and screamed out, 'God, if You are real, please don't let my sister die! Please show her what to do or what to say. Help her! I know You can. Please, give us a chance.' I got back in my car, and as I closed the door, I heard a voice say, 'Linda will suffer greatly tonight, but she shall live and not die. I have heard your cry for help and have answered.'"

Laura continued, "It was hard for me to understand, but I believed that it was God who spoke to me, and I knew that God heard me that night. That's when I knew all those years ago that it was God somehow speaking to me on the day of the fire. I didn't understand it, but I did know that it was not the spirit life that talked to me during the fire, and that is when I finally stopped believing in the spirit life. It was from that point in

October of 1973 that I knew there was a God." Laura told me it changed her somehow… "Knowing there's a God changes things, Linda."

I told her it does change things when you know. I told her how it had changed my life as well and shared with her I had always known that the voice I heard was somehow from God. I told her, "It wasn't like someone talking to me, but more like that sweet inner voice that's gentle and guiding you. Which I know now to be the Holy Spirit, but I didn't know any better back then." We both laughed softly.

Laura shared with me that from the end of 1973, she thought there was a God. She didn't fully understand, but she knew He had spoken to her. She didn't know why God had chosen to speak to her and save us that day from the fire. She shared how she kept waiting for someone to tell her about God, but no one ever did. Laura said when I told her I believed God existed, her heart leaped for joy because she knew I would not stop searching until I found Him or the answer.

Laura talked of other moments and events in her life where she felt that God was there and had helped her in some way. She was lost and confused about where God was and who God was. She said, "The hardest part was, no one ever talked about God."

I agreed. I told her that for so long, I believed it was a well-kept secret, and only certain people knew where God was and could talk to Him. Laura and I laughed at how strange it was the things we once thought. She mentioned how odd it was for us to be sitting there, talking about God openly, when most of our lives we feared saying the word "God." The word "God" for so long brought fear into our lives. Fear of getting taken away. Getting a beating for saying the word or spit on for listening to someone talk of God. Indeed, it was strange for us to sit there in the open and talk freely about the power of our God.

Laura smiled at me and said, "When you told me you were going to go look for God, I was excited; I couldn't wait until you came back to tell me that you found Him. Because I knew you would find God, I just knew you would, and you did. Maybe not the way we were thinking. You really found Him, Linda, and He has changed your life, but there's so much more that He wants for you. Look at you, still wearing those white patent leather shoes. You need to take those things off. Get yourself some real shoes and those dresses; you still make them and wear them. Why? God wants so much more for you, Linda."

I told her, "Let's go to another subject…" I looked down at my dress and shoes and thought, *She is right.* We continued talking.

We talked and talked, and then I told her through tears how sorry I was for my behavior over the last seven years. I broke down. I was so ashamed of the way I had treated her that day in my bedroom and how I walked out and left her so hurt and broken. I asked her to forgive me for what I had said about the speck of dirt on my white shoe and how I didn't care about it or her. I told her that was a lie, and my heart was breaking that day. I really wanted to hug her and hold her. I wanted to reach out and help her, but I didn't want to get hurt anymore. I didn't want to believe her lies anymore. I just didn't know what to do. So, I denied my feelings, pushed them down deep inside, and struck a bargain with bitterness. Oh, how I had regretted it, I told her.

I told her that I wanted us to be sisters and never let anything come between us again. We both agreed and understood we were not perfect and that we would fall and make mistakes. What we needed most was to pray and encourage each other. The afternoon just faded away.

At about ten thirty that night, Laura was getting ready to leave; she spotted a picture that had belonged to Mom hanging on my wall. She looked at me and said, "Mother was a masterpiece, wasn't she?"

I answered, "Laura, she was a wounded soul who, by the grace of God, spent the last of her days seeking His forgiveness. I saw such ugly things come out of her, and then she would turn around and purchase something as beautiful as this and hang it on the wall for all to see the beauty in it. You know, with Mom, everything had a price. Would you like to have it?"

Laura replied, "Oh, yes! Linda, I would love to have it." I took it off the wall and handed it to her. She sat it down and hugged me for a long moment and said, "Thank you, Linda, thank you so much for everything. Most of all, thank you for loving me, even when I was not so lovable. When Dad died, I thought that I had no one left. This morning, I knew in my heart that I had to see you. It was His voice telling me it was time. I love you, Linda."

It was amazing how, in one afternoon, Laura and I had come to terms with our lives and the mistakes we had made. I received forgiveness from Laura and God that day for the years I wasted in anger and bitterness. Healing and restoration had begun in our lives. I walked Laura to her car, and we said our goodbyes. As I watched her drive away, Scott walked up beside me and said, "You two had a good visit?"

I responded, "Yes, we did, Scott, the best! I think we are going to be okay now. I do love her so."

Scott took my hand as we watched her taillights fade in the distance. By the grace of God and against all odds, Laura and I had managed to look beyond all the obstacles of our lives. We each had purchased homes and had established a life for ourselves. Though our lives were not perfect, we had found a place of peace.

We were now untangling the years of our broken childhood, the things done to us, the things forced on us, and the damage done in our lives from the wrong choices we had made. We both knew that the bitter years had passed, and we had survived. Our love for each other had not diminished at all. Instead, it had only been strengthened, and the bond between us had not been broken because of a sister's love and courage to seek and find that which was broken and lost. Laura had found me, and all that hate and bitterness I had carried for seven years melted away.

We both realized that day Satan was the real enemy, and he could not touch our love. He could not steal, kill, or destroy our love for each other. It was God's doing, and it was not of ourselves. For that reason, we thanked God. We praised Him for His perfect love for us and the fact that we were never out of God's hands.

That evening, I was so overwhelmed with God's amazing love. I thanked Him for placing it in my sister's heart to come and find me. I am so thankful He did because that day, I saw in Laura a sister's unfailing love, and without it, I would never have survived!

CHAPTER 12

Love, Truth, and Loss

Over the next few months, Laura and I spent a lot of time together, and our phones proved that they could be valuable to us. I never really cared about having a phone; it was just one of those things I had no use for. My phone had three numbers on it: Scott's number, Abigail's number, and Laura's number.

On September 11, 2001, she called me early in the morning and told me all about what was happening. Laura said, "The Twin Towers have fallen," We prayed and asked God to protect our nation. We stayed on the phone most of the day, back and forth. We read scriptures and talked of things to come. As it was with most Americans, so it was with Laura and me; we were in shock. We cried as we realized the many lives that were lost that day. If there was one thing we both understood, it was loss.

We spoke of 9/11 often over the next few weeks. It was at the top of the list of every conversation we had, and there was something else we also talked about every day. Laura had a three-bedroom Palm Harbor mobile home. She was paying rent to keep her home in a nice addition. I told her she could move her home to my land and stay there for nothing. I had five acres of land that was not being used. She fell in love with the idea, so we were putting the plans into motion. We would be close to each other. We would be able to help each other and be there for each other. September 11 made us realize how much we needed each other.

Laura also wanted me to tell Scott the truth about my past and how we were really raised. I didn't want to face the truth and tell him about the things my mom had done to me. I didn't want him to know I had worked in a gentlemen's club or about the things we were raised to believe. I didn't want to tell him that my father didn't believe in God and that when he died, I was with him, and he rejected Christ.

I would have to face the pain of a lifetime, and I was not up to dealing with any of my past. No, I didn't want to tell Scott anything about my past. I had put all those things behind me. I didn't want to think about them or deal with the pain they had caused in my life. I had buried them and wanted to keep them buried. Laura told me it would not work, that I had to tell Scott, and I needed to do it soon. She told me I would not be able to live this lie. She said no matter what I did, the truth would come out, and if Scott didn't hear it from me, it would hurt him and may destroy our marriage. She asked me if I was willing to take that chance. She said that I needed to see that even though our childhood was not as it should have been, God's hand was on us, and we were His masterpieces. Well, I did not see it that way. I was not a masterpiece, and I was not telling Scott anything. He would never understand, and he would leave me. I told her that the Word of God said to put those things behind and press towards the prize of the high calling. She looked at me and said, "Linda Marie! You are twisting Scripture to justify what you're doing."

I said, "Let's go to a different subject. Let's move on."

One day, Laura told me she believed God had something very special for me to do. She said God had been preparing me my whole life for what He was going to do through me. I asked her what she thought God had created her for. She laughed and said, "To save you, silly, from the fire the day our house burned to the ground and to watch over you all these years and keep you safe. Well, really, to keep you in line." We both just laughed.

Laura got very serious and said, "Linda, what hurt me more than anything was when I felt I had failed you. Seeing you so bitter and angry crushed me and made me take a serious look at my life. It wasn't like you to be so bitter, angry, and hateful. It hurt me deeply and taught me a lot about forgiveness and how valuable it is to our lives. I learned what it truly means to seek forgiveness and to be forgiven. It was at that point in my life I started praying and asked God to put me in prison. I told Him it was one way to clean me up. I think He thought it was a good idea. So that's where He put me—in prison."

Laura had also located her son, Kenneth. She said it was hard to believe, after all the years that had passed, that she was establishing a relationship with him. She had received wonderful news; she was going to be a grandma. So many good things lay ahead for us.

In my life, the grief was just below the surface. I just didn't realize I had never grieved the loss of Daniel, my dad, or my mom. There was really no time to grieve or accept their deaths. Life, death, and so many changes in such a short time had not caught up to my heart. Somehow, I had managed to turn it all off. I was just walking through life in a daze. I was in a dream, and what a wonderful dreamland it was. I didn't want to wake up. I didn't want to face life. I didn't want to think about the past. Not about my family. Not about my parents. Not even about Daniel. In the middle of my grieving, I stopped, I cut it off, I simply refused to. I wasn't going to grieve anymore. I turned those feelings and emotions off. I appeared to be strong and had overcome the loss of my family. Scott would say how brave I was and how his family admired my strength and faith as I moved forward after the loss of my parents. I had gone through such a loss and am still moving forward in life as a wife, a mother, and a Christian, and continuing in the faith. He would tell me how proud of me he was. No, to me, my life was perfect at last. I had love, a husband, a daughter, and my sister. Laura kept telling me I needed to talk to Scott about my past. I would just tell her my past had nothing to do with my future. I buried my past, but it would not remain buried.

On October 3, 2001, Laura and I had planned to meet at the lake with some blankets and hot coffee. We were going to watch the sunrise and share an amazing day together. She said there were some things she wanted to talk to me about. So, we set the date. Made the plan. The whole day was before us.

We watched that sunrise. It was such a beautiful sunrise. It was so amazing. I believe God made it an extra beautiful day for us. We sat on one big blanket, and we wrapped up in about three other ones. We were freezing and drinking our coffee. We were so amazed by the beauty God displayed before our eyes, as if just for us. We prayed together and read the Word.

Laura said there was something she wanted to share with me. I said, "All right, where do you want to go?"

She said, "There's this little place. I checked it out. It's not far from here. I don't want to drive all the way to my place. And I'm sure you don't want to go to yours. We need this time together." I was a little puzzled as to where this was all going. Laura told me she had already set up a place and had everything ready for us.

We went to Emory, a small town not far from where I live. It had a kitchenette, a small living room area, and a bedroom. It was a nice place. I realized she had stayed the night there. She already had everything set up. There was coffee and stuff for breakfast. She cooked everything and was just talking away. I was mostly laughing at her. Then she sat down, and we ate. It was a good breakfast. We sat there and looked at each other. She said, "Just look at us grown women; we did it, Linda; we survived, and we are free and happy. Christ is the center of our life. We must never forget that. You know only God could have done this, right?" I had not taken my eyes off of her; she was my beautiful sister, and, in that moment, I could not have loved her more. I told her she was absolutely right.

We were having a great time. We were having wonderful fellowship. Then she had to ruin it by taking advantage of the moment and started talking to me about telling Scott the truth. She wanted to go with me and us together to tell him the truth about me, about my life, and our family. So that I could begin to heal and live in peace. Laura said, "I know you're living in fear of him finding out every day. You don't have to live like that in fear; it's a lie of Satan. Linda, don't fall for it. Let's tell Scott so that he knows the truth and you have no secrets. He will forgive you for lying, and he will understand. He will protect you and will not humiliate you in front of his family or anyone."

Laura added, "Linda, you are not totally free yet; you are holding a secret from your husband. You need to be open and honest with Scott in everything. Your relationship will be so much more with him. Your love and respect will flourish for each other because of the freedom of walking in truth. I feel you need to be the one to tell him, and you need to do it soon. Let's do it, Linda, together tonight."

Oh no, that was just too much for me. No way was I going to tell him. Laura stressed the point that he would be forgiving and understanding. I told her, "I am not ready." I shared with her that I carried so much guilt and shame over the past. Things I had not even worked out myself yet. I had to have more time.

Once again, she said, "No, Linda, he will help you through this, and I know you still need to grieve. You have buried that with everything as well. There is a huge dam inside of you, and it is going to bust. When it does, everything is going to hit you all at once. Your past, your guilt, your shame. Everything you've done. Everything that's happened to you. All of it, Linda. It's going to come gushing out. And it's going to be mixed with all the grief that you have not allowed yourself to fully go through. Especially over Daniel... You have not grieved the loss of Dad or Mom either."

She raised her hands and continued, "Linda, you must tell him the truth. He loves you, and I can see it in him. I know he will be understanding, and most of all, he will forgive you for lying to him. It may take him time to understand. But in time, he will understand the pain you have carried in your soul for years over the past. The shame and the guilt you carry in your soul over all the things we went through. He will understand why you covered this up and why you lied. He will forgive you."

Laura said, "If you don't tell him, Linda, it's going to hurt him deeply when he finds out the truth, and he will find out. It will destroy almost everything you two have. Please! Let's go to him and tell him tonight."

I told her, "No, I can't. I don't want to listen to this anymore, Laura. I don't want to see that look on his face. I can't face him and tell him. The things we did, the things we went through. I worked in a gentlemen's club for four years. Laura, I can't, I just can't, Laura. Not now."

That's when she asked me what I was going to do if Jasmine showed up. I wasn't worried about that. Jasmine hated me, and she was never going to talk to me again. Her words, I was responsible for Daniel's death. She told me she never wanted to see me or talk to me again. I knew she meant it. I wasn't worried about Jasmine. With that, I dismissed it. I asked her what else she wanted to talk to me about.

Then she said, "Well, I guess it's time to tell you the second reason I wanted to be here with you today. Linda, I want to tell you something. I want to tell you about the passage. Why I wanted you to run away. I didn't want you to get hurt. That's not why I told you to run. I didn't know we would never go back to Kentucky when I told you to run away. I told you to run because I never wanted you to have to go through the passage..."

I stopped Laura by saying, "Please, don't tell me. Please, don't say another word. I know what you are going to say. Please don't. Daddy told me everything the night he died, and I will never understand why he did that."

She asked me what he had told me, and I told her everything our dad said to me that night. I had gone over it and over it in my mind. How could I forget?

Laura said, "I don't think Dad told you everything, Linda. You know what happened at the tent, right?" I nodded my head. Laura continued, "Then you know Dad wrapped me in a blanket and carried me down to the stream, and he put me in the water. He left me there. I am sure he didn't tell you why. It's time you know the whole truth. I told him something when he came into the tent."

Her eyes filled with tears as she said, "I told Dad not to be mad and please not to beat me, but Grandfather and Mom came down in this valley every spring and every fall to spend time together in here in this very tent. I know because Mom told me. She told me Grandfather told her on the night of her passage if she didn't, he was going to have all the men in the family come in one by one and lay with her. Mother told me my time was coming, and she wanted to prepare me. Mom wanted it to be special for Grandfather when he came into the tent. Mom told me that the master grandfather would set her free, and I was to take her place, and I would be the one to meet him there every spring and fall. I told Dad all of it. Everything she had told me about her and Grandfather. He never said a word, Linda."

Laura stopped for a moment and then continued, "I told Dad how Mom prepared me. Mother took me to this place where there were three men. I was sold to the highest bidder. Then the next highest bidder, then the next. The last man paid for his moment. The last man paid a small price to have his way with, as he said, the beautiful daughter. He was the worst; the things he did to me were horrible. When he was finished with me and was leaving, he told me I was worth the wait. How could she do that to me? I had to tell Dad."

Laura started crying and said, "I told Dad I didn't want Grandfather to touch me. I told Dad I was so sorry. I just couldn't let Grandfather touch me, so I fought Grandfather. Then I told Dad what Grandfather said when he was getting dressed after he forced me, hitting me, slapping me, and holding me down. Grandfather told me I had to be punished for my disobedience. Then Grandfather told me I was such a disappointment. He had looked forward to what Mom promised him would be a good time. I told Dad that Grandfather told me Mom would pay for this. Then he said I was unclean. I told Dad that Grandfather had said if I had been like a nasty girl and given it to him well, he would have been the only one, and I would have been honored, but now I must be punished. After a few minutes, Uncle Sam came in. I told Dad it was awful, but I could not stop it, not Grandfather or Uncle Sam. I couldn't stop them. Then I begged Dad to please take me out of there. I begged him, 'Please don't do this to me too. I can't bear it!' I cried. I begged him not to do that to me.

"He never said a word, Linda. Not a word... There was a deadly silence in that tent. He got the blanket and wrapped me in it, picked me up, and started walking. I talked to him on the way to the stream while he was carrying me.

"I was so broken; I thought the spirit life had left me and I was going to die, so I got a little bold. I said, 'Dad, please do not let this happen to Linda. Daddy, she's not like me; she will die if you let this happen to her. She cannot bear it. Linda will not live through it.' He believed me. He didn't get mad. He didn't get angry. He didn't hit me. He just listened. That was all I said to him. When we got to the stream, he laid me in the water and whispered, 'Swim and let the water cleanse you.' He walked away and left me there. I don't know how long I was there. I was cold, so cold, and all I could think was neither this water nor any amount of water would ever be enough to wash away all that was done to me that night."

Laura got this distant look on her face, then said, "When Dad came back to get me, I saw him coming down that hill; he looked so different to me. He looked defeated and torn apart. Like he had been through this horrible battle that was fought and lost in one hour. I could see the pain in his eyes when he finally looked down at me and asked me if I was clean. I told him I washed and washed but that I would never be clean again. Then he said the strangest thing to me. I knew then that he really loved me. He never said the words to me, Linda, but somehow, I knew he did. This is what Dad told me: 'Laura, close your eyes and say I let it go by.' Dad told me it would make it all go away, and I would feel better. But honestly, I never understood why he told me to do that or even what it meant. Then Dad told me we were going home. I lived in fear after that night that we would go back, and it would happen to me again. My worst fear was it would happen to you, but the spring came, and we didn't return. Dad told me to never say a word of it until he was dead and buried. Mom gave you something to make you sleep all the way home. I don't know why because they never said a word to each other the whole trip. Well, when we were almost home. Dad told Mom, 'I should have killed you back there. Be glad I didn't, but I promise you will never see my father again. You will not even go to his funeral when he dies, that's if I don't go back and kill him.' That was all that was ever said in the car on the way home. Dad, well, he never really talked to me again until Mom died, and all he said was, 'She'll never hurt us again.'

"I never understood why Mother did all those things. I told her the night after Dad beat you in the backyard and she burned the book, I would do whatever she wanted if she would leave you alone. When you ran away, I knew Mom had done something. She never told me. I asked, but she was never going to tell me.

"Then life just grabbed us and divided us both. We were on such different paths, but we were taking something in our hearts, our memories, and that was going to get us through it all. Now we have returned, and here we sit together again, like two warriors who have fought battles and won them. Returning to tell each other we fought well. We won battles and lost battles. But we are still standing, victoriously. That's us, Linda. You and me. The two L's. Mighty warriors."

Laura was looking straight at me. And I said, "You want to know something?"

She said, "Sure."

I said, "I know what it means—'let it go by.'"

She said, "Really? You've got to tell me. It's the one thing in my life, Linda, that happened between me and Dad. I felt it really meant something to him, that he was really trying to tell me something, and it was important to him, but I just didn't get it."

When I told her the story of the good man who tended sheep whom I had met so long ago at the building with the cross on top of it, she remembered the story and asked, "Why didn't you ever tell me the part about 'letting it go by'?"

I was not sure why I never included that in the story. I told her that maybe it was meant for this moment. The story refreshed our hearts as we looked at each other and said at the same time, "I let it go by. We let it go by because they knew not what they did."

We just laughed for a moment. Then I finished the story. "Laura, the day of the tea party when I broke Mom's teacup, remember I told her I was going to tell Dad myself? I waited outside for him all day and half the night. That's when I came up with the plan to ask him to let it go by. Just this one time. He was so drunk when he got home. I begged him to let it go by. He pushed me in the bathroom. I knew I was going to get the worst beating of my life. Instead, the belt flew by me. He let it go by, Laura. And it was the most amazing moment. I was forgiven, and even though I didn't understand the full meaning of all that forgiveness engulfed, the impact of that moment forever altered my life. That night changed something in my heart."

Laura got so silent. Then she looked at me and said, "Oh, Linda, Daddy knew about forgiveness. He just told me to let it go by. It must have made him feel something special, something good, maybe even beautiful, when he didn't spank you that night, and Daddy hung on to it. I think he was really trying to figure things out, Linda. There was just so much pain. If only we'd had more time... My heart is overwhelmed. Daddy let it go by, he knew, and he wanted me to let it go by: to forgive such an awful deed, to let it go by. He didn't want me to live in the shame and guilt. Linda, I'm so glad you got to experience that with him. And because of it, I'm a little closer to him too. I love that, Linda. Just let it go by. Don't carry all that baggage. Just let it go by. That is such a special gift that God gave to you, and it's an amazing story. God loves you, Linda."

Laura got silent again. She said she was ready to finish now. I took her hand as she continued. "I have carried so much guilt and shame inside of me, Linda, because of these things. I lived on the streets. I made my living on the streets. I've slept with… I don't know how many men. I have been used and abused all for such a small price, but the price I paid was much higher. I was tormented, living in anguish, full of pain day and night, every waking moment. I've used drugs to forget, but nothing took those memories away. Nothing could make me clean again. There was so much shame, so much self-hatred. I was empty; there was nothing left in me. I was a drug addict, and the drugs were not enough to take away the pain anymore. I wanted to die and was going to kill myself. I had everything ready and set up to do it. I was going to end my life. I had already taken two of the pills when the police busted in the door, and I was arrested and sent to prison again."

She took a deep breath and continued, "On December 19, your birthday, I gave my life to the Lord in complete surrender. My life ended that day, and I was born again that day in 1994. I was truly alive. He cleansed me, Linda. He cleansed me. I never felt so clean, and I was whole, totally forgiven. There was no more shame, no more guilt. It wasn't the same. I mean, I knew all the things that had happened to me, but I didn't feel the shame, the guilt, or even the pain. I didn't see it the same either. It was like I was seeing my life through different eyes, God's eyes, and He was everywhere. I saw so many ways in which He protected us. He protected us. His mighty hand was at work in our lives. Not just to save us but to totally demolish the lies we were taught and believed in. He destroyed those lies in our lives. God destroyed the lie of the spirit life in our family, and He used us to do it. Isn't that amazing?

"Linda, God loves us, and He has watched over us and interceded in so many areas of our lives. He took all my sin, all my shame, and nailed it to the cross. The cross of His Son, the Lord Jesus Christ. He forgave me. He showed me how to become who He called me to be. He went through the process of forgiving with me. I forgave those who used me for their own pleasure.

"I forgave Mom for using me for her own gain. I forgave her for all the lies she told me. I forgave her for trying to make us hate each other. I forgave her for separating us and keeping us separated. I forgave Dad for not being a man, the man God created him to be. I forgave him for never standing up for us, for never standing up to Mom. I forgave him for all the times he unfairly beat me. I forgave him for not protecting me. I forgave him for never talking to me, for never telling me that he loved me. I forgave him, Linda. I forgave him, and I forgave Mom for everything.

"I was there at the house we grew up in after you told Mom about Jesus. In the weeks that followed, I knew she accepted Jesus, and she did repent. I heard her in her room, Linda. I would hear her crying and saying, 'Oh, God, forgive me...' I heard her talk a lot about us, asking God to forgive her for the things she had done to us, and she called those things out. She prayed that we might forgive her. She asked Him to heal our hearts and make us whole. She asked Him to cleanse us of the things she did to us and to set us free from the past. Mostly, she begged Him to take away the hate that was between us to let us love each other like we did when we were little girls."

Laura looked at me with her sad eyes and said, "Dad was so mad at her, Linda. He was so mad at her. She begged him to forgive her. She asked him to buy a Bible. He wouldn't do it. So, I went and got her one. Dad was so mad that he said she was not forgiven until he forgave her, and he didn't.

"I'm glad Mom found her way. I'm glad you came and talked to her. I tried talking to Dad, but he wasn't going to hear it. I went to Mom and Dad's house by myself after the funeral. I wanted you to go with me. I knew not to ask. I wanted you to come with me and help me find that book because I wanted to burn it on the grill in the backyard so that no one would ever be trapped in those lies again."

Laura slapped her knee as she said, "Mom even asked me to do that. I couldn't find it. Maybe it got thrown out or lost. But I'm really confused on that one. Because no one ever touched it. Dad always had it on the dresser, beside the bed, you know."

I looked at her and said, "I did it. I burned that book on that grill and watched it turn to ashes as it burned. I quoted scripture. I felt I had done something of great importance that night. I knew it had no power, none! It was full of lies."

Laura's face—if only I had a camera, I would have taken a picture. I just had to laugh. She asked, "Just why are you laughing?"

I told her, "Because your face is saying, 'Linda, what did you do with that book?' Like you already knew I took it. You were waiting for my confession?"

Laura said, "Well, maybe my face is saying that. But you're just trying to distract me. Let's finish what I came here to do today. And then we can both go home and think about these things. And see the glory of God in our lives because He was there. He was there weaving threads of gold and silver in every area of our lives. I'm almost finished here, Linda, and I want to thank you for allowing me to come visit you that day. And for all the memories that we are creating right here right now. I love you, Linda. I always have Little L. And I always will. And I will see you in heaven."

I said, "Well, don't be planning on going there anytime soon." We laughed.

Laura put her head down, looked at me, and spoke, "I forgive you, too, for lying to me about not being able to sit on the front pew of a church. I wanted to set up there. I wanted to sing. I wanted to walk up to that altar and pray. But that's not what you wanted. You just wanted to sit on the back pew. So no one would know us. So you wouldn't have to face anybody. You wanted to keep it just Jesus, me, and you. Right! That's not life, Linda. That's not even realistic."

Laura pointed her finger at me like Mom used to do and said, "You need to change that. Stop being a coward. Let God's boldness fill you again. He has a calling on your life; He talks to you all the time. He tells you things, but you're not listening. He tells you little things to do, and you don't do them. Maybe you should just start writing down the things He's telling you; then you'll see, and it will all make sense. Somehow, you need to start living life. God's way, not yours. Linda, open your eyes and open your heart. And whatever you do, please tell Scott the truth. And tell him soon. Go home tonight and tell him. Want me to? I will go with you."

I just shook my head, mostly in shame. My heart broke that day. I cried for her, and I cried with her. We cried for our parents. We cried for our losses. We cried for our children. We cried for the two little girls who lived in the house that Satan shook. That day, when we walked out of that little room she rented, we walked out changed and with no more secrets between us. She shared her whole life with me, which I will not put here. That is for my heart, for me to ponder, to remember, and to reflect on. Mostly to learn from and mostly because that's her story.

On Thursday, October 11, 2001, Laura and I had the most amazing day, and the countdown had started: fifteen days until her mobile home would be moved to my land. We were both excited about the upcoming move and the changes ahead of us. On this beautiful day, the past was gone; it was over. Our future was bright.

Laura and I went shopping at one of the stores; Laura found a sixteen-by-twenty-two plastic crate made by Rubbermaid. She wanted to buy it for me.

"What on earth am I going to do with this?" I asked.

"Linda, you have a beautiful way of putting things together. I bet you could take any old box and make something beautiful out of it. You always seem to be so full of ideas and things to do. Linda, you know it's a gift, the things you do—a gift," Laura responded. I just laughed. She said, "Don't laugh, Linda, it's true, and if you can do that with an old box, think of what you could do with this clean, pretty, unused crate."

I just looked at her and said, "Okay, Laura, I do know you by now. Why do you really want me to have this Rubbermaid crate?"

She replied, "For you, honestly, Linda, it's my gift to you because one day, Linda, you will pack a wonderful lunch, bring it to my house, and we will talk, laugh, and cry. We will be little girls again, just little sisters, untouched and undamaged by the world."

As I held up the Rubbermaid crate, I asked her, "What does that have to do with this?"

Laura threw her head back, laughing, and said, "Because, dear little sister, you are going to pack a lunch in this for me on Sunday and bring it to me. We are going to share lunch together, and you get to do all the work."

I just looked at her and smiled. She knew she had won. So, right there, we made plans for our lunch that we would share together on Sunday.

Laura shared the rest of her plan with me, saying, "Then after we have stuffed ourselves, talked until we have nothing left to say, laughed until our sides hurt, and cried until we can cry no more, then you can pack up the mess and take it home with you in the crate. It's a great idea! As a matter of fact, it's brilliant! So, how do you feel about that?"

I said to her the only words I knew, "It's brilliant. What time do you want me at your house on Sunday?"

Laura smiled, satisfied that she had won. "Oh, about eleven, and don't fuss about church. We will have our own little service. We will read a few of our favorite scriptures, pray, and even sing."

I told her, "Okay, I'm ready to do this, but let's make it for eleven thirty."

Laura answered, "Done!"

As I was getting ready to leave, Laura said, "Don't forget—eleven thirty."

I said, "I won't, and it's going to be great; I'm already planning the meal and trying to figure out how it's all going to fit in the crate."

When we hugged each other bye, for a moment, it seemed as if it was a long time ago. I felt as if I had gone back in time, remembering that late October day in 1966, when we came out of the field together, how we had hugged each other after we had spent that afternoon in the field, sharing our hearts. I must have had a look of sadness on my face because Laura said, "Hey, it's okay. I will see you on Sunday."

I stepped forward and just hugged her again. I told her I was thinking about that day when we hid in the field. She told me that it was one of her favorite memories. I said, "It's mine too."

Laura, for a moment, just stared at me. I asked her what on earth she was doing. She said, "I am remembering this moment, and in the future, no matter what happens or how bad it gets, I will think of this moment. I will remember how much you love me and what a precious sister God gave me."

For the first time since she had come looking for me, it seemed like the moment was right, and it was time to tell her what was in my heart. "Laura, I want to thank you for loving me enough to come and find me. I just want you to know how much that means to me. I really missed you; I knew how wrong I had been, and I should have come looking for you."

Laura, with her big, beautiful smile, said, "Linda, I love you. We were very damaged when we were young. But, Linda, we are living miracles, proof that God can and does change lives. Look where we came from and look where we are now. God is amazing, and no matter what happens, you must trust Him. Look how far He has brought you, Linda. You had the courage long ago to set out on your own to look for God." She smiled. "Don't you see, Linda? God honored that heart of yours. With enough faith and passion to believe in Him, you went out into the big world you were so afraid of to find Him. God loves that about you. Linda, you kept your word: you came back and shared your love and knowledge of God with me. We both failed, Linda, not just you. The thing is, God loved me, and at my worst, He found me and showed me His love and mercy. Then, when the time was right, He sent me to find you and all so He could show you what forgiveness really looks like." She hesitated. "Linda, that's what God wants you to understand so you can forgive yourself." She hugged me once again, kissed me on the cheek, and said, "You're right; you should have come looking for me."

That was my beautiful sister, Laura. I'm so thankful for that day. I went over and over it in my mind. What I remember most about that day is how we truly shared our hearts, and we both knew that God indeed loved us. In spite of all we had been through, we did not let hate rule in our hearts. We had learned that the greatest of all was love. Mercy had won over judgment, compassion over unforgiveness, and love over hate. It was a good day and one to remember.

Laura and I had made our lunch date for Sunday morning, October 14, 2001, at eleven thirty. Laura and I talked briefly on the phone on Friday evening. She was looking forward to our little lunch. On Sunday morning, Laura called to make sure I was up. I reminded her I had plenty of time. I got out of bed and started making our lunch. I had a wonderful idea for a salad with all the trimmings. I planned to have albacore tuna with just a touch of mayo. I knew Laura would love it. I made a special iced tea, Laura's favorite: lemon tea with mint. Then, I wanted something special to top it off. Cantaloupe! I would have to go to the store to get one. From that moment, everything changed, and all my plans shifted.

I called Laura at about 10:00 a.m. and explained that I could not make it. We rescheduled for the following Saturday. I told her Sundays were not good for me; she didn't seem disappointed at all. She said, "Look at the bright side; you got to talk to me on a Sunday. That's rare because you go to church and then spend time with your little family."

I said, "You're right; Sundays are family time here, so when you move out here, you will be a part of family time too." We both laughed. The last thing she said was, "I love you. Now, don't you forget that, and we will see each other again soon."

Then we both said goodbye. I thought about what she said for a few moments and then hurried off to church with Scott and Abigail. All through the service, I thought about Laura and how good it was going to be having her live on the same property. No more long drives to see each other. No more long talks on the phone.

On Sunday night, I couldn't sleep. I tossed and turned most of the night. I woke from a bad dream about my dad screaming out from the pits of hell. I went and sat in the living room. For the first time in months, I allowed myself to feel. I had been holding it all in and pushing it down. On the outside, I appeared to be the strong Christian woman I should be, the one my husband thought me to be. I began to think Laura was right. I could not live this lie for the rest of my life.

I prayed and asked God to help me to somehow make things right with Scott. I had determined that when Laura and I had our little lunch, I was going to ask her to come to my house, spend the night, and then talk to Scott to tell him the truth. I thought if everything went well, we would all go to church together on Sunday morning.

All I knew about her job was that she transported cars for dealerships, moving cars from one car lot to another across the state of Texas. She usually went out of town, delivered the car, and returned. She transported for several dealerships and had a steady, regular income, and she liked her job.

Laura had not given me her work schedule for the week. I didn't know when she would leave or what day she would return. I was going to meet her for our lunch in the box on Saturday. I knew we would take care of the final plans to move her home. We would spend most of the day together finalizing all the moving plans and getting everything ready for the move.

Wednesday, October 17, 2001, was a beautiful day. I didn't want to spend the day inside, so that morning, I dressed to work outside, where I spent the day. It was a perfect day to be out in the yard, working in the flower gardens. But my mind was not on the flower gardens. It was a million miles away. All day, I drifted away in my thoughts, and I could not seem to keep my mind on anything.

When Scott pulled up in the driveway, I walked over to his truck. He smiled at me and said, "Hi! How was your day?"

I replied, "It's been a good day. I thought I would clean up the flower gardens today. They needed to be prepared for the fall."

We talked a moment longer, and then I went inside and took a shower. I was sitting on the bed about five thirty, putting on my shoes. My white patent leather shoes. I laughed to myself as I thought, *I really do need to get rid of these shoes. I should have done it years ago. I'm not a little girl anymore. Laura is so right.* The doorbell rang as I laughed again.

I do not believe there was anything in this life that could have prepared me for the events that would follow when I answered the door. It was only by the grace of God that I made it through that evening. It was as if the shock of it put me in a deep trance, and I just floated through everything. In many ways, I believe that is how God took me through the painful, shocking blows, one right after another.

I opened the door; there stood a police officer. He asked, "Are you Linda Prenger?"

I said, "Yes, sir." While thinking to myself, *Whatever Laura has done, I will forgive her, and we will work through this.*

The police officer looked as if he had to force himself to say, "Mrs. Prenger, I am sorry to inform you that your sister, Laura, was found dead at 9:00 a.m. in her home. She had been murdered."

I said, "No, sir, that is not correct. You see, she is out on the road."

He interrupted me, "I am sorry; I am here to inform you that your sister, Laura, was found at 9:00 a.m.. This morning, she was murdered."

Whatever he said after that, I don't remember. I don't remember leaving the house, the drive to the police department. I remembered being at the police department and everything that was said, but I don't remember leaving or the drive home. I just knew I was at home.

It had been a long night, and at eleven thirty, Scott was turning back into our driveway, with me frozen in the front seat beside him. I had not said a word all the way home. The car came to a stop, and he reached over and patted my hand. He said, "We're home, honey. Come on, let's go inside now." I couldn't find my voice, so I just shook my head. Scott said, "Okay, we'll sit here as long as you need to."

The tears began to flow, and I said the words very slowly as if to grasp their true meaning. "Laura is dead. My sister is gone. She was murdered. Who would want to kill Laura and why? She wouldn't hurt anyone."

Scott reached over, put his arms around me, and said, "I know, honey, I know." Scott just sat there holding me and said nothing else. He allowed me those moments to put my thoughts together before going in to face Abigail. I knew how much she loved her aunt, Laura. I knew I would find it next to impossible to look into her eyes and see the pain my little girl was going to experience because of this useless, cruel act of violence.

My thoughts were everywhere. One moment, I was thinking about the last time I saw Laura, and the next minute she was nine or six. I thought of her being murdered, and I would try to push it out. As my mind went over the events of the evening, I could see Laura as a little girl, telling me the story of two little girls in a fire. She would get this amazing look on her face and say, "The flames were everywhere, but I was not afraid because I had to be brave and save my little sister." She would make all these hand motions. *What would I give now to hear her tell me that story just one more time? To see her lifting her hands high, saying, "We are the two L's."*

I sat there in the car as my mind went over the past few hours and the unending questions asked by the police. "Did Laura have a recent breakup with a boyfriend? When was the last time you saw Laura? When was the last time you talked to Laura? Had she mentioned a problem of any kind? The last time you saw her, did she seem distracted in any way? Did you know of any enemies she may have had?" They asked me question after question. Scott did not react to the questions that the police were asking me. He held firmly to my hand and never wavered from the task of getting me through the ordeal.

Then came a shocking blow. "Ms. Prenger, can you be at the medical examiner's office to identify her body at 10:00 a.m.?"

I looked at him and said, "So, there is a chance it may not be her?"

He said, "No, it's her; we could not find any identification anywhere, not a driver's license, nothing. That's why we need you to identify her." The detective gave me his card and the medical examiner's card. The information was sketchy about the murder, leaving me in a state of shock.

I looked across the room at all the people who were untouched by what was going on in my life. My mind was all scrambled and unfocused. There seemed to be an urgency building in the depth of my soul to scream, to tell them, *No! This is all wrong! It's not her! You've made a mistake! Laura is at work... She is—*

My thoughts were interrupted. "You understand what has occurred?"

I looked back at the officer; the tears, at that moment, broke free. "No, I don't understand. I do not understand why anyone would have done those horrible things to my sister. I do not understand such hate or cruelty, and I will never understand why anyone wanted to inflict this kind of pain and anguish upon another human being."

I stood up, and I honestly had no control over my own body. I collapsed and fell back into the chair. I do not know how long I sat there and cried. But when I finally gained control of myself, I said I would identify her body, and after that, I never wanted to think or talk about it again. Those words had come from brokenness and pain so deep that I would never be able to describe it, not then and not now.

The drive home seemed long and aimless. My mind and soul were certainly occupied with thoughts, but I felt numb. I couldn't move. My family was gone. Life suddenly stopped, and it seemed as if God had pressed the pause button to life itself. There I sat, motionless, in the car, as the reality became crystal clear. *What was it they had said? "Stabbed to death." Her body was found by a friend named Tony, who said, "She gave him a key to go in to feed and water her dog on Wednesdays." Where was Little Bit? Nothing was said about her dog.*

Scott disturbed my thoughts, "Linda, it's getting cool. Would you like me to get you a blanket and some hot coffee?"

It was as if, without warning, I had been awakened to the harsh reality. Laura, my beautiful sister, was gone. She was not going to move here. She was not going to get to see her first grandchild. She would never go to church with me. She was gone, they were all gone, and I was all alone. The pain washed in like a wild, raging tide.

There was no one who would ever understand where we came from, our battles, our defeats, or our victories. No one would ever know and understand that once there were two little sisters, those two sisters survived the storms of life, and their names were Laura and Linda. They were the two L's, and against all odds, they had found the strength and faith and walked in the halls of victory. Would we become like grains of sand, our lives washed away with the current? As if we never existed.

How would I ever be able to sift through all of the evil that had been unleashed? How would I ever come to terms with her murder? How was I going to deal with this? At that very moment, I could hear her screaming in my mind. *How would I ever be able to truly understand those final moments of her life? Would I ever know the truth of what happened to her or why?* I crumbled just thinking about the last horrifying moments of her life.

I jumped out of the car. I did not want to sit. I did not want to think. I was just running in circles, screaming. *Why? Why?* I fell to my knees as I screamed, "God, please, please, I beg You, let this be a bad dream! Let me wake up, and this all be over!" I beat the ground with my fists as I was screaming, "Please, God, let me wake up. I want her back; please God, not Laura too!" Scott stood back helpless and watched. All my strength was gone, and I collapsed in a heap on the ground, crying.

I didn't want to think about what had gone so wrong. I wanted my sister; I wanted to tell her I loved her. I wanted to say I was sorry...sorry we had such a horrible childhood. I was sorry for all the things our mom had done to us. I was sorry for the way our father allowed drunks to lay their hands on us and sorry for the way he, himself, treated us. Sorry no one ever told us about God. Mostly, I was sorry that I claimed to know God, and yet I was living a lie. I was afraid of the truth about my past, and just what was it that I was so afraid of? The memories, the pain, the guilt, or was it the shame of a life lived in the shadows of darkness that most would never believe even existed?

There, on the ground, I realized how defeated I was, and now no one else would ever know. Our lives and the story of our lives would be forever lost. I was the only one left now, and it was all buried in my soul.

Then came the earthshaking blow; the truth hit its target, my heart. Without the truth, Laura's life and mine did not exist. All we had lived through and the battlefield on which our lives were lived wouldn't matter. On that same battlefield was a great victory for Christ and the ultimate defeat of Satan. That victory occurred when two girls, who were raised to believe that God did not exist, bowed their heads, repented of their sins, and asked Jesus to save them. Would any of this ever matter? What was God's purpose for our lives? Had we lived in vain? All we had suffered, all our countless ups and downs, would now be forgotten, and our story untold because the story of our lives remained hidden in the dark secret places of my heart.

The greatest tragedy of all was that I no longer knew who I was. *How could I speak what was in my heart?* In the reality of that moment, I wanted to scream, "Oh, God, what have I done?" But there was Scott, and my past was hidden from him. My pain was too deep, my fear too great. *Oh God, would Scott ever under-*

stand? How was I ever going to be able to tell him about the caves of darkness that I had lived in and had come out of?* But here, in this moment, I had to deal with my sister's death. I was overwhelmed as I realized I now had to deal with both her death and my past.

The truth of my life was trickling out like a leaky water pipe that needed to be tightened. I could not stop it. My past was going to pour out and wash away everything I had come to love, the life I had worked so hard to establish. Laura was right; I could not live this lie forever. She knew all along, but I refused to listen. I turned her offer down to stand by me and help me tell Scott. *Why didn't I listen to her?* I felt the chill of the night and started shaking. I told Scott that I was ready to go in. He helped me up. I brushed myself off, and we walked up to the porch. I told him I was hoping Abigail was in bed and that I didn't have to talk to her yet. Then I asked, "How do I look?"

He said, "Honestly, like you have cried all night."

I said, "I have."

We went inside to find Abigail on the couch waiting for us. I could tell right away she had been crying, and the expression on her face told me she wanted to know what had happened and why we left in such a hurry. Abigail has always been bold, blunt, and straight to the point. She said, "Mom, what is wrong? Is Aunt Laura okay? Why did you go with that policeman?"

I told her that her aunt, Laura, was dead and that she had been killed. The police said someone broke in, and Laura must have walked in on the robber. I told her I was very tired and I had to be at the funeral home at eight in the morning to make arrangements to bury my sister. Then I had to go to see the police again. I didn't want to tell her that I had to identify my sister's body. It was all too much for me, and I could not imagine what it was doing to my little girl. I took her to her room and talked to her for a while. I tucked her in and hugged her, cried with her, and told her to get some sleep.

I didn't sleep that night. I had visions of a man hitting Laura on the head and then a fight. Chief Sanders said that she had fought hard. I knew my sister, and I knew he was right. She would have fought, no matter what she was up against. I began to put the pieces together, and in the silence of the night, the words of the police came back in full force. Chief Sanders and the little police officer, whose name I never got, said her body was discovered on Wednesday morning, at 9:00 a.m., by a friend named Tony. He told them Laura had given him a key, so when she was gone, he could check on her dog. She had not called him on Monday to tell him her schedule, as was her routine. He decided that it was possible that she had forgotten to call, so he went to check on the dog and to see if maybe Laura had left him a message on the table. He told the police that when he opened the door, the dog was barking and running around in circles. He called out to the dog, and Little Bit came to him. He picked up Little Bit, and she was covered with blood. Then he noticed blood everywhere. He started going through the house and calling out to Laura. He went into her bedroom and saw her foot sticking out from under a pile of dirty clothes. He called 911 immediately and waited for the police and an ambulance.

The police believed the murder occurred on Wednesday in the early morning hours, on October 17, 2001, around 3:00 a.m. They also believed the killer possibly knew Laura. They had surmised that she had left, leaving the door unlocked. When she returned, the killer was in the middle of the robbery. The intruder may have stood behind the door, waiting for her to enter, and hit her over the head with a glass ball two or three times. They believed that she was severely injured, but she continued to fight. Possibly, three or four different knives were used during the fight. She had been stabbed multiple times and, at some point, had been choked. But none of those things is what killed her.

Laura's body had to be identified. Her body was at the medical examiner's office, where an autopsy was going to be performed. I was told they would know more when they received the autopsy report. The final blow was what they called "the cause of death." The killer didn't just leave Laura to die, even though she was dying from the repeated stabbings and severe head injuries.

Chief Sanders knew there was something else he had to tell me. The evidence showed that the killer walked to the kitchen one last time. They knew this because all the blood in the kitchen had been smeared and distorted during the fight, all except the one set of footprints that led from the bedroom to the kitchen and back again. They believed he picked out the last knife to be used: a large, sharp knife with a serrated edge. He then went back to where she lay dying and cut through her throat, decapitating her. The killer then covered her body with a small blanket and threw dirty clothes over her. Chief Sanders said, "He covered her body. That's how we know he knew her and cared for her in some sick, strange way. If he didn't know her, he would not have covered her body. Killers who don't know the victim rarely cover the body. It doesn't bother them to see the body because they don't care; there is no attachment. The killer was not able to look at your sister's body because he knew her."

Afterwards, the killer stayed in the house for a while. He finished going through her things. The investigators found bloody footprints throughout her home and on the carpet. He took a shower. He washed and dried his clothes before he left. He locked the house up from the outside and took her keys, her wallet, and all her identification. The knife used to cut her throat was found behind the headboard of her bed.

That was it; to the police, it was another homicide case. They just wanted to solve a murder and find a killer. I just wanted my sister back. There were too many things going through my mind. There was so much pain; it was just too much. It was not a dream, and I would not wake up in the morning to a phone call from Laura.

In this life, our time together was over. I knew it was going to take a miracle for me to overcome her death and make it through the raging storm that had descended upon my life. My future was going to be greatly altered because of her death. But that was impossible for me to see at that point in time. I could have never imagined the emotional upheaval I was about to endure. All I knew was my sister was gone; the two "L's" were no more.

CHAPTER 13

The Unexpected

Around three o'clock in the morning, still unable to sleep, I grabbed a blanket and wrapped up in it. I went outside and walked around on the deck for a moment. I curled up in a chair and looked across the vastness of the night sky, the stars, and the moon giving its light to the earth.

It was so very beautiful and peaceful. Even though I did not say it, the thoughts were in my mind. *God created all this. His love for humanity is His signature upon all His creation, and yet He couldn't save my sister. What about that? How am I ever going to understand that?* I thought, *He took Daniel, my mother, my father, and now Laura. I am sorry, but I cannot understand any of this.* I sat there in the stillness and quietness of that moment. There it was, the still, small voice that I knew so well, and yes, I knew it was the Lord. I did not want to hear His words, especially not now, "My love is infinite, and My forgiveness is unmeasurable."

I was honest with the Lord that night. I told Him, "I'm sorry, but I do not understand. Are You asking me to forgive? Please do not ask me to forgive; I cannot do that. I will not do that… Lord, I only want one thing, and that is for whoever murdered my sister to be caught. Take him off the streets before he does something like this again." I asked the Lord for one thing: that the hands of whoever killed my sister, that those same hands would never be given the opportunity to do such a thing again or cause anyone else this much pain.

The next morning, after a very long and sleepless night, I crawled out of bed. The reality hit me again and again as I made coffee, took a shower, dressed, and said goodbye to Scott. I had to do this on my own; it was my choice and the way I wanted it. On my own, I could keep the past where it was. But that meant facing my sister's death alone. It wasn't what I wanted to do; it was what I had to do.

Scott had a very important business meeting that day. He had to at least make an appearance. He owns his own business, and it makes considerable demands on his life and his time. Still, I knew he would have gone with me, but I insisted on going alone. I told him to go on and that I was over the hard part. I said all the right things: "My sister is in heaven. I will go to the funeral home, make the arrangements, and then I'll meet with the police and do what needs to be done. After I am finished, I will come home and take a nap. Honey, I really need to rest. I didn't sleep very well last night. Oh, and about supper..." I laughed and said, "You should bring a pizza home for everyone. I will not be up to cooking."

The laugh was empty and hollow, and Scott knew it. He kept an even tone and said, "Is there anything else that I can pick up?"

I forced a smile and said, "No, I don't think so."

After Scott left, I went to Abigail's room, and she didn't want to go to school. She was very tired from staying up so late.

I gave her a big hug, told her I loved her, and told her to stay home and rest and that she did not have to go back to school for at least a week. The school would understand.

The drive seemed as if it was never going to end, and I was never going to arrive at the funeral home. My thoughts were of Laura. The truth was I found it impossible not to think about Laura alone in the final moments of her life. I could not stop thinking about all she must have endured. I kept going through the whole process of her fighting, begging, and pleading for her life. My mind filled up quickly with unimaginable thoughts of someone stabbing her over and over, just stabbing her without mercy. I could not stop the tears. My soul was in a million pieces, and I was never going to be the same again. There was nothing left for me to do but ask the question that was really in my heart: "Why, God? I don't understand. Please help me. I don't think I can bear this."

The whole process at the funeral home took less than an hour. I knew exactly what I wanted. I wanted the best. It was the last thing I would do for her. I chose a primrose coffin and a beautiful red rose spray. Her coffin had to be covered with a sheer, perfumed silk cloth. I chose her plot under a magnolia tree. I thought she would like that. They said they would call me as soon as her body arrived and would let me know when I could view her body. It all seemed so formal, but inside, I was falling apart while desperately trying to hold on. I told the Lord as I was walking out the door, "Well, I made it through this part." Then, realizing it was the easy part, I added, "In less than thirty minutes, I will have to do the hardest thing I have ever done. I will have to identify my sister's body."

When I arrived at the police station, all the arrangements had been made the night before. I left my car at the police station and rode in a police car to the medical examiner's; my reaction, however, was not part of the plan. I had to be sedated that morning. I collapsed on the floor, screaming, "Oh my God! No! No! Laura! God, no! Why! Get me out of here. Oh, God, what did he do to her!" I don't know what else I was saying. There was no way I could have ever been prepared for that moment or for what I saw. It was a vision that burned into the depths of my soul and would haunt me for years. I begged God to take that vision out of my mind, never to remember it again. My beautiful sister was so bruised with so many wounds. I wanted to put her together; I didn't want anyone to see her like that.

I'll never forget screaming and trying to cover her and make it better, to put her together, but there was nothing for me to do. I remember wanting to run away and, at the same time, trying to hold her. I'm sure they dragged me out, fighting and struggling the whole time. They finally held me down and gave me a shot.

Around four thirty in the afternoon, a police officer picked me up. He took me back to the police station, where I answered more questions. Then, one of the investigators told me that was all and that I had a courageous sister. Then he said, "I am not referring to how hard she fought for her life. I am speaking of how she put her life together after years of drug addiction; she was gainfully employed by an outstanding company. She found a beautiful home, had it financed, and made the payments in a timely manner. She accomplished all of that even though, according to her record, she had five convictions and spent a little over seven years in prison. That does not include jail time of about five years for lesser charges. What you need to think about is she was an overcomer. That is the way you should remember her—as an overcomer."

I thanked him for his kindness and said, "Please do everything you can to find the person who did this evil thing to my beautiful sister. This was a pure act of evil; my mind cannot comprehend it."

They assured me they would do everything in their power to catch and convict the man who murdered Laura.

The next day, October 19, I went to JCPenney and picked out what Laura would be wearing. I purchased a green turtleneck sweater and a straight black skirt. I felt sick to my stomach as I considered clothes that would cover her neck. My heart sank as I recalled them saying if I wanted an open coffin, she would need a turtleneck. I wanted her coffin open so I could see her one last time to say goodbye. I dropped off her clothes at the funeral home that morning around 11:00 a.m., and the staff informed me her body had arrived at 9:00 a.m. They told me that I could come back around 1:00 p.m. for a private viewing. Afterwards, I could proceed to inform family and friends about an evening viewing.

I didn't want to drive back home, and I didn't want to wait around until it was time to see my sister. I didn't want to be there when they rolled Laura into the room in that coffin. I just didn't think I could bear that. I wanted to walk into the room and be able to take my time approaching her. I knew that taking those final steps and preparing my heart for all that I must accept was going to be very hard.

I just needed to get out of there and eat something. I had not eaten in two days. I ended up driving around aimlessly. Before I realized it, I was at the park. Laura and I spent one day there every spring growing up. It was a place I could go where there were memories of her and me together. We played there as little girls. We cried there together on a Sunday afternoon after our first time in church together. We sat on the swings and planned our future. I thought of that look on her face, so determined. I thought about what she said that afternoon. *Why didn't I listen to her back then?* She was worried about what was going to happen and the temptations she would be facing. Instead of encouraging her and praying with her, I laughed it off with words of insignificant meaning. I didn't listen to her plea for understanding, guidance, and help. Laura had even asked me not to give up on her because she might mess up. I was so foolish; I thought we were perfect, incapable of messing up, and I remembered telling her, "We are going to be just fine." I didn't try to understand, and I didn't listen to the words she spoke in truth about her fears. I missed it completely.

I thought about the first time I went to church with Laura. She was so bold, walking right on in and heading for the front. She was not afraid to talk to any of the people there. What of me? I was a coward, sitting in the back of the church, acting like I knew everything when, in fact, I knew nothing about what was really going on. No, I was not bold at all. She was right; I knew nothing about real fellowship, encouraging one another, loving one another, or seating arrangements. When we went to church that Sunday, I made sure she sat on the back pew with me, and I made sure she didn't talk to anyone but me. I told her that I had been going to church since November of 1978, and I still could not even sit in the middle. Of course, I failed to tell her that it was my choice that kept me in the back. It was a lie, all lie's the things I said about church, and she knew it. She never said a word, and she never judged me. When she fell back into drugs, I treated her as if I were superior. I acted as her judge. I condemned her by passing unjust judgment upon her. It was a judgment I was not qualified to make.

A scripture eased into my mind:

Speak not evil one of another, brethren. He that speaketh evil of his brother, and judgeth his brother, speaketh evil of the law, and judgeth the law: but if thou judge the law, thou art not a doer of the law, but a judge. There is one lawgiver, who is able to save and to destroy: who art thou that judgest another?

James 4:11–12

I thought of the times Laura had tried to talk to me about her fear. I had always acted like there was nothing to worry about. Everything was going to be fine. No matter what she said, I had an excuse or gave her a flimsy response. Then, when she fell, I condemned her.

I walked over to the swings, sat down, and repeated the words she had once said in the very spot where I was standing: "We are going to make it. We are going to go to heaven one day." Then I said out loud, "Laura, I don't know why this had to happen to you. I don't even know how I am going to get through all this." I began to cry and call out to God. "Why didn't You stop it from happening? Why didn't You save my sister? Why? You knew it was happening, and You did nothing. She fought hard for her life, and she still died. Where were you?" It was an answer that once again came from Jesus, and it was gentle but strong: "I was with her." I just said, "No, You couldn't have been."

I ran to my car, got in, and could not stop the tears. It must have been about twenty minutes before I stopped crying. I didn't want to think about what had happened or how it had happened. I wanted to get through the funeral. I wanted to bury my sister and go home and sleep. I pulled myself together for about the seventieth time in two days. I started the car and headed for the funeral home.

I arrived at the funeral home at 1:30 p.m. The staff greeted me, and they escorted me to parlor B and told me to take as much time as I needed. I walked in, and they closed the door behind me. I stood there alone in the silence. I tried to move but couldn't. I told myself I didn't belong here and that this was all wrong. Standing there, I asked the Lord once again, "Why? Why did this have to happen? Things had finally turned around for both of us." My thoughts were interrupted with a scripture: "The Lord is nigh unto them that are of a broken heart; and saveth such as be of a contrite spirit" (Psalm 34:18). There in the stillness, I heard Him again, "I am with you." As honest as I could be, speaking from my broken heart, I said, "I love her, Lord, and I truly do not understand. She was my only sister. Deep down inside, the truth is I feel You have taken my family away from me, and I don't understand. Why? Are You still punishing me?"

I was standing in front of her coffin. Everything inside me was screaming, "Don't look!" I knew looking would confirm everything. She had been murdered; she had been beaten and hit on the head with a solid glass ball. She had been choked, and she had been stabbed. At this point, I still didn't know how many times, but I knew it to be so many that the police were still waiting for the count from the autopsy report. My sister was dead. She was gone; I looked down at my beloved sister, Laura. If I could find the words, I do not believe I could write them here. If it has ever been true that time stands still, I believe in that moment, time stood still for me.

I've lived through many trials and challenges. I've walked through the storms of life and been close to death several times. I've suffered many injustices of mankind. I've had wounds that went deep down into my soul. I understood the pain, humiliation, and shame of a life lived in the darkness in a so-called gentlemen's club, where young girls are used and sold for a dollar, and filth from every dark corner pours out like an open sewer. I knew the harsh, cold reality of a life lived in cruelty generated by the two most important people in my life, my parents. I knew the bondage that comes from a life where one is taught that God does not exist, the battles fought on a battlefield I didn't even know existed. Then, I came to terms with the truth that not only does God exist, but He *loves* me. Yet, none of it compared to the broken woman I was at that moment.

The reality of the battle my sister had fought and lost was tearing my soul apart. No matter how much I didn't want to think about that moment in her life, yet it was there in the shadows of my mind, haunting my every thought. I could see her screaming, fighting, begging, and dying. I was incapable of stopping the thoughts flooding my mind. It was a place I had never been. My mind was weaving in and out of thoughts, from our childhood to her final battle, from our last visit to the last time we talked on the phone.

This was my moment of truth. I stood there and looked at her as a thousand memories flooded my mind. There were tears, a deep-down grief that seemed to have a hold on me. I was immovable. I stood there and relived our lives, every moment, every tear, every loss, and every victory. I saw her young and beautiful. I saw her sneaking into my bedroom to tell me a story. I loved watching her tell me stories; she had all kinds of expressions, using her hands to illustrate. "Laura was good at telling stories," I said out loud and then added, "Laura, what I would give to hear you tell me just one more time how you saved me from the fire."

How quickly things can change! Eight days ago, we were laughing and planning a lunch. Now, I was standing in front of a coffin; her life was over. Tomorrow, I would stand in front of her grave. Laura was gone; there was nothing I could do or say that was going to change that. I stood there all alone: no Father, no Mother, no little Daniel, no Sister, no family. They were my family, and now they were all gone. I had no idea what I was going to do when this was all over. I couldn't think past the funeral.

I had gone home and later returned to the funeral home with Scott and Abigail. There were a few people there when we returned. I believe most of them were her neighbors and church friends. All of them were very kind to me. Some of them were friends from her job. There were about ten girls there that she had met in prison. She wrote to them and helped them when they got out. They all shared their stories with me. They all said she had told them about me and what a wonderful sister I was. She had shared the gospel with all of them. They said that was the most important thing to Laura: sharing the gospel and sharing love with everyone she met.

I saw Kenneth, Laura's son, walking out of the room where my sister was. I didn't know her son very well, having met him only a few times. Somehow, I found the courage and strength to walk over to him. We talked briefly. I saw the hurt in his eyes as he said, "Never in my life would I have ever expected this. She was such a loving and caring person. Who would want to do such a thing? My mother suffered all her life due to the things I know your parents did to both of you."

I said, "You're angry right now."

Kenneth stared at me for a moment and said, "Yes, I am, Linda. She was my mother. I was just getting to know her, and I love her. I thought that even though I didn't get to know her while I was growing up, I was going to have her in the best part of my life. She was going to be a grandmother. Did you know that?"

I told him I knew. After I said that, he walked away. I really didn't know very many of the people there. Laura and I, well, we had no family left by the end of 1997. My aunts and uncles had all passed away. Our cousins had died: some from kidney problems, a lot of my cousins were diabetics and died from it because they didn't take care of themselves, not to mention car wrecks, heart attacks, and two, they say, died from accidental overdoses. Several of them had committed suicide, and some just disappeared and were never heard from.

My father said it was the curse. Because the spirit life was not with us anymore, that's what everyone believed in my family, so they all just sat around and waited for death. They all believe they were cursed. Because of what happened in the fall of 1966, the spirit life left the family, and we were all cursed. All of the family would die before the age of seventy because of the curse. I didn't believe it. But they did. I only know because my father told me all of this on the night of his death. He said, "There was none of us left."

What I found to be amazing is that out of thirty-six aunts and uncles, none of them died of natural causes: not one out of thirty-six. I know none of them ever truly recovered from the false beliefs they were taught. It's true; I believe that in the tongue, there is power. The power of life and death. And truly, out of our mouths, flow blessings and curses. What had been spoken over our lives for many years had come to pass. However, I didn't understand because Laura and I did not believe in the spirit life. We had broken that curse. We wanted no part of it. We believed in the Most High God, who gave us the strength and the power to overcome the curse and walk in the newness of life.

It was only by the grace of God that I got through that evening. I stayed until everyone had left, including Laura's son. I went into parlor B and stood there for a few moments. I thought to myself, *Tomorrow, I will be putting her in the ground.* It all seemed so final. The tears began to fall as I said, "Oh, God, how am I going to get through this?" Scott came and told me they were getting ready to lock up. I whispered, "Just one more minute."

The day of the funeral was marked by undercover officers everywhere throughout the funeral home. They believed there was a chance the person who murdered Laura would show up.

I just wanted to bury my sister in peace. People I didn't know told me what a good friend Laura had been to them. Some would tell me about things that she had done to help them. I never really heard half of what was said to me that day. I, too, was looking around for the stranger who just might be the man who murdered Laura. Even on this day, I was not given one moment to bury my sister in peace without the reminders of the events that led me to this point in my life.

At the grave site, I had arranged for bagpipes to be played. The men came up over the hill playing "Amazing Grace," wearing their Scottish outfits. It was absolutely beautiful. The music from the bagpipes could be heard all over the cemetery. They played two more songs, turned, and went across the cemetery and back up the hill playing "Amazing Grace." The casket was lowered into the ground. I wanted to scream as I stood there like a stone statue; unmovable. Visions flashed through my mind. Laura telling me a story, Laura smiling and saying, "I love you, Sis." Then, in a moment, the vision turned to flashes of her as the sheet was pulled back, and the horror of what had been done to her filled my soul. Flashes of her fighting... I whispered, "Laura." As I felt a spear go through my heart, knowing that Laura, my beautiful sister, was gone. I knew that things in my life were never going to be the same. It seemed as if I was numb to all my surroundings. I kept telling myself, "Wake up, just wake up." The funeral was over, and it was time to go home, but I didn't know what "home" would be like for me anymore. In less than three years, I said goodbye to my family, but saying goodbye to Laura was a blow that had devastated my life. Everywhere I looked was a place that seemed to be in ruins.

As I walked away from Laura's grave, I thought about how the unexpected had happened, and it would take years to overcome, if ever. Daniel's death, my mother's death, my father's death, and Laura's death. Grief is surely a valley. It is full of shadows, doubts, darkness, and pain. There are no terms, no conditions, no "when to start or when to stop." It is where memories run like water and regrets fill the soul.

CHAPTER 14

Shattered

I was standing in front of Laura's house six days after her body had been found. The police department made arrangements for me to enter Laura's home. I remember thinking that the worst was over. Now, all I had to do was go into her house, remove her things, and then go home. I was going to spend the day packing her things.

I had made arrangements for two trailers to pick up all of my sister's belongings later that afternoon. Then, I would prepare her house so I could start the long process of selling it. Kenneth wanted nothing to do with her house or any of her belongings. He made it very clear he would not step a foot into her house, nor did he want anything from it.

I was naïve. I had not considered the fact that my sister had been brutally murdered in her home. I had not even considered what I would be walking into. I stood there, listening to the policeman telling me I had to wear a face mask, but my mind was not really grasping what he was saying. The officers would open the windows, but the smell would remain for days. His words faded away as I looked up to her porch and began to reflect on our last visit. I was remembering our laughter as my eyes fell upon the yellow tape surrounding her house. It was clearly marked "crime scene."

I was brought back to reality as the officer handed me a face mask. I was putting it on as he asked, "Are you ready?" I told him yes, but I wasn't really sure I was ready for anything at all. *What am I walking into?* The officers would go in, open the windows, they would give me the keys to her home, and then they would leave. At that time, I would be allowed to go in and begin packing her things. It seemed simple. They had told me that "victims of crime" could clean it all up before I went in. I had declined very hastily, telling them, "No! She was my sister, and I didn't want anyone in her home mulling over her things."

Truthfully, I did not understand what the police officers had tried to tell me. I didn't fully understand their warnings about what I was going to be walking into. They went in with face masks on and opened the windows. They came out, and one of them told me they were sorry and they had done all they could do to prepare me. The police told me that if I found anything that seemed out of the ordinary, I should call right away. They had found only two knives and now believed that at least three more may have been used. They believed the other three knives might be somewhere in the house.

Chief Sanders told me to call if I needed anything else. He said in a stern voice, "There is nothing else we can do here." He asked me one more time, "Are you sure you want to do this alone?" I nodded my head, not really sure of anything at that moment. They got into their cars and drove away. I stood there all alone, with a mask in my hands. I looked at my sister's home. Just eleven days ago, we had been standing on the porch, laughing and talking about me bringing her a lunch in some crazy box. *How strange,* I thought the day we were going to share the lunch. I was standing in front of Laura's grave; instead, I buried her that day. I wanted her back. I wanted all of this to go away. Why did all of this have to happen? I just didn't understand.

I stood there a moment, took a deep breath, and walked up the stairs to Laura's back door. I stopped, took another deep breath, and then walked into her house. Shock! That is the only word that even comes close to describing my reaction when I walked in. I stopped; I could not move. I started gasping for air. I couldn't breathe. I felt like I had walked into an oven. I started sweating as the impact of the violence that took place there hit me in full force. I stood there as the horror sank deep into my soul.

In that fatal moment, my eyes went from one place to another. *Blood!* It was everywhere. I told myself to move, but I couldn't. I told myself to scream, but I couldn't. I just stood there, frozen. It seemed like I stood there for an eternity, and time did not exist. Then I looked down. Her kitchen floor was gone. I stepped back out the door. I was shaking so hard. I was crying and telling myself I could not do this.

I called the police department and told them her floor was gone. Chief Sanders got on the phone and told me I had to calm down. He said he had told me earlier that they had removed the floor and they had taken it for evidence. They didn't want the DNA to be considered contaminated.

Chief Sanders took a deep breath and told me that he was going to send a woman officer over to stay with me for a while.

I told him that would not be necessary. He asked if I was okay. I told him I was shaken a little at first. I told him I was over the shock of it all, and I was ready to go back in and do what needed to be done. Before we hung up, he reminded me and cautioned me that this was something that I did not have to do. There were people who were very organized and skilled, ready and available to clean this up for me. They would be compassionate and sincere in their efforts to clean and make it ready for me. So I would be able to go in. That they would remove everything that had blood on it; once again, I refused. I had made up my mind. Not only was I going to do this, but in my heart, I knew I had to do it.

"Fine," I thought to myself. Who was I fooling? I didn't think that I would ever be fine again. I put the face mask on this time and headed up the stairs. At this point, I stopped and said a prayer. I asked God to help me do what I knew to be impossible. I walked back in, and once again, I was overwhelmed by what I saw, but this time, as I walked into Laura's home, I could smell death and blood. I understood, at that point, that the mask was protecting me from the full force of that odor. It was horrible. I had no idea where I was even going to start. The police had told me that her body had been found in her bedroom. I began to make my way to her bedroom, tears streaming down my face. I could not touch anything; blood seemed to be everywhere. As I entered her bedroom, I screamed, "Oh, God, what happened here?"

Blood had been splattered everywhere. My eyes went from one horror to the next until they rested on the place where her body had been found. There was a large pool of blood, and somehow, I found myself sitting there. I must have sat there for thirty minutes, crying and talking to the Lord. I asked Him to help me and to give me the strength to make it through every aspect of all that Laura's death would bring into my life. I asked Him to forgive me for my foolishness in the beginning, thinking that all I had to do was get through the funeral. I told Him I was blind, and I could not understand why. *Why did He let this happen to my sister?* I asked Him, "Lord, if You love her, how could You let someone do this to her?" The Lord answered, and I have never questioned it since. I knew, without a doubt, that it was the Lord who spoke. I may not have liked the answer, but I knew it was the truth.

"Linda, all mankind has free will. With that free will, choices are made, some evil and some good. I do not interfere with the choices that one makes. However, no matter what choices are made, I can and will work through the results of those choices."

At that point, I finally had the courage to ask the Lord, "What about the man who murdered my sister?" I will admit that I rejected His answer; it was brief and to the point.

"Linda, a tear fell from heaven for sinner and saint alike. You must forgive."

I didn't want to talk anymore. I said, "Oh, God, forgive? Forgive this? How, when in the depth of my soul, I want him dead? I want him to hurt and feel her pain and mine for an eternity. How can I ever forgive this? How could You, a loving God, expect me to forgive this? No, I cannot forgive this; I don't want to! I don't even understand what it is that I am forgiving. I don't even know what he did or why, and *You* want me to forgive him! No! I am sorry, God, but I cannot forgive this!"

I got up off the floor, took a deep breath, and asked the Lord to give me the strength and ability to get this unbelievable mess cleaned up. I had no idea how or where to start. I went back into the kitchen, thinking maybe I could start at the other end of the house. I walked into the living room, and a lady police officer stood there. She was crying. "I'm so sorry; I didn't mean to listen. I just couldn't help but overhear… Forgive me."

A little embarrassed, I said, "No harm done. What are you doing here?"

She told me Chief Sanders sent her so she could assist me and quickly added, "He wants me to stay with you until you're finished here." She hesitated a moment, smiled, and said, "I think he just wanted me here to comfort you during the first few hours of having to face all this. We know how difficult this all must be for you. So, where do you want to start? Have you thought about it yet?"

Where to start just didn't seem to matter. I stood there for a few moments and thought about what I really needed to do. I did not expect to walk into this nightmare, but now it was something I had to face and deal with.

The most gruesome area was her bedroom, but it seemed that there was no area in her home that was not affected in some way. Everything was broken, turned over, or had blood on it, in some cases all three. The carpet would have to be steam cleaned. There was blood all over it and very noticeable bloody footprints as well. I just couldn't comprehend such violence. Where to start just didn't seem to matter.

The lady officer finally broke the silence by saying, "My name is Amy. Maybe you should start in the bedroom that she used for an office." She was pointing to the other end of the house, away from Laura's bedroom. She said, with a little encouragement in her voice, "It has the least amount of damage. You should start easy; it will help prepare you for the tougher stuff."

I thought for a moment and said, "No, I think I will start with Laura's bedroom; I am going to box up anything that does not have blood on it. The things that do, I'm going to trash."

Amy looked a little shocked at my reply. I added, "I have large boxes from U-Haul; two U-Haul trailers will be here this afternoon. The things with blood on them will be thrown on one trailer and taken to a landfill. I don't want to deal with it. You know, all that blood on her things, I would have to wash and...." I stopped, then finished, "It's her blood, my sister's, and I cannot wash her blood off of these things. I will always remember that. I can't, I just can't!"

With great resolve, I told her I was going to do this, and I was going to start in my sister's bedroom. With those words, I headed in the direction of Laura's bedroom. Within moments, I was back in the living room. I had Laura's Bible in my hands and tears streaming down my face. I could not escape the memories flooding my mind, and I could not stop the pain that each memory brought to my soul. I was crushed as I sat down in the middle of the floor. I could no longer stand. I looked around the room and back down at Laura's Bible. The words were fresh from my soul: "Oh, God, I'm overwhelmed; there is so much to do, and everywhere I look, all I can see is the devastation left behind by what took place here. I can hear Laura screaming. Help me to carry this cross; I cannot carry it alone."

The lady officer knelt beside me and said, "Let me read something from her Bible to you." I opened Laura's Bible to the Psalms and handed it to her, and she read it for twenty minutes or so. It was like soothing water to my soul.

When she was finished reading, I reached for the Bible. When I noticed where it was open, I read the inscription: [Note to layout: handwritten font] *"Laura, my prayer is that this will be a great blessing to you. That God will give you wisdom and knowledge in His Word. It is powerful. Hide His Word in your heart. Love always, your sister, Linda, the Little L. Read Ephesians 6:10–18. I dated it October 11, 1993."* She wrote the date she received it: October 14, 1993. It was the Bible that I had sent her when she was in prison.

I looked at Amy and said, "This is so strange. October 11, 2001, was the last day I saw Laura here in this very house, and October 14, 2001, was the last day I talked to her on the phone. This is so hard to understand. I wonder why she wrote this in there. I know it has blood on it; I knew it was her blood. But I had to keep this Bible. I remembered the day I picked this Bible out for her. I wanted to make sure that it had a large print so she could see it. I made sure that it had the golden pages. When I saw this one, I knew it was perfect: Burgundy in color, Scofield Red Letter Edition. I knew she would like it. I prayed about what to write in it, and it took me three days to write. Finally, on October 11, 1993, I finished the inscription, wrapped it up, went to the post office, and mailed it to her. I remember going and seeing her the next week. She went on and on about how beautiful her Bible was and how excited she was when she got it.

"Laura was so amazing, and when she laughed, her laughter could fill a room. I'm glad I was there. My heart is filled with joy that I found this Bible. I will cherish it all the days of my life." There was no hardness or coldness inside of me. There were no tears or fear; it was as if that Bible was placed right there for me. For me to find at the right time, the right moment, my heart was filled with the knowledge and joy that God had indeed answered my prayer. He had given me exactly what I needed to accomplish the task that was before me.

I got up and went back to her bedroom, determined I was going to finish what had to be done. I had mapped out a course. I would start in Laura's bedroom and bathroom, then the kitchen, living room, guest room, office, and hall, and finish with the second bathroom. I would pack and remove everything from each room. I wasn't going to sway from this plan. I was going to be unwavering until I was finished.

I knew I would have to be firm and steady to finish this unpleasant and difficult task that would haunt me for years. I had to do this, and now that I had found her Bible and the joy that flooded my soul because of it, I knew that this was something that not only I had to do but something that God wanted me to do. He was giving me everything I needed to do it. I was not alone. He was going to walk through this with me; I was sure of that. So, no matter how painful it was, I pushed it aside and set out to accomplish the unthinkable.

About every fifteen minutes or so, I had to cry, take a break, or go outside. Around twelve thirty, Officer Amy left and came back with lunch. We went outside to the picnic table to eat and ended up having a very nice talk. She reassured me that she would be staying the rest of the day and would be returning every day until I finished. I told her it was nice having her there but that it wasn't necessary now that the shock had worn off.

I admitted to Amy that all of this was very hard to face all alone. I told her I kept having these thoughts of Laura screaming and begging for her life. I saw an image of a man stabbing her without mercy. I said, "I have tried to stop thinking about it, erase it from my mind, but I can't." Amy helped me that day just by talking to me. I believe that God sent her there just to comfort me during that time. She let me know that I was not going crazy, that my reactions were very normal, but she felt that I should go and talk to someone in the counseling field. I rejected that idea right away. As for this all being normal. There was nothing about this that was normal. I only had a seventh-grade education, but even I was smart enough to know this was not normal. I told myself I would talk to her about that later.

After lunch, I went back in with the face mask on. The stench that filled the air in Laura's house was indescribable. I made my way back to Laura's bedroom and began to pack things again. I had two boxes: one with the word "blood" and one with the word "clean." Once a box was packed, I would carry it outside. I stacked the ones marked "blood" on one side of her house and the ones marked "clean" on the other side.

Laura's bedroom was almost finished; all her clothes from the closet had been removed and sorted. Both of her dressers had been cleaned out, and the clothes had been boxed. All her little knickknacks had been sorted and put in one box or the other. Her bed was stripped, and the bedding was put in the box marked "blood."

The furniture would stay in the house until the men with the trailers came, and they would load it. I didn't want the furniture. It had blood on it, and I didn't want to clean it. I had too many other things I had to deal with, and I just didn't think I could handle the added burden of dealing with bloody furniture. It would be loaded into the trailer that was going to a landfill.

Around three in the afternoon, I began taking things off the walls. I came to the picture I had given Laura when she came to find me in March. I stood there, just letting that memory flood my mind. I reached up to take the painting, resolving that I was going to keep it. I saw the blood; it was splattered all the way across the bottom of the picture. I knew it would always be the tainted. It was a memory I could not erase. The blood could be removed, but nothing could wash it from my memory. I said it louder than I intended, "No! Not on this. Why does this one precious thing have to have her blood on it?"

Amy came into the room to see what was wrong. I told her everything was okay. She turned and left the room. I reached up, not looking at the blood, and was removing it when a bloody knife fell from behind the picture! I started screaming, and Amy came running. When she entered the room and realized what had happened and what I had discovered, she called for assistance. Then she came to where I was and put her arms around me. She took me out of the house as she whispered, "It's going to be okay. It's all going to be okay, sweetie."

It was more than an hour before I could go back inside the house. The moving trailers had arrived, along with two older men and a young man about twenty. I introduced myself, and the man in charge said, "I'm Tom; this is George," pointing to the other man.

I asked, "And who is the young man? It would be nice to know everyone's name."

Tom said, "Oh, that's my son, Daniel. He came along to help us out."

I said, "Hi, Daniel! It's nice to meet you." Turning to Tom, I asked, "You do know what happened here? I explained it to you on the phone. It's really a mess in there, and I'm not sure you would want your son in there. You have to wear a face mask, and blood is just about everywhere." Tears were freely falling from my eyes. "I don't know what happened to my sister in there, but—"

Daniel interrupted, "Ms., I mean no disrespect, but my dad asked me to come. I just got back from Iraq. I'm in the US Army. I've seen a lot of things, and my dad felt I would be better qualified to help if things got touchy. And I'm older than I look."

I wiped my tears from my face. "It's been a long day. Thank you, Daniel, for coming."

People in the neighborhood were coming home from work. A man came up to me and said he had seen me at the funeral. He asked how I was doing and how I was holding up, considering what I had to deal with inside the house. He said he didn't know how I was doing it. I looked at him and said, "I'm not able to do any of this. I have to pray and pray. I fall apart every time I find something that was special between us. Deep down, I know it is only by the grace of God that I am standing here." Then he said he had something to show me. He felt it would bring some joy to my heart.

He left and came back with Little Bit, my sister's dog. God knew I needed that moment. I called out to Little Bit and reached out for her, and she jumped right into my arms. It really put a song in my heart. I patted her and played with her, smiling for the first time in days. The man smiled at me and said, "I guess you will be taking her with you, then."

I smiled back at him and said, "Yes, I have every intention of keeping her dog."

He then shared how his children had fallen in love with Little Bit and asked me if I would allow him to keep the dog until I finished cleaning the house. Agreeing to his request, I told him I planned on having the house cleaned and empty by Friday afternoon. I had to come back on Saturday to go over everything with the realtor. I could take Little Bit on either day. It was agreed that he would keep Little Bit until then. I knew they would miss her, but I wanted my sister's dog. My sister really loved Little Bit. I remember one of the police officers saying that Little Bit may have witnessed Laura's murder. I wondered why the murderer had not killed Laura's dog.

When the police were finished in the house, I was told I could go back in and to call if I found anything else and to be sure not to touch it. Officer Amy told me bye and said she would see me the next morning around nine o'clock.

Chief Sanders took me to the side and said that if I noticed anyone hanging around watching, I should call him right away and not try to second guess. I was shocked. I asked him, "Do you think that the person who murdered Laura will come back? Why?"

He told me that, at this point, they were not taking any chances, and he added, "Sometimes, murderers will return to the crime scene."

After the police officers left, I went back into the house with the movers. I pointed out all the furniture that I wanted removed. I requested that the furniture from Laura's bedroom be taken out first. Her room was all packed, and most everything was off the walls. My plan was to work on her bathroom while they removed the furniture from her bedroom. About an hour later, the only thing left in her bedroom was the bed. I walked in as they were getting ready to move it. I noticed Daniel was pointing to something, saying, "Dad, you should take a look under the bed before just flipping it over due to the trail of blood there."

Tom lifted the bed up and looked under it. He told me it would be best if I left the room while they moved the bed out. I became a little upset at that moment. It wasn't anger, but my words were bitterly firm. I informed Tom that I had seen the worst of the worst. At this point, I did not think that there was anything that would shock me or hurt me any more than what I had already experienced. From identifying my sister's body to walking into her house that very morning, I had already dealt with every kind of fearful, devastating, gruesome, and unimaginable thing, and I was sure I could handle what was under the bed. I informed them that I was not a child and that they should not treat me as such. I told them they were a little late to protect me from any of the things that had gone so wrong there.

I remained in the bedroom, and the bed was flipped. There was a lot of blood under it, as if Laura, at one point, may have crawled under there to hide or get away. There were a few items under her bed: a storage box containing shoes, another storage box that I had no idea what was in it, seemed like some kind of books, construction paper, not for sure, and there was also an old shoebox. It was getting late, and I didn't have time to sort through these items. I asked Daniel to put the old shoebox on a shelf in Laura's closet. It didn't matter what was in it at that moment; all that mattered was that it didn't have blood on it. One storage box had blood on it. Daniel put the shoebox in the closet. I put the storage box with the books and paper in the living room. I would deal with it first thing in the morning. The box with the shoes in it, Daniel put into the box marked "blood." We were finished for the day; I closed the windows and locked the doors.

I stood outside and talked to Tom, George, and Daniel about what I wanted to do. They would take my sister's things to a landfill. The rest was taken to a storage building I had rented, where my parents' things were. I knew that the day would come when I would have to deal with all of it.

The next morning, at six, I returned to Laura's house. I went to work right away. By the time Amy arrived at 9:00, I was almost finished with Laura's bedroom and bathroom. We talked for a few moments, and I told her what I had done, the plans I had made for the day, and what I wanted to accomplish. Then I went back to work, and I continued working until I had completed Laura's bedroom and bathroom. It was about ten thirty; I wanted to take a break and have a cup of coffee before I started working in the kitchen. I brought my own coffee pot, coffee cups, and all the fixings for a good cup of coffee so we could enjoy a cup without having to use any of Laura's things. I just couldn't think about it, not even for a second.

I covered the couch with four blankets I had purchased and was glad that Daniel had talked me into leaving the couch so I could have a place to sit and rest when needed. Now that the couch was covered, I was able to sit on it, but still in the back of my mind was the thought that Laura's blood was there below the blankets. It was hard no matter which way I turned or what I did. Every moment, I was forced to see blood, her blood, and deal with thoughts that shattered the remaining fragments of my heart.

As we sat on the couch, talking, I noticed the storage box containing the pictures. I just reached over and opened it. On top was a scrapbook. I picked it up and opened it to the first page.

My heart skipped a beat, I am sure of it. In big block letters was written: *"For my sister, Linda, my hero!"*

I remembered her telling me that she was making me something very special. She said it was to remind me of who we were and where we came from. I thought, *Oh my God, this must be it.*

I turned to the next page, and there they were: the pictures of us when we were little! The two she had saved from the fire so long ago.

The two she saved from the fire so long ago.

The lettering was all done in gold. The words were bold and strong, piercing my heart: "We are the two L's, and I love you, Little Sis." I repeated the words over and over; at last, I hung my head and said, "No, Laura, we are no longer the two L's."

I sat there, once again overwhelmed by all the events of days gone by, her death, and a scrapbook she would never finish. Sitting there, I held the scrapbook close and deemed it precious. There was nothing else in the scrapbook, just those two pictures.

I asked Officer Amy for a few moments alone. Once alone, I closed my eyes and relived Laura telling me the story of the day our house burned down. A thought that was so subtle I would not have captured it had I not been looking at the two pictures. Those were the only two pictures that had ever been professionally taken of Laura and me. My mother was not in the habit of having pictures of us taken. Our house was full of professional pictures of her. All beautifully displayed throughout the house. I believe it was a second thought to take those pictures of us. Something without her knowledge that the Lord had laid upon her heart to do. Perhaps we just happened to be with her that day, and she thought it to be a good idea. Maybe the gentleman taking the picture made a comment about how cute we were and that she should take our picture as well. Whatever the reason, she did. I know with all my heart that it was the Lord who made sure we had those pictures. They were for Laura and me. Something that we would always treasure. Laura had carried those pictures with her for years and years, always protecting them, always making sure that they were cared for. She had done this for me. I heard the small, still voice that spoke to me that day loud and clear: "My child, the pictures were always yours."

Maybe Laura had always known this too. I remembered; it just blew in my mind like a gentle breeze: Laura and I were sitting on the side of the pool. I mentioned the pictures that day, and she got this expression on her face. I thought it was because she had lost them or something had happened to them, and she felt bad about it. It was like she didn't really want to talk about the pictures. A few days later, Laura told me she was going to be making me something very special and that I would get it soon. She was going to start it, but I had to finish it. *Well*, I thought, *that proves she could be sly*. Well, this scrapbook certainly surprised me. How precious it is, and how precious those two pictures are. The innocence in those little girls' eyes. The innocence that was stolen.

I reflected back on those two pictures. It seems as if it's a vague memory from so long ago. The man was ready to take my picture and told me to smile. I was looking at Laura. She made a funny face, and I was happy in my heart, and I had the biggest smile. *Snap*. I remember Laura telling me some things about the day we had the pictures taken. She said she was after me, and she was staring at me. I made a silly face at her too. *Snap*. The picture was taken. We were both looking at each other when they were taken. *How special is that? No wonder we never forgot!* I thanked God that the scrapbook didn't have blood on it. I wrapped it carefully in some special paper I brought for protecting things; I wanted to make sure it didn't get damaged. I took it outside and placed it in the front seat of my car.

Every day that week, in the early morning hours between six and seven, I arrived at Laura's house. There were tears, and deep down, I knew there would always be moments of tears and feelings of complete loss in a world that made no sense to me at all. I worked until the trailer and the movers arrived.

After that, I would visit and play with Little Bit. The family who was taking care of her lived across the street from Laura. A Christian family was the first in a long time that I had been around for any length of time. The children had watched Laura many times playing with Little Bit outside; she always let them join in on the fun.

One of the little boys, who I guessed to be about six, told me that Laura was his girlfriend and he wanted to marry her when he grew up. But his daddy told him she was so special that God needed her in heaven. The little boy made sure he had my attention and said, "You know what Laura told me? I was her very special friend." His mother spoke up and told me how Laura had made them a cake one day. The strange part was that she said it was their anniversary, and Laura didn't really know them at the time.

Several of the neighbors came to visit with me during the week, and they all shared a special story of how Laura had reached out to them in some way. They shared how she really affected the whole neighborhood. Laura was loved by all those who lived in the mobile home park. She helped many of the families in one way or another: babysitting, going to the store for the elderly, always baking cakes, cookies, and pies, and taking them to different families in the neighborhood. It grieved them that this happened to such a wonderful person. For a moment, I thought that not only was she a wonderful person, but Laura was also beautiful; I don't know if she ever knew that. I like to think that she did.

By Thursday afternoon, Laura's house was empty, and it was time to start cleaning the walls, but by this time, I realized it was going to take another week. The walls had to be cleaned before the carpet. I didn't want to have the carpet cleaned only to mess it up by dripping bloody water on it. I purchased several different household cleaning products to start the long process of washing the blood off the walls throughout the house.

I knew it was going to be a long, difficult chore. There was so much cleaning left to do. So, since I wasn't going to be finished before Friday afternoon, I decided I wouldn't go to Laura's house that Friday; instead, I would take a break. I had to meet with the insurance company at two o'clock on Friday afternoon. Laura had an insurance policy that was paying the house off, and the house had been left to me. I rested most of Friday; I had to force myself to go to the insurance company.

I returned home late Friday afternoon and, for the first time since October 17, ate dinner with my family. I even ate dessert. The next morning, I was surprised when I woke up after eleven. Everyone agreed to let me sleep; I was resting for the first time in two weeks. I woke up feeling really refreshed. Then it hit me that I had to go to Laura's house that day to meet with the realtor. I had planned to get to Laura's house early to see what I could do about the walls. But now I only had just enough time to get ready and meet the realtor there at 1:00 p.m. I arrived fifteen minutes before the realtor. The house still had a horrible smell because of the blood on the carpet. I looked at the walls. It was too late to do anything about them. I had taken the time to stop at a store to pick up two blankets and a sheet. I covered the spot where Laura's body had been found.

When the realtor arrived, I greeted her at the door. She didn't say anything at first, and then she just blurted out, "My God, child, what happened here? Someone get killed? Looks like a blood bath!"

I was stunned by her statements. Now, I have never been one who stands up for myself, or for anyone, for that matter. I like not being noticed, and I am not one to make a big deal out of anything, but something just rose up inside of me as it had several times in the past.

That day, I found out I could be a little on the bold side. I was not a total coward after all. I looked at her and said very firmly, "You, lady, just might be the rudest person I have ever met. As for your remarks, my sister *was* murdered here two weeks ago. I have labored, cleaning blood off her things and removing them from this house. Now, I may not be very smart, nor do I have a good education, but it takes neither to have compassion nor to understand, upon entering this house, that a tragedy occurred here. I want you to leave. Like now! Get out!"

She tried to make amends, but I just wanted her to leave, to be gone.

On Monday morning, I was back at Laura's to finish cleaning. I filled my bucket with warm water and added some Pine-Sol. I bought two dozen cloth diapers. When I was growing up, we always used them to clean with. Diapers weigh less than any towel or cloth; they're easy to handle, easy to wring out, inexpensive, and last a long time. I knew they would get the job done. I decided I would clean the walls in the same order I did the packing. I picked up the bucket and went to Laura's bedroom.

Twenty minutes later, I was in the bathroom, throwing up. There are absolutely no words to express what it did to me as a person, in the depth of my soul, to wash my sister's blood off the walls of her home. Bucket after bucket of clean water turned brownish red, my hands the same color as in the bucket from washing, rinsing, and wringing the blood out, not to mention the smell. On Friday afternoon, I emptied the last bucket of water and rinsed out the bucket and the cloths. I picked up the blanket and sheet from Laura's bedroom floor, wadded them up, put them in the bucket, and took them out to the trash. I tore down the crime scene tape and put it in the trash. I sat the ladder outside the house for her neighbor to pick up.

The following week, the new floor in the kitchen finished by Tuesday morning. Then, the work on the carpet started and was finished on Friday afternoon. The carpet was ripped out after the cleaners explained that the smell of the blood from under the carpet would not go away, the wood could not be washed clean, and that part of the floor should be replaced. All of Laura's bedroom floor would be replaced. During the time the floor and the new carpet were being laid, I rested at home. On Friday, I met with the gentleman in charge of the job and paid him. Then, I went to eat at the place where Laura and I ate the day we planned our little lunch in a box. Memories lined with regrets and moments filled with wonder kept slipping into my mind.

After I ate, I went to the police station to thank Officer Amy. I had gotten her a small gift, and I wanted her to know I would be at Laura's house the following Thursday for the last time. I asked if she would like to stop by to see how it turned out since she had been there the first week of cleaning.

She said, "Yes, but it will have to be on my lunch break."

I responded, "That will be fine."

She replied, "I just want to be Amy, your friend, on that day. Never mind, Linda, I'm going to take the afternoon off and spend it with you."

I agreed that was a good idea. We planned to meet at Laura's house at twelve thirty the following Thursday. It had only been five weeks since Laura's murder, but to me, it seemed as if I had lived two lifetimes in those five weeks.

The following week, on Thursday, I pulled up in front of my sister's house. I walked up to the back door and stood there for a moment. Flashes of all that I had been through over the last month filled my soul in sudden, brief bursts, each one building on the other until the picture was complete. A collision between a murderer and my sister happened; nothing was going to change it, and nothing was ever going to erase it from my memory.

I opened the door and walked into Laura's home, now clean, without a trace of blood anywhere. I looked around the room and thought, *This was her home, her place of refuge, peace, and comfort. She had hopes and dreams when she bought this house, and they died right here with her.* Now, it was all a part of my life, and these memories would take a lifetime to understand. It even seemed crazy to try to understand the senseless, brutal murder of my beautiful sister, Laura.

My thoughts were interrupted by Officer Amy, who had spent that first week with me and helped me get through many emotional outbursts. Our journey together was about to end. I would never forget her kindness to me, nor would she forget the painful ordeal she watched me go through. She told me it was a life-changing experience for her. Amy looked around the room, commenting on what a good job I had done. She asked if it was all right to go into Laura's room. I said, "Go ahead. I'm going to the bathroom." Pointing to the guest bathroom, I added, "Too much coffee this morning."

When I came out, Amy was standing there holding a shoebox. She said, "I think you forgot something. I found it on the top shelf in Laura's closet."

I replied, "I wonder how I overlooked it all this time. I know I have checked and rechecked that closet a hundred times."

She responded, "It was pushed back in the corner on the top shelf; that's the reason you overlooked it." She laughed and said, "You're short, and I am tall."

I said, "Well, it's a good thing you're tall then. I didn't want to leave anything in the house. I wanted to leave it perfect, like the way Laura first saw it. Would you mind taking it back to the station and putting it in the trash? I just don't want to deal with anything today."

Amy said, "I don't think it's trash. It has your name on it."

I looked at it and said, "That's Laura's handwriting."

Amy said, "There is something in it, Linda."

I remembered it and said, "I completely forgot about that shoebox. When George and Tom flipped Laura's bed over that first day, this shoebox was under it. It didn't have blood on it. Daniel put it on a shelf in the closet for me; I just forgot about it."

Taking it from her hands for the first time, I noticed that not only was my name on it but that it was beautifully decorated. I said, "I wonder what it is." She told me to open it and find out. I slowly lifted the lid, and for a moment, the world stopped. I took a deep breath.

Amy said, "Well, what is it? Tell me. I cannot take the suspense."

I looked at her and back into the box as the words rolled out, "It's her letters, the ones she wrote to me when she was in prison. I was angry with her. I refused them, and she just kept sending them. She sent one every week for two years, and I never read any of them; I sent them back to her. I wouldn't even write to her." I began weeping and grieving, holding on to the box. "Oh, God, I'm so sorry for what I did… I don't know if I can read these. It's going to hurt so much."

Never in all my life did I want to go back in time, more than at that moment, to read her letters when she was alive; instead, I found out what those letters said after her tragic death. Amy said she would stay there with me. We sat down on the floor; Laura had taken the time to put them all in order. She had also written a letter on top in a plain white envelope with the words: "Read first." I asked Amy to read it.

> *My dearest sister, Linda,*
> *I want you to know that I love you, first and foremost. I do not blame you for anything. I know that you were angry with me for such a long time, but I want you to know that is what made me see myself, and it put a hunger and a desire in me to want to change. I knew that only God could do that because you told me so (it was the one thing that stuck). I know it is crazy that I kept all these letters, but I*

thought someday you might like to have them and read them. I know that I have never told you, and almost everyone has always said that I was the pretty one, but I want you to know that you are absolutely beautiful to me. I have prayed that you come out of your shell, and stop hiding, because I know that you were destined to do extraordinary things.
Love forever.
Your sister, Laura!

Letter after letter was read. All the changes that Laura went through while she was in prison were amazing. There were letters full of scriptures, teaching me and telling me to get off the back pew. God had more than that for me. Amy read half the letters, it was getting late, and she had to go.

The truth poured into my heart: God brought me back here for the letters. He had saved the best for last, and now it was time for me to go. My job here was done, and it was time for me to go home. I went across the street and asked for Little Bit. After a tearful goodbye, I got into my car with Little Bit and headed home. I will never forget the last four weeks; they were very painful. Now it was finally time to go home, but in my soul, I knew it would take an eternity to understand, or would that ever be possible?

I would like to share some of Laura's letters here.

This letter is the first one Laura sent to me from prison:

Hi, Little Sis. I hope you are doing well and that you will take the time to read this letter. I know that you have been angry at me for a long time, but I am asking you to please let it go. I do know how wrong I was that day when I chose the drugs over you, but more important, I could not see how much that hurt you, until now. I cannot expect you to understand the effect that drugs have on a person, and the battles that are fought and lost every day. It truly does take the power of God to pull one out of such a pit. I have sat in great darkness, Linda, but even there His light shined, and brought hope and healing to my lost and dying soul. I can only tell you that I am so very sorry for the way I treated you, how I used you so many times; yes, I lied to you, and stole from you. I know that I do not deserve your forgiveness, but I ask you to forgive me.

I have been here for almost two months now. God blessed me by giving me a cellmate who has given her life to Christ, and she has been sharing a lot of things with me. She has been studying the Bible for almost five years now, and a lot of women come to her for prayer and with questions. I told her about you, and she said that I needed to ask your forgiveness. She showed me many scriptures, and we have prayed every night for you. I do love you, and I am so sorry for all the pain that I caused you. I hope you will forgive me. This is my first step to make things right. I love you, Linda, and I will keep praying for you.

Remember the big "L" and the little "L."

Love always, Laura.

This letter reveals Laura's love for the Lord and her spirit of hope:

> My dearest sister, Linda, God is so good; today I got a Bible. The one you gave me is at Mom's in some of the stuff I left there. Mom knows it is in the house, and Dad would be so mad at me; you know how it is with him. I have asked Mom to get it and send it to me for over three months, but she will not touch it. She thinks all kinds of crazy things. I have also asked you to send it to me just in case you ever open one of my letters and not send it back to me. I cry and cry every time I see one returned, but God tells me to not give up, and He just says to love you and keep writing, so here's another letter that I fear I will only get back. But I wanted to tell someone about my Bible that I got, and you are the only one I know out there who believes in God. I love it, and it has big letters so I can see; most of the ones in here have small print, and I do mean small.
>
> My cellmate, Nancy, which I have to tell you, her name in every letter now, just in case you open and read it. Nancy got with some of the other women here and they all prayed and each of them wrote their families and asked for a Bible. Out of ten women, one was sent, and I am thanking God. It is very hard to get a good Bible in here, one that is big so you can see the words. I feel so very blessed, I work hard here, and I look forward to getting to my cell and reading my Bible and praying.

> *I would like to mention to you that you are wrong about all this church stuff. Have you ever paid attention to what they say about fellowship? I don't know where you got the front-row thing, but Linda, you need fellowship. Have you read 1 John? Well, you need to! Not that I have the right to preach to you. I pray you will forgive me, as I have asked in all the letters, but you have been sending them back. I am still praying you will open just one letter I send and know that I am seeking your forgiveness. I miss you and hope that someday we can at least be friends, but I have placed that in the hands of God. I feel in my heart that God told me you would read my letters someday, so I will keep writing. I love you, Sis.*
>
> *Love always, Laura.*
>
> *Please forgive me.*

This one letter touches my heart no matter how many times I read it:

> *Linda, you are my one and only sister. I have cried about the distance between us for over a year. I have begged God to touch your heart and change it, to somehow get you into a church. I mean, where you actually go in, sing, meet people, get to know some of your sisters in Christ, have a lunch with them, and pray with other believers. You need to do that; you would be so great serving others. Linda, I don't care how hard you try to be like a stone statue, I know that you are full of compassion. I know you, Linda,*

I watched you grow up, and I saw your heart many times. I know that if you would get in a church, and not on the back pew, you would understand that Jesus wants us to love one another and help each other. I don't know what is wrong with you. How can you keep turning your heart away from your sister, who has sent, you as of last week, fifty-seven letters, all returned back to me? Many times, I say I just can't take it anymore it hurts too bad to send letters for them to be returned. But then the Lord touches my heart and speaks so gently to continue to write to you that you will need them someday. I said, "Of course she will. She will be so old and gray and with nothing else to do. Then she'll just have an old shoebox full of letters from me. I can see it all now Linda will finally take the time to read them. Well, I hope it's not too late, Lord. And if it is, I guess I'm going to ask You to comfort her heart. If she ever finds these letters and I'm not around, let her know that she was loved and cared for. And beautiful in my eyes." That's what I tell Him.

I love you, Linda, but while you spend your time sending my letters back and justifying your un-forgiveness and bitterness towards me, time is wasting. How much time do you want to waste, two years, five years, ten years, twenty years, till one of us dies? Then what? Live in the pain and shadow of regret? Just what do you plan on saying to God about this when you stand before Him? I have learned that time is a gift from God. Don't waste it, Linda; use it for better purposes than sitting around being angry and bitter towards me.

I love you, Sis, and I have begged God to somehow touch your heart and somehow, some way you will open this letter and read it. I have asked God to bless your heart with these words, and for you to see that your need to be loved can only be filled when you stop sitting around saying, "I have never been loved, if only dad and mom would love me." Stop it, Linda! What if something happens to them? Do you plan on crawling in a hole and do what? Give up? Linda, you must take those white shoes off. You are not a little girl anymore and stop trying to be Mom's little girl. You want to be loved, well, there are a lot of people out in the world that need love, so why don't you just go out and start loving them? Like your neighbors. I bet you don't know one of them. Well, bake a cake and take it to them. When you pour your love into others, Linda, you will find what you are longing for, and you will be filled. Get in a church and start loving. I am praying God opens an amazing door for you, even if He has to send an angel to lead you there and show you the door. I only say that because you are being stubborn and it's breaking my heart.

I have written on the outside for you to please forgive me, and that I love you. I hope you see it and open this letter and read it. No matter what, I love you, and I will keep trying. I pray you get into a church where you can learn what you are reading. It's more than words, Linda. I believe that God has a special place *for you and a work that only you can do, but you are too busy being bitter at me over something that happened years ago. Let it go, Linda, before it destroys you. I love you; please forgive me. I don't want to come home with this between us.*

I am still the big "L," and you are acting just like a little "L."

Your sister, Laura.

I love you, Linda, and just like me, I know you want to be loved!

This is the last letter from Laura:

My dearest sister, this will be the last letter that I shall write to you, not because I have given up, but because I am coming home. I know that it will be returned, but I didn't want to miss one week while I am here. I don't want you to think I gave up, and maybe, just maybe, this will be the letter you open.

I want you to know I love you, and I know that you have been hurt by me, and you have also been greatly hurt by our parents, just like I was. I think that when I did that to you and said "the drugs," that it broke something inside of you. I just want you to know, I love you, and I will continue to pray for you, and one day maybe we will find our way back to each other, and you will forgive me for the deep pain that I caused you. Maybe we will laugh again, and have a lunch, and talk. I would love to just once watch the sunrise with you, my beloved sister. Linda, more than anything, I pray that you will find a way to forgive not just me but yourself and our parents. As Christians, we must practice forgiveness.

I am not afraid of getting out this time. I know who I am in Christ, and I know that I have been given the gift of eternal life, and I want to share that gift with others. I know the Word now, and I am ready to share the gospel with our parents. I hope we can still do that together. Please forgive me, Linda. That would be the best homecoming I could ever have. I would be so blessed to have you be at Mom's when I get there, and have you put your arms around me and say, "Laura, I forgive you." Oh, what a joy would flood my soul.

As in all my letters, I ask you to please forgive me. Love,

your sister, Laura, who is coming home!

I do realize how painful it would have been for me to have read these letters if there had been the issue of unforgiveness between us. I thank God every day that Laura came to find me on that beautiful day in March of 2001.

I thought I had endured every kind of pain, everything that a person could ever possibly go through, until the day the doorbell rung and an officer said, "Mrs. Linda Prenger, I am so sorry to inform you that your sister's body was found this morning at 9:00 a.m. at her residence by a friend." With much prayer, I came to the decision not to include the pictures from the murder scene. They were too graphic in nature, and the few that weren't would have taken away from the reality of the murder scene. I believed that it was best to trust in God, who gave me the ability to live through all of this and write my story, giving me the wisdom to describe it in words that would penetrate the hearts of those who read this book.

I did my best here to describe not just the crime scene but to open my heart and describe how unbearable and unbelievable it was to walk through the blood of someone who is a part of your life and family, someone you love so much and so deeply.

As I look back, it's hard to believe that I even made it through the whole process of cleaning Laura's home. Every day, it was the crushing of my heart, and yet in the midst of it, God provided things for me to find and to treasure, to remember, to hold on to: her Bible, the two photos, and her letters. God granted me the privilege of walking away with those things not from the crime scene but from a life lived together, our precious memories.

CHAPTER 15

Exposed

In January of 2002, I received a call from Chief Sanders. He wanted me to come in and talk to him. Scott wasn't working that day and insisted on taking me. We were in Chief Sander's office, sitting in front of his desk, my face like a stone as I sat there motionless. That was the day I had to face the shadows of the past. I wanted to run out the door as shame filled my heart. The leaky pipe was going to bust. I knew it; there was no denying it. All of the past was going to come gushing out. I was going to be exposed. My life. My past. My guilt. My shame.

Chief Sanders asked why I had withheld the fact that Laura and I had both been associated with Seth, a certain man, for several years. Did I know that Laura and Seth were arrested together in November of 1994? Did I know that he was released from prison two weeks before Laura was murdered? He wanted to know if there was some kind of vendetta that this man would have against Laura. Chief Sanders's words were strong and blunt, "Would he have a score to settle with you?"

I knew it was a question I had to answer, and the truth about my life was going to be spilled out in front of Scott. I began explaining, "I worked in a gentlemen's club when I was very young. My mother forced me to; she gave me no choice. Sir, I was only fourteen. She did not care about me. She put me to work, making money for her; the law said I could work there but not drink. The law has since changed, but it was too late for me. Later, I married and had a daughter, Jasmine. After a tragic accident, my daughter was taken away from me by my parents. I left and moved around for five years, and then in 1978, I moved to Tyler, Texas. During the time I lived there, I came to know the Lord as my Savior. I made Tyler my home for the next seven years. During that time, I never saw Jasmine. There was emotional damage in her life from an array of events, as was in Laura's life and mine."

I paused to collect my thoughts as the events unfolded. "By the time I learned Jasmine was working in a gentlemen's club, she had already gone from waitressing to dancing. There were no laws to protect me when I was young, and there weren't any laws to protect her. She had her guardian's permission, and that was all she needed at the age of seventeen. The only law we were told was no drinking for a minor."

I felt as if my life was closing in on me, and I wanted to run out of there, but I continued, "My mom knew where Jasmine was but would not tell me. I looked for her several times at different clubs. The gentlemen's clubs have rules concerning all dancers and waitresses who work in their establishments. It does not matter who you are or if you know a girl's full name, social security number, phone number, and address. If you don't know her stage or waitress name, you don't get to see her. No girls get through the door unless they work there. I could not find her.

"I had a pretty good idea of which two places she might be working at. I asked Laura to help me find Jasmine and get her away from that lifestyle. Laura and I joined forces. We were actually talking and getting along at that time. Laura was not using meth at this time; she had managed to stay clean for over seven months. Laura hated the clubs but agreed to help me find my daughter. We both got jobs in two different gentlemen's clubs in February of 1989. I had reason to believe Jasmine was working at one of them. The club I had chosen to work in was where I found her. Laura immediately came to where I was; I thought together we could convince Jasmine to leave the club and start a different life somewhere else."

I paused for a moment... "We considered ourselves to be on a mission, but Jasmine was not going to leave. She liked working there, setting her own hours, friends, and, of course, the money. She was not going to leave, and she was very firm about it. The money is just unbelievable." I looked at Chief Sanders and said, "What you make in a week is what a girl can make one night. Once a young girl is deceived by that kind of money, she will make choices that will alter her life, and most of them end up on drugs."

The door was opened, and I had to finish the story. "It was at that club where we met Seth, the man in question. He and Laura quickly became friends. They were friends until they were arrested together years later, in 1994, after all of these events had happened in 1989. From April 1989 until February 1991, I saw Laura and Seth on a regular basis. I believed Laura was talking to Jasmine about me and trying to get her out of the club. I found out they were addicted to meth. They never talked to Jasmine and had not seen her or talked to her. They lied to me; they had been using me. I had given them a lot of money."

I looked at Scott, who had not taken his eyes off me. I knew I had to do this because if Seth was the killer, Jasmine's life and mine could be in danger. According to Chief Sanders, Seth had served seven years of his sentence and was now on parole. He should have reported to his parole officer on October 20. He had not been seen since Laura's murder. They had reason to believe he contacted Laura two days before she was murdered.

I knew that this could very well be the end of my marriage. Still, I knew I had to continue. "What I didn't know until March of 2001 was that Seth was the one who supplied drugs to Laura after she got out of prison in December of 1993. Laura was with Seth in a motel room in November of 1994 when they were both arrested. They were both charged with possession and distribution of illegal drugs. Laura was sentenced to ten years in a Texas state prison and was paroled in March of 1998 for good behavior. At the time, I was very angry with Laura. I had absolutely nothing to do with her for seven years because she had chosen drugs over me. It was not until March 2001 that she came to see me, and the gap between us was closed.

"Jasmine had a son born on December 8, 1994. Jasmine had some health issues, and Daniel lived with me. He had been living with me most of his life. Jasmine was in and out." Once again, I paused. "In December of 1997, four and a half years after I went looking for Jasmine, she came to me for help. She moved in with me, and together, we went through the long, hard process of getting her off meth. I understood her pain and how it feels to be so broken and shattered, trying everything to make sense of your own pain and brokenness, and at the same time struggling, making mistake after mistake in an attempt to have some kind of life."

I stop for a moment again. "Like I was saying, Jasmine moved in and stayed with me for a while and got off meth. She moved out, and one month later, Daniel drowned on May 20, 1998. She's angry with me and blames me for his death. I believe she will never forgive me." I took a deep breath and said, "The past and Daniel's death seem to always cast a shadow on our relationship, and like me, she struggles with his death and a past that is too hard for anyone to really imagine."

I closed my eyes to hold back the tears. "I should have never gone to that club. I should have trusted God to bring Jasmine out of that place. I didn't know any of this until Laura came to see me in March of 2001; she came to tell me the truth. She told me she thought I deserved to know how she got mixed up in drugs again. Laura and I worked at that club for five weeks, but that decision changed our lives and altered our futures. She told me that in February 1989, when we met Seth, she was not using drugs of any kind and had been drug-free for over a year and had no desire for them whatsoever. He changed all that and began to supply her with drugs."

I knew I had to finish… "Later, Laura sold drugs for him on the streets. When they were arrested, she told me she was praying for it. She was actually in the bathroom at the motel, getting ready to end her life. While she was in prison this time, she got her life straightened out. She got the truth and started her walk with the Lord. A real walk."

I paused and then continued. "When Laura got out, she had changed. She was stronger and had a real relationship with the Lord. She had studied His Word and said she had learned the power of prayer. She trusted Jesus for the strength and the courage to stand. She trusted the Lord in every area of her life. She talked of God's love in ways that I didn't understand."

I said, "Twenty-nine years I claimed to be a Christian, and I was actually ignorant of many things. Oh, I knew the word, and I could quote it. My life had changed. But I was still missing something. But not Laura. She had a hold of the truth in ways I didn't. I was wrong for the way I had judged and condemned her all those years, and in all that time, she never once told me it was my fault, my doing, or even that I was the reason she ended back up on drugs."

I had to stop for a moment. "Laura told me she hadn't heard anything from Seth and doubted she would. But if she did this time, she knew how to handle it. She wasn't the weak victim anymore. She smiled at me that day as she told me, 'Now I am a child of the Most High God. I am not afraid to face him and tell him I am not interested in him or his drugs. Then I am going to share the gospel with him.' We both laughed about it. After that day in March of 2001, we never talked about him again."

I just sat there, with this deep-down urge to scream, as I realized how truly wrong I had been about everything. I cried, "It's my fault! Everything! I blamed her, but it was my fault! I must deal with the truth. It was all my doing! We should have never been in that club. Her whole life was messed up because I talked her into going there. I was a Christian; what in the world did I think I was doing? She was murdered because of me!" With that, I just hung my head in shame and cried. In the core of my being, the cold, hard fact was that I may have been responsible for my sister's murder. *How am I ever going to live with that?* There was no comfort for me on that day. I had to inform Jasmine of the possible danger that we were in. For weeks and months, I lived in fear, calling and checking on Jasmine daily.

In April of 2002, I received a call from Chief Sanders. I arrived at the police station early the next morning. I spent half the day going through the questions and answers again. They picked up Seth. He had a weapon on him and violated his parole. He had charges pending against him, but murder wasn't among those charges. Chief Sanders said, "He is guilty of a lot of crimes, but he did not murder your sister. He has an airtight alibi, and he has witnesses. He didn't do it, Linda. Let it go."

I said, "But he saw her two days before the murder. Yes, and she told him in front of about ten witnesses that she was not interested and invited him to church, saying he needed the Lord, not drugs." That was the end of it. I was thankful that it wasn't him. It was a heavy load that I had carried. I was thankful that this was a burden that I wouldn't have to carry for the rest of my life.

I went by Laura's house that day. I walked through the house to make sure it was clean and that no empty cans or trash were left in the house by the couples who had looked at it. Around thirty-five couples had looked at it but declined to purchase it.

I walked into Laura's house and headed straight for her bedroom. I collapsed in the middle of the floor and cried for hours. I prayed, and I asked the Lord to forgive me for my actions all those years long ago. How I had come back home thinking I was so wise. I had Jesus! I was saved. I thought I knew everything when, in fact, I knew nothing. I was going to change my family. I never changed anything; my decisions had only made matters worse. I thought of all the opportunities I had passed by, thrown away, and kept on walking. I had ignored all the warnings, and here I was, still sitting on the back pew like a coward at whatever church I was attending at that moment. The worst part was that I had no idea who I was, never did, and maybe never would.

My life was unraveling, and there was nothing I could do about it. Every day, I saw the hurt and anger in my husband's eyes. From one day to the next, I didn't know if he was even going to return home. I had tried to explain it, but nothing seemed to make sense to me anymore. If it didn't make sense to me, how was I ever going to get Scott to understand?

I knew I was on a one-way street, and I was headed for a collision. No matter how hard I tried, there was no way I could determine the damage that it would leave in my already very fragile life. The pain in the very depths of my soul was beyond anything I could have ever imagined. I believed there was no way I was ever going recover to an emotionally whole and complete woman.

I prayed for death; I longed for it. I saw no reason for me to live. My life was destroyed, and all that was left lay in ruins. I thought of the scripture: "Be sober, be vigilant; because your adversary the devil, as a roaring lion, walketh about, seeking whom he may devour" (1 Peter 5:8).

I was painfully aware of the fact that it wasn't talking about alcohol; the scripture was referring to the fact that I was spiritually drunk. I had not been watchful and alert to the dangers that were around me in the world. I had not considered the fact that there were all kinds of dangers that existed in the club that I had talked Laura into working at or the fact that I was putting both our lives at risk.

I should have trusted God. As I lay there on the floor, I knew in my heart that God was more than able to have delivered Jasmine from that place. God had saved and delivered me. I had forgotten the power of God to save, taking it upon myself to rescue her, and I failed. I didn't save her. Instead, my actions resulted in Laura being put at risk by placing her in the middle of temptations. All I should have done was be a witness and an example to those He placed in my life. I was supposed to witness to Laura, but instead, I had her go to a club and led her right into the middle of the war zone. A war that she was not ready to fight.

I didn't tell her about me getting saved or finding God until after she went to prison. Why? Because the first time I tried to tell her, she didn't listen to a thing I said. Instead, she took money from me and left me feeling hurt and rejected. With every day that passed, I had gotten further and further away from God. I asked God to forgive me and to show me how to put my life back together. I asked the Lord for one more thing: to somehow save my marriage. It was late in the afternoon when I got up off the floor. I was emotionally drained.

I walked through Laura's house. It was truly a lovely home. "Lord, You know the right person for this home, and I am asking You to work it all out. I want someone here who will love it and make it into the home Laura wanted it to be. Maybe in some way, her hopes and dreams can live on." I walked out and was locking up when I noticed the couple who lived across the street from Laura's house. They were outside, talking to a young couple with a baby. They motioned for me to come over. They wanted to know how I was doing, about Little Bit, about how the investigation was coming along, and if anyone was interested in the house. They said, "We have been praying for a strong Christian family to buy it."

I said, "No one yet." I shared my thoughts with them about the reason having to do with the fact that my sister had been murdered there. The two women were sisters; I just stood there and listened to them talk.

I had this strange desire for the young couple to see the house, so I asked them if they would like to go inside and take a look. After walking through the house, they said, "We can't understand why anyone wouldn't want to own this home."

Then it occurred to me, and I knew in a second what the Lord wanted me to do. I asked, "Would you two like to have this home?" They said they would love to live there and make it their home, but they couldn't afford it. I said, "I didn't say anything about buying it. I asked you if you would like to have it. If you do, then you can have it. It's never going to sell. It's paid off, and I don't need the money." Two months later, I signed all the paperwork giving it to them. I walked away that day, knowing I had done something that Laura would have wanted me to do.

I would go through all the earth-shattering moments of their deaths. Starting with Daniel, my mother, my father, and then Laura. They were all gone, my family was gone, and I felt so very alone. It all happened so fast; one minute, they were there, and the next, they were all gone. Why did all this have to happen? Daniel's death was still shocking; it tore through my soul like a hurricane. His death was untimely and preventable. The memory of his death brought pain lined with regrets. If only the babysitter had not left him unattended at the pool.

My mother had died in pain, with many regrets. The most beautiful woman I had ever known weighed less than forty-five pounds and didn't have a hair on her head. I was with her when she died, and I truly held nothing against her.

I loved her, and to me, she was more beautiful on that day than in all the years before. Her illness seemed so unfair, coming at a time when she was just beginning to live. She finally had a hold of the truth and was willing to share it in ways I never had.

My dad *never* confessed Jesus as his Saviour. He had no need of one. Those were his final words to me on the night he died. *If only he had more time*, I thought. The pain grabbed at my heart, tormenting me. I had all those years to speak, but I was silent. As my father slipped into utter darkness, I stood there alone, painfully aware that there was nothing else I could do. I beheld the pain and anguish on his face. It was too late; his time in this life was over, and my time to share the gospel with him had vanished into thin air.

Laura... What of Laura? She had a life of pain and was abused in so many ways. She had suffered things far beyond my own pain, only to die in such a horrible manner. Laura had just found joy, peace, and love. She finally had a solid foundation, and it was all taken away.

I wanted her back. I wanted Daniel back. I wanted them all back, all of them. But they were gone, and in this life, I would never see them or hold them again. That pain was more than I could bear. It seemed never-ending. I didn't know what was ahead for me. The future that I saw before me was all too empty and all too cold. I found myself just hanging on and, at the same time, wanting to let go and just end it all. I lived with the fear that just lurking in the shadows was the next tragedy ready to rip Scott or Abigail out of my life. This was my punishment. My punishment for what I did all those years ago.

I would spend my days just sitting on the couch from the early morning hours until late in the night. I had nothing left to do. I spent my days looking at pictures and newspaper clippings, crying for hours. I cried until I no longer knew who the tears were falling for. It was not the only thing wrong in my life. My life was falling apart at every level. There was nothing I could do to stop it. All I could do was sit there and wait for the crash.

The crash came in June of 2002 when Scott confronted me. Why would I lie to him? I was not raised in a Christian home. Not even close, I was a part of an occult! I had not graduated at the top of my class. Why would I tell him that when I had barely finished the seventh grade? Severe pain shot through me as I heard his final words: "Accident? What accident? You did not get those scars from an accident! You were raped! You almost died! Who was it? One of the men you met and used from a club? You worked in gentlemen's clubs! For almost six years, Linda! You are sinful. Those places are filthy, nasty, and full of sin. Do you have no shame? No guilt? Who are you? You are not an angel; God did not send you into my life. You came in like a snake to lie, steal, and destroy my life." He threw a pile of papers at me, and I just stood there like a stone statue, speechless. "Well," he said, "say something! Defend yourself! Don't you have anything at all to say?"

I knew in my heart that there was really nothing I could say to make him understand. I said the words that I myself had denied Laura so many times. "Forgive me" was all I could say. There were tears flowing like a slow, steady stream. I stood, waiting for my final judgment to fall, a judgment that I knew I certainly deserved.

Scott walked away. He was broken, and I was responsible. I stood there, not knowing what to do. *Does he want me to leave? Or is he going to stay with me?* I didn't have any answers. I prayed, "Oh, God, help us...help us to find our way back to each other and back to You. Somehow, bring us out of this valley of death and restore us. Take all that has been shattered. And put us back together again. Make us whole and complete. Allow us both to find the joy that comes when we truly understand that mercy rejoices when it wins over judgment. Forgive me, oh God, for what I have done here."

Scott talked to me about two weeks later and told me, "I am staying with you because I made a vow, not to you but to God, the day I married you. I am going to keep my vow to Him. I am going to honor Him by keeping the vow that I made to Him alone, and He knows what it was, and just maybe He can bring something good out of the mess *you* have created." I felt like Eve standing there with him, glaring at me as if I had just taken a bite from the forbidden fruit that created this mess. Scott stood there as if he were trying to determine if I should be granted forgiveness or run out of the garden and executed.

I got a job at Denny's as a waitress because I needed to get out of the house. I felt that if I had just gotten out of Scott's way and given him some time, it would have helped. I couldn't hurt Abigail by ending my life. I knew it would damage her for a long time, possibly the rest of her life. Somehow, I managed each day to get up, put my clothes on, and go off to work. It was during this time that Scott and I moved out of the house that Abigail and I had called home for so long, one we picked out together and moved into seven years ago. We were so full of dreams and hope.

We moved into a frame house close to a lake in a nearby town. Scott kept his word and stayed with me, but there were many times I wished that he had left me and completed my punishment. It seemed as if God had just pushed the pause button in my life. I was alive but dead. I smiled, but I was crying. No matter which way I turned, there was something right in front of me that brought me crashing into the past. There was a constant pain that just seemed to be unleashed in my life without warning. I was completely shattered.

I was contacted again by Chief Sanders in August of 2002 to meet him at the Texas ranger's office. I wondered what was going to be unleashed in my life next. I met John of the Texas rangers, a very straightforward man, who informed me that the possibility of finding the person who murdered Laura was vanishing. I walked away defeated, lost, and believing that God was punishing me. I could not understand why He did not answer my simple prayer. I got in my car, realizing the person who murdered my sister had indeed gotten away. The investigation was coming to an end; it was rapidly turning into a cold case. There were no more arrests, no warrants, and no suspects. It was the end of line, and there was still no reason why my sister had been so brutally murdered.

As for my life, I had been exposed; all my past poured out without warning. Laura was right. You cannot hide your past. You cannot hide who you really are. Maybe for a brief time. But your past is what made you who you are. And who you are cannot be hidden. You must face your past because you are the product of all the events in your life. Lying about your past and hiding your past means living life without being fully yourself, and that creates deep-seated shame and guilt.

CHAPTER 16

Judgment and Justice

When I walked away from the Texas ranger's office, I felt there was no reason left for me to live. I drove around for hours. I went to the park, the one place where there were precious memories I could hold onto. I felt the cool evening wind, and in my heart was the firm reassurance that I was alone. I felt so empty, and the fragments of my life were scattered like leaves in the wind. There was no rhyme or reason to my life. I was screaming inside, "How did I get to this place in my life?" In that moment, I was ready to die. My family was gone.

I was a failure as a daughter. I was a failure as a sister. I was a failure as a mother. My marriage lay in ruins; I had failed at everything, including being a Christian. The weight of guilt and shame blocked out the words that would have brought comfort. I refused to hear them or consider them. "Come unto me, all ye that labour and are heavy laden, and I will give you rest. Take my yoke upon you, and learn of me; for I am meek and lowly in heart: and ye shall find rest unto your souls. For my yoke is easy, and my burden is light" (Matthew 11:28–30).

There was nothing left for me. The only way out was to just end it. I drove around looking for a place to end my life. I had no direction, no certain place to go to; I just wanted a private place. I drove for about fifteen minutes, and then I spotted a parking lot and a large building. I pulled in and parked in front of the building. I sat there for a moment, and I asked God to forgive me. I reached over and picked up the bottle of sleeping pills that was in the passenger seat.

I had a bottle of water and was getting ready to open the bottle of pills when I looked up and realized that I was at a church. *Oh no,* I thought to myself, *I don't want to kill myself in front of a church. I have enough problems without dying in front of a church. What about the people who attend here? Oh, this is definitely not a good idea.*

I started the car and pulled out a little bit faster than I should have, not going very far. I saw the lights. *Yes,* I thought to myself, *this is just what I need in my life right now: a speeding ticket! My just punishment.* I was speeding, so I slowed down and pulled over. I waited for the officer to come and give me my just reward.

The officer asked, "Do you know why I stopped you tonight?" Before I could reply, he knelt by my car and said, "I just saw you pull out of that church. Are you a member there?"

I said, "No, I am not."

He asked, "What were you doing there at this late hour?"

I looked down at the pills in my lap and then back at him. I wanted to pour my whole life out to him. Suddenly, I had this urge to tell him everything. I couldn't help it, and I couldn't stop it. I started saying, "A lot of things have gone wrong in my life during the last four years. My grandson drowned, then I lost both my parents, and my sister was murdered. They cannot find the person who killed her. Today, they basically told me it was possible that they would never solve the case. I don't know what I am doing anymore, and nothing in my life seems right. Even my marriage is, well, I don't even know what it is anymore. I feel lost, and I really wanted to end my life tonight, and then I realized I was at a church."

He said, "You missed the most important thing there."

I looked up at him as he stood up, and I asked, "What was that?"

He smiled and said, "Hope, young lady. Hope. People talk a lot about faith, but God's Word says these three remain: faith, hope, and love. All three are important to the Christian. Now, from what I have just heard you say here tonight, love is not an issue. You love and have a desire to be loved. I see you have faith, but, child, you have no hope. 'Now faith is the substance of things *hoped* for, the evidence of things not seen'[1] (Hebrews 11:1). Why don't we go back to that church and see why, of all the places you ended up there tonight, God led you to that particular church for a reason."

As I turned around, I was trying to figure out what had come over me. I don't talk like that to anyone. It was as if I wanted to pour my whole heart out to him, tell him all my problems and everything that had gone so wrong in the last few years. I followed him back to the church, where he prayed for me. When he was finished praying, he told me to go home and tell my family, including my husband, that I love them.

Then he got this big smile on his face and said, "Remember this: God knows right where the man is who murdered your

---

[1] Hereinafter, emphasis added.

sister. God is able to work in his life as well as yours. You may not understand, but God desires to fulfill His will and purpose in both your lives. You must forgive the man who murdered your sister. Just start by saying, 'I forgive him.' Say it four or five times a day. Now, don't let me find you back out here again unless, of course, you are attending this church. You go home and live the life God has given you, with purpose."

I drove home, walked inside, and looked at Scott and Abigail. I said, "I had a hard day. I met with the police; it was the end of the line. They are going to close the case. I almost got a ticket. I love you both. I'm going to bed; I have to work in the morning." I said it just that way and in that order, and then I went to bed.

I woke up the next morning, and I covered my head when the alarm went off. I didn't want to go to work. I didn't want to get out of bed. I called in and took off work for a couple of days. I spent those days sleeping.

Nothing changed; I was lost in this endless world of pain without hope. It was, as the officer said, I had no hope. No hope that the man who murdered my sister would ever be captured. No hope that my marriage could be restored. No hope of friends or a future where I would really know what it meant to live in the fullness of God's love and what it meant to really laugh. I went back to work, feeling cold and empty deep inside.

Abigail was having problems, lots of problems, that were quickly coming to the surface. I knew I had to get my life into some kind of order. I had to do something to help myself so that I could help Abigail. I had to do something about my marriage. I truly loved my husband. I knew what I had done deeply hurt him. I didn't know how to deal with my past. I knew I needed help, so I asked God to guide me and help me to do the right thing. I told God I wanted to help my daughter, and yes, I wanted Him to show me how to put my marriage back together.

On a Friday morning in September of 2002, I told Abigail I could not explain it, but I knew I had to do something. I tried so many times to understand what was wrong with me. I was trying to fix something I knew was broken, but I could not understand why it was broken and how it got that way. She told me she felt the same way. As I listened to her talk, I was astonished. My little girl felt the same way I did when I was young. She had no reason to feel that way. She was raised with love and everything I could give her. I had taken her to church all of her life. I read the Word of God with her and to her. I shared stories with her. She was loved. And she knew it. She had friends and things I never had. She wasn't raised in lies, deception, fighting, and drinking. She was taught there was a God, and yet she felt the same way I did when I was young. How could that be?

Suddenly, it was crystal clear: I had taken her to church, but I did not live the life we heard about. I kept her on the back pew with me, going in late and leaving early. She had seen my display of bitterness towards Laura, and she had seen my actions toward Scott. When she needed me the most, I drowned myself in sorrow and never once thought about what she might be going through.

I picked up the phone, dialed information, and asked for the number of a church. I called and left a message. Within twenty minutes, I received a call back from the pastor. He confirmed that he would meet with me in an hour. I told Abigail to get ready, that we were going to church, and that we would be talking to a pastor. She was full of questions. I told her, "I don't even know what I am doing; I'm just doing it. If I'm ever going to get my life straightened out, it's going to take a little effort on my part. I want things in our life to be better. I don't know how to do that right now, but I have to try."

Abigail and I met with the pastor. We spent the whole afternoon talking. We talked about my marriage, Abigail, the death of my family, and even some about my childhood. That afternoon, I made a real connection with another human, and I spoke honestly and openly. I received positive input for the first time in a very long time, which I could take with me and apply to my own life. My daughter even had a real smile on her face when we left. I told her as we drove off, "I really like this church."

The following Sunday, I went back to that church. I sat on the back pew, as I was so accustomed to doing. I really enjoyed the service, and I decided that I wanted to start attending church there, at least for a while. The people were a little friendlier than I was used to, but I could adjust my timing a little and miss the hand-shaking time.

Scott had been out of town during this time. When he returned, I took the pastor's advice, along with the police officer's advice. I fixed a nice supper, and while Scott and Abagail were at the table, I told them both I loved them very much. I told them both I knew I was messed up, but in time, with their love, prayers, and lots of hope, maybe the battle could be won. I said, "I'm hoping for a great victory."

I let Scott know I understood how he must feel, thinking he had married this wonderful Christian woman only to find out she was a fake. I told him I may not like it, but he had a right to be angry. I thanked him for staying with me. I assured him of my love and the hope that maybe someday he would forgive me.

Scott had a few questions. He said he noticed something a little different about me and wanted to know if I had secretly taken a bunch of pills and was going to go to bed and die that night. He said it would not work because he checked my breathing and my eyes all the time. I said, "You do, why? You really care about me?"

Scott didn't answer but asked, "So what did you do while I was gone? Just work and come home?" I looked at him, smiled, and said, "No, I went to a church and talked to a pastor. We went to a real church, sat down, and talked to a real pastor. I went to church there last Sunday. Think you might like to go there with me?"

Scott was a little puzzled, to say the least. "What do you mean you talked to a pastor? Like you sat down and had a normal conversation?"

I was kind of proud and said, "Yes, Scott, I did. I took Abigail, and we went to a church and talked to a pastor the whole afternoon. I told him about losing my family, about you, and some things from my past."

Scott said, "You did?"

I answered, "Yep, I did."

I don't think he believed me. He wanted me to call the church the very next morning and meet the pastor as well. By the end of the next day, Scott said, "We are going to start attending that church." That Sunday, we went as husband and wife for the first time in over a year. That was the day Scott began to talk to me. That Sunday was a new beginning for us.

On November 15, 2002, I woke up to a cold morning, and my mind settled on the idea of not going to work. I didn't want to get out, but I forced myself to go. At work, as I took my coat off, one of my coworkers said, "You were on the news last night and in the paper today." A coworker walked up to me and said, "Don't you know? They caught the man who murdered your sister. He confessed, and they are asking for the death penalty."

I just stood there shaking for a moment. Then I ran to the newspaper stand. I was shaking so bad I couldn't get the money into the slot. A coworker walked over, put the money in, and got the newspaper out for me. I asked, "Can you read it for me?"

She pointed. "There it is, 'Man Arrested in Woman's Slaying October 2001, a Bizarre Twist with a Spectacular Ending for the Police Department.'"

There he was. As I looked at his picture, I realized how young he was. If I had to guess, I would say he was maybe twenty or younger. I stood there, staring at his picture, thinking that it would have been impossible for him to kill Laura by himself. She was strong, and I knew she could stand on her own. No, there had to be a mistake. He is too young. Maybe there were two of them. This was all wrong; he was just a kid!

My cell phone was ringing. I answered, "Hello?"

"Linda, we got him!" Chief Sanders was saying.

I interrupted him, "Yes, I know; how did this happen? I thought you were closing the case."

Chief Sanders said, "Slow down. Can you come to the police station? I'll tell you all about it."

We made an appointment for that afternoon. I left work early; I couldn't think about work anyway. I had a lot on my mind. Who was he? Why did he murder Laura? Why? That was the real question that had haunted me for over a year. The waiting was finally over. I was parked in front of the police station, and in a few minutes, I would walk up the stairs, open the door, and walk in. Chief Sanders would come out and greet me, we would walk back to his office, and he would tell me what happened to Laura and why.

Chief Sanders was telling me to have a seat. I wanted to stand, but I took a seat and waited for him to speak. He cleared his throat as if what he had to tell me was more disturbing news. He started out slow and steady, "The man who murdered your sister is Billy Lopez. He is a twenty-three-year-old Hispanic. When your sister was murdered, we could have run the DNA through the state's database, the 'Combined DNA Index System.' Due to the cost, we didn't get the DNA processed at that time; we were going to wait until we were at least 99.9 percent sure we had the right man in custody."

Chief Sanders took a deep breath. "After you met with John, the Texas ranger, he took an interest in the case. He was convinced we had to get the DNA analyzed. We went through the long, drawn-out process and got it approved. Three weeks ago, it was processed. All DNA is put through the state's database, the 'Combined DNA Index System.' A match was found that linked Billy Lopez to the crime scene. This was truly a strange turn of events."

Chief Sanders looked at me and said, "Billy had been arrested less than three weeks after he murdered your sister and was sentenced in May 2002. He is serving a six-year sentence. Good behavior and he would have been out in a year or two—"

I interrupted, "So, did he break into her house, she walked in, and he killed her?"

Chief Sanders said, "No, that is not his story."

I asked, "Well, then, what is his story?"

Chief Sanders looked down. "Well, Billy knew her; he did yard work and odd jobs around the outside of her house. He said mostly fixing things up and taking care of her yard. He says he did her yard work for about a year or more for extra money. We have two confessions signed by him, and both are very different stories. We really do not know why he killed her. He is lying, and we may never know the truth. Linda, look at it this way: we got him, and he will get the death penalty."

I sat there for a moment, looking at him. "Chief Sanders, I deserve better than that. I want to know why my sister was murdered. Why was she ripped from my life? I need to know the reason. I don't believe that's too much to ask for."

Chief Sanders looked down and said, "I don't believe these statements. None of that will matter. He will go to trial, and he will get the death penalty. He is never going to tell anyone the truth about what happened that night. Do you understand that?" I looked at him as he continued talking. "Linda, look at it this way: We got him, and he signed a confession. We have DNA, the weapons he used, and the autopsy report. He will get the death penalty. He will pay for what he did. Isn't that what you've waited for? Isn't that what you wanted?"

I was honest. "I don't know what I want anymore, except that I want to know why he killed her."

Chief Sanders shuffled through some papers, held up one sheet of paper, and said, "This is one of Billy Lopez's signed confessions. Linda, I've seen his type before, and I don't think he knows how to tell the truth. I know what he says in this confession is a lie. He thought it would excuse his actions." I looked down at the paper Chief Sanders was holding as he spoke, "Linda, I'm sorry, but you will hear all of this later. You just remember that he will not get away with it. He has already said he killed her. Do you understand that?"

I said, "Yes, I do."

I could see it was messed up handwriting; things were written then scribbled through. Chief Sanders read it. I couldn't stop the tears as I heard the words. "She asked me to kill her; she was unhappy, she had no family, and she wanted to die—"

I interrupted Chief Sanders and said, "That is not true. She was moving to my land in the country with me. Why is he saying this? I don't want to hear any more of these lies!"

Chief Sanders told me I would be subpoenaed to the trial and have to appear in the courtroom. It would take months, maybe even a year. As I walked away from the police station that afternoon, I had an awful, empty feeling. It wasn't at all like I thought it would be. There was a sudden awareness that Laura's death would always remain a mystery. There would never be a great victory, and nothing good could ever come out of this mess.

I went to Laura's grave. I don't know why I went there. It may even seem foolish in many ways. I understood that only her body was there. I knew that her soul, the part of her that loved, laughed, and cried, was in heaven. According to God's Word, to be absent from the body is to be present with the Lord (1 Corinthians 5:3).

I didn't stay long; I would not give up until I knew the truth. Neither her life nor her death would be forgotten. I wanted to make some kind of sense out of all that had happened. I wanted to make her life matter. I needed to know she didn't live and die in vain.

I was not sure how much more I could take. I wanted to say I was doing better, but that was not true. I had to face the trial now, and that was something that I was truly not ready for. I wanted to forget, put it all behind me somehow, and find a way to live.

I looked toward the heavens as I thought, *Oh, how they declare the glory of God. Just as the scripture says in Psalm 19:1.* I told the Lord, "I do not believe that I have really lived. I've been alive, and I have existed, but I have never truly lived, not the way Your Word speaks of life. I have not lived with hope, joy, love, or peace." Words spoken by Jesus came to my mind: "I am come that they might have life, and that they might have it more abundantly" (John 10:10b). I asked, "What does that mean, anyway?"

I was driving home, thinking about how they had caught Billy. It was strange indeed how he had been captured, and then it struck me: I had prayed the night after I got home from the police station, asking God to just get him off the street and keep him from hurting anyone else. He was arrested! It began to sink down into my soul. God had not only heard my prayer, but He also answered it in a mighty way. All the months, I had told God I couldn't understand why He, as my loving Father, wouldn't answer such a simple request. He had already answered my prayer! It was a glimpse of God's love for my sister and for me. He wasn't going to allow Billy to get by with what he had done to my sister. I asked God why He hadn't revealed it sooner that Billy was already in prison. It would have eased my pain.

He spoke to me and said, "Because you were not ready to know until now."

Time began to pass, and nothing really changed like I had assumed it would. I still had the same feelings, the same fears, and the same nightmares. Scott, well, the truth was, some days were good, and some days were bad. However, he had spoken of his love for me and the fact that I stayed with him instead of leaving. He said he understood that I could have left.

We were still going to church, but Scott started changing our routine. Even though we were late more times than not, Scott wanted to start getting there on time. He changed my seating arrangements as well. He had found his way to the middle section of the church and dragged me there with him.

I found myself constantly hiding from one particular lady. I had come to believe that she had radar and was able to detect me as soon as I walked into the building. Her name was Sheila. Not only did she remind me of my sister, but with her smile and outgoing nature, she also showed a determination equal to that of Laura. She was not giving up.

One Sunday, I went to the restroom just to avoid Sheila. I waited until I heard the music start and then slipped out of the stall. Immediately, I heard, "Oh, there you are. I knew I saw you come in this morning!"

I was saying to myself, *No, don't say it, please don't say it.*

Then out came the words, as she smiled, "Well, how are you doing?"

I managed to look up for a minute. I replied with my usual answer, the famous word: "Fine!" Of course, as I was trying to get past her, she grabbed me and gave me a big hug. Even though I never wanted to admit it, I was thankful for her hug that Sunday. It was just what I needed.

It was June of 2003, and I just found out it was time to go to court. I had received a subpoena; now, the waiting was over. Sheila's hug meant a lot to me because it was like the Lord sent her into the restroom for me to let me know it was going to be okay and that He knew right where I was. He had a plan, and I was ready to accept God's will, whatever it was.

The end of this long journey was within sight. The Lord had been speaking to my heart about the trial. He had been preparing me, even though I didn't know it until the day I walked into the courtroom. The word "forgive" was fresh in my soul. God had forgiven me, and now I had a chance to extend forgiveness. Even though I knew Billy was going to get the death penalty, I could still let him know I had forgiven him. Well, we can fool ourselves sometimes. I had not forgiven him, but God was going to use me anyway.

I entered the county courthouse at eight that morning in June. The trial was expected to last more than two weeks. I wore the black dress I had worn to Laura's funeral. I felt it would be an appropriate way of saying, "It is finished."

When I walked in the courtroom, I knew right away something was wrong. Chief Sanders greeted me and said, "Billy has had a change of heart. He is pleading guilty and asking for a life sentence. What do you think?"

I looked around, unsure of my surroundings, "I don't know, I have to think a moment."

He said, "Everyone has to be in agreement, or it is going to trial. They're waiting for you, and they want to hear what you have to say."

I walked into a side room and was introduced to Samuel, the district attorney. Everyone in the room was arguing, saying there was enough evidence and that after the trial, we could hit him with more charges. "No, let's just go to trial and not accept his plea; let him get the death penalty."

Laura's son, Kenneth, had his teeth clenched and said, "I want his death." Jasmine agreed with him.

I said, "No! She was my sister, and I love her, but his death will not bring Laura back. I will not live with his blood on my hands. I want to accept his plea." I was stunned at my own reply; it wasn't exactly what I had set out to say. However, I felt a peace come over me after I had said it.

For two hours, the arguing continued. Finally, the district attorney said, "We must decide. If you cannot all agree within ten minutes, we will start the trial."

I looked up after being silent for more than forty-five minutes. I nodded my head toward Samuel, the district attorney, and said, "I have sat here and listened to what all of you have said. I believe all of you are wrong. Have any of you really thought about what Laura would have wanted? I know Laura, and she would not want any part of what you are doing here today...

"What of God, and the very words of Jesus, about forgiving those who trespass against us, as He forgives us? I am begging all of you not to do this. Let's accept his plea of guilt and let him spend the rest of his life in prison, where he will live with the memories of his deeds. When we stand before God, we will not do so with his blood on our hands."

Jasmine, Kenneth, Samuel, and his assistant, as well as I, agreed, and twenty minutes later, we were in the courtroom. Billy Lopez was brought in. He was small and seemed more like a frightened child than a murderer. He stood as he pleaded guilty to capital murder and was sentenced to life in prison without the possibility of parole. I watched as all color left his face. My heart was still asking the same question: *What happened that night? What really went so wrong that he brutally murdered Laura?* He sat back down. Then, the judge asked him if there was anything he wanted to say to the family. He declined. At that moment, I saw fear in him. I saw it in his eyes as he looked back when the judge had pointed to me. I was well acquainted with fear; I knew when I saw it, and Billy was in its grasp.

I remembered a year ago, in June of 2002, when Scott threw some papers at me and asked me a very similar question: "What do you have to say for yourself?" I remembered realizing the only thing I could do was ask for forgiveness. Was Billy unwilling to do even that? I wanted to hate him at that moment. The Lord spoke to my heart, "He is my child too." I wanted to scream, "No! No! How can that be? He has no remorse at all! Do you even know what he has done and the pain he has caused?" Silently and lovingly, the Lord said, "Yes, Linda, I do. I was there. You must go up and speak to Billy now."

I was quick to reply, "Oh, no! Lord, not me, not me, someone else, Lord. Please, not me." I didn't realize that I had spoken out loud. I was shaken by the sound of my voice, the loud banging of the gavel, and the judge saying, "I will have order in this courtroom, or you will be removed." I apologized and bowed my head. I told the Lord in a whisper, "I can't do it."

Then the Lord spoke to me in such a loving way, "No one else here will speak to Billy on My behalf today, Linda, and he needs to have some kind of hope, or he will die. You must speak to him. I will go with you, and I will give you the words." I told the Lord I didn't care if he died, and I certainly didn't care if he had no hope. *Why should I care what happens to him?* I told the Lord I had done my part. I talked the others into accepting a life sentence instead of death, and I said the words, "I forgive him." That's more than anyone else would have done. My life was torn apart because of his actions. *I lost everything, and You want him to have hope when I don't; that's not fair.*

There was a raging battle going on inside of me. I tried to stop it, but right there in the courtroom, I was having one big spiritual battle. The storm was raging inside me. "Forgive him." I knew it was the Lord.

I said, "I have."

"Have you?" the Lord asked again.

"Yes, I have."

The Lord was clear. "No, Linda, you are just saying the words."

My heart felt a sharp pain; the Lord was right. I was just saying the words. I asked the Lord right there, "How do I get past just saying the words? How do I get to that true place of forgiveness?"

He spoke again, "My ways are not your ways."

I knew that to be true. I felt His presence in a way I never had before. It was as if He sat down right beside me, took my hand, and said, "You must act upon it. Saying and doing are two very different things. His life depends upon you. I am with you."

Once again, I responded, "But, Lord, he killed my sister..."

He said, "I know."

I asked, "Why does it have to be me?"

God said, "Because he killed your sister."

Tears began to flow, and for a moment, it seemed as if God wiped away my tears and said, "This one is for Billy." I was speechless as I remembered my mom's last tear rolling down her cheek, how I said it was mine.

Then I said, "Why would I shed a tear for Billy? There are no tears for Billy?"

Words came, "He is lost; you can show him the way."

It was then I knew exactly what God wanted me to do. But could I do it?

Kenneth was asked if he would like to say something. He walked to the front, stepped onto the witness stand, and took a seat. He talked about the love and goodness of his mother. He directed his hate, anger, and bitterness towards Billy Lopez. Last of all, he told Billy that he didn't deserve to live and that death and hell would be waiting for him. He spoke for ten minutes or more. Every word was lined with hate.

Then, I was asked if I would like to say something. I walked to the front and sat down. The words, as God said, just rose up out of my spirit. I looked down at Billy, who had not once looked up at Kenneth, and said, "Billy, look at me." He kept looking down. So, I said it again, *"Billy Lopez*, look at me! I am not leaving here until you look at me." He lifted his head and looked at me. This moment of truth was not just for him. It was for me as well.

I kept my focus and continued to speak. "I have been haunted by the vision of the condition you left my sister in. I cleaned her home and washed her blood off the walls. Now you come to me, her sister, begging me to give to you what you denied her: 'the right to live.' I know she begged for her life, and instead, you brutally murdered her. Your life has been granted to you. Something you wouldn't do for my sister. I hope that you will use the life that has been given to you here today for good and not evil. What you do in prison will be your choice. Take a look at your life and the truth; I know my sister wanted to live. Billy, your testimony was false. Maybe someday you will face the truth about what you have done and the lives that you destroyed. You will live the rest of your life in the shadow of what you have done. Rest assured that there will be a day when it will not be a judge in a courtroom you will face, but the true judge that has the power to destroy not only your body but your soul as well. You will face God someday. How you face Him is up to you. But right here and right now, I want you to know that I have forgiven you."

I stopped for a moment, realizing the words I had spoken. I hung my head because they tasted sour and bitter in my mouth, but I said them anyway as I raised my head and spoke again. "I have forgiven you, but you will have to live with the results of your actions the rest of your life, and the painful truth is, so will I. This, however, is not the end. If by some miracle you are given the gospel and accept Jesus Christ as your personal Saviour, Laura, you, and I will walk side by side in heaven, and what has happened here will not even be a thought. I will pray that God will send someone to you in prison to share the truth of His love and that the truth will set you free. Please understand that person cannot be me. May God have mercy on your soul." With that, I stepped out of the witness stand and walked back to my seat.

The judge said, "All rise, in the said case of Billy Lopez, it is hereby...."

The words faded as I drifted into a solemn moment. Realizing that God, indeed, had answered all my prayers. Not exactly the way I thought He would, not even in the order I had asked, but He had definitely answered. The man who murdered my sister wasn't only captured but was, at this moment, being convicted to life in prison. There were tears: tears of regret, tears of loss, tears of pain, tears of sorrow, and tears for what could never be in this life.

Afterwards, the reporters and the district attorney wanted to talk with me. The courtroom was suddenly full, and I just wanted to escape. I watched as Billy was handcuffed and taken away. I saw his family out in the hall. I noticed his sisters and wondered what they must be feeling.

The day's events would be with me for a long time. I walked away from the courthouse that day, realizing that there were no real winners, no great victories; we had all lost something. The chain of events that led us all to this place and the reasons why were sealed in the heart of one man who had chosen this path for all of us one night when he took my sister's life for reasons I would never know.

Lives had truly been shattered by one man, Billy Lopez. I noticed the expressions and the pain in his family's eyes; it was familiar to me. I saw it every morning in the mirror, and that day was no different. I understood that all the answers I had looked for that I had hoped to find were not going to be found or answered. He had been captured, and he had been convicted, but it had changed nothing. Judgment and justice were not found in the courtroom that day. Maybe our view of judgment and justice is not what we feel or think in the here and now but truly in another time and another place.

CHAPTER 17

Time to Dig

I was on my way home after the trial, lost in thoughts about the day's events. I asked the district attorney if he had talked to Billy about the reason he had killed Laura. He just said no. I asked, "Does anyone know why he killed Laura?"

He told me, "No, and it wasn't a matter of why."

It just seemed like no one even cared why this young man had killed my sister. Was it such a hard question? I felt that it was very important to know why one would kill and so brutally take a life.

I went by the cemetery. At her grave, I thought about the day's events, how Billy had been sentenced to life in prison with no possibility of parole. I wondered what that meant to him and now even to myself. I wanted to feel something, but I didn't. I simply felt nothing. I didn't stay long at the cemetery; it was late, and I needed to get home. Scott had told me he would be home early. I was in a rush because he was expecting the trial to last longer than two weeks, and he was very concerned as to how it was going to affect me. He knew I was on very shaky ground, and I knew he would be surprised that it was all over.

I got into my car and headed for home. I was trying to rid myself of the guilt and deadly silence, so I turned on the radio. The song on the radio was "The Anchor Holds," so I turned off the radio. It was more than my shattered soul could handle. I thought about how I didn't go to Laura's that Sunday with the lunch in the box as we had planned. If only I had gone that day, things might be very different right now. I hated the guilt I carried in my soul about not going that day.

I started going over that day in my mind. It would have been my last time to be with Laura. Scott had stopped me from going. He wouldn't let me go; instead, he made me go to church. I was dealing with all kinds of feelings that I didn't even realize I had until that moment. All I knew was that I was going to pack a lunch on a beautiful Sunday morning, take it to my sister's house, and have a wonderful afternoon. But Scott stopped me and wouldn't let me go. He took that away from me—my last time to be with her—and he took that away from me!

Why did I not go that Sunday? I should have gone, no matter what. I had been planning on asking Laura to spend the night; she needed to pick a place where she wanted to have her mobile home put on my land. But I didn't go; I just called her and canceled. I wanted to go, but Scott told me no. It was his fault I didn't go. It was his fault that I missed my last chance to see Laura. *If he hadn't stopped me from going,* I reasoned as I screamed out loud, "My sister would still be alive! It was all his fault." From that day forward, I blamed Scott.

I remembered the day I went to identify her body. I was alone after she was murdered. Why? I began to think, *Why was I alone that morning? I should not have been alone, no matter what I had said. Why did Scott even allow me to do that alone?* I reasoned it was because he knew he was wrong about that Sunday. Once again, it was all Scott's fault.

Things were very difficult for me after the trial. I quit my job, and my sleeping patterns changed. I slept all the time. My house was a mess, my family was suffering, and all I wanted to do was sleep. When I wasn't sleeping, I was crying. I had fallen into a deep, dark pit. There was no light or glimmer of hope in my life anymore. Day after long day, I wandered aimlessly. It felt like all life had been stripped away from me, and I was in a deep trance, unable to wake up. The rest of the time, I wanted to die. I was sleeping a lot. I would sleep anywhere: in the closet, in the bathtub, under the table, in the car, behind the couch, anywhere I could hide. I would just lay down and sleep. I admit that I even slept an entire day on my sister's grave, then went home, showered, and went to bed. Sleep was my only way out of the pain. I was trying to numb myself; I didn't want to feel anymore.

One morning, about two months after the trial, I pulled the couch out, got behind it, and went to sleep. When I woke up, I lay there listening to sounds, wondering what time it was. *Has anyone come home? Am I still alone in the house?* Somewhere along the way, my questions began to change. *What am I doing here? Why was I ever born? Why didn't my parents love us? What did I do that was so wrong that even my mother could not love me? I hate living, and I…. I hate myself!* Something shifted inside me and rose out of the ashes of my pain. There was a fierce anger that grabbed hold of my heart. I jumped up and started walking back and forth. I was screaming, "Why can't anyone love me, God?"

What happened next just poured out of my soul. There was nothing to stop it; I didn't even want to stop it. The years of pain and damage had surfaced. I exploded, *"I hate myself!"* I said it again, this time hitting myself in the stomach. I did it again and again.

I walked over to the cabinet, took a plate out, and threw it across the room, screaming, "I hate what you did to Laura and me, Mother." I grabbed another plate and screamed as I threw it, "I hate what you did to us, Daddy." I grabbed another plate, threw it across the room, and screamed, "Forgive him? What about me?" Another plate: "My husband can't forgive me." Another plate: "You want me to forgive a murderer?" Another plate: "Do You forgive me, God?" Another plate: "I want to know, do You forgive me?" Another plate: "God, are You still punishing me?" Dish after dish was thrown across the room: plates, saucers, and glasses.

All the dishes I had were broken that day, except my bowls; I never made it to that cabinet. I'm glad I didn't because all of those bowls were so special to me; some of them were my mother's, and a few were Laura's, so I'm glad I never made it to that cabinet. In truth, I would have had no dishes left. It wasn't that I didn't know what I was doing. I knew exactly what I was doing. I simply didn't care. The pain was just too much. I stood and looked at the result of my anger, my pain, and the suffering of a lifetime. I stared at the mess I had created. I just sat down on the floor and cried.

That was my life I was looking at. I was that broken pile of dishes, and there was no way they could be put back together, and neither could I. From such an early age, the hurt and the pain had begun. It was a lifetime of brokenness, fear, doubts, rejection, loss, and, most of all, realizing that my life had absolutely no value, just like all those broken dishes.

As I was crying, the Lord spoke to me, "You are forgiven. My Son died for you. You cannot see it now, but joy will come in the morning. You must walk by faith."

I said, "But, Lord, I don't know how."

His words were clear; I knew the Lord was giving me a choice. He said, "I want you to paint, and as you paint, you will heal."

My reply was simple: "Lord, I don't know how to paint. You know me, Lord; I don't even know how to draw."

The Lord responded, "Noah never built an ark before I asked him to build one. Paint your walls. I will guide you."

I replied, "Paint my walls? What about Scott? He will have a thing or two to say about that."

His response was soft and firm: "It's all about faith and believing. What you desire, you will find when you paint the walls."

I asked, "What about the dishes?"

The Lord is so good… He said, "What dishes? They are not eternal, and they will never be missed."

I went to the store and got some boxes, paper plates, and plastic glasses. I went back home and cleaned up the mess. I took the boxes full of broken dishes to my car and put them in the trunk. I told myself they were just dishes and they could be replaced. *What am I going to tell my family? Nothing*, I thought, *I am not going to tell them anything.* Just like the Lord said, "What dishes? They are not eternal, and they will never be missed." As I walked inside, I said, "We shall see."

Abigail came home, and I fixed us something to eat. I put our food on paper plates. I set the plate and a plastic glass full of tea down in front of her, fixed mine, sat down, and we ate. Not a word was said about the paper plate. It was like she didn't even notice. Scott was out of town; when he came home, at dinner, I put his food on a paper plate and gave him Sprite in a plastic glass. Not a word.

To this day, no one ever asked me what happened to the dishes, and I have never told anyone about that day until now, and to this day, we still use paper plates and plastic glasses.

Well, when they read this, they will know about the broken dishes, and I hope they understand. If I know Abigail, she is thanking God for all the dishes she never had to wash over the years. Scott, well, he is probably laughing to himself and thinking, "Wow, I really missed that one."

I talked to Scott about painting the walls. I told him I believed, for some strange reason, God wanted me to paint, and I thought it was crazy. After that, I said, "Scott, the Lord said that if I would paint the walls, I would heal. Please don't think I'm crazy. I know it sounds crazy because I have never painted in my life."

Scott looked over at me, his big blue eyes just shining. "Well, you know, Linda, that Noah never built an ark, either, when the Lord asked him to build one."

I was stunned at his reply and answered back with, "Well, I guess we need to go get some paint."

Scott asked, "What are you going to paint?"

I answered, "I really don't know what I'm going to be painting. It seems strange to me that you believe me, and I am kind of curious as to why."

Scott just smiled. "Because I know you never would've thought of this on your own. It's not something you would do or even want to do. I believe that God wants you to do this. Who knows? Maybe we will both heal."

The painting began in October of 2003 and has continued. I painted, and Scott stood by me in every way. He helped by picking up supplies for me and bringing me several tree stumps to use as step stools. They helped me move easily from one area to another. I painted, and I *healed*.

It was a long and painful journey. I wasn't sleeping all the time anymore; I was painting. As I painted, I listened to Christian music and to the Bible on CD. Scott and I were getting along. He was talking to me, and we were reading the Word of God together again. My life was changing; I spent more time in prayer, and I prayed for specific things. I was really healing, and in the middle of healing, I was walking down the amazing path of finding and understanding forgiveness.

One day in April of 2004, I finished painting my kitchen, giving each cabinet its own word and a painting that illustrated the word. The kitchen had a vine weaving in and around scriptures, which I had spent over two weeks painting. I decided to clean the kitchen that day, just a little spring cleaning. I pulled out a plastic Rubbermaid crate. I knew what it was the moment I saw it. The pain in my heart was still fresh as I looked at the plastic crate.

The thought that occupied my mind that day, however, was the fact that my life was still as empty and unused as that plastic crate. That's when it came to my mind; it was just my empty box. A few days later, I sat down with a black marker and wrote on the lid of the crate: "My empty box."

I said a long prayer that day and asked God to help me. That is when the Lord spoke and said, "Pack this box with a lunch for two. Take it to someone and share a meal with them."

My immediate response was, "No! That's not fair! Lord, I will do anything but that. Please don't ask me to do that."

Once again, I was asked to do something I didn't want to do. But this time, it was because it involved *the crate*, the same one that Laura had wanted me to bring to her house with our lunch in it. That was our box, and I would not share it with another. I would not pack a beautiful lunch in our crate and take our crate to someone else. Someone I didn't know. Someone who would never know that the beautiful lunch they were receiving came with a great cost. That the lunch they were enjoying, first and always, would be the lunch that was intended for my sister. How would they know, or ever understand, the pain and loss of the very first lunch in a box? That was unfair, as far as I was concerned. That was Laura's crate and mine. I would never surrender to placing a lunch in it for someone else, and so the battle began.

I was asked to fill *our crate* with a wonderful meal and take *our crate* to someone else. Oh, and by the way, I didn't even know who the someone was. First, I had to agree to do it, and that was not going to happen. If I agreed to do this, I wanted to do it the other way around: First, tell me who I would be sharing the lunch in the box with, then, I would decide whether I wanted to take *our crate* with a wonderful meal in it to them. Or I could decide to just drop *our crate* off and pick it up later. I had all kinds of answers and reasons for not wanting to do this simple little request. There was also the fact that I had asked the Lord for a baby step, and He was asking me to take a giant step. I was reminded of the crate over the next few months, every day in all kinds of big and small ways.

I really tried to get it off my mind. I couldn't get rid of the crate; it meant too much to me. I couldn't get anyone in the house to see that it was useful, that they could use it to store their things. Nope, they didn't want any part of that old Rubbermaid crate. I tossed it from one place to another. I finally put it outside on the front porch to catch dust and rain. I thought that the weather and the elements of nature would destroy the crate. In my mind, it was Laura's and mine, and no one else was worthy to take her place. I would rather see it destroyed. I had no intention of ever using *our crate* for lunch with someone else. I had asked Jesus many times, "Why do You want me to do this?" I talked to Him about how I felt. "The first lunch that was fixed in that box was for Laura. I wanted to go see her that day, but Scott stopped me."

The Lord always answered the same way, "Be still and know that I am God." I had my battles, and I would ask Him sometimes, "What is that supposed to mean? I don't understand." One time, when He spoke those words to my heart, it was the last thing I wanted to hear that day. My reply was, "Okay, Lord, I am still, and if I remain as still as I am right now, I will become a statue." I think I heard Him laugh.

Finally, in June of 2004, the battle ended, and I told the Lord I would pack a lunch in the old crate and take it wherever he wanted it to go. I don't know why I fight so hard when I know that I am supposed to do something. It's like I think that it is the worst possible thing when God says "go" or "do." I know I should have responded, "Yes, Lord, here I am, ready and willing to do what You have asked me to do."

Instead, I struggled and tried to figure it all out. *What's going to happen if I do this?* I struggled long and hard with this idea. I wanted to pack lunch in that crate and have an amazing time with my sister the way we had planned. However, it was never going to happen.

It was truly a big step of faith for me. I walked into church one Sunday morning in June of 2004 as if I were on a mission. I didn't stop. I knew God was going to lead me to the lady for whom I was going to prepare the lunch. My heart was free that morning; I was unafraid and unstoppable. I knew the Lord was going to show me who. The most amazing thing was that I didn't care who she was; all I knew was that someone was hurting just like me, and the little lunch in the box would warm her heart and give her hope.

It's just like God to amaze you in ways that take your breath away. He led me straight to Sheila. That's right, the lady who had radar. The first lunch in a box was for Sheila, the one who showed me great kindness in a world that, for the most part, didn't even know I existed. She found me and was kind to me when my life was full of pain. I never really thought about it until that day, but I was really looking for her every Sunday too.

I took the box to Sheila's house with the lunch in it. What an amazing day. When I left, I knew my life was never going to be the same. The Lord opened my spiritual eyes. He began to show me things that had been hidden from my natural eyes. When I got home, I took a black marker and wrote something on the bottom of the crate. Something I never wanted to forget; I believed it was a special message meant for me as a reminder that, as humans, we forget, but God never does. This is what I wrote: "God's plan, Laura's gift, Linda's choice."

God showed me that the box was His plan. It was Laura's last gift to me, and now it was my choice. I had to make a choice whether or not to use what God had placed in my hands and fulfill the purposes for which it was intended. I would let Laura's gift be opened and used, or I would let it die in the ashes and ruins of our shattered lives. I chose to take a single step of obedience and let God show me that joy comes in the morning.

Over the next two years, my life changed drastically. The lunch in a box was more than an idea; it was a miracle. I carried that sixteen-by-twenty Rubbermaid crate with a lunch in it to 216 women. I even had a name for it, "A Lunch in a Box." Today, in many of the surrounding areas where I live, the lunch-in-the-box idea has caught on. I talked to women who were hurting, lost, afraid, lonely, angry, bitter, and isolated. Sometimes, I would think that Laura was smiling down from heaven as I walked up to each door with our little box.

I had finished painting my living room by this time and had moved on to other areas of my house. I was at peace for the first time in my life. I was beginning to understand what it meant to be loved. I had some real friends, which was new to me.

Oh, I made lots of mistakes, but I learned not to let it control me to the point that I locked myself away. I found out that sometimes it's okay just to say, "Oops! Sorry about that; I didn't mean for it to turn out that way." But to punish myself for weeks and months, crawl into a hole, and bury myself is not what God wants me to do.

I still missed my family, and I thought of Laura all the time. I thought of Billy too. It was all still there in the corners of my mind. I would just tell myself, "I don't understand it all now, but someday, I will." Of course, I was referring to when I got to heaven.

In August of 2004, I went to a Women of Faith conference; it was one of the boldest steps I had taken up to this point. It was one amazing weekend, and I met some very special women who would become my friends. Over the next few years, they were the women who encouraged me, loved me, and corrected me. Women I learned to trust and respect. They have been there for me as I have journeyed on this road of healing and restoration.

When I returned home from the Women of Faith conference on Saturday afternoon, Scott was full of questions. I shared the events of the weekend with him. After we talked, I fixed a little something for us to eat. We had the house and evening to ourselves because Abigail was staying the night at a friend's house.

I can still recall how very restless I was that evening. I had some painting that I wanted to do, but I couldn't get focused enough to get any real painting done. I tried to read but was still not able to focus. Finally, Scott and I went to bed. It was raining outside, and I lay there listening to the sound. I don't know what hit me or why it happened; it just did. I sat straight up in bed and said, "I've got to get out of here."

I got out of bed and took a look at what I had on. *It will do*, I thought to myself. I had on a long granny gown that was loose on me. I grabbed my keys and headed toward the door. Scott grabbed clothes and put them on, telling me to wait. I wasn't waiting; I walked out the door and was backing out of the driveway when he screamed, "Stop! Let me in. I'm going with you." I don't remember what time it was, and I didn't even realize where I was going.

Over an hour later, I pulled up in front of the house I had grown up in. There was a "for sale" sign in the front yard. Laura and I had taken it off the market in July of 2001, and Jasmine had lived in it for a little over two years. After Laura's death, I told her it was hers. She was selling it and had already purchased a home near me. I looked at the sign, and then I looked over at Scott and told him I would be back. I stepped out of the car and onto the grass. I was barefoot and could feel the wet coolness of the grass as I walked across the yard. Flashes from my childhood went through my mind. I could hear Laura, and then I would see her lying in the middle of her bedroom floor, covered in blood. I could hear my dad screaming at me. Daniel in the pool, facedown. Everything was flooding into my soul like the fresh rain that was upon the ground.

I walked toward the back of the house. Looking down, I saw a little handheld shovel, and I grabbed it. I walked through the gate into the backyard and sat down under the pecan tree. Then I began to dig. It was raining, and I was digging and digging. I was throwing dirt everywhere when I heard Scott say, "Oh my God, Linda! What are you doing?"

I looked up at Scott, and I said, "I've got to find it, I've got to find it." I kept digging and digging.

He said, "Find what, Linda?"

I said, "Scott, don't you know? I got to find the candy because if I can find it, I know that I'll be all right… If I can just unbury it, I'll be all right; I will be whole again."

It was then that I began to weep. I cried for the lives of the two little girls who had been so bruised physically and emotionally in the confines of that house. Scott sat down on the ground beside me and put his arms around me as I shared with him all that was in my heart: the pain, the shame, the guilt, and the fear. I told him, "Two little girls lived right here in this house, on this land, in a world of fear, hate, deception, drunkenness, and perversion. A world that you could never imagine. We lived without hope and without love. There was no light that shined in the darkness for us. I was so young on the day I was sliding down the hall in my little white socks. That was the day I caught my mom in bed with another man. I had bought her some candy. I didn't know what happened to me. There was this pain deep down, and I buried it here somewhere. I buried it. I buried myself when I did it. Every time something happened, I buried it until there was no place to bury anything else. No place to hold the things I was trying to bury. Then everything just began to spill out, everything! I am so damaged, and I am so sorry for what I did to you, Scott."

I continued talking because I knew he needed to know the truth. "I am that girl in the stack of papers that you once threw at me, demanding to know who I was. Everything you read was true. I just didn't want to be that girl anymore. I hated myself. I hated who I was. I wanted to be the good girl, the Christian woman. I wanted to be a Sarah. I wanted to be a Mary, Elizabeth, Leah, maybe even a Hannah, and I wanted to be accepted and loved."

I stopped and told the truth, "I didn't think that anybody could ever love me. I wanted to know what it was like to be loved, even if it was just for a moment. The only thing that your investigation left out was that I have a heart, and it was shattered right here in this home. Forgive me, Scott, please forgive me."

Scott stopped me, "You are forgiven."

I looked away and said, "No, Scott, that is not what I mean. I know God has forgiven me. *I need you to forgive me.*" He gently cupped my face in his hands. I knew in my heart at that moment he was seeing me for the first time. Me, the real me.

Tears filled his eyes. As he looked at me and I looked at him, face-to-face, eye to eye, I saw the anger and hate disappearing and compassion taking its place. His voice was gentle as he softly said, "Linda, I forgive you, and I love you."

I remembered a time when Scott had said those very words to me just a few months earlier, but only because things were changing, and he didn't want to rock the boat, so to speak. I knew then he didn't mean it; he was just saying the words like I was saying: I forgive Billy.

This time, I knew Scott meant it. I knew it was from his heart. I knew that I was truly forgiven by him. I don't know how long we stayed there or how long the rain fell upon us. I was being washed and cleansed, there in the shadow of forgiveness. I still hold onto the beauty and the fragrance of the forgiveness that filled my empty soul that night.

On Scott's birthday, in November of 2004, I had made up my mind that I was going to ask him about the day that he would not let me go to my sister's house. I was ready to face and deal with the endless circle of guilt and blame. His birthday, of course, was probably not the ideal time to confront the issue, but I just didn't want to put it off any longer. I knew if I didn't talk to him, it would be another year of me flip-flopping between feeling guilty that I didn't go and blaming Scott because he stopped me from going.

After we ate supper, we sat around the table and talked. It was late in the evening by the time he opened his gifts. I was about ready to let it go when Scott said, "So, what's on your mind tonight?"

I asked, "What makes you think I have something on my mind?"

He answered, "I know you pretty well, little girl."

He calls me that sometimes, and I kind of like it. I decided this was it; it was time. "Scott, that Sunday, I was supposed to go to Laura's house; why wouldn't you let me go? You made me go to church, and that was my last chance to see her alive. Do you know that she would be alive if you would've let me go?"

Scott seemed a little shocked at my accusation, but I continued, "I was going to ask her to come home with me. She was off the next few days; she would have come. We had things to do preparing for her move. She would have been at our house when Billy broke into her home."

He began rather slowly, like he couldn't believe that I possibly thought he was responsible for Laura's death. "So... you... blame... me.... right?"

I told him what I thought, "Well, yes, I do. She would have been here and not at home when he broke in."

Scott defended his actions, as I knew he would. "Linda, you cannot go back and change things. One: if you recall, we had made an agreement that we would go to church together, no matter what, unless I was working out of town. Two: you made plans to go to Laura's on a Sunday morning at 11:30 when you knew we would be in church at that time. I told you that you could go to her house after church. I never told you not to go. You did that all by yourself. You could have gone, Linda, so don't blame me. You called her and told her you weren't coming. That was your choice."

Now, in my mind, that was not the way I remembered our conversation, but I wanted Scott to know that I had forgiven him for not letting me go. I thought I would approach it differently this time. "So," I said, "then why wouldn't you go with me the day I had to identify her body and plan her funeral? I will tell you why—because you felt guilty for not letting me go that Sunday to see her."

I realized that I was talking louder than normal. I pulled myself together and started talking in a softer tone. "You could have canceled your meeting, but instead, you let me go all by myself. Why? I know why, and you know why too. Because you knew you were wrong! I was all ready to go, and I had fixed a beautiful lunch for us. It's all your fault!" I was yelling again and crying. *"You knew I should have gone to Laura's that Sunday; it was my last chance—"*

Scott interrupted me, and he was very firm, "Linda, you have come a long way. I like the direction we're going in; don't do this to yourself, and please don't blame me. I begged you to let me go with you that night after we got home. Don't you remember? You told me no, you wanted to go by yourself. You didn't want me to go. The next morning, you even told me to just bring pizza home for supper.

"You want her death to make sense, and it doesn't. You want to blame someone for you not being there. Linda, you cannot change what happened. You know that Sunday, I started to let you go, but you were already talking to Laura on the phone, and you put your hand in the air, informing me not to speak.

"Linda, don't do this; let's pray and ask God to help you remember those two events more clearly. You were deeply hurt by what happened, and it is normal to have feelings of guilt and blame. I don't want to fight with you, and I don't want to walk around knowing that you blame me for taking away your last chance to see your sister."

I was very upset because I just wanted to forgive him, and he wouldn't admit he was wrong. He stopped me from going to her house, and he didn't go with me to identify her body. I said, "*Fine!* Let's pray, but I think God will show you how wrong you have been. I am not responsible for her death."

I stopped where I was standing. I looked at Scott, and the look on his face was one of shock and disbelief, "Linda, no one has ever said you were responsible."

He reached out and touched me on the shoulder. I jumped back. "Don't you touch me, it's your fault she died, you made me go by myself, I had to look at her broken body, I saw.... I saw her head... Oh God! It wasn't....it was cut off! Oh God, I still see it and dream of that moment when they pulled the sheet back as if I were going to watch a play. It was horrible. There were bruises and stab wounds all over the upper part of her body. Why? Why did they do that?"

Scott reached for me. I screamed, "Don't you ever touch me. It's all your fault! I have to live with that; I shouldn't have been alone."

Scott said, "Linda, you're upset, and you're not thinking clearly. Please, honey, let's pray." We got on our knees where we were, and Scott started praying.

As he prayed, I began to calm down, and gradually, my mind slipped back to that day. The whole scene played out in my mind. I didn't have a cantaloupe. I was getting ready to go to the store when Scott said, "Where are you going?"

My reply was, "To get a cantaloupe for the lunch that I'm taking to Laura's."

Scott said, "Well, just get it on the way home from church."

To which I replied, "That would be a little late; I am supposed to be at her house at eleven thirty."

Scott said, "No, we made an agreement; we go to church together. I thought you meant you were going after church. That is what I thought when you told me you were going to fix a lunch and take it to her today. Just call her and tell her you will be there at one thirty. You can stay the rest of the day. You can stay as late as you want, but you are going to church with me this morning." I had forgotten all that conversation. I realized that I didn't want to remember. But why? The truth was painful. It was my own doing because after Scott said I had to go to church, I just tuned him out because I didn't get my way. I could have gone to Laura's after church. I was blaming him for no reason and had for over three years. Blaming him for a choice I had made because I wouldn't listen to my husband and hear him out.

That night, I began to remember things more clearly. Scott was also right about me going by myself to identify her body. I didn't want him to go because I was afraid of my past. I knew after I identified her, I had to go back to the police station, where I would be asked more questions, and there were going to be questions about Laura's past and mine. I shut Scott out then, and I continued to shut him out. I had blamed him for everything while I balanced my guilt and carried the responsibility for Laura's murder.

I asked Scott to forgive me. He amazed me with his response: "No, Linda, it is I who should be asking for your forgiveness this time. I should have trusted God. I should not have dug up your past like that. I should not have talked about you to my family or my friends. I have said things about you that should not have been said. I know that I did things to hurt you.

"What grieves me the most is that night in August at your parent's house; you were not the only one there who needed to ask forgiveness. I should have asked you that night for forgiveness as well. I had sinned against you too. I had done things and said things to you out of anger. Linda, what I am trying to say is, *will you forgive me?*"

Words cannot express what was in my heart at that moment. I believe that if I were to try, it would be a heavenly language with words beyond all comprehension. Sometimes, within the depths of our hearts and in the midst of our pain, there are simply no words. That night, as I lay in bed, I remembered Laura's very last words to me. I cried, but not out of pain and loss. I cried with tears of joy, and that joy was lined with hope.

I remembered our last conversation clearly. That was what Scott had asked God when he prayed, "God, I am asking You to allow us to see clearly, show us those things that will bring healing and hope to our broken lives." I had blocked things out, things I didn't want to think about, things that were too painful, things I blamed Scott or myself for when there was no way either of us could have been responsible.

I let the next thought flow freely through my mind about the last time Laura and I talked. The last thing she said was: "I love you; now don't you forget that, and we will see each other again soon."

I thought about that for a moment and realized all the hope she had left for me in her last words. She loved me, and she wanted me to remember that. Her final words gave me hope. I knew my sister, and never in all our years of goodbyes had Laura ever said to me, "We will see each other again soon." She would say things like, "Love you! Bye" or "Give me a call later." Just little sayings, but never like that. I thank God for putting those words in Laura's heart that day. I needed to hold on to that.

God truly answered Scott's prayers that night. Scott and I received much more than we had asked God for. We both begin to see clearly. Our eyes were opened, as were our hearts.

We did not see each other with our natural eyes. Nor did we see each other with all our imperfections. We saw each other with spiritual eyes. God had given us an amazing love story, and that night, we saw each other through God's eyes. I knew I was loved by Scott. He knew he was loved by me. We both knew we were loved by God. We suddenly found ourselves in the shadow of God's amazing forgiveness.

I was a child when I buried the candy; such a broken little girl. I walked away from that buried candy and never looked back. I lived on, but the time had come to dig up what I had buried. A time to dig up all the stuff and let God heal and restore me. So I could move forward into a future that He had planned for me. Yes, there comes a time to dig up the candy that's been buried so deep within our soul and face it. A time to dig it up and say, "No more buried candy!"

CHAPTER 18

Will You Go?

I continued to paint, and I was very busy taking my lunch in the box to any woman whose name had been given to me or was placed on my heart. I was moving out of the pain of the past and moving forward into a life that was full. I had friends, I was active in church, I was painting, taking care of our home, and I visited the elderly in our neighborhood. I took the lunch in the box to at least three women a week. I was busy, but I always made time for Scott. Every morning and evening, we always read God's Word together, and afterwards, we prayed together.

In August of 2006, I served my lunch in the box. I cleaned it out and put it away. A new season in my life was about to begin. I was going to have luncheons in my home, now known as "Just a Little Luncheon." Once a month, seven ladies are sent an invitation. I do not know most of these ladies. They are invited to come for a one-time luncheon and share on one special topic. I prepare all the food and trust God with the details. The first luncheon in my home was on October 21, 2006. By the end of 2009, I had served over 210 women a luncheon in my home.

That would not be a big number to most, but that was huge to me.

Women have come into my home from every walk of life. Women have sat at my table and have experienced an amazing journey of sharing, connecting, fellowship, and, of course, food. Women have laughed, cried, and opened up and let go of the hurt they had been holding onto very tightly for years. I call the luncheons a small miracle, and the lunch in the box is a gift, a joy to those who open it, as it continues today.

However, no matter how much I did or where I went, the pieces of a scattered puzzle that could not be put together remained in the corners of my mind. The question in my heart remained unanswered. *Why?* Thoughts of Billy would slip into my mind, and I would tell myself, "I have forgiven him. I went to court and spoke to him. I even told him in court that I had forgiven him."

One day, I asked the Lord, "What more can I do?" I am not one for riddles, and I never liked jokes. If I ask a question, I just want a straight answer. So, when I asked Jesus what more I could do, I just wanted an answer, but instead, I got a riddle, "I was in prison, and ye came unto me." I knew the words well; they were spoken by Jesus in Matthew 25:31–40. His words continued, "In as much as you do it unto the least of these, you do it unto me." I wanted to push those words right out of my thoughts. However, I didn't allow myself to do so. I stopped and let the words fill my soul and asked myself, "What does this strange reply mean?" I wanted to solve the riddle right away, so I asked the Lord, "What do you mean? Lord, You're not serious, are You? You want me to be in some prison ministry and visit women in prison? Well, I'm not saying anything bad against anyone, but, Lord, I just don't see myself in some prison ministry. But I will do it if that's what You want me to do."

It was blown into my spirit like a very soft and gentle breeze, "Go see Billy Lopez."

I jumped up, and I began to walk in circles. "Oh, no, You got the wrong person. Go tell a preacher to go see Billy, but not me. Anyway, I don't think it is possible for me to get into the prison to see him. Have You forgotten that he killed my sister? They are not going to let me see him. I will not do this. Oh, God, You just cannot ask me to do this. Not me, please, not me. I am doing good; don't take my peace and joy away."

It was with those words that the battle began. I knew right from the beginning that it was going to be a long, hard battle. "I was in prison, and ye came unto me. Inasmuch as ye have done it unto one of the least of these my brethren, ye have done it unto me" (Matthew 25:36b, 40b). The words stayed with me. Day after day, as usual, I struggled and fought, and I had all kinds of excuses. I had all kinds of things to say to the Lord, like, "No, I will not go see him. It would accomplish nothing. He is a killer. He brutally murdered my sister. I cannot understand why You would want me to go see Billy. I cannot do this thing that You have asked of me. It is too hard." I even asked, "Why me? Why not some preacher, someone who hasn't been hurt by his actions?"

No matter what I did, those words still haunted me. "Go see Billy. I was in prison, and ye came unto me. Inasmuch as ye have done it unto one of the least of these my brethren, ye have done it unto me." There was a "how?" to all of this. Like how would it ever happen? How could it ever happen? There was no way anyone would let me walk into that prison and sit down and talk to Billy like nothing had ever happened. Like I was an old friend just dropping in to see how my buddy was doing and have tea.

In October of 2006, the Lord tugged at my heartstrings until I was ready. I got my Bible, sat down, got comfortable, and read the passage.

> When the Son of man shall come in his glory, and all the holy angels with him, then shall he sit upon the throne of his glory:
> And before him shall be gathered all nations: and he shall separate them one from another, as a shepherd divideth his sheep from the goats: And he shall set the sheep on his right hand, but the goats on the left.
> Then shall the King say unto them on his right hand, Come, ye blessed of my Father, inherit the kingdom prepared for you from the foundation of the world:
>
> For I was an hungered, and ye gave me meat: I was thirsty, and ye gave me drink: I was a stranger, and ye took me in:
> Naked, and ye clothed me: I was sick, and ye visited me: I was in prison, and ye came unto me.
> Then shall the righteous answer him, saying, Lord, when saw we thee an hungered, and fed thee? or thirsty, and gave thee drink?

When saw we thee a stranger, and took thee in?
or naked, and clothed thee?
Or when saw we thee sick, or in prison, and came unto thee?
And the King shall answer and say unto them, Verily I say unto you, Inasmuch as ye have done it unto one of the least of these my brethren, ye have done it unto me.
Then shall he say also unto them on the left hand, Depart from me, ye cursed, into everlasting fire, prepared for the devil and his angels:
For I was an hungered, and ye gave me no meat: I was thirsty, and ye gave me no drink:
I was a stranger, and ye took me not in: naked, and ye clothed me not: sick, and in prison, and ye visited me not.
Then shall they also answer him, saying, Lord, when saw we thee an hungered, or athirst, or a stranger, or naked, or sick, or in prison, and did not minister unto thee?
Then shall he answer them, saying, Verily I say unto you, Inasmuch as ye did it not to one of the least of these, ye did it not to me.
And these shall go away into everlasting punishment: but the righteous into life eternal.
Matthew 25:31–46

When I finished reading the passage, I prayed. I reasoned everything out and weighed it in the balance of my mind. I didn't know how I could possibly do what the Lord was asking me to do.

Scott was out of town, and that evening, after we had our nightly talk and prayed over the phone, I decided to read the passage again. This time, I saw it a little differently. The King called the sheep on His right "blessed of the Father." The sheep had no idea they had ever done anything for the King. They had not kept track of the deeds they had done in reaching out to others, nor did they consider doing these things as a means of gaining favor from the King. It wasn't even a matter of whom, when, or even where they ministered. It was a matter of serving and meeting the needs of others with genuine love and concern. They kept no record of their deeds since they replied, "When did we?" It is obvious they didn't have any idea when, where, or even who they had served.

The goats were told to depart, and they were cursed. The goats, however, thought they deserved some kind of special treatment, and they had kept track of their deeds. This is clear when they demanded of the King: "When did we ever see you without, for we would have taken care of our King?"

Another thing that I considered was the animals. There are differences between sheep and goats; these were the ones that interested me. Sheep are easily led; they submit to others. Sheep are gentle and innocent. They are very calm and without resistance, even in the face of something that is unpleasant. Goats are stubborn; they are very alert and move quickly with skill and control, thinking and reacting. A goat will find one spot and keep hitting it until it weakens, and they break through. A goat remembers weak spots. This is important because it proves that goats are smart and active and calculate their moves. They are also very selfish. Sheep follow, and goats lead.

I didn't think of myself as a goat, and I knew Billy was not a Christian. I didn't see him as a "brethren." I realized I was justifying my actions. I told the Lord, "I want to be a sheep, not an ugly goat. They are selfish and eat everything. But what You are asking me to do, Lord, is just too hard. I am not the one for this task; it's just simply impossible." It was very quiet that night as I waited for a response. There was nothing, just the quietness; there was no response.

Three hours passed, and I got ready for bed. Nothing... I got into bed, waiting for a response, and still nothing. Finally, I said, "I am waiting for You to talk to me." There was nothing; He was not talking to me. I got out of bed, walked over to the window, and looked up at the sky.

It was a beautiful night; the stars were shining brightly. I said, "Is something wrong?" I waited, and still nothing. "Please talk to me... I am sorry; I just don't know how to do this. I want to know what happened. I want to know why he killed her. I want to forgive, and I felt I had. He was right there in the courtroom. He was given a chance to ask my forgiveness, and he didn't. I know, Lord, You know my heart. The way I call him Billy, You know that is my unforgiveness and bitterness showing itself. I don't call him *Billy* for the same reasons. I cannot say *Billy* in forgiveness."

Tears were now revealing themselves as I continued sharing my heart with the Lord. "I am torn between the memories of the past, the life I lived, and the life I long to have. The life that is before me now that I am living in love and joy. You know the truth: I still cannot let go of the past. The truth is, I still miss my family, little Daniel, my parents, and, yes, Laura.

"If I let go in some way, I feel that I will forget them and that their memories will vanish. Lord, their lives lived and died in vain. What could be learned and understood from the lives that they all lived? Is there some hidden wisdom that can flow from lives lived in such lies and darkness? Is there truth that can be revealed that would cast a shadow of hope and healing in the life of someone else? If so, how? God, how do I get from this place of brokenness to a place of completeness? I want to believe that I am valuable and usable. Help my unbelief, Lord!

"If, by some miracle, there is a way to see Billy, I would feel like I am betraying Laura. I am sure Scott would never agree to me going to a prison to see Billy. One important detail is *why* I am going to see him. It makes no sense to me." I wiped my eyes and waited; all I got was, "I was in prison, and ye came unto me. Inasmuch as ye have done it unto one of the least of these my brethren, ye have done it unto me."

Two months went by, and the passage stayed on my mind constantly. One rainy day, mid-morning, Abigail was lying on her bed, complaining that there was nothing to do. She said it was "boring."

I said, "Okay, Abigail, let's go have some fun. Let's play in the rain."

We went outside, and the rain was coming down steadily. At first, we just walked around, not really knowing what to do. Then the rain started pouring down, and we laughed and ran from each other. We found big puddles of rainwater and jumped in them, splashing and laughing, seeing who could make the biggest splash. It stopped raining about twenty-five minutes later, and by then, we were muddy and soaking wet.

As we were drying off on the porch, Abigail looked at me and said, "Mom, you are the greatest; you know more about things than anyone I know. I think you know everything sometimes. Thank you for today; I will never forget it. It's like I looked at rain as bad, but without the rain, things would not grow. It's like the rain washes and makes everything clean and fresh. In your life, some bad things happened. I know it hurt you badly, and you slept a really long time, but now you stay awake, you paint, you take those lunches out in that box, and I see you smile sometimes, and it makes me happy. Being out here today, playing in the rain, running, laughing, jumping in mud puddles, taught me something."

I asked her, "What did you learn?"

Abigail looked up and waved her hand. Oh, how my heart leaped. It was like seeing Laura as a little girl telling me a story and waving her hands all about. Abigail brought her hand down with a finger pointing upward and said, "I could have told you no, that I didn't want to play in the nasty cold rain. I didn't think it would be any fun, but I saw your smile, so I just did it to make you happy at first. Then everything changed, and it was like the rain washed and made everything clean and fresh in us."

Then she said, "What I learned is sometimes the things we are asked to do make no sense at all, and we think it's all bad, but then if we just do it, we find out that it really was exactly what we needed to do. And it becomes the best part of our day."

I was smiling and said, "Abigail, you are a smart girl. Today, we have both learned something."

She said, "What did you learn?"

I replied, "Well, I learned that you are never too old to play in the rain."

We both laughed and went inside, took a shower, and had a bowl of hot soup and a glass of tea.

After our soup, we laid down to take a nap. I whispered, "Lord, I am ready. Talk to me, please."

The words were different and direct. "Will you go?"

I replied this time, "I don't understand why You want me to, but I will go. I don't know how, but I am willing to do this. I am going to say this out loud, and I mean it. I know it has taken me a long time. I am willing to go see him, and I believe You will prepare me. I will go for You; I will be a sheep, a helpless sheep in the midst of wolves. I know You shall take care of me. I don't desire to be a stubborn, selfish goat anymore. I will take the gospel to him, and I will go the extra mile. I need You to be the one to open all the doors and lead the way, and *I will go*."

That was in June of 2007. I began by having a friend check some things out for me on the internet. I learned that I had to be on his visiting list, and the only way to get on the list was for him to put me on it. In December of 2007, I let it go. I had tried several things and hit a dead end with every avenue. I tried. I decided I was just being tested, but even that didn't make sense to me. I knew now that it had to be God who opened the door and was the one to lead the way.

A light had come on in my soul. The lies, the deception, and the darkness that I had been raised in were vanishing. They no longer had control of my heart. I was not letting guilt and shame rule in my heart anymore. God's Word was coming alive in my soul. I wanted my King to say to me, "Come ye, blessed of My Father."

I didn't want to miss the opportunity to serve someone or help someone. I didn't want to pass up an opportunity to witness to someone or to share with them the love of my King. When someone was hungry, thirsty, sick, naked, a stranger, or even in prison, I wanted my heart to be open to their cry, my hands ready to meet the need to the very best of my ability. Would I always do that? Would I make mistakes? Would I fall down? Would I blow it from time to time? The answer was yes to all the questions. The one thing that mattered, however, was what I had learned. I may not always do what is right, but deep in my heart, in the core of my being, I wanted what was right.

I was waiting for the door to open; I prayed for a way to go visit a prisoner. I needed to visit the one man who had brought so much pain into my life. Pain so deep that I thought I would never get past the emotional damage. I had crawled into a hole and never wanted to come out. Now, here I was, praying for him and asking God to send someone to him who would share the gospel with him, even if that someone was me. In a world full of impossibilities, I believed the impossible could become possible.

The years 2005 and 2006 had proven to be years full of mistakes, downfalls, a few minor potholes, and a ditch or two. However, I had defied the odds; I survived it all. I no longer wanted to play "guilt and blame" like a musical composition on a grand piano. I no longer saw myself as the victim. I was a child of the Most High God, and I was loved by Him. I was learning to rise above the circumstances of life and see my faults from God's perspective. I no longer wanted to hide from my problems and act like they did not exist.

I wanted to face any sin in my life and deal with not only the sin but also the effects that it had not only on me but also may have had on others. I learned that it is important to admit when I am wrong. It is very important that confession is made not only to God but to those around me whom I may have offended. I had learned to humble myself and ask for forgiveness when my actions had resulted in the unforeseen hurt and pain in someone else's life. These were not easy lessons to learn.

Yes, during those two years, I had faltered, and mistakes were made, but I had learned the basic principles: confess, forsake, and seek forgiveness. I also learned to pick myself back up, dust myself off, and be open to all that God could teach me through the experience. I had learned a wonderful secret. I would never outgrow the ability to learn. God has given us the capacity to acquire knowledge, understanding, and wisdom, and experience is the best teacher. God has given that capacity to all mankind.

The greatest lesson I have learned is not to allow myself to become the victim of circumstances or allow mistakes to paralyze me. Finally, I came to the place where I understood that pride and destruction go hand in hand, and pride always comes before a fall. The greatest of all is love, and love will cover a multitude of sins. I was maturing in many areas of life, both spiritually and emotionally. One of those areas concerned Billy. I was now praying for Billy on a regular basis. I asked God to begin to prepare his heart for the day we would meet. I didn't know how, but I was going to walk into the prison he was in. I was going to sit down, and we were going to talk.

A year had passed since I had told the Lord I would go see Billy. My desire to visit him had gotten stronger. I desired to share with him what I went through, not out of hate and anger, but to allow him to see how the mighty hand of God brought restoration and healing, not because of what he had done but in spite of what he had done. I wanted him to understand that the brutal crime of murder he had committed didn't just affect him, nor was his crime just against Laura.

What he had done affected the lives of his family and friends, Laura's friends, and what was left of our little family. We had all been touched and changed by his actions. My greatest desire was for him to know I did not hate him. However, because of God's great law and because God is not a respecter of persons, he was going to be held accountable to God for his actions. He needed to know that out of the most horrible scene of his life, God could and would paint a masterpiece. Wrapped up in that desire was my longing for him to see and understand what God had done in my life as a result of his actions. I desired for him to know that he could be forgiven by God and that there was hope and healing for him. It was all his to receive through Jesus Christ; all he had to do was ask.

It was November of 2007 when a ministry called Disciples 4 Christ came to our church. It is a ministry that helps women after they get out of prison. All through the service, the Lord just kept tugging at my heart, "Just go ask one of the ladies if she knew whether or not it had ever been done, a victim meeting an offender." When the service was over, I headed towards where they had set up to hand out information about their ministry. They were surrounded by the members of the church. I was going to forget it when one of the ladies stopped me and handed me something, saying, "Hi! Here is a little information about our ministry. Also, there is a list of some needs we have at this time. Did you have any questions?"

I told her, "Not at this time."

We started talking about the prison ministry. She was very open about the fact that she had been in prison and how God had changed her life. She shared what the ministry was accomplishing. She just had an air about her that made me feel comfortable enough to share some of my story with her. Within moments, I was asking her about visiting prisons. I told her that my sister had been murdered and that for the last two years, I had been trying to find out if there was any way I could get into the prison to meet the man who murdered my sister. I explained how the trial had ended so quickly, and there were so many unanswered questions. She smiled and said, "Hang on." She went and talked to another lady and then came back to where I was and said, "Come with me; you need to meet Susan."

She introduced me to Susan. I went through the whole story again. She gave me a number for the Texas Department of Criminal Justice Victim Services Division in Austin, Texas. I had the number in my hand, reminding myself of the words that Susan had spoken to me. It was possible through this program called "The Victim Offender Mediation/Dialogue Program." I had not heard of it before, and I was very excited. On my way home from church, I kept thinking, *It is possible.* I took the number and laid it on my desk. *I will call first thing in the morning.*

I felt that there had been an awakening in my soul and that I was ready. I knew I would not be meeting him with my old desire to know what happened and why. I would be going as an ambassador of Christ to take the gospel to him. I knew I would have to share with him at some point how his actions had affected my life. I would also be able to share the great victory that came as a result. God had worked in amazing ways to bring good out of such a horrible crime.

I had not shared the news with Scott; he was in Nebraska. He goes every year in November to hunt and spends ten days there. I knew he was in the mountains, and it would be impossible for me to talk to him about it. Realizing that I wouldn't be able to tell him until he got home, I decided that my best course of action was to pray about it first. I decided I wouldn't call the number until I had talked to Scott. I wouldn't even call and ask questions. Scott might have a few questions he would want me to ask about the program when I called. I wanted Scott to feel like I had included him in this decision. So, I waited.

When Scott got home, I waited a few more days so he could rest and get caught up on his work. Finally, the moment came on a Saturday afternoon. Scott and I sat down, and I shared with him the story of how I got the number and that it was possible for me to go see Billy through "The Victim Offender Mediation/Dialogue Program."

Scott had been all for me going and seeing Billy and talking to him up until he realized that it was indeed possible. We talked for hours. I told him I would not go without his consent. I told him that I hoped that he wouldn't make a hasty decision but that he would consider my desire to be able to face Billy and get the answers that I so desperately needed from him.

After that, he had lots of questions, questions I had no answers for because I had not called the number or talked to anyone yet. Scott was very clear on where he stood. He would not go to the prison with me. He told me he wouldn't go if it had been his sister. He was very honest about how he felt. In the end, he agreed to it, and his final words were, "I will not stop you because I believe this is something you have to do, and I know it is what God wants you to do. Call them Monday morning and find out what steps you need to take. Let's pray."

It was a Monday morning, September 10, 2008, almost a year after Susan had given me the number. I have been asked many times why I waited so long. The first reason was that I had learned that making quick decisions without getting all the information, without godly counsel, without prayer, and without truly seeking God can lead to mistakes. Sometimes, those mistakes are very costly, not just hurting you but others as well. I learned it is better to wait on God's timing and get the right answer. The second reason was that I was still battling to forgive Billy.

I had dialed the number, and the phone was ringing. For a brief moment, I thought, *What am I doing? Hang up!* A voice on the other end said, "The Victim Offender Mediation/Dialogue Program, how may I help you?" The lady on the other end of the phone was very polite. She answered all my questions. She needed some details of the case before she gave me any information. It would not be an easy process.

When I got off the phone, I was thinking, *Jesus, do You ever make anything easy?*

I heard Him say, "To every thing there is a season, and a time to every purpose under the heaven" (Ecclesiastes 3:1).

There were several steps in the program, and it would be a long, difficult process. First, I would be placed on a waiting list.

It would be a four- to six-month wait. Then, someone would be assigned to my case. After a mediator was assigned to my case, he would go see Billy and tell him that the victim's sister wanted to meet him and talk about his crime. The idea behind this is that the offender must be willing to face up to what he did and be accountable for his actions.

He could refuse to admit that he committed the crime, or he could choose not to meet any of the victim's family. In either case, I would have to wait another year and file again. In order to proceed, Billy had to be willing to admit to the crime and would have to agree to meet me. At that point, the mediator would start the process by meeting with Billy and me separately over the course of three to six months. This was set up to give us both a chance to talk about the crime and how it affected our lives.

During the mediations, you don't get to know about each other. The mediator is to prepare you for the actual meeting. I would go through months of mediations. It would give me a chance to speak openly and honestly about my feelings and about what I had been through. I thought this would be good for me because I had never really talked about it with anyone. I was also informed that there would be a lot of paperwork. Which I was not good at, remembering I only had a seventh-grade education.

After the mediations and all the paperwork were completed, a time would be set up to go to the prison and meet the offender. I would have as long as I needed on that day: two hours, three, six, or even ten. After that, I would meet twice with the mediator, one month after and again six months later. It would be a time to talk about whether meeting the offender helped me or not. It would be a time to talk about how it affected me, and of course, they wanted my input on how I felt the program might be improved.

The program is a great one, and I would highly recommend it to anyone who has worked through their bitterness and anger. I have not talked in depth about the program in this book because I am not at liberty to do so. I believe that the program works, but I also know that it depends on where each individual is in dealing with what occurred. Each person is different, and of course, it would be based upon the extent of the crime. I just wanted people to be aware of this program and the benefits of going through the mediations and meeting the person who committed a crime against them or someone they love.

I felt that it was a very good program right from the beginning. It was the waiting that I considered to be a problem. I had already waited one year just for this step, and from the looks of it, I may have to wait another year. I knew if I didn't do it, I would always wonder. On the other hand, would I live to regret meeting him? For a moment, I wondered, *What was in the heart of a killer? What would make one person take another's life?* Then, there was that old familiar question, "Why?" I wanted to settle it right away. Yes, I still had that desire to know why Billy killed my sister. However, I didn't want to get sidetracked or wrapped up in that. I had to stay focused. I stopped everything I was doing at that moment. I went and got my Bible and read from the Psalms, and then I read from the book of James. After that, I spent some time in prayer. I gave it all to the Lord. I would trust Him in this matter, and if the time ever came that it was revealed to me why Billy killed my sister, it would be by my Master's hand. I was at peace with that.

That evening, I explained the program to Scott. The whole process of waiting and all the mediations I would have to go through, and of course, it all depended upon Billy. He would have to be accountable for his crime and be willing to meet me. After I had finished telling Scott, he asked me, "Are you willing to go through all that? Do you want to open those wounds up again?"

I looked down and said, "Scott, those wounds have never been closed. Those wounds are still open, and every day, I hurt in one way or another. It's just that I am different now. There is a place I go every day. It is there that God puts healing balm on the wounds of my soul. I am healing, and in time, I will be okay. I have a hold of the hem of Jesus's garment, and I know that one day, I will be made whole, and I will be complete."

Scott answered, "Linda, it's time you call and put your name on that list. Let's pray about it this evening. I want you to make that call first thing in the morning. I am telling you that you have my full consent to go through the program. Go meet Billy; maybe you will find peace and the answers you long for. I do want to tell you something, and I don't want you to take this in a prideful way, but you are the bravest woman I have ever met. I admire your courage and your ability to trust God in all situations. I have seen you stand when I would have run. I have watched you face impossible things I would have hidden from until they passed. I believe that God is going to make you complete and whole, so don't let go of the hem of Jesus's garment."

The next morning, I called the number again, this time to put my name on the waiting list. After that phone call, the rest was in God's hands. I had done my part, and I didn't want to assume anything at this point. I reminded the Lord that this was not my idea; it was His idea, and therefore, I trusted that He would bring it to pass in His timing. Deep down in my soul, a little nagging was going on in spite of what I knew to be the truth. I was haunted by the words spoken to me, "It will be the offender's choice. Billy may not want to meet you. If that is the case, you can walk away and forget it. If you are a patient person, you can file every year. Who knows? Maybe one year, he will be ready. You can file as many times as it takes."

Things in my life have always happened rather quickly, leaving very little time between powerful events and situations that once spun my life out of control. It seems I was always changing directions, changing my focus, or looking for some new way to numb my pain. I believe many times, God's mighty hand held back the evil forces that could have destroyed my life with just one more out-of-control situation. It was only by the grace and love of God that I had a few rare, brief moments of stillness in my life. For that reason, I call those moments the "silent moments."

Now, here I was in a new arena, waiting for word from the man who murdered my sister. I was not what I would call "at peace." I was in the middle of a "silent moment." My spirit was waiting on what I knew would be a moment of truth in my life. I couldn't help but wonder, *Is this what it means by the calm before the storm?*

If Billy agreed to meet me, it would be either a triumph or a moment of defeat. I prayed every day for God to reveal the truth and set us both free. I didn't feel like the brave woman my husband had described a few months ago. I think it's easier to say, "I felt like I had planted a garden, but the seeds were unfamiliar to me, and I, like a coward, was hiding, waiting for them to spring forth to reveal their true identity. They would bring either joy or sorrow, but which one? The answer was just below the surface." I didn't know what was in Billy's heart. Was he ready? Was I ready? Had I opened a door that should have remained closed?

It was January 23, 2009, when the call came. It was mid-morning, and I had just finished reading over the passage from Matthew 25:31–46. There was a beauty in the words I had read, a sweetness that was surrounded with love, correction, and warning. How had I missed it before? I bowed my head and said, "Lord, I will go."

The phone rang as I finished saying those words. I glanced at the number. The call was from Austin; I picked up the phone and thought, *Lord, let this be it.* I answered, "Hello?"

The voice on the other end was a male. "Is Linda Prenger there?"

I answered, "I am Linda Prenger. How may I help you?"

He introduced himself: "I am David Flores, with the Texas Department of Criminal Justice Victim Services Division. I have been assigned to your case."

We talked for a few moments, and he explained what the next step would be. He would go and visit Billy Lopez in a few weeks and let him know that the victim's sister wanted to meet with him and speak to him concerning the murder.

It was at this point that I was once again made aware of the fact that Billy had to admit to the crime and have a willingness to seek forgiveness and accept accountability for his actions. I responded to David, "So, in other words, it is all left up to Billy?"

David said, "Yes, it would be up to Billy."

I didn't really know how to feel. I just stood there as if I had been frozen in time. My mind began reeling back to the day I answered the door, the police officer, the police department, the drive home, the funeral, her broken and bruised body, her bloody home, the pain, the dreams, the loss, and all she must have endured as she fought to live. I screamed, "Oh, God! Please help me; don't let me be overtaken again by the painful remembrance of those days. I have buried them in the depths of my soul. I have finally moved past the pain. I don't want the memories or the pain to be awakened again in my soul."

It was there, in the stillness, that God spoke to my heart, "It is I who healeth the broken in heart, and bindeth up their wounds. Joy will come in the morning" (Psalm 147:3, Psalm 30:5b; paraphrased). It had been a long time since I had heard those words spoken to my heart. I remembered the days right after Laura's death and during so many painful, shattering moments that the Lord brought those scriptures to me, and I clung to them. They were my hope and my comfort during so many hopeless, overwhelming days of loss and emotional upheaval.

"He healeth the broken in heart, and bindeth up their wounds" (Psalm 147:3). "Weeping may endure for a night, but joy cometh in the morning" (Psalm 30:5b). I asked myself, "Why are these scriptures once again washing over my soul like the midnight tide?" The Lord did not have to speak because, in the very depth of my soul, I knew that God was going to bring the wounds into the light, reopen them, and dig out the infection. I said very softly, with tears flowing down, "Lord, I honestly do not know if I am ready, nor do I know if I can bear this. I don't know what is ahead, but I am trusting You and Your Word."

There was an awakening going on inside my soul. There was a flood of renewed questions that still had no answers. *Is Billy ready for his awakening? Is God preparing his heart?* The real question that tugged at my heart was one I would have to answer very soon: *How am I going to face him? As a judge or with compassion and forgiveness? Am I really ready for any of this?*

After all, I had stepped out in faith and started a ministry called "Healing for the Wounded Heart" in September of 2008. At that time, I sponsored my first retreat. It was a two-day event, with over a hundred women in attendance. I will always remember 2008 as a year of amazing challenges and the freedom of walking in Christ. It became the year that fear was no longer the hidden driving force of my life.

Suddenly, I didn't want to change anything; it was too close to the pain. I didn't want to go back into all that. *Why go through this when I am happy and my life is fine? I am at peace with things. Do I really want to do this?*

Then the Lord spoke to my heart, "Linda, you seek the truth, do you not? You have been seeking, and now it is time to find. If you walk away from this, you will be walking away from finding the truth. You have asked Me to set Billy and you free. The *truth* is what will do that."

God was going to take me back in time. He was awakening me spiritually and emotionally. He was going to open a fatal wound, one that was deep in my soul, and He was going to heal that wound. Then, He was going to heal and restore the broken areas of my life that were infected because of that wound.

I had always believed that time heals all wounds; maybe you believe that too... However, I was about to learn that time does no such thing. Time had gradually eased the pain, giving me the illusion that the emotional damage was healed. Time had only eased the pain and made it become bearable. But time had not healed my wounds; they were still there, just below the surface. God wanted to heal my wounds completely so I could be set free to walk in the fullness of His love.

Seven long years had come and gone since Laura had been murdered. In many ways, it seemed like it had just happened. I missed her smile, her laughter, her telling me stories, and most of all, I missed her and all that inclines.

I missed her presence in my life. I missed my parents, but they were not violently taken out of my life. I missed Daniel so very much, but even his death was not violent. He drowned and was suddenly ripped from my life because of a tragic accident that could have been avoided. But Laura was murdered, and that "word" changes everything.

I was being awakened; my soul was being awakened to the life I could have had as I once again caught sight of the life I had lost. I was awakened again to the reality of what Billy had inadvertently chosen for the both of us when he murdered my sister. Now, in my heart were the words: "Will you go?" My answer was, "Yes, Lord, I will go!"

CHAPTER 19

The Letter

On February 26, 2009, I received a second phone call from David Flores. He told me that on February 20, he had seen Billy and had a very long talk with him. David was silent for a moment, and then he said, "Linda, I have bad news: Billy said he didn't commit the crime."

My mind just could not receive that. I had thought of many different responses that I could have received from Billy, but that wasn't one of them. "What else did he say?" David informed me that Billy did want to see me and talk to me. However, the main part of the program requires the offender to confess to the crime he committed, and he must seek forgiveness.

The harsh reality rushed into my mind like a mighty undertow, pulling me down to the very bottom, and I was drowning! It was over, and I would have to wait another year. All the waiting, the hoping, the praying—this is how it was going to end. I told David, "I don't know why he is saying he didn't kill Laura. He did, and he knows he did! He even signed confessions saying he did. He pleaded guilty, knowing he could have gotten the death penalty. It doesn't make sense to me. Why, after all this time, would he say he didn't kill her?"

I just could not grasp what was taking place. I was having a hard time understanding the current situation, and I could not stand the thought of more waiting. The silence was broken again as I spoke, "I have to wait another year, but I am not sure that I can go through this again." I paused for a brief moment and continued, "The waiting is unbearable, and I just don't think I want to go through another disappointment like this again. I know I am taking a risk by asking this, but if I don't, I will always wonder if I really did everything I could and if I left no stone unturned. Are there any other alternatives? Anything that can be done that might help change Billy's mind? Is there anything I can do? Because I really don't think I can do this again…"

David said, "Write him a letter and mail it to me. Just be honest and tell him how you feel. I'll take it to him, and maybe he will change his mind and confess to the crime. You never know; it just might be the push he may need. It's just hard to tell sometimes; I don't think he will change his story, but it's worth a try."

It took me about a month to write the letter. My wounds were brought out into the open. It was too late to close the door; it had already been unlocked. I prayed about every word in the letter. I asked the Lord if Billy didn't commit the crime to bring the truth to light. Perhaps he knew what really happened because his DNA was found at the crime scene. Maybe he was there, but he didn't actually kill Laura. I was so hurt and mixed up. I had convinced myself I had foolishly gotten messed up in something I should have left alone. Yet, within my soul, there was such a longing for the truth that I pressed forward.

During that month, I had a lot of highs and lows. I felt like I was stuck on a roller coaster ride without a ticket. I did a lot of soul-searching and spent hours every day in the Word of God and in prayer. I knew the letter would be my only chance to speak to Billy. The letter had to be right and written with an attitude of forgiveness. I did not know if I had the strength to go through all of this again. I was still hoping that somehow God would touch Billy's heart and change his destiny, his eternal destiny, that is. There was something else that hung in the balance. Deep in my soul, I still longed for the truth. As I look back now, I realize I was unwilling to even admit that I wanted to know what happened to my sister and why. So, to say the only reason was to forgive Billy face-to-face would not be the whole truth. However, I did claim it to be the only reason at that time.

Before I mailed the letter to David, I called him and let him know the letter was on its way because it had taken me so long to write it. I had to trust the Lord with this letter, and I prayed it would touch Billy's heart. I prayed it would stir his soul and bring him to a place where he was willing to talk about what happened. It was part of the agreement that he would have to make, which was he would have to confess to what he had done and seek forgiveness. I mailed the letter, and David Flores received it on March 27, 2009, and the waiting began again.

David Flores would take the letter to Billy on his next visit to the prison a month later. Billy was in Huntsville, Texas. On April 28, 2009, David walked into the Ellis Unit. On that day, he talked to Billy and told him I had written him a letter and handed it to him.

The letter:

Billy Lopez, I just got off the phone with David Flores. I am very hurt and disappointed after waiting for such a long time just to get to this point.

Now that I have come this far, you do not want to admit to what happened that night. The night my sister was murdered, you were there, and you know what happened. Making this step was very difficult for me. Still, it was small in comparison to what I have gone through since October 17, 2001, when my sister's body was discovered. I find it hard to believe that after all this time, you do not want to face up to what you did. However, I ask you to consider this. I am willing to meet with you to give you a chance to talk about what happened honestly and openly. Not so I can judge or condemn you, but so both of us together might find forgiveness and healing. That cannot happen if you will not accept the responsibility for your actions. I pray that you will read this letter and that God will open your heart so that you may see the truth that lies within these pages.

Why do you keep changing your story? If you think for one minute that I didn't go over and over everything that I saw and what the police, investigators, detectives, and the Texas rangers said about the evidence, you are wrong. I ask you to think seriously about this. They had enough evidence to convict you.

There were four people, including Laura's son, Kenneth, Jasmine, the attorneys, the district attorneys, and me, in that room who did not have to accept your guilty plea. They wanted the trial and the death penalty. They had enough evidence to convict you of capital murder. There was no doubt you would have gotten the death penalty. I think you should know that it was me who begged those in that room to accept your guilty plea. You really need to think about this. You took my sister's life, and I begged for yours.

Your statement about Laura asking you to kill her because she had nothing to live for was a lie! I knew different. I had five acres of land and was planning to move her home on to it. I was going to meet with her on October 19, 2001, at 9:00 a.m., to get her mobile home ready to move on Monday morning. So, when you said she asked you to kill her because she had nothing and no one loved her, I knew it was a lie. However, it seems that was not your first lie, or your last, concerning what really happened that night.

I know that my sister fought hard for her life that night. I love Laura very much. There was a bond between us. We always knew when something was wrong with one another. I tried to call her, but there was no answer. I had this feeling, but I just pushed it out of my mind. I just kept thinking, no, everything is all right. Instead, on Thursday morning, I was making plans for her funeral, talking to the police, and trying to make sense out of it all. You did it, and you know you did, just like I know. I am trying to give you a chance to face up to what you did. To confess to me what you did and what really went so very wrong that night. It's not like I can do anything to you that has not already been done. I am her sister, and I want to know what happened.

Tell the truth, Billy; Jesus said, "The truth shall set you free." Let's look at the facts: You knew that you were guilty when Chief Sanders came to see you in prison. They had all the evidence. The only thing they didn't have was your DNA, which turned out to be a perfect match. They took the kitchen floor out of her house. Did you know that? Did you think you didn't leave a trail? Do you think your blood wasn't left anywhere in the house or skin particles under her nails? Do you think you didn't leave any smudges that would be identified as yours?

Wrong, you left more behind than you think. You left traces everywhere. There were bloody fingerprints and blood all over the thermostat and wall where you turned the temperature down. Your bloodstained footprints were left on the carpet all through her house. Remember the bloody white sock? It was found by me! Remember where you put it? You threw all those clothes over her body so you didn't have to look at her while you finished robbing her home. I am sure that this burns in your soul every day. Maybe you are haunted by the images that you left behind for me to clean up.

You need to stop with the lying. You're saying her ex-husband murdered her is the wrong answer also. He was in another state on a job site where he had been for two weeks. Proven fact. He also attended the funeral with his wife. All you need to do is tell the truth. You need to understand no lie will ever make you innocent.

That day in court, you chose to plead guilty because you knew you killed her. You knew there was enough evidence to convict you, and you knew you would get the death penalty. However, did you know that we didn't have to accept your plea of guilt, nor the bargain for your life?

We could have made you go to trial, and you would have gotten the death penalty. You took my sister's life, and as strange as it may sound, you were granted your life because I accepted your guilty plea and begged those who were in the room that day to do the same. You would have gone to trial for capital murder had I not begged for your life even after you killed my only sister, Laura.

You are alive today because of the work that God has done in my life. All because of His amazing love, you have been given a chance to come face to face with the one who had to deal with all you left behind. It is because of the work that I allowed Him to do in my heart that you didn't get the death penalty. You have a chance to see me and thank me for that. Oh, but I forgot. You will see me, but you will not tell me you killed my sister or why. The only way you will ever see me is when you agree to tell me the truth about what happened that night.

They have laid out the rules for you as they have me. I don't want you to think about this as one of man's interventions. I want you to think about it as one of

God's small miracles. God has made a way for us to see each other face to face. That's God's grace. What you do with that is up to you.

Something else you need to understand: you cannot ever have a retrial. Ever! When you make a deal with a guilty plea, it destroys all chances of you ever having a retrial. You told David you were coerced into saying you murdered my sister. I don't believe you are that stupid, saying you murdered someone when you didn't. When you are ready to get honest with me, then and only then will they allow you to see me. There is nothing I can do to you. Nothing! You have already been sentenced for her murder. What could I do to you? I tell myself to forget it, that I am crazy for wanting to see you and help you. However, deep in my soul, I know that this is something I have to do. I need to know why. I need to know what went wrong that night. What went so wrong, Billy, that made you take her life? I understand that you were in the middle of robbing her house that night, but why did you have to kill her?

I believe that God wants to bring something good, and maybe even amazing, out of all of this mess. However, that can only happen if you're willing to face the truth and deal with what you did. It cannot be any worse than what you have already lost and what was taken from me. I live with many harsh, cold facts about the way you brutally murdered my sister. I live with the memory of walking into her house and finding what you left behind. As for you, I am sure that you have your memories and nightmares as well.

I want to forgive you face to face. Please think about all of this. I do hate what you did, but I do not hate you. I know you did it, and so do you. Let's see if we can get past this part of you being afraid to look me in the eye and tell me what you did. You could not tell me anything worse than what I have imagined for over seven years.

I know that in some cases, it wouldn't be possible for there to be a face-to-face meeting, but I believe there can be, in some cases, like this one. You need to see me and just admit what you did. I had hoped that talking to you would also help you accept the fact that you did murder her and realize that maybe you are having a hard time dealing with the fact that you did indeed kill her. To say the words, "I killed her, and this is what happened," to you may seem impossible, but you can do it.

I am told that if you do not agree to tell me the truth and admit you did it, then I will have to wait another year to reapply, wait for someone to be assigned to the case, then another four months for them to talk to you. I'm not sure that I want to go through all of this again. I don't want to go through all the waiting again, knowing that you have already turned down the opportunity once.

Consider this: you face me, you openly and honestly share with me what went so very wrong that night. I will listen to what you have to say and hopefully hear

you ask for forgiveness and, after all this time, be able to forgive you face-to-face. I ask you to reconsider your answer. Tell David Flores that you are willing to see me and tell me the truth.
But that is your choice! Isn't it?
Laura's sister,
Linda

David Flores called me on April 29, 2009, which happened to be Laura's birthday. He told me the news. Billy had read the letter, hung his head, and said, "She is right; I did it." David was truly amazed at Billy's change after he read "the letter."

It was remarkable that the chain of events occurred from that first phone call to the Victim Services Division to that moment when Billy agreed to the visit. I thanked the Lord for all He had done in our lives and for giving me the right words to write in the letter. Billy and I were ready for the next step of the program. I had no idea what was ahead of me, but I was ready. I knew I had to trust the Lord every step of the way. I would have to go through at least three months, possibly more, of mediations. The first mediation was set for May 12, 2009, thirteen days away. At first, I didn't understand why this was necessary. The truth was, I didn't want to go through the mediations. I just wanted to walk into that prison and demand to know "why?"

Sometimes, I was not sure why I even wanted to meet him. I told myself that he had murdered her brutally, and he got less than he deserved. It was a very rough thirteen days. I was going through an array of emotions, but I just kept telling myself when this was over, I would be free. God had promised me I would know the truth, and that truth would indeed set me free. I was holding on to that.

There was something else that was very important to me, and I was being very cautious. I didn't want to fall into an easy trap that I was sure the enemy had set for me. I mean, when I was in the beginning stages, all I could see or even think about was me walking into that prison and saying, "Billy, I forgive you, and God loves you, and all you have to do is ask Him to forgive you." Then, I would share the gospel with him, laying out the plan of God's great salvation. He would either accept or reject that salvation. No matter what, I would be free, and I could just walk out and be finished, having done my part.

The mediations were all about forgiveness. I had to be willing to talk about the crime, and that made it all too real to me. Meeting the man who had done the things I would be talking about was going to be a tough battle. I didn't know all that from the beginning. I didn't want to relive all of that again.

Whenever I needed someone to talk to about these things, or I needed someone to pray with me, there were twelve women that I knew whom I trusted to hold me accountable. I could call on any of these twelve women any time, day or night, and I did on many occasions. I knew I could rely on them for support.

Tiffany met with me on Tuesdays every week for over seven months. Cheri wrote me letters and called me often. Kathy, Sheila, Bonny, Lori, Trish, Charlette, Debra, Miriam, Mary, and Louise, these women prayed for me during the long months of waiting and through the months of the mediations. These women, with great resolve, journeyed with me on this road.

They prayed with me and for me. They encouraged me and sometimes corrected me. They helped me to stay focused on the race, the goal, and the finish line. They were more than my friends; they were my teachers and tutors. They all worked with me, teaching me reading and writing skills. They were my friends and did not make me feel ashamed because I could not read or write well; instead of judging me, they taught me how.

The first meeting would take place at a restaurant. David was already there when I arrived. I talked to him earlier that morning, and we had both given each other a brief description of ourselves. As I was walking up to the door, I saw him sitting in a rocker. He stood as I approached, and he introduced himself right away.

Once inside the restaurant, we were seated. After talking for a few moments, we ordered something to drink and eat. David filled me in on how the program was laid out and what was expected from that point on. He also explained that a study was being done by the University of Texas on a volunteer basis only. He informed me that I didn't have to participate in the survey. I decided that it might help me, so I agreed to participate. It was at this first meeting that I was put at ease. When I walked away from that meeting, I knew I was doing the right thing. Apart from the University of Texas study survey, there were also assignments for me to do at home. There were lots of questions, but they helped me in many areas of dealing with the crime itself.

Going through the mediations wasn't at all what I had imagined it would be. I was given a chance to express my feelings. For the first time since my sister's death, I had the courage to talk about it and how it had truly affected my life. I was finally emerging from the ruins of what Billy had left behind for me to clean up. Without realizing it, I had become stuck in that place.

The experience of walking into my sister's house had such a profound effect on my life, and I had not realized it. I was still standing at her front door, looking at the horrible scene that unfolded before my eyes. My mind could not conceive the evil that had taken place there. It was during the mediations that I began to allow myself to visit that place again. I was able to talk about it for the first time in over seven years. As the truth of those days, weeks, and months poured out of my soul, I was no longer numb; I was able to feel the pain, express it in a tangible way, and then release it.

There was one experience during the mediations that God used to speak to my heart and teach me one of the most valuable truths I have learned as a Christian. It happened during the second mediation meeting. David placed an eight-by-ten picture of Billy Lopez before me. I had seen Billy before. I saw him in court. I had seen his mug shot before and even pictures of him in the newspaper, but there was just something about seeing that picture of Billy. It was as if it shattered my world just seeing his picture.

I excused myself from the table and went to the restroom. Once in the restroom, I broke down. "I cannot do this. Why did I ever get involved in this program to go see Billy? I am sorry, Lord, but I cannot do this!" By this time, I was crying. "No! He killed her in cold blood, with no mercy. He stabbed her over and over. I washed her blood off of the walls in her home. Do You remember, Lord, how I stood where they found her body?

How much it hurt me? You saw it all, how he killed her, blow by horrifying blow, and You want me to go there and see him? Why? Why me? I cannot go. No, I know now that I cannot go! I don't know what I was thinking, but I know now that I cannot do this. I will not go! I just want to go home now."

I knew that the Lord was going to speak, but I told Him I didn't want to hear that I needed to go. God is always ready to reply. However, I have learned that hearing is the main problem between God and mankind. One thing I did know was that God wasn't going to leave me in the restroom that day. He spoke, and I heard, but not what I expected to hear. He asked a question, "What is eternal, Linda?"

I stopped. "What do you mean?"

He said it again, "What is eternal, Linda?"

I really didn't know how to answer that question. "Well, I guess heaven is."

The Lord's response burned in my soul, leaving its mark as I grasped a truth that I should have already known. "No, heaven is a place where the eternal dwells. The soul is eternal, Linda. Your soul, your daughter's, your friend's, your mother's, Daniel's, your father's, Laura's, and so is Billy's. All that you see in this world, no matter how big or how small, will pass away because it is not eternal, but the soul is eternal."

We, as Christians, must get a hold of this truth. Heaven is a place where the eternal dwells. The soul is eternal; our souls are eternal and made to dwell in heaven. The earth was not designed to be eternal. I finally understood. I washed my face, freshened up, and went back to the table. We scheduled the next meeting and talked a few moments longer, and then David hurried off to his next meeting.

On July 1, 2009, David said he believed I was ready to go meet Billy. The date was set for August 7, 2009, almost a year since I had made that first phone call to the Victim Services Division. It was hard to believe that in a month, I would meet Billy, and we would sit down and talk face-to-face.

Before I wrote the letter, I had written several letters. The first one was full of anger, and bitter words were poured out onto more than twenty pages. The second letter, the third, the fourth, all the same. I wrote so many letters, and out of my soul poured the bitterness, the pain, and the damage of a lifetime. I saw such ugly things come out of my heart. Things I had never known were there. Thirty days later, I realized my soul was cleansed of all the things that were hidden in the darkness. Things that needed to come to light so I could be free from hatred, anger, unforgiveness, and bitterness in my soul. I was trapped like sand in an hourglass. I needed to be set free, and when I was, I wrote the letter.

CHAPTER 20

The Shocking Truth

There I was, standing in front of the prison, knowing that in a few moments, I would be walking through those gates into another world, one I had never known. Oh, I knew the prison existed, but not what truly lies behind the gates, for it is indeed another world. I wanted to run away, and at the same time, I knew that I had to finish what I set out to do. It wasn't a path that I had chosen; it was one that was chosen for me.

It was August 7, 2009, at eight in the morning, when David Flores, Abigail, and I walked through the gates. The sound of them shutting behind us was like no other on the face of this earth. It sounds so final. It was as if we were shut away from life itself and walking into an unknown world. I had chosen to take the option of touring the prison. It was truly amazing. I saw firsthand how life is on the inside of those high fences with razor wire on top. The tour lasted around an hour and a half.

The meeting with Billy would take place in the visiting area. There was a table and chairs that had been set up for us, with a pitcher of ice water and glasses. There were vending machines in the room, so snacks and soft drinks were available to us. I looked around the room slowly, so unsure of my surroundings.

Abigail would not be able to talk to Billy or sit at the table, so she brought a book to read and would sit across the room in a small area, out of hearing distance.

I was required to have a list of questions that I would ask Billy, and I had them with me in a folder. I sat down at the table and glanced over them; then I stood up as Billy entered the room. He was in chains, hands and feet; there were chains that went from the ones on his hands down to the ones on his feet. They loosened the chains, and for Billy, it was a moment of freedom.

I watched his face and his expression as they released him. His head hung down; even as he took his place at the table, he kept his head down. It was silent. I looked over at the guard, then at David, and then at Billy. I could tell he was uncomfortable, and I knew it wasn't because of the guard. I saw the look and the actions of a person who was living in shame and trapped in guilt.

We were both aware that the prison guards would remain in the room during the visit as a matter of precaution. Billy didn't know what to do. He wanted to look at me, and he tried to raise his head a few times, but to look into my eyes must have caused him unimaginable guilt and condemnation. I told him that it was all right, that he needed to raise his head and look at me. He spoke and said he wrote me a letter and asked if I would like to read it first. I said, "Yes, I would; it might be the perfect way to start."

Billy handed me the letter that he had written on June 20, 2009, but wasn't allowed to give it to me until our face-to-face mediation. His letter would break the silence and be the beginning of a long day, a day that would bring about the untangling of a past that was full of twists and turns that had brought the two of us together at this time in this place. It was indeed an unlikely meeting as we looked into the past, a past that was full of pain for both of us.

I reached out and took the letter from Billy's hand. He quickly released the letter. I slowly opened it and began to read.

Billy's letter:

> Linda, how are you doing? I guess that is kind of crazy, me asking you that kind of question. I just didn't know where to start or how to start. I've just been here thinking of what to tell you. I'll just start off by telling you that I am really sorry for all the pain and heartache I have brought to you and your family.
> It has been almost eight years since the crime occurred, but it feels like it just happened because I relive it every day. I know I don't deserve this opportunity to meet you and seek your forgiveness. I hope that you can forgive me. I still have a lot of shame and guilt because never in my life did I think I could ever kill somebody. I do not want to excuse what I did, but I was under the influence of alcohol and drugs. I wasn't in my right state of mind. I had been eating meth for weeks, and during the weekend, I continued doing the same, along with drinking and partying with my friends. It didn't even occur to me until after it was all over what I had really done. I don't know what made me snap except the drugs.

I don't know if you have a lot of hatred against me, and I cannot be mad at you if you do. I just want to bring closure to your life. I cannot change the past, but I know that you need to know the truth. My crime changed the outlook of our futures. I want to be responsible for my actions. The shame and guilt have held me back. Those dark clouds still hang over my head. We all suffer in many ways in this world, but it seems senseless that you have had to suffer because of my actions.

I know that it is because of you that I am alive. My lawyer told me what you did. I do appreciate what you did. I know that I could be sitting on death row right now, waiting on the needle. I have been in administration segregation for the last seven years. That means I have not had any human contact; I have been in my cell day and night. However, by the time we have our mediation, I will be in population, and for the first time in seven years, I can have contact visits.

I know I don't deserve what you have done for me. But I want to thank you for accepting my guilty plea and giving me the chance to live.

I was born on January 14, 1979, in Florida. I was twenty-two years old when I murdered Laura. I have been in prison since May 2002, and I will spend the rest of my life here.

I hope that you will forgive me.

Billy Lopez

Tears filled my eyes as I folded the letter back up and placed it in the envelope. I didn't look at Billy right away. I had to gather my thoughts.

I didn't expect to receive a letter as a way of starting out. I looked down, and in front of me, there lay sheets of paper, with the words typed across the first sheet: *"Questions to ask Billy."*

How am I ever going to get through this? I have over seventy questions to ask, and I can't even form the words for the first question, let alone ask the ones that followed. Have I made a mistake?

Then, the Lord spoke to me in a very tangible way. "Linda, this is the way; walk ye in it." There was such a calmness that came over me. I looked over at Billy, sitting there looking down, crying, and saying, "I am so sorry, forgive me."

I asked Billy to look at me and to stop looking down. I told him it would be impossible to talk to him, with him looking down and away from me. We had to make eye-to-eye contact. I said it as gently as I could, "Billy, you need to look at me; I didn't come all this way to talk to you with your head bowed. I need to see your eyes. You know they say the eyes are the window to the soul?"

Billy looked up and said, "No, I didn't know that. Is that true?" I told him that I believed that it was true. Tears filled his eyes as he said, "Laura had beautiful eyes."

I said, "I know."

Question number one rolled out: "How did you know Laura?"

Billy wiped the tears away, "I installed a new stereo system in her car. After that, I went by almost every week. She always had some kind of work for me to do. It was always outside, mostly yard work, mowing, pulling weeds, and planting flowers. I made flower beds for her. Changed the oil in her cars and kept them clean."

Question number two: "How long did you know Laura?" Billy bowed his head and then looked at me and said, "It was sometime in March of 1999 when I installed the stereo in her car. I guess I knew her for about a little over two and half years."

Question number three, I asked with tears in my eyes: "Have you ever had a fight with Laura before?"

Billy replied, "No, I really cared for her; we were friends. She helped me out a lot. That weekend in October, I did a lot of partying at a club. I drank so much that Saturday night I didn't remember leaving the club. On Sunday morning, I was still drinking and partying with friends. A friend gave me some meth, and I ate it.

"Meth was just floating around that morning; every time I turned around, someone was giving me a little more meth, and I just kept eating it, like candy. I wasn't myself. My friends wanted me to go get the money that Laura owed me for some yard work I had done for her on Friday. I thought it would be nice to see her, and I could pick up my money so I could buy some more alcohol. I walked over to her house at about nine o'clock, and I saw a guy leave her house. I was upset because she told me she was not seeing anyone and would not be dating."

Billy cleared his throat. "I was so high, I couldn't stop thinking about that guy and her. She lied to me, I thought. She told me she had made a promise to God to wait for three years before getting involved with a man. She said that her relationship with God was important to her, and He was still working in some areas in her life at that time. I walked away thinking she had a reason and she was a good person. There were other thoughts of her, but nothing bad, and I knew she did care about me. I partied some more. Then my friends said something about the money; I went back to talk to Laura and get the money she owed me."

Billy said, "Before I say anything else. I need you to know that this will be very hard for me. I have lived and relived every second of what I am about to tell you. I live every scream, every hit, every stab, and every cut I placed on her body, even cutting her throat to decapitating her. I live it over and over again. It is embedded in my mind—every detail. I have no peace. This is not going to be easy, but it's the truth. I never wanted to speak of it, but you came all this way to hear the truth, not half-truths or some imagined thing to make it easier to understand and forgive. Because even though I long for forgiveness. I do not deserve it."

I felt that it was going well at that point, and he was ready to tell the truth. I would be done with these questions in no time. I asked question number four: "The Wednesday morning you murdered her, you went back to her house; how did it all start? You broke in, or what?"

Billy cleared his throat and said, "Linda, you misunderstood me. I didn't break in, and it *was not* Wednesday. *It was Sunday morning.*"

I took a deep breath, bringing my hands to my face, and shaking my head, I said, "No, that cannot be."

Billy said, "Yes, Linda, it was Sunday morning. That's what I was telling you. I went there the first time at nine in the morning. I went back the second time around ten. She was on the phone—"

I interrupted him, "That was me she was talking to. I was supposed to be at her house at eleven thirty."

Billy said, "She told me it was you, but I was so high and angry......"

His words trailed off as I thought, *I was supposed to be there. Oh my God, if I would have just been there, nothing would have happened.*

I quickly regained my composure. I knew I had to be calm and keep control over my emotions, and I was determined to, no matter what was said. I asked another question not from my sheet: "What happened after she hung up the phone? How long were you there before it started? Where did it start?"

Billy was crying; he wiped away his tears as he answered, "She went to the bedroom to get the money to pay me for the work I had done. I was so high on meth. Suddenly, all I felt was anger and jealousy because I wanted her, but she didn't want me. I thought she was talking to that man on the phone, the one I saw leaving her house, and that they were making fun of me. I thought she was lying to me, just telling me it was you she was having lunch with. I had eaten so much meth I couldn't think straight. I kept thinking she was just trying to get rid of me, and that's when it happened. It was like a door opened, and something evil came into me."

He paused... "I asked her who she was really talking to, and she told me her sister, Linda. I called her a liar and asked why she was making fun of me. Then I pushed her against the dresser, grabbed her around the neck, and started choking her. She passed out, and I thought she was dead. I was getting ready to run out the front door when I heard her moving around in the bedroom. I went back into the bedroom; she was getting up and asked me to leave. She said, 'It's over; I'm okay; we're going to forget this ever happened, and you need to leave. I promise you I will not call the police, and Billy, I want you to know that I forgive you, but it would be best for you not to come back when you're high on drugs.' Her words have haunted me for almost eight years because after it was all over, I knew she meant them, but at that moment, I didn't. I called her a liar and called her some very bad names. I didn't realize it. Everything just happened so fast. There was a knife lying on her dresser…"

He stopped for a moment. "I was high and thought she was messing with me, and as soon as I left, she was going to call the police. Then, I would be arrested for attempted murder. I was afraid, confused, and angry. I grabbed her by the arm, and as I spun her around, I stabbed her the first time. I didn't even realize I had a knife in my hand until she stepped back. It was from that point on that I felt I just had to kill her. We fought, and I stabbed her again, around nine or ten times, then she went down. I thought it was over, and I walked away to let her die."

Billy looked down, shaking his head. "She was still alive… I got a different knife, went back, and did it again. I stabbed her again as we fought; she begged me to stop. She told me I was killing her and asked me to call for help. I just kept hitting her with my fist and kicking her. I was telling her to die, and she deserved this. I still had the knife, and I did stab her again."

Billy was crying as he said, "Every time I went into the room as we fought, we went from one room to another, throughout the whole house, and somehow, we always ended up back in her room; she was trying to get out. I know this sounds horrible, and I hate having to tell you this, but I know you came here to hear the truth. Not a day goes by that I don't think about this or hear her screaming and begging. I can still hear her praying. For such a long time, I kept telling myself that it wasn't me; it was somebody else. I walked out of that room again and thought it was over, but it wasn't. That was the third time, but there's more, Linda."

He paused to regain his composure. "Laura was begging me to call for help. She wouldn't shut up, so I went back, and we fought again. This time, I did stab her over and over, but she still fought. She kept begging me to stop and call for help. She told me I was killing her. Blood was everywhere, and she went down again. I walked away and thought it was over. I had started something, and I had to end it. I thought it was over, but she started talking again and kept saying—"

I asked Billy, "What did she say?" I could tell he didn't want to answer. I told him it was all right...

So he replied, "She said, 'Oh my God, oh my God, I am dying.' She sounded like a frightened child at first. Then it got silent; it was a deadly silence. Then, through the silence, I heard her say, 'Lord, I am not afraid. My sister, please help her, Lord.'"

Billy was crying, and it was getting hard for him to speak. I asked him if he wanted to stop and take a break. He said, "No, I want to finish this now." Billy then looked at me and said, "I am so sorry. Will you forgive me, please?"

I looked away from him, then back, and said, "Let's finish this."

Billy wiped away the tears and said, "I went back in the room because she wouldn't stop talking. I could hear her; I knew she was suffering and dying slowly. I just wanted it to be over, so I picked up a large glass ball. It was solid, kind of like a paperweight, but it was much larger. I walked over to her. She was begging, 'Billy, please don't do it. Please stop.' She told me she was dying, and to let her go without any more pain, and that I could sit there with her while she died. I sat down, and she told me she forgave me and that God would forgive me too. She asked me not to kill the little dog, and then she said, 'Oh God, my sister will not understand. We should pray for her.' Laura asked for my hand, and she started praying. I felt something evil, and I could hear something telling me, 'She is tricking you; finish it, kill her now.' It was like a song playing over and over in my mind. I could not hear Laura praying anymore. I stood up and told her she deserved to die. She screamed, 'No! Billy! No! Please don't do this, Billy! Stop!'"

Billy took a deep breath. "I hit her with the glass ball, two, maybe three times on the head, and then I kept hitting her, on her back, legs, stomach, arms, everywhere. I don't know where all her strength came from, but she was still fighting me; again, we went from one end of the house to the other. I don't know how many times, but we ended back up in her bedroom again. I took the glass ball back into the living room. I looked at the clock. It was eleven thirty, and Laura was still alive. I walked over to the front door with the glass ball, and it was like I had a demon all of a sudden. I could not stop the anger and rage that was pouring out of me. It was there that I dropped the glass ball."

I looked at Billy and said, "I was supposed to arrive at that time; I would have just walked in. I had a key."

Billy stopped talking; it was as if he couldn't say another word. He started crying, and he put his face in his hands, then he raised his head and looked at me with such fear and pain in his eyes and said, "*I would have killed you, Linda. If you would have walked in that door, I would have killed you. Without question and without thought, I would have beat you to death with that glass ball, and only God knows what else I was capable of doing to you that morning.*"

The room started to spin, and I couldn't think. What he was saying was impossible. The police said...they said it was Wednesday morning, but then I knew Billy was telling the truth. It hit the very center of my being. Suddenly, I understood the truth; it was uncovered, the scales fell off my eyes, and I did see. He killed her that Sunday morning. The morning I was supposed to be there. The day Laura and I were going to have our little lunch in the box. I wanted to scream, I wanted to run, I wanted to cry. I wanted to find a place to hide. I wanted a hole to crawl into. The guilt I had carried for years, and I had blamed Scott. I had tormented myself for so long, but the truth and facts were I would have changed nothing, absolutely nothing. Well, that also wouldn't even be close to the truth. Things would have been different, but not in the way I had dreamed of or fantasized about.

I asked for a moment as my mind reeled back in time to that Sunday morning, October 14, 2001. For the first time, I saw the mighty hand of God to save and deliver. I saw the hand of God upon my life. I saw the look on Billy's face, and I knew he meant what he said. He would have killed me. If I had gone after church, I would have arrived at Laura's house around two thirty. According to Billy, that would have been fifteen minutes after he left. I would have walked into her home, and I would have found her. I do not believe I would have ever gotten over that, but that, too, is just more speculation, isn't it?

I was crying as I realized that Abigail, who was sitting across the room from me, had grown into a beautiful woman. Abigail would have had no mother. It would have affected her life in such a harsh way. Then there was Scott.

I realized all that God had spared them from that day and all that God had given to me. I, who had acted like a spoiled, selfish child who didn't get my way, who thought that it was me that could control the beginning and ending of a thing, I had been so foolish; sitting there, I realized the awesome power and wisdom of God, and I knew it to be far greater than mine. "His ways are not my ways, and His thoughts are not my thoughts. His are higher, wiser, and of deeper understanding" (Isaiah 55:8; paraphrased).

After a few moments, I was ready to continue. "So, Billy, you were standing by her front door with a glass ball in your hand at eleven thirty; what happened next?"

Billy shook his head as tears filled his eyes. "I dropped the glass ball there at the front door. I walked back into the bedroom. She was crawling toward the bed. She was trying to get away from me; she knew I was coming—"

I stopped him and asked, "Why do you think she knew you were coming?"

Billy said, "She was saying, 'Please don't do this, don't hurt me anymore. I forgive you. I forgive you, Billy; God will too. I'm dying; let me go in the stillness and quietness, not fighting, and please, no more pain, no more pain. I'm dying, let me go in peace, please.'"

Billy stopped and wiped his eyes again. "She forgave me, and then she asked me why I was doing this. Then she said, 'Oh my God,' again. She was very still for a moment. Then she started crawling again, trying to get under the bed. There was so much blood, and it seemed like it was coming out from everywhere all of a sudden."

He paused, and he was crying and shaking his head. "I'm so sorry; I don't know what happened to me. I have tried for so long to figure out why I didn't just leave. From the moment I grabbed her and choked her, something inside of me changed. I was standing there, and I knew she was dying. I knew she only had moments left. I should have walked away and let her have her last moments in peace. That was her only request for me not to hurt her anymore. She had forgiven me, and I still don't deserve it. She said, 'I forgive you, Billy.'"

Billy paused again and then continued. "She had crawled halfway under the bed. I grabbed her feet and pulled her out from under the bed. She was still talking, but I couldn't understand her anymore. There was so much blood; she was gurgling; it was horrible. I flipped her over and got down beside her. I saw this big hole in her throat. I put my two fingers into the hole and applied some pressure, and I heard her say, 'I forgive you, Billy.' I jerked my fingers out. I was horrified as I heard her final words."

Billy was having a very hard time talking at this point. He had to stop and start over. "Those were the last words that I understood. She was talking a lot, it seemed, but I couldn't understand because of all the blood; that's when I knew I had to end it. I went into the kitchen, grabbed a large knife, and went back into the bedroom."

Billy stopped and wiped tears from his eyes as he continued, "When I got back to the bedroom, Laura, with the last strength she had, rolled over and started crawling again. I stood beside her. She was trying with all the strength she had left to get away from me. I stepped over her body with one foot on each side of her. I reached down and grabbed her by the hair, pulling her head up. With the knife that was in my other hand, I brought it down across her throat and cut and cut. There was so much anger and hate in me. I just kept cutting. I felt evil; it was like I was someone else. I had never in my life felt that way."

Billy stopped for a moment, then said, "When I realized what I had done, I was so scared. I sat by Laura's body for a long time. I began to think about all that I had done and what I was going to do. I had to hide it and cover it all up. Then I thought that I would make it look like a robbery. Someone broke in; they tried to rape her, then killed her, and robbed her house. So, I took her clothes off; then I covered her with some blankets that were on top of a chest at the foot of her bed. I also grabbed some clothes from her closet and put them on top of her body. I thought that I should turn her thermostat down to keep her body from..."

He stopped and had this painful look of remorse on his face. "I am so sorry; I did it to keep her body from stinking. I was thinking it would be a long time before anyone found her. As the drugs wore off, I began to get sick as I saw the awful things I had done. I had walked around and around, tearing things up and going through her things. I was just trying to mess things all up in her house, so it would be hard to figure out what happened. I was afraid that I was going to have to stay in her house until dark; I just wanted out of there. I regretted going over there so messed up on meth after partying all weekend. Even right before I went back to her house, I had eaten more meth."

He stopped, and I asked, "You need a moment?"

He nodded his head yes. He put his head down and cried, begging for forgiveness. At that point, I couldn't understand what he was saying, nor could I understand what he was saying on the recorded tape so that part of our conversation is not here.

After a moment, he continued, "I walked by a mirror; there was so much blood in my clothes; I knew I couldn't leave her house wearing them. When I saw myself in the mirror, I looked like someone else. I hated myself, and I hated what I had done. I was afraid of what would happen to me now that I had done this horrible thing."

Billy paused again, then said, "I washed my clothes. I don't know why I didn't wash my socks. They were wet with blood; I put the knife I cut her throat with into one of the socks and put it behind her headboard. I figured out a way to get out of her house without being seen. There was blood all over me, so I took a shower before I left."

Billy looked at me and said, "By that time, I was sober, and the meth wore off, and I had come to the full realization of what I had done. The worst part was when I realized that I had cut her head...." He couldn't say it, no matter how hard he tried. He stuttered and looked down. "Even now, I find it impossible to say the words. I didn't know I had done it until I uncovered her, to make sure she was dead and to take just one last look at her. I realized her head was not...." He looked down and just cried. "I ran to the bathroom and vomited; afterwards, I went back to put her head so it looked right, but it was at the foot of the bed. I couldn't touch it, I couldn't, so I kicked it on under the bed and covered her back up."

Billy had to pause for a few moments again. "After my clothes were clean and dry, I put some of her clothes in her washing machine, added bleach and laundry detergent, set it to wash, and left. I went to my sister's house. I had taken one of the knives that I had used to kill Laura with. I don't know why, but I got rid of it on the way to my sister's house. I had some meth in my pocket that I had been eating the whole time I was at Laura's. When I got to my sister's house, I ate the last of it. I was so scared. I didn't know what to do."

Billy just shook his head, then looked back up at me and said, "I never knew why I did that. I tried and tried to figure out why I did it; what made me snap like that? I tried to not think about it, but it kept flashing through my mind. I could hear her screaming and begging; even now, I can still hear her, and the dreams are unbearable. I wanted to make it stop, to make it all go away, but I can't. I know what I did was awful, and it deeply hurt you. My actions also hurt my family. I know I have destroyed two families, all because of drugs and alcohol. I can say I am sorry, but it doesn't sound like much after all the pain I have caused you. I can ask for forgiveness, but I fear it will never be granted to me. I know that I don't even deserve to be alive, and I will never understand why you accepted my guilty plea when you knew I did it and I was going to get the death penalty. Why would you come here to see me and to talk to me? I don't understand."

I am ashamed to admit that even though I heard his words, I ignored them because it was just too much for me. I had come with such a different idea of what had happened and how I would feel. I looked down at all my questions, and it seemed kind of useless to ask all of them now. Still, I told Billy I had some more questions I needed to ask. If he would like to take a break, it would be all right, and now would be the perfect time. He said no break for him, but if I would like to take one, he would agree to go back to his cell until I was ready.

There was so much pain in his eyes. I looked away from him and said, "No, I don't want a break. I would like to finish this. I have waited a long time for these answers." I looked down at the questions and said, "Okay, I will start with this one: Why didn't you just walk away?"

Billy answered, "Linda, I was so high on meth, I had been drinking all night and I was so angry. I don't know where all that anger came from. I just snapped. I believe that it was the meth. I had been eating it for weeks, and I was so strung out. I am not trying to make an excuse for what I did because there is not one, and forget trying to understand; no one can, not you, not even me. I have tried."

My next question: "Billy, to the best of your knowledge, how long did the whole ordeal last?"

He took a deep breath, "While it was happening, it seemed like it was never going to end. Laura was on the phone when I got there, and after she got off the phone, we talked in the living room before she went to her bedroom to get my money. I remember her looking at the clock and saying it was 10:10 a.m., and then she said that the morning had just gotten away from her."

Billy looked down and said, "As she walked away, she said she was going to drive out to visit her sister and surprise her. I thought she was lying, and my heart changed to hate. That is the only way I can explain it because that's when I really got angry. I thought she was lying because she didn't want to spend time with me. The meth and alcohol had full control of my mind, and I was not thinking. All my thoughts were not complete, and thoughts of Laura were full of hate, and that hate overtook me. The last time I looked at the clock, it was 11:30 a.m., and about forty minutes later, I killed her. I had to end it, her suffering. The whole fight, from start to finish, lasted about two hours and fifteen minutes. When I got the last knife, it was 12:15 p.m., and it was over right after that. The next time I looked at the clock was 12:25 p.m. She died during the ten minutes."

My heart just sank in a sea of hopelessness when he said that. I was stunned at his reply. As I listened to him speak of the things that took place that morning on October 14, 2001, I knew how Mary, the mother of Jesus, must have felt at His death. She was told that a sword would pierce her heart. That day, sitting there listening, I, too, felt a sword go through my heart. That day, I understood the depth of pain that Mary must have felt as she watched them murder her Son, Jesus. I felt I had watched Laura being murdered at that very moment. I could mentally see it happening. It took me several moments to compose myself again.

I looked at my next question and asked, "Billy, did you care for Laura? You know, did you love her?"

He sat there for a few minutes. He looked down and then back at me, his eyes red from crying, "I did; I knew her for almost three years. She would talk to me, not down to me, like most people. She was always very kind to me."

Billy paused and wiped away the tears. "She told me she prayed for me every day. She tried to talk to me about God, but I never really paid much attention to that stuff. I always thought that after I was finished with the partying. I would go back and finish college. Get a wife and a few kids. Then, I would go to church and get things right, like Laura talked about. Start doing things the right way, like she kept telling me that I needed to. Now, all that is gone, and it is too late for me. I was going to college. I was going to be an artist. But none of that really matters now. I want you to know I really cared about Laura; she was my friend. She would talk to me, and she never treated me badly, and I believe she did look at me as a friend."

I was upset at his answer, so in haste, I asked, "Well, if that is true, how could you have done what you did to her? You killed her and never for a moment showed her any compassion."

His response was: "Like I told you, I was very messed up on meth. I was so strung out that even days after it happened, I kept telling myself, 'It was just a bad dream.' I had never so much as hit a woman before. I was taught to respect women. I believe it was the way that the meth affected me, from eating so much of it and mixing it with way too much alcohol. Linda, I had been partying and drinking all weekend, just out having some fun. Lots of kids do this, but now I realize how wrong it is to take things that alter your mind in any way, and that includes alcohol."

I made no response but looked down at the next question and asked, "Did you see them bring her body out? Did you come around when I was there cleaning up her house?"

Billy said, "No, I didn't see them bring her body out. Someone told me that Laura had been murdered. I went to my sister's house, packed my bags, and went to Lubbock, Texas. I didn't think she would be found so soon—"

I didn't let him finish. I didn't care how he felt. My eyes filled with tears as I asked, "Do you ever think about her?"

There was a quivering in his voice as he replied, "Yes, I think about her every day. I wish every day I could change what I did. It is like a heavy chain around me that I carry with me twenty-four hours a day—"

Before he could finish, I asked the next question: "So, do you ever think about what you did to her?"

Billy looked away, his pain too great. "Yes, Linda, I do; every day, I think of her, and I think about what I did. I live with it every day, knowing I can never go back and change it. I relive the screams, the begging, and her praying. I was killing her, Linda, and she was praying for me. What I carry in my heart is unbearable. Many times, I have wished that I had not taken the guilty plea and let them put me to death. I think about why I am even alive after what I have done. I don't deserve to be."

I was very serious about the next question. I think when I asked it, I sounded a little harsh: "Did you rape my sister?"

Billy looked shocked that I would even ask him that kind of question. He looked straight at me and said, "No, I did not."

I was ready to ask another question when I looked at Billy; he seemed a little different than when he was led into the room in chains. He seemed so broken, not knowing how to fix what was wrong in his life. I said, "Billy, I have more questions, but they don't seem so important now. I am not going to ask you anymore, but I do have just one question I would like you to answer. I believe this is the one that really counts. If you could go back to that day, would you now give your life for Laura's?"

Billy looked at me, and his eyes brightened up. "If I could, Linda, I would give my life right now for her. I hate living with what I did. I do not regret getting caught because I am in prison. I regret what I did that put me in prison. I was wrong, and my punishment is just." That was the one answer I really needed to hear.

Sometimes, things are not what they appear to be. There are those who are trained and are experts in their field. They have skills and knowledge; they are the ones with the answers. We listen to their wisdom because we long to understand when things are past our understanding. However, they can pass on information that is incorrect. They are human and can stray from the truth in their quest to be the best at what they do. We should pray more often about the reports we receive because, as I have learned, it is God who knows the truth and reveals the truth. God is the only one who has all the facts and all the evidence because He sees the whole picture.

I had the answers that I had waited so long for. It would take time for me to really process all his answers. I looked at that day so differently for eight years, believing it was a robbery and it happened early Wednesday morning. The visit between Billy and me had uncovered the truth. The truth that was now penetrating my soul, God had indeed spared my life on October 14, 2001. The visit had already started changing my entire perspective.

CHAPTER 21

Secret of My Heart

My emotions were not as I had thought they would be. It seemed most of the day, I felt downcast and defeated. I thought that I would walk into that prison strong and sure, and I felt that in the end, I would walk out with confident assurance that, finally, I had won some kind of battle. However, as I faced the truth of my sister's death, there was no great battle to be fought or won, except the spiritual battle that was going on over Billy's soul. He was lost and dying, not physically, but in another way. I knew in my heart that if he died in that spiritual darkness, he was doomed to eternity in hell. I looked at him and thought, *God, why should I care at all what happens to him now?*

There it was, that old familiar question, and I truly felt it unfair. I was very uncomfortable at that moment, so I began to shuffle around in my seat as I asked the Lord, *Why do I have to be the one through which You tell him that You love him? What about me, and what about how I feel?*

My chain of thoughts was interrupted by Billy asking, "Is that all, or is there anything else that you want to ask me about?"

I looked at Billy and saw such a deep anguish in him as the Lord said, "Linda, you know the end of bitterness and unforgiveness." I didn't know what to do. I put my hand up and asked for a moment.

I thought that I had let go of all that bitterness and that I had forgiven Billy. I just didn't expect all I had heard that day, and it was so painful. It was as if my soul had been awakened again from a deep sleep and brought back into that world of horrible memories and unimaginable pain. All that I had ever imagined was not even close to the pain my sister had endured nor the courage that she had as she faced death. Yet I knew that even Laura would want me to complete the last part of my task. She would want me to do it out of love, but I honestly had no love at all for Billy. I saw his pain, his fear, and his regret, but I didn't know how to let go of all I was feeling at that moment and find a gift called mercy. Even though I knew that there were other reasons for me being there, I knew why God allowed me to come. I knew the primary reason was to share His love with Billy, whether I understood that or not.

Once again, Billy asked me, "Linda, is there anything else you have to say or ask?"

I looked at him once again and asked for a moment to collect my thoughts. I asked Billy if we could take a moment to pray. He said, "Yes, Linda, I would like that before I go back to my cell."

I prayed, and my focus was redirected, and my heart was a little lighter. I had this amazing feeling that God had a perfect plan, and He was in control of what was going to happen during the rest of the visit. All I needed to do was trust Him. After I prayed, I began to share the love of God with Billy. Very boldly, I said, "Billy, 'the wages of sin is death, but the gift of God is eternal life' (Romans 6:23). God loves you and desires that you have this gift of eternal life. It's a gift, Billy, a gift that is being offered to you right here, right now, today. You can accept this gift or reject it. That is your choice, just like with Laura; it was a choice you made. You, going to Laura's house and killing her that day, was not what God wanted you to do. Somehow, I believe that God tried to reach you, in one way or another, to stop you."

Billy looked surprised. "I believe that too, Linda, but I didn't look at it as God trying to stop me until now."

I asked, "What do you mean?"

Billy said, "The first time I went to her house, I saw the guy leaving, but I wasn't mad then. I was upset, but I wasn't angry. I just thought that I really didn't want her to see me all messed up and drunk. I walked back to where everyone was partying. I began to eat more meth that is when I started getting angry. I picked up the last bottle of beer and drank the entire contents after I had taken at least a four-ounce shot of Ever clear. Then someone said, 'Go get your money from that lady like you said you were going to do.'"

Billy stopped for a moment and shook his head. "Everyone kept nagging me and telling me to go get the money and not to come back without it. I finally said, 'All right, I'll go, but she has already left for church.' On the way to Laura's house, I felt something deep inside me telling me not to go to her house, to just go to my sister's and sleep it off. Just for a second, I thought I should go to my sister's house and do some kind of work until all the meth and alcohol wore off or just go to bed and sleep. I had not slept in more than eleven days. My head was so messed up. Then I thought of that guy at her front door, and I let the anger and hate take over. It seemed like within seconds, I became someone else."

Billy stopped and then looked over at me. "That was God telling me not to go over there, wasn't it?"

He wanted me to answer, and I thought, *Oh, God, how?* The Lord spoke to me with such love and compassion, "Billy needs to hear this, and you are the only one who can speak this truth to him. Billy needs to hear the truth so he can know that he can be forgiven. You can do this because I am with you, I love you, and I love Billy."

I told Billy that I believed that too. Just listening to him, I knew that God had tried to keep him from going back to my sister's house. It was then that our conversation changed, and I began to share God's plan of salvation with Billy again; it was time for him to hear all of God's truth.

I said, "See how awesome God is? You can go to heaven; Laura, you, and I can enjoy an eternity with our Lord and Savior, and all that has happened here will not even matter. All that we see here will be gone; it's not eternal, Billy. The things in this world will all vanish, but you and I are eternal beings, and we will spend eternity in one place or another. There are only two places that have been prepared for our eternal soul: heaven and hell; these are the only two choices we have. No matter what you did, you still have a choice; right here, where you are, you can make a difference."

Billy said, "But murder?"

Maybe it was the way he said it, or it was just time for the secrets of the heart to be revealed. I chose to believe that it was time for me to be released from the prison that *those secrets had kept me* in for so long. My mind went back to a time during the investigation when the Lord was speaking to me about His love for Billy. I looked at Billy, and I knew he needed to hear about that event in my life. "Billy, I battled for a long time about what you did to my sister. I hated you at first, but one day, God showed me that He loved you. That was very hard for me to grasp. It absolutely made no sense to me. God showed me that when Jesus died on the cross, He died for *all sins*, and that included murder."

I stopped; I didn't want to finish. Everything inside me was saying no, but God's voice was speaking louder. I looked back at Billy and said, "During the time that I was in the battle with hate and unforgiveness toward you, God asked me a question. He asked me what sins He should forgive me for. Then He told me to look deep into my soul, to look honestly at which sins I had committed, that I was seeking forgiveness for."

I looked down. "Billy, I have sinned. I am not so different from you. There are many things I have done that I am so ashamed of, and still, God loves me. God has given me a life and a future. God is constantly at work in my life to complete His work, and I trust Him every day. He is the one that took away the pain from my heart. He will do the same for you if you trust Him. Let's pray and ask Him to help you."

I went to reach for Billy's hands, which were stretched out on the table. He pulled them back quickly out of my reach. He started crying, unable to hold the tears back. "Oh, no, these are the hands that killed your sister. How can you even look at them, let alone touch them?"

I just froze, and I couldn't respond to him. I was just sitting there staring at him. I wasn't prepared for what happened next; my past came into my future. My heart was pounding, and God was speaking, "Tell him, Linda, you have come for this purpose. Your life has brought you to this moment. It's time, Linda."

There was no sound in the room except for Billy crying. I reached all the way across the table and took his hands in mine and said, "No, Billy, these are the hands that have been forgiven. It's all right, I forgive you." At that very moment, it was like a massive explosion took place in my soul. The darkness was expelled by light pouring into the depths of the darkest places in my soul. God's light, God's love, and God's truth flooded my heart and filled my being. I spoke again, "I have lived a life of many twists and turns. I have walked down many a road that led me to places I should have never gone. We all do things we regret; we all have shame and guilt that we bear in our souls and live with every day of our lives. I am not innocent, Billy, and I, too, am guilty of horrible sins."

I paused. "You see, Billy, I belong in prison too. I, too, am guilty of a crime that I committed many years ago. I thought I got away with it, but it has haunted me for thirty-seven years. You see, I, too, am guilty of murder!" There was a rustling in the room, and then it became still and deathly silent. Billy and I had tears streaming down our faces, our eyes fixed upon each other. The words were no longer prisoners in my soul; they began to flow out in perfect harmony… "Please hear me. I don't know what will happen after today, but I know that God brought me here today to tell you this so you can be set free."

I looked directly into Billy's eyes. "I cannot carry this in the depths of my soul any longer. I know why God chose this day for me to come and see you. It is a day that holds so much pain for me. You see, Billy, it was on this day, thirty-seven years ago, that because of my actions, an innocent baby died. I was so young, and these are very painful memories for me. Let me tell you about my beautiful baby; he could hear sounds and was startled by loud noises. He was very active and would curl up and rest after he had been very active. My baby could hear my heart beating and went through the motions of crying, but without making a sound. His favorite thing to do was suck his thumb. He had hands and feet, toes and fingers, and his heartbeat with perfect precision. He was ten inches long and weighed one pound, and on August 4, 1972, I went to have him ripped from my womb, but something happened, and the procedure failed. At the time of this so-called abortion, the doctor told me that I was in the first trimester, but I was almost five months pregnant. My baby fought for his life for three days, and on August 7, 1972, he lost that battle, and he ended up in a toilet." I shook my head, still in unbelief of that moment. "I stood back in shock and watched as a nurse flushed the toilet. That memory has haunted me every day for the last thirty-seven years. I never told anyone about it. I pushed it deep down into my soul and left it there. I never talked about it to anyone. I had nightmares for years and still do. There were times I would hear my baby crying. There were even times that I woke up in the middle of the night and found myself somewhere, and I knew I was looking for my baby. Every time I saw a baby, I thought about my baby. The one I killed."

I paused for a short moment. "I have to say this, Billy, or I may never say it. I know that there are many women and men who believe that abortion is all right. You, too, might think that

I did nothing wrong, but life is not for us to will and choose who shall be born and who shall die. It's a decision that was never intended for mere humans to make. I know firsthand from my own experience the depth of pain and anguish of such a choice."

I could not stop the tears as I continued; I brushed them away. "I didn't even believe that there was a God at the time I got the abortion, and still, my conscience told me I had killed my baby and what I had done was wrong. I had no right at all to decide whether my baby should be born or not. I just didn't see it. Maybe I didn't want to see it. Maybe no woman wants to see it, and I have learned you can put any name you want to on it. They can call it a procedure, a D&C, or an abortion, but it is murder when you rip a baby from the only safety and protection the baby has in the mother's womb. My baby was in the midst of being fearfully and wonderfully made, and I had him ripped from the safety and protection of my womb. I took my baby's right to live away from him. I didn't have the right to do that any more than you had the right to take Laura's life. We are both guilty of murder, and as such, we both deserve to be punished. We have committed a great sin in spilling the blood of the innocent."

I had no strength left; I dropped my head and said the only thing left to say: "God, forgive us."

I was crying, and Billy was crying. I heard him say, "God, forgive me." I didn't even realize it, but I still had a firm grip on his hand. I asked him if it was all right for me to pray with him again, and he nodded his head yes. I prayed as tears ran down my face. I asked the God who loves us to forgive us for killing and destroying the lives of those that He created and loved. I prayed for Billy and me to have courage to stand up and do the right thing for the days and nights ahead when our vision may be blurred by our own ways that God would allow us to have twenty-twenty spiritual vision so that we could see the truth, know the truth, and that we would not fail or be deceived by the enemy. I asked for peace and love to reign in our hearts. Last of all, I asked God to open doors for both Billy and I to share our testimonies and witness to others about the love and forgiveness of our God. After I finished praying, Billy and I continued to talk. I finished sharing God's plan of salvation with him. Then, he miraculously bowed his head and asked Jesus to forgive him. Billy openly confessed he was a sinner in need of a Saviour, and he asked Jesus to come into his heart and cleanse him; right there, he gave his life to Jesus.

Billy was saved that day. I watched as he raised his head, and I saw a man that I knew in my heart was forgiven. He was twenty-two years old when he killed my sister. His whole life was laid out before him. He had gone out with some friends on a Friday night to party; then it turned into a weekend of drugs and alcohol that ended in murder. He was now thirty years old and in prison for life. He cannot go back and undo what he did; no more than I could go back and change the events that led up to the death of my baby. No, all we can do is repent, confess, and ask God to help us overcome the pain and heartache caused by the wrong choices we have made. We must learn to trust Him as He fills us with His peace, a peace that surpasses our own understanding. Walking in that understanding gives us the knowledge and the wisdom to warn others of the dangers and the pitfalls that lead to the place of regret and shame.

The air was lighter. Everything seemed brighter. I felt so free; that's the only way to phrase it. I was impressed by the Holy Spirit, how Billy had said he was going to be an artist. That's why he was going to college. I sat there for a moment, letting my thoughts flow so I could speak freely what I believed God wanted me to say. I had to say what was in my heart in a way that I believed Billy could understand. I told him about the day that I broke all my dishes, my plates, my saucers, my glasses, and my soup bowls. All of it, I slammed them up against the wall and broke them.

"Billy," I said, "I sat in those broken dishes, and God spoke to me; He told me to paint. I was a little confused; I'd never painted in my life. Yet now God was telling me to paint. God said if I painted, I would heal. I could not understand it then. But I did begin to paint. I've painted for years. My walls are painted, and now I paint on canvases. I think that's amazing, don't you, Billy? Your heart's desire was to become an artist, a painter, and paint on canvas. Put the things that were in your heart and make them real and beautiful on a canvas. You did not get to do that. God put your dream in my heart and made it a reality. God is so good. I love to paint, Billy. Something I thought I would never do now brings peace and joy to my life. I am so grateful that I obeyed that day. My husband was right along with me, making it possible, encouraging me, and pushing me until I picked up the paintbrush and started painting. I just want you to know how it fills my heart with joy at this moment to know that I am doing something that you wanted to do. Something that has been taken away from you and how it breaks your heart that you no longer can paint. It's like coming full circle. God gave me your gift. It seems so very strange that you wanted to be an artist and you loved it, but because of your actions and according to what you told me, you can't even pick up a paintbrush. According to your own words, you cannot even have paint in this prison. I am sorry for that because it was something put in your heart by God; it was your gift. I know how much it calms the soul; you must miss it greatly. You never got to do what you set out to do. Your dream in life was destroyed the night you killed Laura; because of your actions, you no longer can paint. God made your dream come true in me. He gave me something that was taken from you. God took your gift and gave it to me. God did it to help me heal because of what you took from me." We talked a while longer.

Billy and I said goodbye after we both prayed again. Abigail had asked special permission to speak to Billy before he was handcuffed and taken back to his cell. Her request was granted, and it was her time. She had so loved her aunt, Laura, and she had been patiently waiting for her moment to talk to Billy. I don't know what she said; that is between her and him.

I walked to the area where she had been waiting and sat down. With a heavy heart, I was ready to face the pain of my past. I was ready to accept the fact that I, indeed, had sought to end the life of my baby growing and developing in my womb. I had, indeed, murdered my own child.

My mind went back to the year 1972. After my daughter, Jasmine, was born on February 5, 1972, I continued to visit my parents at least once a week. My parents were all I had, and I loved them.

I knew my roommate would be moving out soon, and I would be alone again. I had no other friends, and I didn't want to be alone, so I kept in touch with my parents. I knew I still needed to have someone to talk to. I knew my parents would hurt me, but even if they hurt me, it was better than having no one. I was hoping to see Laura as well. I kept asking about her, but my mother wouldn't tell me anything. One day in February of 1972, I was visiting my mom. She told me that for a small price, she would give me Laura's phone number and take me to see her. The bargain and exchange took place a week later, on March 14, in the afternoon. Mom would give me Laura's phone number first, and then I paid her "small price."

She took me to one of the biggest hotels I had ever seen. It was so fancy and extravagant. Everywhere I looked, there were expensive vases, lamps, and decorations. There were tables and couches that I was afraid to even touch. We went into a very large, elegant restaurant in the hotel. I smiled to myself, and I thought, *It is beautiful here and very much my mother's taste and style.*

It seemed that the people there knew my mother. The hotel staff catered to her in special ways, and of course, she loved it. We had been there about thirty minutes or so when a man in a very nice suit showed up. What I remembered most about seeing him in the restaurant was his suit. It was a soft-looking gray; it was the first time I had ever seen a suit like that, even though I had seen a lot of men come and go over the years in our home. I didn't think that I had ever met this man. He seemed different from the other men I had known Mom to see. I couldn't place him; he had charm, but still, something just didn't seem right. I don't know why it stood out to me or even why I recalled him saying, "So this is little Linda. You are right; she doesn't look like she is a day over fourteen. She will do just fine." That's when I realized why my mother dressed me the way she did. At that time, he handed my mother an envelope and said, "As we agreed, this is the first half. You will get the rest after."

My mom asked, "What time do you want me to pick her up?"

The man answered, "We agreed on four hours."

My mother said, "Well, where do you want me to pick her up: here or in the room?"

He said, "The room would be best in four hours. Here's a key; I'll take the *do-not-disturb* sign off when I'm finished."

He handed Mom a key, and I knew it was to one of the rooms in the hotel, but I never knew which one. It was when he handed her the key that I knew I was his prize for the next four hours. But this was what I had bargained for? Mom had given me Laura's phone number when we arrived at the hotel, and I had it in my purse. I was doing this for my sister so I could find her and talk to her. I told myself that four hours was not long, and it was worth it. I had Laura's phone number, and Mom was going to take me to see Laura on Monday morning. I told myself that it would be over soon.

As we were going up the elevator, he said, "Would you like some candy?"

I told him no.

He said, "Sweetie, you are supposed to say, 'Yes, sir.' Now, let's try it again. Would you like some candy?"

I said, "Yes, sir." He handed me a piece of candy. Once I was in the room, the man changed, and he was not charming at all anymore. The four hours were long and painful, and after it was over, I went back to my apartment and buried it all in my soul. It became the secret of my heart. I refused to think about it; I acted like it never happened. That day simply did not exist.

In July of 1972, I discovered that I was pregnant. The doctor gave me a complete exam, and afterwards, he said, "There is no need for you to have it." I didn't really understand, so I asked what he meant by that. The doctor said, "It's not a baby; it's a fetus; nothing as of yet, an embryo, just tissue, that's all. The law says if you would bring harm to yourself to keep from having it, then a doctor can get rid of it for you."

I asked if it hurt. The doctor said, "No, but you have to sign a paper saying that you would rather end your life than have this baby." I told him that I didn't want to end my life. He said, "Of course you don't; you just have to say that for me to fix your problem."

I said, "I didn't know that I had a problem. What's wrong? I mean, what is the problem?"

Then the doctor said, "This is the best I can do until the laws change. You do have rights; after all, it is your body and life that will be affected by this unwanted fetus."

I said, "Okay, but you're sure it's not a baby?"

He said, "Young lady, I'm very positive. I am the doctor, and you are the patient, and I believe that this is the best course of action for you."

As I was signing the paper, the nurse said, "That's a good girl, and you are helping thousands of girls in the future have the right to choose what they do with their own bodies."

I said, "What do you mean?"

She replied, "This paper, along with thousands just like it, will go to the White House in January of 1973 to help legalize abortion."

I have never forgotten those words, but still, I really had no idea what the nurse was talking about at that time. She told me that the law kept women from doing what they wanted to do with their own bodies. She said that was wrong. "Like now, you should be able to walk in here and, on demand, get rid of that fetus, but you have to wait two weeks after you sign in case you change your mind. Then, by law, you can get the abortion."

I said, "You mean I will have to come back? You're not taking the fetus out today? What if it turns into a baby by then?"

She looked at me and said, "Honey, you really don't need a baby."

Over the next two weeks, I tried not to think about it. I made arrangements with Rhonda to take care of Jasmine while I was gone. I told her I had something very important to do and would return as soon as I could.

The abortion was scheduled on August 4, 1972, at ten thirty in the morning at the hospital. I arrived on time and was taken into a room. I put a robe on and lay on the table. The doctor came in, and a machine was rolled in. I felt a forced pressure, and then I heard a sound coming from the machine. I looked over at the tube that ran into the machine. The doctor smiled and said, "That is the fetus, and you're done." He left the room, and I thought this was all wrong. I had this feeling that I had done something really bad, but I didn't understand what it was. The nurse came in and said they would come for me in about ten minutes and take me to a room where I would stay overnight, and then I could go home.

I developed a fever sometime during the night. Over the next three days, the fever kept going up. I was in a lot of pain, and nothing was helping. The same nurse kept coming in and giving me medicine. I asked her what was wrong with me. She said that the doctor had ordered some tests for the next day. She told me I had a severe infection somewhere in my body for some unknown reason. That night, I woke up in severe pain and called for the nurse. I was in so much pain. I hurt so badly I could barely move. I asked her if she could give me something for the pain. She left the room and came back and said I could have something at 4:00 a.m. I asked her what time it was, and she said it was 3:00 a.m. I asked her what day it was, and she said, "August 7. Get some rest; I'll be back in an hour."

About fifteen minutes after she left the room, I got out of bed to go to the bathroom. I was hurting so badly that I crawled on my hands and knees to the bathroom. I pulled myself up on the toilet. I felt this excruciating pain shoot through my body, and I felt like I had to push. A few moments passed, and I had another pain, and then it stopped, leaving me in a cold sweat and cramping. After about ten minutes, the cramping eased up, the sweating disappeared, and it seemed that I had improved in less than thirty-five minutes. I still felt some cramping, but it was very light and not as intense.

I stood up and reached over to flush the toilet, and there was my baby. I saw my baby there in the toilet. I collapsed on the floor in total shock. I just sat there and stared at my baby. I could see his hands, his feet, his head, his little body; it was my baby, fully developed, just very small. The nurse came in with a shot for my pain and asked what I was doing on the floor. I told her to look at my baby in the toilet. She looked into the toilet, and as long as I live, I will never forget the heartless words she spoke. She said, "Yes, that is your baby; it seems you may have been about nineteen weeks. Hard to believe he hung on for three days." With those words said, she reached over and flushed the toilet. Then she got this look on her face and said, "I should not have done that; I may be in a little trouble. It will be all right. We will just tell them you flushed it. Just look at you; that is the afterbirth. We need to clean you up and get you in bed. Now, remember you flushed the toilet."

I started screaming, "Oh no, it is my baby. You lied to me. Why would you do that? It's a baby, my baby! Why did you lie to me? I would have never done this." The nurse cleaned me up and gave me the shot. Then I went to bed and collapsed in tears, my heart broken. I wanted to undo it, but I knew nothing was going to change what I had done. I felt I had murdered my own baby. I could not figure out why. What made me do such an awful thing? I was a bad person, and I deserved to be punished.

The next morning, the doctor came in and told me I needed to have a surgical procedure, commonly called a D&C. The surgery was scheduled for the next morning at four. I had the procedure done the next morning, and three days later, I left the hospital. I went home, knowing in my heart that I had done an evil thing. I pushed it down deep inside my soul and tried not to think about it. I knew it was something to be ashamed of, something to hide, never tell a soul, bury it deep, and never think of it again, just like the candy, to be forgotten; it was best just to forget it altogether. At least, that is what I told myself the day I went home from the hospital. It was never forgotten. I tried to, I really did try to forget over the years, but it was always there in my heart and in the shadows of my mind, always haunting me and tormenting me. I kept telling myself I was a young girl and soon I would forget.

Two months and twenty-three days later, on October 31, 1972, I was brutally raped and beaten; among the devastating injuries I sustained and the damage done to me, I would never have children again. I could no longer have a baby. For thirty-seven years, I believed that God allowed me to be raped as punishment for killing my baby. I also believed it was God who took away my ability to have children to seal my punishment. I truly believed in my heart that it was the one thing I could never be forgiven for. It was the one thing I never talked about to anyone, not even God. However, the night I was raped was the night my eyes were opened to the truth that there was a God, and somehow, in some way, I had to find Him, even though I thought that He was punishing me for killing my baby. I still had to find Him!

Years passed, and even after I was saved, I would never talk about it, not even to God. I could never bring myself to even mention it, not even in my prayers, not even to ask for forgiveness. No one knew this secret except me. I was never going to tell anyone. It was the one truth that I never had to worry about being exposed because I was the only one who knew. It belonged in the secrets of my heart. I could never even bring myself to admit that I had ever gone to that hotel or that I was pregnant a second time. The most painful memory for me to face was the fact that I had signed a paper that said I would rather die than have my baby; if forced to have the baby, I would have taken my own life! I lived with the memory and the pain of that fatal choice for thirty-seven years. Tortured and tormented, in my mind, in so many unimaginable ways. Nightmares, night sweats, waking up in constant fear, shame, guilt, and regret, walking around crying in the middle of the night, looking for my baby. Asleep or awake, it didn't matter. Seeing my baby over and over and over again in a toilet, being flushed like he was nothing, haunted me for years and years.

"Mom! Mom! It's time." Abigail was calling to me. I looked up, shaken from my thoughts. "Mom, they're ready to take Billy back, and he has something to say to you before they put the shackles back on him."

I knew that was something he did not want Abigail and me to witness. I walked to where Billy was; he looked at me and said, "Thank you, Linda; I will never forget what you have done here for me today. I know the courage it must have taken for you to come here to see me. Thank you for writing that letter; I will keep it always. Most of all, thank you for sharing the truth of your past and God's amazing love with me. Because now more than ever, I know He loves me. I know God brought you here to share that with me today. God knew I would never believe that I could be forgiven until I saw you take my hands. I know that I have been forgiven by God and by you. I will never forget this day or the forgiveness I have received here today. Just remember, today we are both free; you are forgiven too. Don't forget that, okay? I will pray for you, and please pray for me. One more thing: Laura is in heaven, and I believe she is holding your baby. We will see them both again someday. We must hold on to that. Please keep me in your prayers, and thank you so much for coming here today and sharing Jesus's love with me. Goodbye, Linda. God be with you."

Before that day, Billy and I were both standing behind huge bars in a spiritual prison, one that physical eyes cannot see. We were prisoners of our own making and held there by the enemy of our soul in chains of guilt and shame. For thirty-seven years to the day, I had been in that prison, but on August 7, 2009, I was set free. I find it absolutely incredible that God selected that day to birth Billy Lopez into His kingdom. God took a day that held nothing but death and darkness for me and turned it into a day of celebration. That day, God revealed to me that my baby was in heaven, safe, with Him, and Billy was born again. He had a new life; he was in the Master's hands now, and I trusted that. Those bars that held me captive were shattered and busted wide open; I was set free.

Billy and I were no longer in spiritual bondage. We were set free from the secrets of our hearts, free from the darkness that held us in its grips. On that day, August 7, 2009, forgiveness poured down upon us from heaven, washed us, cleansed us, and set us free. It was God's forgiveness. I knew then what it truly meant to let it go by as forgiveness poured down upon two lost souls, the truth was uncovered, and the secrets of the heart were revealed.

CHAPTER 22

Reflections

Home! I thought as we pulled into the driveway. I was so glad to see that old, familiar place that I had come to love. *"Home" is a word that we seem to look at as a place of safety, a place where families dwell. Home is the place where we come together and share a lifetime of love, hope, and faith.* I thought to myself, *Well, at least that's the way it should be.*

It was such a long weekend, and it seemed as if I had been away for a very long time. I had walked through a dark valley on a journey where few ever go. I needed to find a safe place where I could cry, to grieve for all that I now fully understood.

I thought briefly about the prison that I had just walked out of. Not the one with bars, high razor fences, and shackled prisoners. I'm talking about the unseen prison, the one that holds its captives in spiritual darkness, in caves and dens of shame and regret. They are held firmly by the unseen shackles of the hidden secrets done in darkness, unable to come to the light. It's an unseen prison of darkness, where all joy is drained from the prisoners, who then become unseen among us. I thought to myself, *I was one of those prisoners, unable to escape because of what I had done in darkness.*

God had proven that His light is greater than any prison, seen or unseen. God flooded the soul of a prisoner with His marvelous light, a prisoner who had been held captive in dungeons of darkness. That prisoner was me. God, with cords of love and kindness, had encouraged me many times to come into His light. But time after time, I had chosen to hide in that prison of darkness with my secrets because of my fear of judgment and condemnation. Yet, in His light, my deed was manifested, bringing the death of my baby out into the open. I was able to repent; I found forgiveness and healing. God had pursued me with love, and it was in Him that I found mercy and compassion.

My mind quickly reflected on Scott. How was I going to share with him all that had been revealed to me over the weekend? There was so much in my heart that I needed to share with him. However, at that moment, I didn't feel it was the right time. I didn't feel I could walk into the house, sit down, and tell Scott about *all* my experiences over the weekend.

I just didn't feel I was ready to do that. I needed to rest, and I thought we could sit at the table in the morning and talk over coffee. I knew it was going to take at least four hours, and that was just to start. The truth was, I didn't know where to start. I was physically and mentally exhausted. At that moment, the only thing I really wanted was a hot bath and a good night's sleep. I was completely worn out.

Scott was preparing a nice hot bath for me while I unpacked my suitcase. I moved slowly and steadily, realizing I was holding back the tears. The reality of the weekend grabbed hold of my heart. The shock of all I heard flooded my soul in an instant.

I took my bath and went straight to bed. I woke up at about three in the morning. I went outside to a small deck on the side of our house, and I thanked the Lord for all He had done. I asked Him to forgive me for my foolishness. I told Him how wrong I had been about everything. I thanked Him for the prison visit and for preparing me for the time that I spent with Billy. I was very thankful for the truth that had been revealed to me, and I was very thankful that God trusted me and gave me the opportunity to meet Billy and to hear everything he had to say, even though it was very hard. What I was most thankful for was the forgiveness I had received.

God had certainly taken me places that I would have never gone on my own. I believe God opened the doors when I became willing to go through those doors. He spoke to my heart about what He wanted me to do, but the choice was mine. He asked me to go see Billy; I find it amazing that God, maker of heaven and earth, trusted me to deliver His message of love and forgiveness. It was God who opened the door and made it possible for me to visit Billy.

One of the things that I came to understand that weekend is how God truly does open and close doors. I now understand God opens the door when we become willing and obedient to what we know is truth because of His light. The more truth and light I allow in my life, the more doors He opens, giving me unbelievable opportunities to serve, love, witness, and minister to others. At the same time, He closes the doors that are no longer necessary for me to go through.

The next morning, my thoughts were crystal clear, not the normal mixed-up, mingled, self-absorbed memories of the past. Scott and I sat at the table having our morning coffee when he finally asked, "So, what happened?"

I normally would have just spoken out and told him the whole story, using my storytelling techniques to get his attention and keep it. I don't know how to explain it, but something happened. In an instant, my eyes were opened, and I saw my life, my whole life, as it was in the hands of God, and I saw His amazing showers of mercy raining down on my life.

Instead of answering Scott's question, I said, "Scott, you know when I first met you, I wanted to be somebody else? I didn't want to be me. I wanted to be like everyone else. Everyone else seemed so normal and happy; I wanted to know what that was like. I thought there was something so wrong with me."

I took a sip of my coffee and smiled. "God has shown me that I was so busy looking at others and trying to be like them that I could not see who He had created me to be. All the good things He had given me, all the gifts and talents He had given me, were being wasted because I wanted to be like someone else, just another carbon copy. There are so many women who are just imitations in this world, who have given up so much to be like someone else while denying the very special life that God has given them. All to be noticed, loved, and accepted in this life, based upon the latest trend. I no longer want to be like everyone else, and I don't want to be a carbon copy. I believe there are enough of those in this world."

I took a deep breath and said, "I am just now beginning to realize all that God has done in my life. There was a time when I couldn't look at myself in a mirror; I hated everything about myself and my life. I saw other Christian women, and I tried so hard to be like them. They were my models, my examples, and I thought I was supposed to be like them. I wanted to dress like them, walk like them, talk like them, and the more I tried, the more I failed. Today, I see how truly blessed I am, and when I stopped trying to be somebody else and acting like everybody else, God showed me who He created me to be."

Scott was smiling as I said, "God has taught me how to use all the gifts and talents He has given me. He has shown me that I am used most when I am who He created me to be. In short, Scott, I love God, and I know He is the creator, and He created me. I love who I am today. I love being your wife, and I love serving and reaching out to others."

Scott said, "Is there anything else?"

I laughed and said, "Yes, God has indeed opened my eyes, Scott. He is showing me that He is the great I Am! He has always been working on my behalf to show me His goodness and mercy, only I have been so stubborn and blind that I couldn't see.

I wanted things my way. I thought that I knew what was best. However, it is God who has been picking and prodding, allowing and disallowing things in my life; God is the one who knows what is best for me." I smiled at Scott, who seemed to be just a little surprised. "He has the blueprint to my life, and I am His creation. What He creates, He loves, and He longs only for His creation to love Him back. He pours His love into each one of us, desiring only to make us into the image of His Son. That image is not what we see on the outside, the images that we portray, but of a much deeper content. It's the image of love and forgiveness, and nothing short of that will do."

I took a deep breath. "The sad part is, when we reject God's blueprint, then we set out on a different course, one of our own making. We fail to realize that Satan also has a blueprint—his is full of evil plans and desires for each one of us. Satan gives us small bites, making sure we will take the bait. Once we take the plunge, the enemy is there, waiting to instill his false images in our minds. Once we accept those images, we believe them, and eventually, we become their prisoners in a world of spiritual darkness. What I am so excited about at this moment is the fact that God loves me enough to trust me with such truth and will hold me accountable for this truth as well. To me, that's amazing."

After taking a sip of coffee, I said, "I know now that God brought Laura back into my life. Scott, He arranged it. He moved in Laura's heart, and she was obedient. She came looking for me, she did not give up, and she trusted God to turn my heart."

I reached over and touched Scott's hand and said, "I will never forget when Laura and I were in the driveway, with empty space between us, and how quickly that space between us disappeared. We were sisters; we had endured so many things, and we had been so broken, but we loved each other so very much. God did an amazing thing when He brought us together again. He healed us and restored us both as sisters. Then He gave us the best eight months of our lives."

I smiled as I told Scott, "I have a treasure of memories, of laughter that we had never had as sisters, cooking together in freedom, laughing and sharing our hearts in the kitchen, meeting in the early morning hours, wrapping up in blankets to keep warm as we huddled together watching the sunrise, and how truly beautiful it was."

I smiled as a memory came to mind, and I could not help but share it with Scott. "One afternoon, we met just outside of town. It was the perfect plan; from there, we drove out to the lake. We found a nice spot, spread a blanket out on the ground, took a seat, and watched the sunset on the lake. We held each other's hand as we beheld just a small part of God's glory. Scott, it was magnificent! The most beautiful colors we had ever seen in the sky. I believe He painted it just for us that day. We never had such an opportunity to sit still and enjoy God's handiwork together."

I brushed away tears, tears of joy, because of the beautiful memory God had given me. I told Scott, "God allowed Laura and me to find our way back to each other. There was a bridge of love and forgiveness that we crossed together. We found the true meaning of sacrifice, the value of life, and the foolishness of wasting our years in bitterness and unforgiveness. I have to believe that was God's gift to both of us, a time and place for us to find and experience love, forgiveness, and healing."

I lowered my head for a moment. "Scott, I look back, and I remember now how many times God touched my heart and spoke to me about Laura. He told me so many times to go to her and to just love her. He told me to find her and put my arms around her. Many times, I knew that I should have gone to her and talked to her. I wouldn't do it; I was so prideful and arrogant. I had let anger, bitterness, and unforgiveness keep me from obeying the Lord and doing what I knew to be right."

I sat in silence for a moment, then continued, "I now understand that if Laura had not come looking for me, the guilt would have been unbearable for me. I cannot even begin to think about the emotional damage and pain I would have carried in the depths of my soul. Laura's death was horrible, and as bad as it was, it could have been so much worse for me. It would have destroyed me to find all those letters Laura wrote to me when she was in prison. The guilt would still be ripping through the center of my heart and would have torn me apart. I do not believe I would have ever been able to bear it, and I never would have recovered."

I couldn't stop the tears, and I really didn't want to. I looked at Scott with tears in my eyes and said, "Scott, I would have read those letters and been haunted and tormented by the words of love and forgiveness that she wrote about. The memory of her writing all those letters to me and how I sent them all back unopened would have added more damage to my already painful existence. I thank God that He touched Laura's heart, and she came and found me. Because she sought me out and found me, I have wonderful memories, and I thank God she kept those letters. I am so very thankful that they were there for me."

I wiped the tears from my eyes. "If I had not gone to Laura's house and faced the unimaginable, then I would never have been able to face Billy. It was there at her house, in her bedroom, where her body was found, that the Lord first began to speak to my heart about forgiving the person who created the mess that I had to clean up. Being there and seeing how horrible it was put the one question in my mind, 'What happened there and why?' That question was used by God."

The tears and words continued flowing... "It was hard at her house, seeing all that blood, her blood, but in all my weakness,

I discovered God is indeed strong because I know now, looking back, that going there and facing all that I faced and dealt with for those four weeks at her house was not in my ability at all. That strength and courage came from God. There were so many things that I would not have discovered. I wouldn't have found her Bible, the scrapbook with our two pictures in it, or her letters, and reading them gave me the courage and strength to hold on and even to forgive. Her letters were full of scripture, encouragement, words of forgiveness, stories of her life and things she had been through, and so many other things."

I looked down. "No, Scott, I cannot even begin to think about the guilt, the torment, the unforgiveness, and the shame I would be walking in right now had Laura not come looking for me. I would be in a valley of darkness I would not have ever recovered from. God indeed spared me from that."

I looked back up and smiled. "Instead, God gave me all those wonderful memories to hold onto, memories that pulled me out of that dark pit. Laura and I had all those amazing moments together. I have some of the most amazing, incredible memories from those eight months that we shared together in love and freedom. Laura and I talked a lot about our childhood, and it helped me to talk to her about how things were when we were growing up. She knew and understood more about our trips to and from Kentucky. She helped me understand Dad and Mom a little better. No, it would have destroyed me had Laura died with all that brokenness still between us."

I looked down and then back up, and I realized how much I loved sharing my heart with Scott. I smiled at him and said,

"I have so very much to be thankful for. Laura and I laughed together one afternoon for over an hour. We had never really laughed together, not like that. We had always loved each other, but we were never allowed to express that love. It was during those eight months that we were able to break down the walls and barriers that our mother and life had placed between us."

I smiled at Scott as I took another sip of coffee. "You know, she warned me about hiding my past from you. She told me you would find out. She told me the best thing to do was just tell you the truth. She even wanted to come with me and talk to you. I just told her that there was no way you could ever find out. She begged me to tell you. She told me you would find out, and it would be best coming from me. I just wouldn't listen to her. I can be stubborn from time to time."

I laughed. "You know something else? On that last day with Laura, we relived the best moments of our life together. It gave me something to hold onto during the darkest days right after her death. The strange thing is I wasn't even planning on going over there that Thursday."

Scott reached over and took my hand as I said, "It just sort of happened, and it was the most amazing day. We ate out; we went shopping. That's the day she brought the Rubbermaid crate for the lunch. It was her idea, Scott, the lunch in the box. Anyway, after we had finished shopping, we sat around and just talked. Our goodbye that day was very special. We just kind of lingered and held onto that moment. You know what she told me that day? Well, with her big, beautiful smile, she told me that we were just very broken when we were young. She said, 'But we are living miracles, proof that God can and does change lives.' She told me to look where we came from and to look where we are now."

I stopped talking, got up, and fixed myself another cup of coffee. I sat back down and continued. "She told me that day that God is amazing, and no matter what happens, I had to trust Him. She said for me to stop and look how far He had brought me. She told me I had courage, *me*, Scott, the coward who couldn't even face the truth. Laura told me I had the courage, long ago, to set out on my own to look for God, and God honored that. She told me I had enough faith and passion to believe in Him and had gone out into the big world I was so afraid of to find Him. She told me that God loves that about me. She wanted me to remember something and to hold onto it."

I looked at Scott and said, "It was important; it was our last time together. We stood face-to-face when she told me this; she believed that God had sent her to find me so He could show me what forgiveness really looked like. She said that's what God wanted me to understand so I could forgive myself. She didn't know I had done something long ago that I had never forgiven myself for doing. I lived in shame and guilt because I had done this terrible thing."

I hung my head and said, "God brought me all this way because He loves me. He wanted me to walk in His love and forgiveness so I would be able to truly love and serve others. But until I understood forgiveness, I only had a small piece of the truth. That's why I was so defeated; I lived and walked in that defeat because I did not understand that He would forgive me. I didn't understand His forgiveness, and because of that, I was unable to forgive myself and others. I now see the riches and the depth of His forgiveness, and it is all because of His amazing love."

I finally shared the truth with Scott about the abortion and the pain it had brought into my life, the years of unforgiveness, and the emotional damage I had experienced because of it. I shared the truth about how Billy had killed Laura, the whole ordeal she had faced, and how she had forgiven him. I talked of how I had taken Billy's hands to pray. Scott listened as I talked for over four hours, and then I said, "You remember how I had blamed you for not letting me go to Laura's that day? Scott, God's mighty hand was in that to save me."

Scott looked away. "Linda, I am so sorry I didn't let you go have lunch with her that day. I've blamed myself a long time for that. The strange thing is, I was going to tell you to go ahead and go. But....." His voice trailed off into silence as he hung his head.

I said, "Scott, you need to look at me. It's all right! God didn't want me to be there that morning because one of the things that I learned from Billy was that he killed Laura that Sunday morning, right after I got off the phone with her. He was already there, and he told me that if I had walked in, he would have killed me too! So, please don't blame yourself anymore."

Scott had a look on his face that I had never seen. He sat there silent, then finally said, "That is hard for me to believe; I don't know what I would've done. I am trying to grasp it, but I don't think I can even think about that. It seems impossible, are you sure?"

I told Scott I was very sure.

He said, "My God, Linda, I could have lost you! I've never once thought about that. I would have been lost in all of this and a visit to Billy. I could have never done that. God knows I am not built that way."

Scott and I spent that day together, talking and praying. We both had so much to be thankful for, and we both knew it was all because of God's love and forgiveness.

As the days began to pass after the visit with Billy, I began to sift through all that was deep inside my heart. The visit with Billy had brought many things to the surface. There were still things I questioned regarding my sister's murder. The one question that was in my mind was, why? Why Laura and not me? I felt it was a good question, one that I really wanted to understand. I knew that God had protected me that day. I knew, according to Billy, that he would have killed me, without question, had I walked into Laura's house that Sunday morning. Still, couldn't God have warned Laura? It did seem to be a fair and reasonable question.

As time went by, the question gradually slipped from my mind. I found myself in the midst of writing this book and talking to Chief Sanders, going through the files, police reports, pictures, court reports, newspaper clippings, confessions signed by Billy, and statements made by neighbors and those who were called in and questioned. I went over and over the tape of my meeting with Billy. Suddenly, one day, in the middle of all this, the Lord spoke to me, "See that, Linda?"

I looked again at the paper I was holding in my hand.

The Lord spoke again, "Remember, Linda?"

Then I saw it; there it was in plain sight, a list of phone calls made to and from Laura's home phone that Sunday. I had missed it. My mind flashed back to that morning. The phone was ringing. "Hello?"

It was Laura, and she said, "Are you still in bed? I'm coming out there today!"

I said, "Yes, Laura, I am still in bed, but I was getting ready to get up. It's like eight thirty in the morning. I am going to be on time, twenty minutes to get a shower and dress, about forty minutes to prepare our little lunch in a box. Don't worry; I will be at your house at eleven thirty. We are going to have a great day!"

Laura was silent for a moment. "I was wondering if you would like for me to come out there today instead of you coming all the way out here."

I said, "You think I'm not coming because I'm not up yet, don't you? I will be there."

She replied, "All right, I will see you when you get here."

We said goodbye to each other and hung up. It wasn't like I had forgotten that phone call. It was just so quick and unimportant. The most important call, according to the police, was the last conversation we had on the phone because it was the last call that was answered by Laura. No outgoing calls were made after that, and the only incoming calls after that were from her friend Tony, who took care of her dog, her place of employment, and me.

I flipped through some more papers until I found the statement from the young man who had borrowed milk at her house that morning. He said that he was there at nine o'clock, and he was sure about the time because Laura had said, "No problem, it's nine o'clock. You didn't wake me up. I've been up since seven."

He also stated that he told her she looked very nice that morning, and she had replied that she was going to drive out to her sister's house for a surprise visit. She gave him the milk, and he left. It was a sworn statement. He had no reason to lie. I looked back over the statement; it was like it just jumped off the page. In the young man's statement, he said that Laura told him she was going to drive out to see her sister. But that was not our plan.

I pulled out the recorded tape of the visit with Billy and played it. Billy said he was walking to Laura's at nine o'clock that morning when he saw a young man at Laura's back door. He turned around and went back to where he was partying. He had said that he was going to go to her house earlier that morning, but how much earlier he never said. The guys he was partying with had started harassing him around seven o'clock Saturday night, before they left for the DMX club, for him to get some money owed him. The harassment started again early that Sunday morning. He said he did not want to go to Laura's because he was so messed up, and he did not want Laura to see him that way. He said that his thoughts were confusing because of the meth, and the guys were making him angry at Laura.

I pulled out the list of all the calls to and from Laura's house again. I had called her house at 10:03 a.m., and we had talked for exactly seven minutes and twenty-seven seconds. I hadn't noticed before that the minutes for each call were listed as well. I looked up at the call she had made to my house at 8:32 a.m. We had only talked for one minute and forty-five seconds, much less than I had thought earlier.

Billy returned to Laura's house at 10:00 a.m. He was in her home before we even said goodbye. I knew while we were talking that someone had come into her house. I even asked her if she was seeing someone on the sly, and we laughed about it. Then she said, "No, it's just a friend." I had never thought about it before because we believed Laura was murdered on Wednesday, October 17, 2001. I had never even mentioned that first phone call to the police, and they had never really asked me about it either. It was just lost and forgotten in the midst of all that had happened.

As I began to put it all together, I saw it for the first time. Laura called me at 8:32 a.m. to make sure I was up and going to come, or *was* that the real reason? She asked me if I would rather her come to my house, and the first thing she said to me was, "Are you still in bed? *I'm coming out there today!*" I told her I was coming to her house. However, thirty minutes later, she was already dressed and told a young man she was going to visit her sister. A surprise visit, she told him. That was before she even knew I wasn't coming to her house!

Laura told both the young man who borrowed the milk and Billy the same thing, that she was going to visit her sister. I checked through everything again. I knew what the Lord was showing me, that Laura wanted to come to my house that day. She didn't want to be at home. However, I will never know this side of heaven. But I believe the Lord showed me that Laura wanted to come to my house at 8:32 a.m. when she called me.

Laura must have gotten up early to get ready to come to my house, even before she called me. I know my sister; she would not have been dressed that early in the morning unless she was planning on leaving her house. Otherwise, she would have taken her shower and stayed in her robe, relaxing with a cup of coffee, until it was time to get dressed, right before her company was expected.

When I called her at 10:00 a.m., she didn't even sound surprised that I wasn't coming. I also remember the last thing she said was, "I love you. Now, don't you forget that, and we will see each other again soon." Then we both said goodbye. I now believe she said those words because it was her intention to come to my house. I also believe she was going to leave as soon as we got off the phone, and she would have arrived at my house about the time we would be getting home from church. I do not want to second-guess or allow my mind to go into overtime. It's only a deep-down feeling that I have. With all the information that was placed in my hands, I believe that I was given insight into the reality of the thoughts and intentions of Laura's heart that morning. I believe Laura was going to come to my house. Laura never said goodbye to me that way. Whether or not it is true, I don't know, but her last words still give me great hope I shall see her again. As for the rest, was it her intention to come to my house that day? I believe so, but only God knows for sure.

Today, I know that God has worked in many ways, in and through my life, as a direct result of Laura's murder.

I know that God has brought good out of the most horrible thing that I, as a human, have ever had to face and deal with.

I am thankful for the reflections that come from God to help us see things in a different light, to help us understand how He has moved mountains, calmed storms, and brought peace to the raging war inside of us. He has taught me how to love the unlovable, forgive the unforgivable, and live a life in service to others. There is no greater aim and no greater privilege than to lay your life down for others.

CHAPTER 23

The Journey's End

I was coming to the end of my journey, and the things I had learned to value most were not so much the things that I could hold in my hand but those that one can never own: the smile on the face of a child, the first breath of a newborn baby, children playing in the sand, the sound of waves in the ocean, the wind on a cool evening, and the soul that just accepted Jesus as their Saviour.

We sometimes place such high value on homes, cars, jewelry, and so many other material things that only have temporal value, yet in all honesty, have no value at all. Value can only be placed upon that which lasts. The things that are eternal have great value, and that value does not depreciate because the eternal will last forever. Our souls have great value because we are eternal, and a great price was paid for our souls.

I was not turning back; I had come too far, and it was time to go to the one place where I could finally lay it all down and say goodbye—Laura's grave! It would be a long and difficult day. I had not been to Laura's grave since the meeting with Billy, and the first time, I would go with the full knowledge and understanding of what had happened to her. I wanted to say goodbye to her and let her go into our Master's hands. There will always be those special memories of her, and I will always miss her. I miss her every holiday, and on her birthday, I still whisper, "Happy birthday, Laura."

It was a beautiful day, and I believe that the Lord made it that way just for me. He knew, even though I didn't ask, that I hoped the sun would shine down on me the day that I had chosen to say goodbye to my sister. It was hard to say goodbye; I had not done so until that point in time. It was like I couldn't let go until I knew, or at least understood, what had happened to her and why. I think it's just part of my crazy nature, which now I consider a blessing.

I have thought a lot about what to share about that moment in my life and what not to share. Moments like that are rare, and oftentimes, they sweep through my mind as I feel the gentle breeze on a warm afternoon or sometimes as I smell fresh honeysuckle on a hot summer day. Laura so loved the smell of fresh honeysuckle.

I have so many beautiful memories. I watched the sunset the other evening, and I could hear her laughter and see her throwing her head back, saying, "Just look at it, Linda, we are the only ones who will ever see this sunset, just this way."

I did have a lot to say that day, more for myself than for Laura. It was more like a mighty rushing river at first, with mixed emotions and garbled words. However, the winds shifted and brought a calm and peaceful breeze, and the mighty rushing river became healing waters. Our lives had been so broken: our journey long and hard. I cried over our childhood as I realized that we never really had one. I talked of our teenage years and the many things that were taken away from us and lost forever. My words just flowed out, "Laura, we lost our innocence, but our bond as sisters could not be broken. We were broken, but long ago, we were little girls, and we loved each other so much. Together, we survived the years that were lived in confusion and fear."

I wiped away the tears as I said, "The years just seemed to go by unnoticed until one day I woke up and I was forty-seven years old, trying to figure out how I got there, with no parents, no sister, no answers, lost in a world that somehow I felt that I never belonged in." My thoughts shifted as I realized that it was true. I don't belong in this world; it is not my home. I am only passing through.

After sharing a lifetime with her, it was time to do what I had come to do. I looked at the headstone one more time: "Laura, Beloved Sister." I said the words, "Laura, my beloved sister, you are not here; you are in heaven. I will not be coming back to this place again. I do so love you and miss you, so much more than words can say, but this is a place of death, and I don't see you that way anymore."

I took a deep breath. "This place is for those who may still be searching for answers, or they have no hope, or those who are still grieving the losses, but I have moved past that now. I shall always remember our time together, all of it, the battles and the victories. Oh, Laura, there were victories, so many of them, but I didn't see them for so long. Laura, I want to thank you for the Rubbermaid crate, your last gift to me, and what a blessing it turned out to be. But you already know that."

I bowed my head and whispered, "I love you, Laura." I stood up and looked down for the last time and said, "Goodbye,

Sis; I'll see you again soon." I turned, and as I walked away, I brushed the falling tears from my cheeks.

There was such a peace and serenity in my soul as I drove out of the cemetery late that afternoon. It was such a beautiful day; I noticed the colors of the leaves and the shadows of the trees. My eyes were opened to a beauty I had not noticed before, or maybe it was because, up to that moment in my life, I never really understood who God was. It was at the journey's ending that I looked back and discovered who God is, and He is Love in the truest form.

The last visit to my sister's grave was on October 31, 2009.

I thought of our last words to each other. We both laughed, and the last thing she said was, *"I love you. Now, don't you forget that, and we will see each other again soon."*

Her last words to me, and now they are the words that fill my heart with joy and hope. I will see her again in heaven. In the meantime, I only want to use my life to honor God and serve others. There are so many ways in which to do that. Even in the smallest ways, we can reach out and touch someone's life and possibly change them forever. The ability to share the gospel and witness to a lost and dying world was something that I thought I would never do. Speaking boldly to those around me was simply unimaginable. I would have never thought of myself as one to stand in front of others and tell my story. I never thought that I would pack a lunch, "my empty box." Take it to a woman's house that I had never met, sit down, and have lunch with her. Yet I have done it over 2,964 times in the last twenty years. I could never see myself opening the door to my home and allowing seven women to walk in and sit at my table. These were all impossibilities to me, far beyond my reach, and now they are the joy of my life.

Looking back, I realize my life was full of mistrust, deception, and the inability to respond to love. Moving forward has brought the beauty of love and trust, which I had never known. As I moved forward, not only was I responding to love, but I was also able to show love in a real and tangible way. I was able, for the first time in my life, to be touched and actually feel that touch. I was able to sense the love that came with the hugs I had been receiving at church for over three years. From 2002 until 2005, I was incapable of understanding why anyone would want to hug me. Because of that, I could not feel hugs, nor could I respond to love. I simply didn't know how.

Now, love flows freely in my life; it is not the desire to be loved but to love others and reach out to them. Where once there was no feeling in touch, now I have the joy that comes when my husband reaches for my hand. And when my daughter gives me a hug and says, "I love you," I can receive it. Trust, love, and feelings are the beauty that God has raised up out of the ashes in my life. No, it didn't happen in a day; it was a long, hard road to the freedom I now have to love without fear. It has been a healing journey, letting go of my own desire to be loved because without truly understanding what love really is, how can you receive love, let alone love others? It is just a desire and, at best, a selfish one. I had to allow God to show me love, His love, and when I truly understood, my desires changed.

There is one thing that stands out as a constant reminder of just how far God has brought me and the amazing work that He has done in my life: the paintings that now fill my home, the walls covered in scriptures and murals that inspire those who see them, and keep me focused on the things of real value. The paintings on the walls have touched the hearts of hundreds who have visited my home.

As I call to remembrance where I was when I started painting, the shattered, broken woman who sat on the floor, looking at a pile of broken dishes, I see a woman who had no hope and no direction. I sat alone in a valley of depression, where the only remaining decision to be made was whether to face one more day in a pile of broken dishes or death. I was that woman, and now I stand in the beautiful place that God brought me to. As I *painted, I did indeed heal.* He healed me and restored my life.

God brought me through the valleys that I had walked in during my life. He showed me how He was with me, even before I knew His name. He showed me the raging storms of my life and how He had calmed them. He showed me the mountains I could climb and the clouds I could soar above. He showed me how to stand, even in the midst of the greatest battles of my life. We all face them, sooner or later. However, we must come to the place where we begin to hate the lies we live in, cast out the lies we have believed, and search for the truth. That truth is found only in Jesus Christ, the Son of God. As Jesus stated in John 14:6, "I am the way, the truth and the life."

As God said, Sheila and I did serve together in various ministries. We have served luncheons together. We have sung together at church. We spent many afternoons together, just talking, praying, singing, and enjoying our friendship.

Sheila stood by me as I moved forward into the ministry. She sang on the praise team with her husband for events that we had put together for "Healing for the Wounded Heart Ministry." God sent her to me at a very special time in my life. It was a time of great loss and also a time when God was taking the ashes of my life and turning them into something beautiful.

What is not to be forgotten or overlooked is that God did a mighty thing. He took a useless crate and brought to life the beauty of the "lunch in a box." That useless crate, as I once called it, has been used in the lives of more than 2,964 women, bringing laughter, friendship, trust, and healing to those who opened their hearts to the empty box that really wasn't so empty after all and is still on the road these days with destinations, to homes, to women, who just need to know they are loved. They are needed, and they have a purpose in life. Something so undefined, just a crate to store things in, a simple box that my sister wanted me to bring her a lunch in, was instead used by God to bring healing to others. Two years later, God began to move me in a different direction. So it was that out of the "lunch in a box" that the "luncheons" in my home arose. Since the luncheons began, over 1,260 women have experienced luncheons in my home. I call it "Just a Little Luncheon." These luncheons are truly the miracle out of all of this. They are the real beauty that came out of the ashes of my life.

Sometimes, I feel as if I have been through the desert, as if I have traveled through a very dry and thirsty land where there was no water and no way to nourish my dying soul. I had to come to a place where I understood the emptiness of my own soul, to be able to see that my greater need was not something I could see or touch but something unseen; I had to realize that I was a sinner in need of a Saviour.

His desire was for me to turn away from my ways and learn His ways. That is what it means to repent; it means to change your mind. In other words, I was wrong. I was going in the wrong direction, and now I am turning around and going in the right direction. I am a disciple, and I am learning how I should live and act as a Christian. It took me a long time, and I wasted so many years wandering around in the wilderness when God wanted more for me than that. I have come to the water, the living water, and I know that I can freely drink the water that Jesus offered to the woman at the well, in John chapter 4.

For such a long time, I could not understand why God allowed me to go through so much and then asked me to forgive Billy. Why, at the trial, God spoke to my heart and asked me to speak up and beg for his life. Looking back, I can now see God's handiwork everywhere. Only God, in His wisdom, could have known and understood what it was going to take to make me the vessel He could use. God knew what it would take to save Billy's soul. God had prepared me to be there to beg for Billy's life. I find it amazing that *God knew Billy had killed my sister, and then God placed his life in my hands*. I found myself in an unknown place; I was given the choice to ask for his life or a chance for revenge, and I do not believe that it was just a coincidence. God does work in ways we cannot understand. I believe that He trusted me with a lot.

Today, I am thankful that I chose to ask for Billy's life and accepted his guilty plea and that God gave me the strength and the courage to stand against the others in the room that day. I thank God every day that I didn't let anger, bitterness, and hatred blind me because I would never have been able to talk to Billy on the witness stand that day. I never would have set out to meet him or even known that the opportunity existed for us to meet. I would not have been able to walk into that prison and visit with him face-to-face. No, if I had let hatred win, Billy would have gotten the death penalty, and we are both sure of that. I also would have never known the truth. I would not have been set free. I would still be carrying the secrets in my heart that kept me a prisoner. Most of all, Billy would have died in his sins, and that would have been a great tragedy because my sister's last prayer would have gone unanswered due to my unforgiveness.

The prison visit was God's way, not mine. It was a long and painful journey, but one worth taking, to find forgiveness, healing, restoration, and a clear understanding of God's amazing gift of salvation.

I did walk away from the prison that weekend as a free person, not just because I wasn't locked behind the bars, but because I was released from a spiritual prison that I had been in for thirty-seven years. I could have walked into that prison on any day, but God knew the exact date that I needed to walk through that gate. God knew the overwhelming guilt and shame I had carried in my soul for thirty-seven years to the exact date. God knew the weight that held me down, and He knew when I walked through those gates, I would be hearing in my heart, "This is where you belong; remember August 7, 1972? You killed your baby. Go ahead, judge him, but remember the way you judge him will be the way you will be judged. Do not forget, you murdered an innocent baby thirty-seven years ago today, Linda." As the sound of the gate shutting interrupted my thoughts, I walked into a prison that so defined the punishment for breaking man's laws. However, I understood in that moment that there is also a prison for breaking God's laws. It was such a soft whisper as I heard His words, "So what shall I forgive you for today?"

As I walked through the prison on the tour, my soul was overwhelmed with grief for Laura, for my dad, for my mom, for Daniel, for my baby, for myself, and yes, for Billy too. I grieved for all of us, the choices that we had made that had brought such pain and suffering to others and to ourselves. Realizing that sometimes we build our own prison, I began to understand that there are many kinds of prisons. There, in the halls of the unit at Huntsville, Texas, it seemed to be a world within a world, and the choices that one makes in life define which world they will live in. Darkness or light, truth or lies, life or death, it's all just a matter of choice.

God has been true to His promise to me. Every day, I see His amazing love and His handiwork in my life. I know that there have been times I've fallen down, and I have missed the mark more than once. Yet, there have also been times I've done the right thing and hit the target with an amazing bull's-eye, and I've heard God say, "Well done."

At one time, I wanted the approval of those around me, including the ladies at church that I looked up to and respected as godly women who set the example of the high calling in Christ. But what I have discovered is that there is no greater approval than God's stamp of approval upon my life. I am very content with who I am and with the work that He is doing in and through my life as I choose to yield and trust in Him.

This is a very hard issue to talk about. I am aware of the many different views on abortion. However, I believe that God has only one view, and that is, "It is murder." I do not seek anyone's approval concerning this issue. I am only speaking from my heart, what I believe to be the truth.

This book is not about the issue of abortion, but abortion has a lot to do with what I had to endure and one of the reasons I suffered for many years. I do believe that there are many women in the world today who live with the same guilt and shame that I lived with for many years because of abortion. They can be forgiven and end the guilt and shame they live with. What makes it so hard to be free from that guilt and shame is admitting the truth. What is so hard about the truth? It is very hard to say, "I killed my baby." I know how painful that is to say because I had to say it, and I know it is very difficult to admit that you are responsible for the death of your own baby. However, it is in the speaking it and confessing it that we truly find the forgiveness and the healing that we are longing for.

We must begin speaking the truth and calling things by their name. Sin is sin, and we must name it and seek God's forgiveness. As I said before, I cannot and will not "white lace" this issue or skip over it. It is a sin to kill a baby in any language or by any name you want to call it.

Taking a baby from the only life support system they have to sustain their life and ensure their well-being is murder. I realize that there are going to be those who will be offended by what I am saying about abortion, but I pray that they will come to an understanding about what abortion really is. You can agree or disagree, but none of that really matters because it is God who will have the final say in this matter when we stand before Him.

Texas first enacted a criminal abortion statute in 1854. Texas Laws c. 49, § 1 set forth in 3 H. Gammel, Laws of Texas 1502 (1898). It was against the law to even seek to get an abortion for any reason in the state of Texas. However, it was in the state of Texas that Roe v. Wade was filed in March of 1970, when Roe alleged that she was unmarried and pregnant, that she wished to terminate her pregnancy by an abortion "performed by a competent, licensed physician, under safe, clinical conditions." She stated that she was unable to get a "legal" abortion because her life did not appear to be threatened by the continuation of her pregnancy. It was taken all the way to the U.S. Supreme Court. Case # (410 U.S. 113, 120).

The laws on abortion have changed over the years; Texas state penal code Arts. 531–536; G. Paschal, Laws of Texas, Arts., 2192–2197 Texas Revised Statute, c. 8, Arts. 536–541 (1879) Texas Revised Criminal Statute, Arts. 1071–1076 (1901), and the final Article 1196 stated that a woman may receive an abortion by medical advice for the purpose of saving the life of the mother.

James Hubert Hallford, a licensed physician, sought and was granted leave to intervene in Roe's action. In his complaint, he alleged that he had been arrested previously for violations of the Texas abortion statutes and described conditions of patients who came to him seeking abortions. He claimed that for many cases, he, as a physician, was unable to determine whether they fell within or outside the exception recognized by Article 1196.

Article 1196 became the law used by physicians all over the United States from the early months of 1970 to 1973, stating that those women who sought abortions were in danger because of threats to end their own lives because of the emotional instability created by the unwanted pregnancy. This law was used as a means of killing unwanted babies. A baby in the womb is not a blob of tissue or a "product of conception." It's a human life.

It was 1969 in a small Texas town, where a young woman who was seeking to have an abortion was denied. She filed a suit against Henry Wade, the district attorney in the Dallas court. She was represented by two female attorneys. As plaintiff, she was known as Jane Roe. It went all the way to the Supreme Court. Actually, there were only three hearings. One in 1970, 1971, and January 22, 1973, the day abortion became legal; in history, it became known as Roe v. Wade. In truth, it was Satan versus the life of the unborn.

Once abortion was legalized, the doors were opened for abortion on demand, and it has claimed the lives of millions of unborn babies. The proof of this is in these tragic statistics: In 1973, an estimated 132 abortions were performed in the United States each day. After abortion became legal, that figure greatly changed. Abortion was legalized on January 22, 1973, and to date, over 50 million babies have been killed. At present, over 4,000 babies are being killed every day all over the world. I am part of that; I helped pave the way for millions of women to say they have the right to rip their babies from their wombs. They may legally have the right to do that by man's law but not by God's law.

I believe that it is too late to change the laws of man; however, it is not too late to repent and educate the women who seek to kill their babies. I realize that some will not agree with me about this. However, I still have to stand for what I believe to be right in the sight of God. One day, I, too, will stand before Him, so I will not, and cannot, justify my actions. The term "abort" means to cancel or end abruptly. One definition declares that it means to end or stop something before completion.

I have asked God's forgiveness, and I'm forgiven. I would say this to any woman who comes to me and tells me she has had an abortion: "Repent, admit to God what you did, and ask God to forgive you." After that, I would softly remind her, "You have been forgiven, and you will see your baby in heaven face-to-face."

It is also noteworthy that Jane Roe, whose real name is Norma McCorvey, never had an abortion. She gave birth to her baby and gave it up for adoption. Norma also had a change of heart and repented of the part she played in Roe v. Wade. In an interview, Norma said, "I thought that I was doing the right thing, but I was wrong. I have been forgiven; I just do not have a lot of forgiveness for myself right now." She died on February 18, 2017.

I am looking into what can be done about the paper that I signed in August of 1972, that went to the White House in 1973 with signatures from women who sought abortions and were able to get an abortion by signing a form stating that they would rather die than have their baby. I was one of those women, and I now seek to have my name removed from the list of more than 97,000 names of women who signed such a form. I have discovered that it can be removed.

One day, I will see my baby, and I will behold his face. I cannot imagine a more humbling moment other than standing before the throne of God. I know God will take this part of my life and give me beauty for the ashes, but that is a journey I've yet to take. Here I am at the journey's end. With what I have learned and carry in my heart, I shall press forward in journeys that are just over the horizon.

Based on a true story...

My empty box... I still do the lunch in the box. It's October of 2023, and yesterday, I packed a lunch in the box. I took it to a beautiful lady; she just needed a friend. As always, we had an amazing time. I am thankful for the lunch in the box. It is no longer an empty box; it is full, and so is my life. I still host luncheons in my home. I am in the middle of getting some home improvements and remodeling done and will continue to do luncheons again after the work is finished. Healing for the Wounded Heart Ministries closed its doors in February 2013. I speak at conferences and retreats. I still paint, which I love to do. It's such an amazing gift that was given to me.

I am a wife, mother, and grandmother, but above all that, I am a Christian and a servant of the Most High God. I never thought that I would say this, but I am so very thankful for the extraordinary life that I have lived. I am thankful for the journey that I was able to take with my sister; it was incredible. Oh, what victories we had.

CHAPTER 24

Forgiveness: Just Let It Go By!

What is forgiveness anyway, and what does it mean to really forgive? After years of struggling, I realized that forgiveness is something we seek from God. Yet, rarely have the capacity to experience or extend to others. What is so amazing to me is that most people have never truly allowed themselves to experience God's forgiveness. The real problem is that we have never really forgiven ourselves for our own weaknesses and failures. How do we get past that so that we can indeed experience God's forgiveness and then be able to forgive ourselves and others?

Life offers many roads, and some of those roads are very wide, with all kinds of temptations. The roads are brightly lined and paved with fun, pleasure, and promises of happiness, with no consequences for our actions. But they quickly turn into traps full of lies, darkness, and potholes. Some potholes are so big that only the power and grace of God can pull us out.

Every minute of every day, choices are made. No one ever wakes up and says, "Well, today I think I will go have an affair and destroy my family," or "I want to become a drug addict today." No, it starts with a choice to vary, just a little off the path onto a road that looks so inviting. One might tell themselves, "It can't hurt, just one little moment." We tell ourselves that this one time will be all right. Once we have yielded to the one-time temptation, we remember how much we enjoyed it and how we got away with it. We deceive ourselves by believing: "Oh, just one more time won't hurt." We act as if God does not see or even notice.

When we think about something long enough, we slowly begin to accept it. Once the "just one more time" lie has been accepted, it becomes easier to take the plunge the next time. Without realizing it, we are doomed and headed into an addiction, habit, affair, or whatever brightly paved road we have chosen, and the list is long. Before we know it, we are trapped, begging for a way out and wanting a quick, easy escape without any consequences. It's hard to even admit we sinned.

It's heartbreaking as well as true, but millions will make a wrong choice today. They will end up going down one of the brightly paved roads that this world has to offer and will end up in the middle of nowhere, broken down and stuck in the middle of a bad habit, left with a drug addiction, or their family laying in ruins and turmoil because of an affair that seemed to be so irresistible. Thousands have ended up involved in some form of sexual perversion and a host of other things that they never thought they were capable of because they made one wrong choice again and again and again. Before long, it became an addiction, with overwhelming cravings and the uncontrollable obsession of "just one more time."

There are so many people being held in bondage because, in one brief moment, they willingly went against what they knew was right and chose one of those brightly paved roads for a moment's pleasure. Many of us have loved ones who are traveling down some of these roads as we sit back and painfully watch while they destroy their lives.

We feel unable to help them, and we feel used and hurt, time after time, as we try to pull them off of the road they are traveling down. In many cases, we believe we are helping when, in fact, we are only enabling them. We must come to terms with the fact that we are not capable of changing them; as a matter of fact, we are not capable of changing anyone. No, that's God's business. Our business is to love them and be there when they are ready and truly need us. We must let them know we love them, we are praying for them, and we forgive them. But we are not going to be a part of what they are doing in any way. We should warn them that the road they are on is a dead end and will take them nowhere, then trust God to reach out to save and deliver them. If we continue enabling them, we will eventually become bitter and angry, and unforgiveness will begin to fill our souls. When, and if, the time comes to reach out to them, we will not be able to because we have become filled with unforgiveness towards them.

There are many roads, and among these roads are some that are viewed as harmless. These roads are very easy to end up on. They consist of a variety of things like anger, pride, hatred, gossip, envy, jealousy, bitterness, and even unforgiveness. We tend to think that these things are harmless; it seems so easy to justify them. They can be so easily hidden behind our smiles. Maybe we even believed these paths are so small and unimportant that they go unnoticed and unrecorded by God. It's as if we think God doesn't know our hearts. We tend to justify these harmless roads with excuses. We overlook the potholes and never admit we have sinned by allowing ourselves to end up stranded on one of these seemingly harmless roads. After all, these things cannot be compared to sexual perversion, adultery, drug and alcohol addiction, or even murder, right?

These seemingly harmless roads are well traveled, and the hidden dangers are rarely seen until it is too late and the damage is done. These "harmless" roads have destroyed lives and brought death to friendships, marriages, families, and even churches. Just because they are easy to hide and cover up does not mean the damage and pain they cause are overlooked by God. Nor does it mean repentance and forgiveness should not be sought. Search the Word for yourself, and you will find, as I did, that if you break one commandment, you have broken them all. We cannot, nor do we have the right, the wisdom, or the ability to measure and compare each other's sins, Christian or non-Christian. Sin is sin, and the person who knows to do good and does it not, to them, it is a sin, James 4:17. We have all sinned, and we all fall into some pothole at one time or another. We must show love and compassion as we help each other out of these potholes without judgment.

Forgiveness is the only answer for all of this. Bitterness and pride are just as sinful as adultery or murder. Stealing and lying are sins also, but so are anger and gossip. We tend to put sin into categories, yet I cannot find one place in the Bible where it is recorded that murder is a sin that is worse than adultery, and anger is not as bad as stealing. How can we expect God to forgive us of our many sins while we hold such unforgiveness in our hearts against others and ourselves? We cannot seek forgiveness while we judge and condemn others.

We turn our faces against those who do not measure up to our expectations, yet we are told that those who compare and measure themselves among themselves are not wise (2 Corinthians 10:12). The truth is, all roads lead to the same place: the throne, which is where we shall all be judged. There is no exception to this; *everyone* means *everyone* (Revelation 20:12). We ask God to forgive us of our many sins while we hold such unforgiveness in our hearts against others, and more times than not, find it even hard to forgive ourselves.

God is gracious, kind, loving, and very forgiving. He woos us in many ways. He gives us the chance to face the consequences of our actions. What we do with that chance is up to us. Will we use it to seek forgiveness or to extend forgiveness? Sometimes, we are given several chances. God knows if we are going to change and repent. And He knows when we have hardened our hearts and have become too prideful to admit any wrongdoing. God knows when we refuse to seek forgiveness, and He knows when we are unwilling to extend forgiveness.

We can't go back and undo the unkind things we did or said. The most loving, humbling thing we can do at the end of the day is seek forgiveness from God and from those we know we have hurt or offended. Sometimes, the hardest step of all is to admit to ourselves the wrong we have done. It is much easier to sit back and look at the wrongs of others while we justify our own actions and feelings. Have we become so bold as to think we shall escape the judgment of God? We overlook verses like

"Judge not, that ye be not judged. For with what judgment ye judge, ye shall be judged: and with what measure ye mete, it shall be measured to you again" (Matthew 7:1–2). It's as if we think that these verses do not apply to us. We ignore the truth that everything we do and everything we say, be it bad or be it good, has a final result. In James 1:14–15, it says, "Every man is tempted, when he is drawn away of his own lust, and enticed. Then when lust hath conceived, it bringeth forth sin: and sin, when it is finished, bringeth forth death."

We fail to consider and take seriously what the Word of God declares: "The heart is deceitful above all things, and desperately wicked: who can know it?" (Jeremiah 17:9) Our hearts, which we never want to admit, can be deceitful and wicked. We truly do not know how deceitful and wicked we can be until we end up on a dead-end street or in a pothole, unable to deal with the mess caused by the choices that we have made.

What we need to do is cry out to God and clean up our mess as much as we possibly can. We need to face the consequences of our actions, repent, and seek forgiveness. But, instead, most of us just cover! We refuse to admit any wrong on our part and will not ask for forgiveness or even repent. The only reason we call out to God is to ask Him to help us get out of the mess we have created. The rest of the time, we blame Him and others for where we have ended up. What I have come to understand is that no matter what road you are on or how you got there, *the only thing that matters is the next choice you will make.*

I took life so lightly, never considering that the things I had said and done may have hurt someone very deeply. I never thought that the unkind words I said to someone might be the last words I ever spoke to them. It just seemed to me that certain things would never happen to me. No one that I loved would ever drown or die of cancer and certainly not be murdered. No, that would never touch my life. That is something that happens to other people, not to me, and not to my family. I lived as if I had outsmarted death, and I took life for granted. I failed to cherish life and the gift of time that God had so freely given to me. When death did touch my life, I dared to blame God. I asked, "Why?" As regrets grabbed hold of my soul, I buried myself in guilt and blame. I didn't want to admit that sometimes wrong choices play a part in the end of a life. The choice of drugs and alcohol has claimed the lives of thousands. Drugs are a tool in the hand of Satan, and he cares not whose life they claim, a Christian or a nonbeliever; it makes no difference to him.

I did not want to admit that defiance against God and the free will to make choices are responsible for the conditions in the world today. God gave us free will. Simply put, He gave the freedom of choice to the whole human race. The freedom of choice is nothing more than the free will to choose between right and wrong. We decide for ourselves what is wrong and what is right and then base our actions on that. However, when we ignore the standard of what God's Word says is right and wrong, it becomes a formula for failure.

In our sin-torn world, murder, rape, adultery, robbery, suicide, and abuse in every form happen every ten seconds, according to the statistics. Today, in our world, man no longer views sin as sin but as some mystic form of self-gratification while indulging in whatever is pleasing to look upon, touch, taste, listen to, and smell. Once a day is gone, it's gone. No matter how much we long to go back and do things differently, we can't. We have to accept the things we have done and believe that when we ask God to bring beauty out of the ashes of our broken lives, to give us the oil of joy for mourning, and the garment of praise for the spirit of heaviness, He will do just that (Isaiah 61:3).

In a world where we long to have our ears tickled, we have missed the greatest message of all. The message of forgiveness. God longs to forgive us and desires that we share that forgiveness with those who trespass against us. The proof of God's love and willingness to extend forgiveness to a lost and dying world was confirmed by the death of His only Son on the cross for the sins of the whole world. His forgiveness is extended to liars, drunks, drug addicts, adulterers, the bitter, the thieves, the prideful, the angry, backbiters, gossipers, and murderers. Jesus died for all our *sins*.

When we truly experience forgiveness, it changes our lives. I mean, to really know you have been forgiven changes you. Billy knew I had forgiven him, and it allowed him to see that God could forgive him as well. Billy now walks in the freedom of forgiveness. That forgiveness did not change or alter the consequences of his actions. Forgiveness changed his eternal destination and altered his future actions.

For such a long time, forgiveness was just a word. I said it many times, I heard it said many times, but then I truly experienced it in the very depth of my soul. I have embraced forgiveness, and it has changed my life. That was what the thief on the cross understood that day when Jesus forgave him. He understood the death that he was suffering at that moment was exactly what he deserved, yet Jesus told him, "Today you will be with me in paradise."

I believe that the thief knew how great his sin was and what great power, authority, love, and forgiveness Jesus had. The thief not only repented, but he received the forgiveness that was granted to him. Here we are, two thousand years later, standing at the foot of the cross, when in the reality of it all, we should be aware of the fact that we ought to indeed be the ones on that cross. We should be so grateful and humbled by the great sacrifice He made on our behalf, the price He paid for our forgiveness.

That's what happened that day with Billy at the prison. I experienced God's great salvation, His forgiveness, and His love all rolled up in the most powerful words ever spoken to my heart: "I let it all go by. Linda, you are forgiven."

When I spoke those same words to Billy, I saw a heaviness lift from Billy and a face that was stricken with pain turn into a face full of expressions of thankfulness, and I knew he was seeing the same thing happening to me. For a moment, I could see myself standing in the bathroom as a little girl, as my earthly father let it go by. As a little girl, I didn't understand all of that wonderful moment that I held on to and never forgot. Now, as a woman, I understand the amazing power, freedom, and love of letting it go by.

There we were, two murderers. That day with Jesus, He told us we were forgiven. Our penalty was paid by His blood and His death, and because of that, we received God's forgiveness. Before that day, I thought I knew what forgiveness was, but after that day, I understood that forgiveness gives us the freedom to love in spite of, not because of.

What broke the chains? What happened that forever changed my perception of forgiveness? On August 7, 2009, when I was sitting across from Billy in one of the silent moments, I visually saw Jesus in my mind's eye, on the cross. I noticed the two sinners who were crucified with Jesus, and as I took a closer look, I saw myself as the repenting sinner. There I was, asking Jesus to forgive me and speaking words of praise and thanksgiving. I even told Him that I deserved to be on the cross He was hanging on; I deserved those lashes and crown of thorns, not Him. Then I looked to the other sinner on the opposite side of Jesus, expecting to see Billy, but it wasn't Billy; it was *me!* I was the bitter, unrepenting sinner lashing out at Jesus and mocking Him. I spoke cruel words of hatred while justifying all my actions.

I questioned the vision, and Jesus said, "Linda, you have a choice; which one do you want to be: bitter and unforgiving, tangled in a web of justification and self-righteousness, or do you want to be with Me in paradise, living in My love because you humbly asked for forgiveness, then you grant that same forgiveness to others, forgiving them, because you were forgiven a debt that you could not pay?"

That vision changed everything. A week after the visit to the prison, I went to my parents' grave and sat down on the ground. I know they were not there and that only their bodies remained just below the surface. I know that they could not hear me or see me. It was just something I had to do, a way of saying, "It's all right, I forgive you."

I had never admitted that I was bitter and angry with them because they had hurt me and used me. I was their child; I was their daughter, and they didn't teach me or prepare me for the world. But I was guilty, too, because I wanted their love and approval so desperately that I did not make a stand for Christ in their presence. In doing so, I failed to be the one person who could have possibly reached my dad and made a difference in his life and in his eternal destination. Could I have made a difference? That remains unknown. But I never want to ask myself that question again regarding anyone who crosses my path. No matter where I go, I only have one desire: that Christ, the hope of glory, is seen in and through my life, that I never fail to share the gospel with those around me, and that I never fail to show love or kindness to anyone. Most of all, I give my life to serving others because I know that even Jesus did not come to be served but to serve, and we are to be examples of Him. I believe there is no greater aim than to love and to serve those for whom Christ died.

Another thing that I have learned about forgiveness is that no one can teach you how. It is a choice that you make, and there are no guidelines. Every day, you decide to grab hold of the forgiveness that has been extended to you, lay claim to that forgiveness, and extend it to others. You exercise it by doing things you would not normally do, like sending a card without relating it to the offense or sending a gift card of some type and letting them know you are committed to them and desire God's best for them. When you do that, you are investing in their lives. What you invest in, you care about, and it changes your focus. You are no longer focusing on the negative but turning the negative into a positive. An investment in the life of someone says you believe that they have value. It is also noteworthy to know that when someone believes you see value in them, many times, it changes their heart and their perspective. That is an eternal investment.

Forgiveness is seeing the debt you owe as greater than any debt owed to you. It is to release them of the offense in the same manner that God has released you of your offenses. That is forgiveness, and when you truly experience it, you will never forget it. It becomes the fuel that burns within your heart to share the gospel. Forgiveness of sins comes only through the power of the death, burial, and resurrection of Jesus Christ, the Son of God. Once you embrace that, your life will never be the same. As I have discovered, forgiveness is the bridge between the offended and the offender, which heals, restores, and sets you free!

Jesus said that if you will not forgive others their trespass against you, His Father in heaven will not forgive you your trespass.

Jesus said that even murderers would enter heaven before some of us.

Moses was a murderer, and God used him to lead an entire nation out of bondage.

Paul was a murderer; God used him to write over half of the epistles in the New Testament. "For the wages of sin is death; but the gift of God is eternal life through Jesus Christ our Lord" (Romans 6:23).

What I have come to understand about forgiveness is that, in the end, when I stand before God, it will not be about how much I learned. It will not be about how much money I made or even the works I may have done or have not done. What will matter most is whether or not I extended forgiveness to others, as He forgave me. Did I love others as He loved me? Did I serve others as He served others? Did I lead others to Him and spread the Gospel? With this as my focus, everything else just doesn't seem to matter so much anymore.

At the end of my life, I want to look back and know that I can stand before God, knowing these simple truths that if I ever hurt or offended anyone, I took the time to seek forgiveness, and I did whatever was within my power and ability to make things right. That I not only repented and asked for forgiveness but also forgave those who hurt me or offended me. That I never failed to reach out to anyone around me in love and never failed to serve those in my home, my neighborhood, my church, my town, or anyone in my life, no matter who they are, with a genuine spirit of hospitality and love. And that I sought out those who were lost, hungry, hurt, and alone just to share God's love with them and the hope of eternal life.

As for forgiveness? It is truly a journey, one that we must go on. For me, that journey began as a little girl. When a pastor who was a shepherd who tended sheep said, "'Forgiveness' means you let it go by." Those words stayed within my little girl's heart. For years, I searched for the true meaning. As I saw, my daddy let it go by one night so long ago. The love and the feelings it placed in my heart could not be forgotten; there was so much power in what happened that night; so vivid was the scene in my mind. I really experienced a father's love and a father's forgiveness. That's what the real journey was all about in my life. The journey of forgiveness.

I believe, in essence, that's what we are all looking for. It's what we all crave: love and forgiveness. It's what we long for. It's what we need the most: To be able to see the beauty of this life that we've been given, we must experience the love and the forgiveness of God to be able to forgive ourselves and others as we walk through this thing called life; we must allow ourselves to say it loud and clear, "I let it go by." In truth, that's what forgiveness really is. Just letting it go by. No judgment, no condemnation, no guilt, or shame. Let Jesus take that weight; we were not meant to carry such loads.

That is truly what unforgiveness is. We hold on too tight, and we carry such heavy loads that wear us down, causing us to become bitter and angry. It causes us to resent others and to fall into judging others and condemning them. We become harsh judges. When all we had to do was let it go by and allow forgiveness to bring the peace, joy, and healing that we need as we journey through life, experiencing genuine love because we walk in His light, the light of forgiveness. We experience true forgiveness as we let it go by; then, we are able to allow the love of God to flow through us, genuine love that enables us to forgive ourselves and allow room for mistakes. We then can love others and allow room for their mistakes, forgiving as we have been forgiven.

We do not live in a perfect world. And yet, we expect perfection from ourselves and those around us. We make the mistake of setting someone high on a pedestal, hanging on to every word they speak and everything they do. Then, when they let us down, we condemn them and make sure that all of those around us know that they failed, they sinned, they made a mistake, they did something we did not like or approve of. Because of our anger and bitterness, we cast them off. They become castaways. There are many women who feel that they have been cast away and forgotten. Unforgiveness is one of the main reasons gossip takes place in our churches, and it is destructive. Gossip can and has destroyed families and friendships. Gossip has devastated our churches; it has brought pain to so many and caused many to falter and walk away from the church and, sometimes, from the faith.

Another tendency that we have is putting people under microscopes, looking for flaws and imperfections, or watching and waiting for them to make a mistake; that is not what we were called to do. That's God's business. We are to love, to forgive, to encourage, to lift up, and to help all those around us. And we are to do it in love, understanding, and forgiveness, as He has forgiven us.

I went outside the other night and was looking across the vastness of the night sky, the stars, and the moon giving its light to the earth. It was exceptionally beautiful, and peace just flooded my soul. It reminded me of one night long ago when I had gone outside and viewed the night sky with similar thoughts, and I remembered what God spoke to me that night. He said, "My love is infinite, and My forgiveness is unmeasurable." Today, as I find myself in the closing pages of this book, I can honestly say, "His love is infinite, and His forgiveness is of a truth unmeasurable."

I finally did what Laura asked me to do. Actually, told me to do it several times. "Grow up! Take off those white patent leather shoes and get you some real shoes." I did it; I took off the white patent leather shoes. I still keep them as a reminder of where I was and just how far God has brought me.

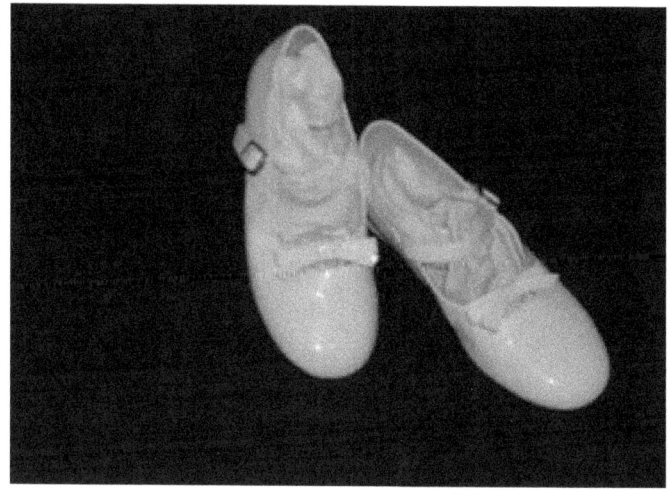

I didn't get to share the lunch in a box with Laura, but there is a wonderful, amazing supper that I look forward to sharing with her at the marriage feast of the Lamb. I am so thankful that God has saved the best for the end!

But then again, it's not the end at all, only the beginning of... eternity! *Until then, I will be about my Father's business!*

In memory of my sister, Laura
April 29, 1952, to October 14, 2001
Special thanks to:
the officers who investigated Laura's murder,
the Texas rangers,
Victim Services Division for the mediation program,
David Flores, TDCJ Mediator.

Printed in the USA
CPSIA information can be obtained
at www.ICGtesting.com
CBHW061125171124
17562CB00013B/235